# *Pineapple* GRENADE

# *Pineapple* GRENADE

## TIM DORSEY

*wm*

WILLIAM MORROW
*An Imprint of* HarperCollins*Publishers*

PINEAPPLE GRENADE. Copyright © 2012 by Tim Dorsey. All rights reserved. Printed in the United States of America. No part of this book may be used or reproduced in any manner whatsoever without written permission except in the case of brief quotations embodied in critical articles and reviews. For information address HarperCollins Publishers, 10 East 53rd Street, New York, NY 10022.

HarperCollins books may be purchased for educational, business, or sales promotional use. For information please write: Special Markets Department, HarperCollins Publishers, 10 East 53rd Street, New York, NY 10022.

A hardcover edition of this book was published in 2012 by William Morrow, an imprint of HarperCollins Publishers.

FIRST WILLIAM MORROW PAPERBACK EDITION PUBLISHED 2012.

The Library of Congress has cataloged the hardcover edition as follows:
Dorsey, Tim.
    Pineapple grenade : a novel / Tim Dorsey. —1st ed.
        p.   cm.
    ISBN 978-0-06-187690-5
    1. Storms, Serge (Fictitious character)—Fiction.   2. Florida—Fiction.
I. Title.
PS3554.O719P56 2012
813'.54—dc22
                                                                2011022711

ISBN 978-0-06-187693-6 (pbk.)

13  14  15  16   OV/RRD   10  9  8  7  6  5  4  3  2

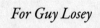
*For Guy Losey*

A life is not important except in the impact it has on other lives.
**—JACKIE ROBINSON**

# PROLOGUE

**A** prosthetic leg with a Willie Nelson bumper sticker washed ashore on the beach, which meant it was Florida.

Then it got weird.

Homicide detectives would soon be stumped by the discovery of the so-called Hollow Man. Empty torso with no external wounds, like all his organs had been magically scooped out. Little progress was made in the case until a TV station began calling him the Jack-O'-Lantern Man, which immediately doubled the number of nicknames.

But right now, the victim had yet to be found. In fact, he was still breathing.

A finger tapped a chin. "Should I kill the hostage back at our motel room?"

Coleman surveyed topless sunbathers and swigged a secret flask. "You never asked that question before."

"I know." Serge looked at his sneakers. "But this would make four guys in the last two months. I wouldn't want to be accused of over-reacting."

"I did notice you've been wasting a lot more dudes lately."

"I blame my environment." Serge picked up a piece of litter. "Oil spills in the Gulf, foreclosed homes in Cape Coral, voting machines held together with paper clips, rising crime, falling landmarks, that structured-settlement asshole on TV yelling, 'It's my money and I want it now!'"

"Who can take it?" said Coleman.

"I live for Florida." Serge stuck the piece of trash in his pocket. "And she's been disintegrating for decades. I've tried sounding the alarm."

"Remember the time you actually used a real alarm?" said Coleman. "That handheld siren and a helmet with a revolving red light on top. Everyone scattered and screamed when you ran through."

"They've become blind to the darkening spiral."

"But it was a baby shower in a restaurant."

"Because I care about future generations," said Serge. "If we don't act fast, they'll never know the majesty of this sacred place. But recently, the decline has accelerated far beyond anything I imagined possible, and the Florida of my youth may be gone in my *own* lifetime. I won't survive—it's like oxygen to me."

"Then what will happen?"

"I could become unstable. So to keep pace with the deterioration, I'm forced to kill more of the fuck-heads who blight my fine state." He turned and looked at Coleman. "Is that selfish?"

"I say the guy back in our room has it coming."

Serge nodded. "And I respect your opinion because you smoke marijuana. You're chemically biased against violence and job applications."

"I'm only against taking part. But I still like to watch."

"Which? Murder or people working?"

"Both." Coleman picked up a prosthetic leg and tucked it under his arm. They continued walking along the surf.

"We need to get back to the motel and prep the patient," said Serge. "I'll call the county agricultural department to learn who handles bull semen."

"What's jism have to do with croaking him?"

"Ever make a jack-o'-lantern?"

## THE DAY BEFORE . . .

12 DEC—0800—MIAMI SECTOR

URGENT

Echo: Intercept unsuccessful. Sanction proceeding. Repeat.
  Sanction proceeding.

Target: Unknown

Asset: Unknown

Protocol: Omega

Germination: Data Corrupted

ALL SECTIONS: TOP PRIORITY

Rush hour.

A river of headlights inched through the humid dusk along the Palmetto Expressway. An inbound Continental jet from Houston cleared the highway and touched down at Miami International. Then a United flight from Oklahoma City.

Serge snapped a photo out the window of a green-and-orange 1968 Plymouth Road Runner. They took the next exit.

Coleman looked around a dark neighborhood of burglar bars and darting shadows, then back up at the parallel, elevated expressway with a row of reassuring streetlights. "I'd feel a lot safer if we were still on that other road."

"And that's exactly why we're down here." The needle dipped under thirty as Serge leaned over the steering wheel.

Coleman leaned over his bong. "Why *are* we down here?"

"Miami's gotten an unfair reputation just because of all the tourist murders. I blame the media."

"It's not right."

"And ground zero of this herd-thinning epidemic is the ancillary roads around the airport, where roving bands of land pirates cruise for unsuspecting visitors in rental cars who get lost and take the wrong exit. So we took the wrong exit."

"But we're only two guys," said Coleman. "How can we change things?"

"All it takes is one headline."

Coleman looked down at himself. "Is that why we're dressed like this?"

Serge floored the gas and cut his lights.

"What are you doing?"

"Here's our headline."

On the shoulder of a dim and deserted access road, a retired tool-and-die salesman from Bowling Green stood next to his wife behind their rented Taurus.

At gunpoint.

The carjacker heard something and turned. "What the—?"

A screech of brakes. The assailant went up over the front bumper, then bounced off the windshield and landed at the feet of the shaken couple.

Serge jumped out with his own gun.

The couple's hands went back up.

"Put your arms down," said Serge. He grabbed the wrist of the would-be thief for a pulse. "I'm not robbing you. I'm rescuing you."

The man squinted in the darkness at Serge's leotard and flowing red cape. Then his chest. "Superman?"

"No, that's a different $S$. I'm Serge."

The woman stared at a passenger climbing out the other side of the Plymouth. "Who's that?"

Serge glanced over the roof at Coleman, wearing a plain white T-shirt with flames drawn in red Magic Marker. "The Human Torch."

Coleman waved cheerfully and lit a joint.

Serge dragged the carjacker by the ankles and threw him in the trunk. Then he walked back to the driver's door. "Shit, I got a run in my tights." He looked up. "Welcome to Miami! Please tell the media."

"Tell them what?"

Serge gathered up his cape and put on a helmet with a revolving red light. "Everything's normal."

A Plymouth Road Runner raced east on the Palmetto Expressway.

Another overhead thunder of Pratt & Whitney jet engines.

Outside the airport, people on cell phones covered free ears. Arriving passengers looked up from the curb as an Aeroméxico 747 roared on takeoff.

The airliner quickly gained altitude. It reached the edge of the Everglades and banked over a patchwork of water-filled, limestone quarries.

Between two of the quarries, a dozen men in jumpsuits looked up at the drone from the Cancún-bound flight. Its moonlit contrail disappeared in the clouds. The sound faded to crickets.

Back to work.

It was an old barn of a warehouse. Sunbaked, remote, corrugated aluminum. Used to be an airplane hangar with two huge doors that slid open on rusty tracks. The doors had a single row of windows, long since spray-painted black.

Three white vans sat in the back of the building. Magnetic catering signs suggested they knew what they were doing with wedding cakes. Men unloaded wooden crates under fluorescent lights. Every tenth one went to a table for inspection.

Crowbars, sawdust.

Two large hands pulled out an SKS assault rifle, the cheap Chinese knockoff of the Russian Kalashnikov. The man shouldered the weapon, checking sight lines and placing his ear close as he dry-fired the trigger. Then back in the box. A slight nod. Jumpsuits replaced the lid and hammered flat-head nails.

The man reached for the next crate. He stood six three, with one of those massive stomachs that started just below the neck and involved the chest. It was covered by a custom, five-XL Tommy Bahama tropical shirt, which hung loose at his waist like a tarp covering a vintage Volkswagen. An unseen wrestling-style belt buckle said VICTOR in sparkling diamonds. Light olive skin, not quite the local Latin, maybe Mediterranean. He was thinking again of quitting the Hair Club.

The warehouse doors creaked open. Headlights. Another van.

A jumpsuit: "Mr. Evangelista, here comes the rest of the shipment."

Victor set the rifle down and rubbed his palms. "The good stuff."

This time, all crates went to the table. Everyone gathered round.

Out came a much larger weapon that pressed down on the shoulder of the tropical shirt. A bulbous, pointed projectile perched on the end of the muzzle.

The men finished their count from the crates. Forty-eight factory-fresh RPGs diverted from an army base in the Carolinas.

Victor slapped the side of the last box. "Move it out!"

The only other person in the warehouse not wearing a jumpsuit was a young man wearing gold chains and a single stud earring. He compensated for his uncommonly short stature with tight slacks, wispy mustache, silk nightclub shirts unbuttoned to the navel, and tall hats.

Victor turned toward the young man. "Scooter, are you standing on your tiptoes again?"

"No." He slowly eased down onto his heels.

"Just don't touch anything," said Victor. "It's like I can't take my eyes off you."

He took his eyes off him.

When he looked back: "Scooter! That's not a toy! Put it down this instant!"

"Shut up, old man." Scooter rested the weapon on his own shoulder. "I've handled these a thousand times."

"Don't touch that switch!" Victor lunged. "It's armed!"

*Woooooosh.*

Luckily, the rocket-propelled grenade threaded through the slit in the warehouse doors. Unluckily, the gravel parking lot was a target-rich environment.

*Boom.*

A chassis blew ten feet in the air and crashed back down. Tires sailed like discus.

"You idiot!" Victor snatched the weapon. The front hood of a Ferrari clanged down onto the warehouse roof. "That was my car!"

Scooter nonchalantly strolled away. "My uncle will buy you a new one."

"You're damn right," yelled Victor.

One of the jumpsuits came over. "Shouldn't we get the hell out of here? That was loud. And a big fireball."

Evangelista shook his head. "It's Miami. People don't even notice anymore."

The jumpsuit looked toward the departing Scooter. "Why do you let that pussy come along?"

"Politics," said Victor. "It's the business we're in."

## THE NEXT AFTERNOON

A scorched tropical motel with an empty signpost sat behind the demolished ruins of the Orange Bowl. An old chain-link fence that surrounded the swimming pool had been pushed down in places, but the pool was drained and filled with broken bottles. The office showed hints of a recent altercation that involved shovels and fire. When it rained, the guests subconsciously thought of childhood, but not theirs.

Tourists didn't stay at the motel, although it was quiet, except when junkies knocked on random doors with a range of requests representing the width of the human condition. In the swimming pool's deep end was a ripped-in-half poster of a sailboat crew that said TEAMWORK.

A knock on a door.

Serge answered. "Hello, junkie!"

The man swayed off balance. "Have any yarn? Blue?"

"No, but here are some postcards."

The door closed.

A minute later:

*Knock, knock, knock . . .*

"Another junkie?" asked Coleman.

"Probably the deliveryman." Serge opened the door and his wallet. "Right on time. Just leave the tank there. And here's a little extra for your trouble."

The deliveryman hesitated at the sight of Serge's cape. Then took the money and left quickly.

"What now?" asked Coleman.

Serge headed out the door. "Welcome our guest."

A key went into the trunk of a Plymouth Road Runner.

The hood popped.

Blinding sunlight.

Serge waved his gun. "Rise and shine!"

A bruised carjacker shielded his eyes with one hand and raised the other in submission. "Don't shoot!"

"And ruin all my fun?"

Serge marched him toward the motel.

"I swear I'll never rob anyone again!"

A poke in the back with the gun barrel. "I know you won't."

The captive stopped just inside the motel room. "What's the metal tank for?"

"Cow jism." Serge grabbed a mug of cold coffee off the dresser and downed it. "Actually *bull* jism. Cows are chicks, I think. Who cares? It's a cryogenic tank, but there's no bull spooge in there either. So I put in some of my own, because when do you ever really get the chance? I'm just that kind of cat. It's my new hobby. The tank, not the other. Hobbies are important. And you're about to become the star in my latest episode of *World's Most Dangerous Hobbies*!"

"You're insane . . . Ow!" The man grabbed his shoulder. "What the hell?"

Serge pulled back the syringe. "Just a prick for a prick."

"What was in that? . . . Whoa . . ." He grabbed for the bed.

"Better sit down," said Serge. "It gets on top of you pretty fast."

Moments later: The hostage lay stretched out across the bed, eyes fixed on the ceiling. Still breathing.

Moments after that:

"Far enough," said Serge. "Now roll him back the other way."

"He's heavy."

"We need to go slow anyway." Serge reeled in the hostage by his belt. "The key is to keep him constantly turning like a rotisserie."

"For how long?"

"A few minutes each time."

"Time?" Coleman grabbed the man's sleeve. "How many times?"

"At least twenty." The captive reached the edge of the bed; Serge rolled him back the other way. "This must be a layered, even application, or we have a serious breach in our guest that'll ruin my hobby."

"Which hobby?"

"The human version of building a ship in a bottle." Serge slipped on thick rubber gloves. He reached in a shopping bag, removing an aluminum cooking tray and a turkey baster.

"What are those for?" asked Coleman.

"Just hand me that gas can by the door and grab his feet."

## MIAMI INTERNATIONAL AIRPORT

Assorted travelers scurried along sidewalks and ignored the deep boom of a distant explosion. The fireball rose above the parking decks.

A bonded courier in Miami for the first time looked out the back of a cab. "What on earth was that blast?"

"I didn't notice," said the driver.

Others rolled luggage as wind carried the smoke plume toward Hialeah. Families huddled at curbs and studied rental-car maps. The loading zone abuzz in eleven languages. A police officer made a car move by blowing a whistle.

Then more cops on motorcycles. Flashing blue lights. Limos arrived.

News teams from local affiliates already there. TV cameras on tripods.

A woman raised a microphone.

*"Good afternoon. This is Gloria Rojas reporting live from the airport*

*with the latest on the upcoming Summit of the Americas. As you can see behind me, heads of state and top diplomats from across the hemisphere are beginning to arrive at this historic event, which is returning to the Magic City for the first time since thirty-four nations attended its inaugural gathering in 1994 . . ."*

The terminal's automatic doors opened. Air-conditioning and security people rushed out. They made a quick sweep of the street, then hustled a man with a bushy mustache into the back of a stretch.

*". . . I believe that was the president of Bolivia . . ."*

Another security detail. Another limo. So on.

*". . . The presidents of Uruguay and Belize . . ."*

Police held off onlookers as the rest of the dignitaries were swept into backseats.

The motorcycle cops sped away, followed by limos. TV crews packed up.

Non-VIP airport hubbub resumed. Luggage and courtesy vans.

Automatic doors opened again.

A pair of dark Ray-Ban sunglasses looked left and right. Picking up surveillance cameras. The man crossed the street for the Flamingo parking garage.

He stopped on the opposite curb and removed his glasses, wiping the right lens while mentally mapping police locations. He put the shades back on.

Another typical afternoon, everyone rushing about in that irrational state of mild alarm from being at an airport, checking watches, rechecking flight times, worried about the length of X-ray lines, herding toddlers and golf clubs. Distracted. Except the stationary man across the street. Minor details tallied behind designer sunglasses. A briefcase with a broken latch, a suitcase with a sticker from Epcot, license plates, levels of suntans, duty-free bags, the brand of cigarettes a Taiwan executive rapidly puffed after a Detroit flight, a chauffeur with the left side of his jacket protruding from a shoulder holster. Whether the shoes of skycaps and other badged employees matched their station in life. Anyone else in Ray-Bans.

He was satisfied.

The man crossed back to the original side of the street and stood at the curb. His shirt was sheer, formfitting, and Italian. The form said athletic. Could be mistaken for a European cyclist or soccer goalie. Three-hundred-dollar loafers with no socks. A stylish crew cut, dyed blond like the bass player for U2. He didn't waste motion and seemed like one of those people who never laugh, which was correct.

A cell phone vibrated in his pleated pants. He flipped it open. A text message:

"+."

He closed it and waved for the next taxi.

## BISCAYNE BOULEVARD

"Know what else pisses me off?" said Serge. "Calling customer care: 'Please listen carefully as menu items have changed.'"

"It's always that same woman," said Coleman. "Who the fuck is she?"

"The Tokyo Rose of automated messages," said Serge. "She wants us to believe they're hard at work around the clock improving menus."

"They're not?"

Serge shook his head. "Since I became aware of the phenomenon, I've been calling dozens of menus every few days for over a year to check, even when I'm neither a customer nor need care."

"And they don't change?"

"Only the wait time changes. But you're busy thinking: 'Holy Jesus! A new menu! And I just got used to the old one—better pay close attention or I won't receive ultimate pampering.' And you're so rattled you miss the real issue of not talking to a live human."

"That always bites." Coleman continued up the sidewalk.

"And when you *don't* want to talk to a human, some solicitor calls right after I've poured milk in my cereal, and I say, 'Can't talk now,' which among their people means keep talking, so I interrupt and say, 'Serge isn't here. Cereal's happening.' And they ask what's a convenient time to call back, so I say, 'I don't know. The police are still looking for him. Somehow he got the home address of a telemarketer and they found a bloody clawhammer. Where do you live?'"

"What else do you hate?" asked Coleman.

"Segues."

The shark was a man-eater.

Probably a bull, at least ten feet nose to tail.

It had somehow strayed from Biscayne Bay into the mouth of the Miami River, where people weren't expecting sharks.

They expected sharks even less in the downtown business district, where it now lay on the hot pavement in the middle of Flagler Street.

But it was a busy lunch hour. Office workers in suits walked purposefully along the road. Others in guayaberas sipped espresso at sidewalk sandwich windows. They offhandedly noticed the shark, but it wasn't bothering them, as it was dead, and it was not their concern.

"Serge," said Coleman. "There's a dead shark in the middle of the street."

"It's Miami."

Taxis and sports cars swerved around the fish. Above, commuters looked down from the windows of a Metro Mover pod that slid silently along elevated monorail tracks winding through the downtown skyline and south over the river to the Brickell Financial district. Serge unfolded a scrap of paper and crossed something off a list. He raised a camera sharply upward, snapping photos of a forty-story office building, all glass, glistening in the sun.

Coleman glanced around and sucked a brown paper bag. "You've been taking pictures of buildings all morning."

"Correct." Serge reached in his backpack and removed an envelope. "Stay here. I won't be long."

He ran into the building, then returned.

"What did you just do?" asked Coleman.

"Delivered a message." Serge checked his address list again and strolled half a block. He raised the camera.

"What's *this* building?" asked Coleman.

*Click, click, click.* "Argentinian consulate. Last one was Germany."

"Consulate?"

Serge held up his page of notes. "That's this whole list—sixty consulates within a two-mile radius." He resumed west. "Outside of Washington, Miami is the diplomatic capital of America. Even the Canadians have a consulate here."

"The Canadians! Christ!"

"No shit. They scare the hell out of me," said Serge. "I mean, what on earth are the Canadians doing with a consulate in Miami?" *Click, click, click.* "Nothing good."

"But why do you need so many pictures of the same buildings?"

"I don't need any." *Click, click, click.* "These are to provoke a response."

"Response?"

*Click, click, click.* "Take enough photos of consulates, and people act fidgety. That's how I intend to make contact."

"With who?"

Serge stowed the camera. "What's the one thing every consulate has?"

"Desks?"

"A spy." Serge pulled another envelope from his backpack. "And in case my photos don't work, there's Plan B." He ran across the street again and returned.

"Who are you delivering those messages to?" asked Coleman.

"The spy."

"What's the message?"

"Just a generic greeting. Brighten up their day."

"No secrets?"

Serge shook his head. "I'm not out to pass information. Just raise curiosity."

"What for?"

"To get hired."

"By the consulate?"

"Or whoever has it under surveillance."

"You're losing me again."

"All consulates are under constant surveillance." Serge pointed at a black SUV parked up the street. "Looking for defectors, secret agents, keeping track of their own to see who's career is moving up. If you loiter around enough of these buildings, you're bound to show up on an internal report. 'Say, who's this new guy at ten consulates on Tuesday? That's seriously connected. Maybe he should work for us.'"

"Can I see one of the messages?"

Serge grabbed another envelope from his backpack.

Coleman unfolded the note. "But it's blank."

"Exactly."

"I mean, there's no message here."

"Oh, there's a message all right."

"I don't understand."

"Spies will. You pass a note with regular writing and it goes right in the junk-mail pile." Serge took the paper back and returned it to the envelope. "But they can't resist a blank page. It's like crack to a spy: 'This must be super important! Get the lab guys right on it!'"

"What kind of message are they supposed to find?"

"If they're remotely competent, they'll be able to raise the invisible ink."

"Where'd you get invisible ink?"

"Grocery store." Serge walk another block. *Click, click, click.* "Stay here." He ran across the street again.

"Wait! I want to come."

Coleman caught up with him in the lobby. "What kind of job are you looking for?"

Serge stared at a wall, reading plastic letters inside a glass case that listed offices by floor. "I've always wanted to be a secret agent. From now on, I'm completely dedicating my existence to the art of spycraft. And it fits snugly with my new Master Plan, Mark Five."

"You never said anything."

"Just found out. Watched that spy-movie marathon on TBS and kind of fixated." He tapped the glass case. "Here it is, seventh floor." They dashed across the lobby.

"So you're really going to be a spy?" asked Coleman.

"I already am one."

"But you don't work for anybody yet."

"And that's exactly what they all think." Serge waited outside an elevator and stared up at lighted numbers. "Where's the rule that says you can't just unilaterally declare yourself a spy and snoop around for no reason? That's the whole key to life: Fuck explaining yourself to people. Plus Miami is the perfect place, absolutely crawling with self-employed, freelance agents in dummy corporations ready to join any government that can't have direct involvement with an illicit operation. I'll just act suspicious until the highest bidder comes along."

The doors opened. They got in. Coleman sucked his paper sack. "But how do you get hired as a spy?"

"By acting like you don't want to get hired. If you just barge into some office asking for a spy job, they'll think you're a double agent with disinformation. Or worse, a conspiracy kook off the street. That's how the conspiracy works."

Elevator doors opened on seven.

Ahead, glass doors with gold letters: CONSULATE OF COSTA GORDA.

Serge grabbed a handle and went inside.

Flags and travel brochures and the national crest.

Serge whispered sideways to Coleman, "What you need to do is play hard to get, which makes *them* want *you*."

"How do you do that?"

"Behave inscrutably. Then contact will be made on a park bench by a man in a hat feeding pigeons."

They entered the consulate. "This next part's critical," said Serge. "I better drink lots of coffee." He walked over to the reception area's coffee machine and poured a cup.

Coleman drained his paper sack. "Serge, the woman behind the reception desk is staring at us. Not in a nice way."

"My plan's working." He chugged the Styrofoam cup and approached the desk.

The woman narrowed her eyes. "Can I help you?"

Serge quickly glanced around, then leaned closer. "The code word is *smegma*."

## CHANNEL 7

*"This is Cynthia Ricardo reporting live outside the Miami morgue, where police are still baffled by the so-called Hollow Man discovered in a run-down motel behind the former Orange Bowl. Also known as the Jack-O'-Lantern Man, he has since been identified as Juan Vizquel, whose fingerprints implicate him in numerous tourist robberies near the airport. Most puzzling is the cadaver's empty chest cavity, missing all internal organs, but with no external surgical marks. Meanwhile, authorities are seeking the whereabouts of mysterious vigilantes responsible for the murder. Two surviving witnesses from Bowling Green credit the suspects with saving their lives during an attempted carjacking, and further believe that the pair—clad in superhero costumes—are on a crusade to rid Miami's streets of crime and legalize marijuana."*

Inside the morgue . . .

A homicide lieutenant burst through lab doors.

"Got anything yet?"

The medical examiner didn't look up. "Hold your horses."

"The chief wants this solved fast," said the lieutenant. "The press just came up with another nickname."

The examiner was a gnomelike public servant with a habit of girlish giggles when handling close-up gore. It got under the lieutenant's last layer of skin, and the examiner explored the possibilities.

"We got another problem," said the lieutenant, staring curiously at the gray body on a cold metal table. "There's an information leak somewhere."

The examiner picked up a sharp instrument. "Not in my department."

"*Some*body's talking to reporters. Have you seen the headlines?"

The examiner nodded.

"Do you have to giggle?"

The examiner reached for safety glasses. "I thought you'd be happy."

The beginning of an incision at the collarbone.

"Happy?" said the detective. "I'm not feeling the joy."

The examiner chuckled to himself. "You cleared at least fifteen car-jackings, including a fatal with that Dutch tourist."

"But now we've got vigilantes cruising the airport." The lieutenant picked up an X-ray and held it to the ceiling light. "The chamber of commerce hasn't stopped calling."

"People on talk radio seem to like him. Especially the part about the cape."

"We look ridiculous."

Slicing continued in classic autopsy Y-pattern. A giggle.

The lieutenant held the X-ray to the light again. "I see I'm talking to the wrong person."

The examiner set down his instrument and looked up. "What do you want from me?"

"A conclusive ruling." He extended a palm toward the table. "What's taking so long? You're usually done way before this."

"It's a complicated case." The examiner reached toward his desk and opened a file. "Seemed open-and-shut at first. Fractured femur and tibia from when the car hit him, embedded windshield glass in his scalp. Almost positive I'd find internal punctures and hemorrhaging from a rib. Then I saw these . . ." He held up his own X-rays. ". . . I thought our machine was broken. See how the entire chest cavity is empty? All organs removed."

"You're shitting me," said the lieutenant. "I thought the papers were just being sensational, like Squid Boy."

The examiner shook his head. "He's literally hollow. So then I thought his lacerations from the car were covering surgical entry. You heard those urban legends about a guy waking up in a hotel bathtub full of ice, no kidney and a telephone?"

"Some surgeon did this?"

The examiner shook his head again. "No incisions. And none of the lacerations penetrated the hypodermis. Some mysterious new technique I've never seen before, like building a ship in a bottle. That's why it's taking so long." He slapped a cold shoulder. "We can't hurry into this guy, or I might destroy evidence of the method."

"You wouldn't say not to hurry if it was your ass in city hall this morning." The officer wiped his forehead with a handkerchief. "We need to stop all the wild speculation. You should hear the rumors: voodoo, supernatural, UFOs. It's like the freakin' *X-Files* out there."

"How am I supposed to stop that?"

"Bring it down to earth. Surely there's some reasonable explanation that's boring and will get the reporters—and the chief—off my back."

The examiner grabbed his knife again and finished the Y-cut. "Don't get your hopes up."

"What's that supposed to mean?"

"I've looked at this from all angles, and a flying saucer is as good as anything I've come up with." A bone saw buzzed to life.

"You're not making me feel any better."

"And you're crowding me." The saw went back on the tray and the rib spreader came off.

The lieutenant winced. The examiner stuck his head down. "That's more like it. Clue city."

"What'd you find?"

The examiner scraped inside with what looked like an ice cream scoop and held the results toward the officer.

"That's disgusting. Get it out of my face."

The examiner set it aside. "Extensive internal burns."

"You mean like he was in a fire?"

The M.E. took another scoop from the abdomen. "There are many kinds of burns besides fire, and no indication here of external heat trauma."

"This just gets worse and worse."

"When I make some slides from tissue samples, we'll know a lot more." The examiner bent down again. "Now, if you leave me alone, I can work faster."

"You'll call?"

"Got you on speed dial."

The lieutenant put his hat back on and headed out. He stopped in the doorway, neck muscles seized. Behind him, giggling. "A cape."

The receptionist glared at Serge.

He produced an envelope and glanced around again. "Give this to your spy."

"Spy?"

"Every consulate has a spy."

"But we don't—"

Serge winked. "They trained you well. And since you hold such a low position, *you* might even be the spy, like the submarine cook in *The Hunt for Red October.* If so, open that envelope and read it yourself." Serge chugged the rest of his coffee, then held the empty cup to his left eyeball. "Some spies have to put things in their butt. I don't want that job, unless it's something very, very small. Coleman would do it, but his bowels are unreliable whenever you need to count on them. In the 1965 James Bond movie *Thunderball,* the skydiving frogmen are supposed to be jumping into the Bahamas, but downtown Miami is in the background. Or am I lying? See how I turned that around? That's critical in the shadow world: The truth is the lie, and the lie is the truth. Sometimes it's a limerick or a productive cough. I saw a werewolf with a Chinese menu in his hand. Dead shark in the street. The code word now is *monkey-pox . . .*"

One of the building's elevators reached the ground floor. Five beefy men rushed Serge and Coleman out the front door and threw them down on the sidewalk.

Coleman got up and rubbed his hands on his shirt. "Don't take it too bad. Maybe the next people will hire you."

"What are you talking about?" Serge checked his backpack and threw a broken thermos in the garbage. "Those guys hired me."

Coleman looked puzzled. "I haven't been hired much, but when it has happened, they don't rough me up and throw me really hard on the ground."

"Everything in the spy world is opposite." Serge hoisted his backpack. "Remember the constant surveillance? If they took us out to dinner and had loads of laughs, *that* would mean I wasn't hired. This way, anybody watching would mistakenly think we annoyed them. Standard protocol to distance themselves before they activate me."

"But who would be watching?"

Serge shrugged and headed east toward the waterfront.

A city truck pulled up. Workers threw a shark in the back like they were picking up a discarded sofa on the side of the highway.

The truck drove off, revealing a black SUV with tinted windows parked on the other side of Flagler. The back window rolled down and a telephoto lens poked out.

## MIAMI MORGUE

A door flew open.

"You said you had something on the carjacker?" asked the lieutenant.

"And how," said the examiner. "I'd love to meet the killer."

"I'd love to kill him. So how'd he do it?"

The examiner clapped his hands a single time. "Okay, this is really cool. The mind that thought this up . . ." A whistle in admiration.

"Will you just spill it?" The lieutenant glanced at the foot of the autopsy table and tilted his head like a cocker spaniel. "Wait, what's that metal canister with the evidence tag?"

"After I checked slides in the microscope, I went back to the police report. Your guys got lucky. During their neighborhood canvass, one of the uniforms found the canister in a trash bin behind a convenience store. He thought it was unrelated, but because of what it is, and the location, he logged it into evidence anyway as probable stolen property. More on that later. Take a look in the microscope."

The lieutenant bent over and adjusted focus on twin eyepieces. "What am I seeing?"

"Chemical burn. Liquid nitrogen."

The officer stood back up. "That's all Greek."

"It is to most people, so I set up a demonstration . . . This makes my whole month!"

"Can you get on with it?"

"Right . . ." The M.E. slipped on his thickest gloves and went to cold storage, retrieving a round thermal container the width of a punch bowl. Then he grabbed a disarticulated cadaver hand. "Don't worry, we were going to throw this out anyhow. Now watch closely . . ."

The lieutenant didn't need to be told. He leaned with rapt attention as the examiner unscrewed the container's lid. Wisps of vapor wafted out the top.

The examiner held up the lifeless, severed hand, then giggled and dipped it wrist-deep in the jug. He listened to a wall clock tick. Then pulled it out.

The lieutenant scratched his head. "Looks the same, just a different color."

Another giggle. He grabbed a tiny surgical hammer off the instrument tray and smacked the hand just below the knuckles.

"Jesus!" The officer jumped back as frozen slivers scattered on the floor. "It shattered like an ice sculpture." A closer look. "There's . . . nothing left."

"And that's liquid nitrogen, minus three hundred Fahrenheit." The M.E. grabbed a dustpan and swept up the pieces. "But here's the critical step." He dumped the pan's contents in a sink and turned on the hot water.

The lieutenant watched the remains melt and circle the drain until they were gone. "I still don't get how he did it."

"Easier than you'd think—if you're as sharp as this guy. He probably poured the nitrogen down the dead man's throat with a long funnel. But had to roll him around so it wouldn't settle and freeze through a cavity wall. And for even distribution, he needed to repeat the process over and over, each time pouring in hot water to melt what he had just iced over, suctioning it out."

"Suction?"

"You could do it with items as simple as a gas-can tube and turkey baster."

"But where the heck does somebody get liquid nitrogen?"

"Anyone can get it," said the M.E. "Just call the agricultural agent in any county and ask who maintains cryogenic chambers for animal husbandry, usually prize bulls." He pointed at the metal tank near the foot of the autopsy table. "They even deliver, refills as low as thirty bucks."

"Mother of God! I thought this might calm those reporters, but it's even worse." The detective grabbed the M.E. by the arm. "I don't know who's leaking to the press, but we cannot under any circumstances let this get out. Can you imagine the headlines?" He released the examiner and rubbed his own forehead. "How on earth am I going to identify the killer?"

"Might be able to help you there." The examiner walked over and patted the top of the tank. "The sample chamber wasn't empty. We can do a genetic test."

"What? You mean you can identify the bull semen and maybe track down where he bought it?"

The examiner shook his head. "Not bull semen. Human."

The lieutenant felt sick. "This definitely can't get out."

"Mum's the word." The examiner turned his back. "I'll send it for DNA immediately after I write up the official cause of death."

"Please tell me it's something that won't make a good headline."

The examiner saved his biggest giggle for last.

"He froze to death in Miami."


## PALMETTO EXPRESSWAY

"Damn, it's hot."

The driver of a white van switched on a small, battery-powered fan glued to the dashboard.

The front passenger looked up from the *Herald*'s sports section. "Take the next exit."

They got off the highway, and two others trucks followed.

Opa-locka is one of the rough older areas, just north of Hialeah. Often tops national crime charts. Like driving through Baghdad. But not the violence part. Back in the 1920s, local founders kind of got hung up on *Arabian Nights,* and it now boasts the country's highest concentration of Moorish architecture. City hall looks like a flying carpet might sail out a window. One of the streets is named Ali Baba Avenue.

There's also a small airport that used to be big. The Graf Zeppelin paid a visit. Amelia Earhart took off on her fateful flight from here, and there's now a public park in her name where people honor the pilot by playing Frisbee golf and visiting the insect museum.

Three white vans skirted the north side of the park and passed through galvanized airport gates. They raced toward the civil aviation side of the runways, across from the Coast Guard air-sea-rescue helicopters.

A twin-engine Beechcraft waited with its side door flopped down. Vans parked. A bucket brigade passed wooden crates up the airplane's steps.

Behind the tail, a stretch Mercedes. Four solemn men in a row. Banker suits and haircuts. Arrogance. Victor Evangelista strolled across the tarmac with a loud smile. "Is that for me?"

The suits looked down. A briefcase handcuffed to a wrist. A key went in the lock. Airplane engines sparked to life.

Victor's hair whipped from the propellers. He grabbed the briefcase in a deafening drone and tossed it to one of the jumpsuits. Victor never counted. And the men never looked in the crates. That level of business. Not trust. Certainty of consequence.

They stopped to watch the Beechcraft take off into the setting sun. The plane banked hard south until it disappeared behind rain clouds, casting long angular shadows over the glades.

The suits stared across the runway at the Coast Guard detail, staring back. "After all this time, how do they not suspect?"

"Because they know for sure," said Vic. The smile broadened. "And under specific orders to stand down. But don't worry: You're paying a lot for those connections."

The tallest suit: "Dinner? Versailles?"

Vic shook his head and pointed up. "Got another shipment."

"Do you ever stop?"

"I'm the best."

Four men laughed and climbed in the Mercedes. It headed for the exit as another Beechcraft cleared the limo's roof and touched down in waning light.

A cell phone rang.

Evangelista excavated it from a pocket under his flowing Tommy Bahama shirt. He checked the number on the display and flipped it open. "I thought you didn't like to make phone calls. Hear it's snowing in D.C."

"Vic, Jesus, what the fuck blew up at our warehouse?"

"My car."

"But how'd it happen?"

"How do you think?"

"Scooter again?"

"My cross to bear."

"You let that moron near the shipments?"

"You're the one who forced me to bring him along," said Vic.

"Because of politics," barked the voice on the other end. "Doesn't mean let him play with the rocket launchers."

Vic turned and shielded himself from the wind as another plane landed. "Thanks for caring about my car."

"This ain't a joke! We got budget hearings Monday. And this is just the sort of thing that could expose everything."

"You worry too much."

"That's my job! A few more shipments and we're in the clear."

Twin propellers jerked to a stop. "Another just landed."

"No more screwups," said the phone. "Have one of the boys take Scooter to get a milk shake or something."

"Speaking of which, what happened to that reporter who was poking around our offshore accounts."

"I don't know what you're talking about."

"The one who went missing after getting drunk in Costa Gorda."

"Accidents happen."

"You're the one who's so worried about drawing heat," said Vic. "Holy God, taking out a reporter—"

"Not on the phone! How many times do I have to tell you? No more phone calls!"

"You're the one who called me."

*Click.*


## THE NEXT DAY

Downtown Miami.

Two pedestrians reached the corner of Flagler and turned left toward the basketball arena. "There's Bayside Market," said Serge. "They have a picture of Shaq next to a powerboat that takes tourists on runs past the Scarface mansion."

"What's that UFO-shaped building by the marina?"

"The Hard Rock Cafe."

"Didn't it have a giant guitar on the roof?"

"Hurricane blew it off and sank a yacht."

Across the boulevard: bright sun and a gusting breeze off Biscayne Bay. Colorful flags snapped atop rows of just-planted aluminum poles. An army of landscapers manicured hedges, drove lawn mowers, and rode skyward in hydraulic cherry-picker baskets to snip away any palm frond with the least tinge of brown. Behind them, others in yellow hard hats erected scaffolds around the amphitheater for lighting, sound, and news cameras.

In the middle, an eternal flame.

TV correspondents loved it as a backdrop.

*"Good afternoon. This is Gloria Rojas reporting live from downtown Miami, where workers are putting the final touches on the landmark Bayfront Park in preparation for this weekend's Summit of the Americas, which promises to be a cultural high point . . ."*

A passerby jumped up and down behind her. *"Wooo! Dolphins number one! . . ."*

Serge and Coleman walked in front of the television crew. They climbed in an orange-and-green '68 Plymouth Road Runner and drove down Biscayne Boulevard. All around them, factory-fresh BMWs and

Lincolns with the a/c full blast, heading for high-rise hotels. On the other side of the median, more luxury sedans sped toward Miami International, guided by commercial jets flying down from the north and private Lears soaring up from South America.

At the airport's international arrivals wing, the customs line was unusually stacked up and snaked back through the concourse with random curves as people saw fit. No waiting in a separate VIP line, where visiting dignitaries went unchecked thanks to diplomatic status. They flowed through the terminal circled by entourage knots radiating out in strict pecking order: immediate family, cabinet members, campaign donors, political strategists, personal assistants, distant family—passing newsstands, shoe shines, and airport bars with TVs set to local news.

"... *On a lighter note, Tuesday's mystery has been solved and no charges will be pressed against three Honduran fishermen who caught a wayward shark in the Miami River and carried it through downtown in a futile attempt to sell it at local restaurants. Witnesses reported the trio taking the shark aboard the Metro Mover for a loop around the city before finally getting off the monorail near the Museum of Art and throwing the fish in the street ...*"

Outside, along the pickup curb, a waiting row of limos with small flags on the hoods.

Another Latin entourage reached the curb near sunset. Security agents went first, making a visual sweep in mirror sunglasses, then urgently waving the rest forward.

The president-for-life of a country the size of Connecticut approached one of the limos. A bodyguard opened the back door.

An explosion.

The security detail threw the president to the sidewalk and piled on top. They peeked up from pavement level. Everyone else nonchalantly tending luggage and hailing cabs.

Agents stood up.

"What just happened?" asked the president.

A skycap looked in the distance at a black column of smoke. "Probably shooting *Burn Notice.*"

The president's suit was brushed off. He climbed in the limo and headed for the Dolphin Expressway.

At the rear of the pickup line, an orange-and-green Road Runner sat at the curb, next to a row of newspaper boxes with large headlines:

CARJACKER FREEZES TO DEATH IN MIAMI

COLORFUL CAPES NEW RAGE ON SOUTH BEACH

HUMAN SPERM FOUND IN BULL SEMEN TANK

ETHICAL DEBATE: SHOULD HERO-VIGILANTE BE CLONED?

In the street, five lines of exiting airline traffic merged with designed chaos. Brake lights. Hand gestures. Horns honked and echoed off the terminal. A police whistle blew. Serge pulled away from the curb . . .

Night came quickly. Long rows of headlights at the tollbooths near the former site of the Orange Bowl. A limo hit a blinker for the cash lane.

It was one of those twin skies. Light blue behind, where the sun had just gone down over the Gulf of Mexico. Ahead: impenetrably black toward the Atlantic.

Serge handed change to one of the collectors and spun rubber.

Coleman bent down and fired a fattie. He blew a cloud out the window. "What are we doing again now?"

"Fighting crime."

"I thought you were spying."

"Coleman, there are many things that naturally go together and you can do at the same time, like receiving oral sex and organizing post-cards."

Coleman stared out the window. "We're just driving in circles around the airport again."

"You are correct, fact-boy."

"But we did it the other night. Remember nabbing the carjacker and saving that old couple? Problem solved."

"Coleman, there isn't just one guy behind it all. Think of the ground he'd have to cover in one night."

"Like Bad Santa."

"We're fighting a pandemic," said Serge. "Out-of-towners don't realize the dicey area surrounding the airport."

Coleman took another hit. "I didn't think the neighborhood was that bad."

"Not the neighborhood specifically. But there's a massive predatory element that lurks in the shadows, looking for any car that's not local, especially rentals."

"Why?"

"The reasons are like the sand on the beach. But to name a few: Criminals know most tourists can't afford the hassle and cost of returning to testify, especially since it's an international city and many are from overseas. Two: Visitors get lost faster than our Silver Alert seniors wandering from retirement homes. Three: They don't have the Miami Survival Skill Set."

"Skills?"

"They pull up at a stoplight and don't know to leave a space for evasive maneuver from a box-in robbery. And if they get rear-ended, they *definitely* don't know not to get out of the car to exchange insurance information like everything's lollipops in Candy Land."

Serge's eyes made another scan of traffic. They locked onto a vehicle ten cars ahead: limo with small flags flapping on each side of the hood. He changed lanes.

"I didn't know it was that bad," said Coleman.

"Used to be worse," said Serge. "One summer it hit the tipping point, and an embarrassing number of Europeans had their return flights upgraded to coffins in the cargo hold. So the state legislature passed a law sanitizing license plates."

"What's that mean?"

"Tourist robberies around the airport became so commonplace it spawned a widespread slang called 'Z-ing.'"

"Z...?"

"Rentals used to be designated with a *Z* or *Y* on their license plates. Or 'Manatee County.' Criminals must have a newsletter or something."

The limo drifted into the far right lane. Serge matched it. They crested an overpass, and the skyline grew near, giving the night air a phosphorus glow.

"Serge?"

"Yes, Beavis?"

"I get the part about circling the airport, but why did we park at that curb, just to pull away two minutes later?"

"I wanted to look at flags on the limo hood. Needed to make sure we're following the right car."

"What's the right car?"

"The one from the country whose consulate just hired me. Spies are expected to take initiative." Serge checked all mirrors. "Plus the Summit of the Americas is coming this week, and my beloved state is reaping the prestige she so richly deserves. The last thing I want is for her to get a black eye."

"You're worried something might show us in an inaccurate light?"

"No, the accurate light." Traffic backed to a standstill. Serge craned his neck to find the limo. "If that stretch stays on the expressway, they should be okay. Just as long as they don't get off the wrong exit."

"Serge, their blinker . . ."

The limo got off the wrong exit.

The Road Runner sped up, then screeched to a halt.

Red taillights came on in sequence.

"We're stuck in a traffic jam," said Coleman. "What are we going to do?"

"This is what." Serge swerved into the breakdown lane and raced toward the exit with two wheels in the dirt. They hit the bottom of the ramp and looked around.

"Where are they?" said Coleman.

"We lost 'em."

A dozen blocks ahead, a limo drove slowly down a deserted access road. The visiting president reclined in the back, pouring brandy from a Swarovski crystal decanter. "Are you sure you know where you're going?"

"Yes, sir," said the driver, glancing back through the open partition. "Biscayne Boulevard should be coming up soon."

They stopped at a red light.

"But I thought Biscayne was downtown, on the other side of the skyline." The president looked out the window. "There aren't even any streetlights. It's totally dark—"

*Bam.*

The president pitched forward. A flying brandy glass conked his food-taster in the forehead.

"What the hell was that?"

The chauffeur looked in his side mirror. "I think someone rear-ended us."

"Great." The president's head fell back against the top of his seat. "Just take care of it."

The driver grabbed his door handle. "Be right back . . ."

. . . A Plymouth Road Runner rolled quietly along the access road.

"Still don't see them," said Coleman.

Serge pointed at a distant intersection. "There they are."

"The light turned green, but they're not moving," said Coleman. "And there's another car behind them."

Under Serge's breath: "Please don't get out of the car. Please don't get out of the car. Please don't—"

"Look," said Coleman. "The driver's getting out of the car."

Serge cut his headlights.

Ahead, the chauffeur walked to the rear of the limo. He glanced at the crumpled bumper, then over at the other vehicle's two occupants walking toward him, almost featureless in the absence of light, except for respective silhouettes of dreadlocks and a shaved head. The chauffeur opened his wallet and fished for a foreign license. "You guys got ID?" He looked up. The answer came in the muzzle of a MAC-10 between his ribs . . .

Two blocks back: Coleman hit a joint and strained to see ahead in the darkness. "Doesn't look like things are going so well for the chauffeur. What do you think will happen?"

"Someone's probably going to die."

"How do you know?"

"I just have this uncanny feeling." Serge shook his head. "It's such a tragedy."

"Do you have this feeling because you're the one who's going to kill them?"

"That's why it's such a tragedy. I'm trying to eliminate negative energy from my life."

"Look," said Coleman. "There's *two* bad guys this time."

"At least that'll make it more interesting."

"How?"

"Because one will get to see the other go first." Serge parked on the side of the road. "That's always a conversation starter."

# PART I

## A SPY COMES IN
*from the* HEAT

## Chapter **ONE**

### THREE DAYS EARLIER

A field of tall, dry grass. Brown, hip level.

The grass rippled through the middle. Could have been wind, but it continued in a narrow, straight line.

Then serious rustling.

Whispers.

"Coleman, stop thrashing around."

"I'm trying to, but I can't see anything." He crawled on hands and knees. "The grass is too high."

"That's the point." Serge slid forward with expert stealth. "We're hunting."

"What are we hunting?"

"I already told you."

"Was I fucked up?"

"You still are."

"The streak continues."

"Shhhhh! We have to approach downwind in complete silence." Serge inched ahead. "Coyotes have acute senses."

"Coyotes!" Coleman's head popped up through the grass like a groundhog.

Serge jerked him back down by the hair.

"Ow!"

"Stay low or they'll see you."

"But I hear they bite. I don't want that."

"Not to worry." Serge resumed his crawl, dragging a zippered bag. "I speak with the animals."

"That's why I don't understand this hunting business." Coleman marched on his elbows. "You're usually so gentle with critters."

"Still am." Serge reached back in the sack. "That's why I only hunt with a camera."

"Now it makes sense," said Coleman. "Except I wouldn't think coyotes came within fifty miles of this place."

"Neither would most people." Serge dug through the bag again and removed an airtight foil pouch. "New migratory phenomenon from the state's exploding development encroaching on their natural habitat—"

Serge froze with laser focus.

Coleman peered through the blades of grass. "What is it?"

"There they are." He silently raised his camera. "Looks like three or four families. Which is good because in order to survive, they must rip their prey to pieces with coordinated ambushes from swarms of their adults." *Click, click, click.*

Coleman's head swiveled sideways. "Ambush."

"It's really something to watch." *Click, click, click.*

"Do they have it on TV?"

"And miss it in person? Do you realize how fortunate we are to have this rare opportunity?" Serge stowed the camera. "Come on. We have to change direction and head that way."

"Why?"

"To get upwind." Serge crept forward. "So they can detect our scent."

Coleman grabbed Serge's ankle from behind. "You're deliberately trying to get them to attack?"

"Of course. Otherwise what's the point? . . . We're upwind now." Serge broke open the foil and removed a pump bottle.

"What's that?" asked Coleman.

"Coyote bait." He heavily sprayed the ground and grass. "In case they don't like our smell, this stuff has the scent of their favorite food. And makes them more aggressive."

"Have you lost your mind?"

"I know what you're thinking: Baiting a field is illegal. But only if you're hunting with rifles." Serge looked back. "The bigger ones are getting restless and beginning to circle. Means they've picked up our trail. We'll need to move fast."

Coleman scrambled over the top of Serge.

Serge continued spraying as he crawled. "Now to launch phase two of my—"

He was drowned out as a large jet flew low overhead and cleared a fence.

Coleman looked up. "I can't believe all these coyotes live around the Tampa airport."

"*National Geographic* sails down the Amazon and climbs the Matterhorn. Anyone can do that." Serge dismissed the idea with a flick of his wrist. "But tracking wild predators in the middle of a major American city is the real adventure."

"But how did they pick this place?"

"World-class litterbugs. The bastards attract coyotes to the city's west side, where they've begun straying onto runways, imperiling both themselves and frequent fliers. Serge cannot allow that. Airport workers are firing blank guns to scare them off, but I have a better plan."

"One of your secret master plans?"

"Actually an impromptu mini-master plan, not to be confused with the fleeting notion, half-baked idea, or emergency room spin-story for a masturbation mishap."

"You had one of those, too?"

"No." Serge pocketed his spray bottle. "My current plan simultaneously draws the packs away from Tampa International *and* discourages littering."

"But who's doing the littering?"

"Those guys we walked past on the way out to this field."

"The ones in red jerseys by those pickup trucks with the gun racks?"

"That's them," said Serge. "And you know how I hate litterers. No circle of hell is too low."

Another roar in the sky.

"Whoa!" said Coleman. "That was really loud. Must be landing on a closer runway."

Serge shook his head. "It's the military flyover for the national anthem before the football game. Planes take off from the MacDill base in south Tampa and follow Dale Mabry Highway north. One of my favorite local traditions. I love to stand in the middle of the highway and salute as they fly above. We can get up now."

They stood at attention and watched a quartet of F-16 Falcons blaze over the filling stadium.

"At ease." Serge looked at his watch. "It's almost kickoff."

The pair reached the edge of the grassy field. Serge leaned down and extended the telescoping handle on his zippered bag, which was a suitcase.

"Look," said Coleman. "There are those guys in the jerseys again."

"So they are." Serge rolled his luggage onto a dirt parking lot. "This is the new overflow parking area, which is how the whole coyote thing got started."

Coleman followed with his own bag. "Jesus, look at all the trash! There was just a little when we arrived."

Serge's face turned redder than the jerseys ahead: guys whooping it up, faces and chests painted team colors, flipping burgers, chugging beers, rummaging fifty-gallon coolers on the tailgates of pickup trucks with Marlin hunting rifles in the window racks—"Buccaneers Number One!"—throwing garbage over their shoulders.

Serge and Coleman were noticed.

A fan in a red-and-silver Afro wig elbowed his pal. "Hey Ralph, get a load of the goofy guys with the luggage." He cupped hands around his mouth. "What's the matter? Get lost on your way to the airport? Ha ha ha ha ha . . ."

"Ha ha ha ha ha." Serge laughed. "Actually we're sales reps."

"Sales reps?"

Serge nodded. "You know how companies are always dispatching employees to give away free samples outside stadiums?"

"You got free samples of some shit?"

Serge grinned. "Are the Bucs number one?"

"Fuckin' A!"

Serge reached in his suitcase and pulled out an armload of foil pouches. "Bugs will eat you up something fierce in Florida, especially this side of the stadium with all the marshes."

The Afro scratched his painted belly. "They've been biting all morning."

"And what have you been doing about it?" asked Serge.

A plastic mug rose in the air. "Drink beer!" The Afro high-fived a man wearing a construction helmet with cup holders.

Serge rapidly flung foil pouches to the gang, left to right, like dealing cards. "Apply liberally to chest and arms, and your scratching days will be reserved for instant lottery tickets."

They began spraying. "You say this stuff really works?"

"You'd be surprised."

"Gee, thanks, mister."

The pair rolled suitcases until they reached a sidewalk along Dale Mabry.

"Serge, where's the airport entrance?"

"Around the right, five miles."

"Five freakin' miles! That's a long way to walk in this heat!"

"Won't have to. Tampa is the strip-club capital of America. You're never more than spitting distance."

"What's that got to do with walking?"

"Every time we land a national convention or Super Bowl, TV pundits mock us for our titty bars, but you never have to worry about where to find a cab in this city." Serge gestured at a nearby building with a giant silver disk on the roof, where people paid extra for lap dances inside a flying saucer. "There's the closest taxi stand."

Coleman stared at a fleet of yellow cars on the other side of the road. "But why couldn't we have just gotten a cab in the first place?"

"Because we're about to take a great vacation to Miami for the fabulous Summit of the Americas." There was a break in traffic, and Serge trotted halfway across the highway to the concrete median. "Except everyone else just *goes* to the airport. I like to take the path less traveled."

An ambulance raced toward shrill screams from an overflow parking lot, and Serge and Coleman dashed across the street to a flying saucer.

## WASHINGTON, D.C.

Office of Homeland Security.

Glass doors, card readers, metal detectors. Bright walls and shiny floors. The lobby displayed the department's official seal of a bald eagle in a fiercely protective pose, giving citizens increased peace of mind on the approximate level of a smoke detector.

Malcolm Glide navigated a maze of hallways toward the center of the building, passing cordially through ascending security-level checkpoints. Even though he had no official identification.

Because Malcolm had no official title in Washington. And total access.

Because he was a puppet master. And no one was better.

In the last midterms alone, Malcolm was the brains behind the election of six senators and fifteen congressmen, despite voter registration heavily favoring their opponents. Malcolm was the ultimate political partisan. To money. Eleven of his candidates were Republican, ten Democrat.

Footsteps echoed through waxed halls. Glide dressed like his clients: tailored black suit, red or blue tie, banker's haircut, and teeth-whitening treatments requiring ultraviolet beams and eye protection.

At six one, his dark-haired pretty-boy looks had gotten him the pick at any sorority. In three decades since, they'd matured to nonthreatening leading-man standards, like Cary Grant or Jimmy Stewart. He could have done TV commercials, but he did this.

Malcolm took another left down another hall. He had actually done one TV ad for aftershave.

Glide made a final turn in the last hall and entered the department's inner sanctum. He cheerfully waved at a personal secretary and strolled into the director's office without knocking. The aftershave was Hai Karate.

The director was on the phone. "I gotta go." He hung up and smiled. "Malcolm!"—practically running around his desk to shake hands.

"Mr. Tide!"

"How many times have I told you to call me Rip."

Rip detested Malcolm, but Glide held the strings to key votes that controlled his budget, so he loved him.

"Rip," said Glide. "Hate to ask since you're so busy guarding the safety of every man, woman, and child in America, but I need a big favor."

"Name it."

"I want you to raise the threat level."

"What? Did you hear some overseas chatter? Is it the ports? Airlines?"

"No. Three of my candidates just dipped below forty in the polls. They've unfairly been linked to the latest oil spill in the Gulf."

"Are they linked?"

"Yes. I need something to take over the news cycle."

"No problem." Rip reached behind his desk for the big vinyl threat thermometer. "Uh-oh."

"What's the matter?"

"We're already at the highest threat level." Rip pointed at the top of the thermometer. "Remember? You asked me to raise it last week when one of your candidates apologized to the oil company because *they* were the real victim."

"So make up a new color."

"I can't. The colors are set."

"You're the director of Homeland Security. You can do anything you want."

"Malcolm, don't get me wrong," said Rip. "I'd do anything for you. But my hands are tied. Red's the top color. There's nothing scarier."

Malcolm opened his briefcase. "What about a darker red? I brought some color swatches."

"You might have something there." Rip grabbed a sample and held it up for comparison. "This one seems more upsetting."

"Then it's done."

"I still don't know," said the director. "Two reds. They're pretty close in shade. Won't people get confused?"

Glide snapped his briefcase shut. "Confusion's scarier."

"You're the expert."

Indeed, Glide was.

His motto: All politics is marketing. And in marketing, there are but two variables: product and salesmanship. Malcolm had the best of both worlds.

He'd cornered the market on fear.

And when it came to sales, Glide could package utter terror like a tit to a baby. During campaigns, it was his hottest seller.

It hadn't always been that way.

Just a few short years earlier, the firm Glide founded, Nuance Management Group, was renowned throughout the nation's capital for thorough policy research, unflagging accuracy, strident ethics—and losing a record volume of elections.

It changed overnight.

It was a Tuesday.

Four A.M.

Malcolm Glide sprang up from his pillow in a cold sweat. Heart pounding like a conga drum. Another nightmare about zombies. Except now they'd learned to walk faster.

Malcolm grabbed his chest. "Holy Mother! I'd vote for anybody who could stop that!"

The next morning, Malcolm charged confidently into the boardroom. "Throw away everything." He walked to an easel and ripped down a chart of international exchange rates. "It's all fresh."

Murmurs around the conference table.

"We've been going at this completely wrong." Glide crumpled the chart into a ball and threw it at a secretary's head. "You know how we excruciatingly track swing voters, the base, independents?"

Various levels of nodding.

"Fuck that margin of error!" Glide grabbed a marker and scribbled rapidly on the washable easel. "Behold, our new business model."

They stared in blank thought:

It's the stupid vote, stupid!

Furtive glances across the room.

An intern dared raise his hand. Veterans gasped. "What's that supposed to mean?"

Malcolm pounded his fist on the table. "Everyone tries to get elected by leading. Instead we follow."

"Follow what?"

"The emotions of the people." Malcolm stood and began pacing. "They're a massive disenfranchised class out there who feel abandoned."

"That's awful!"

"Tell me about it," said Malcolm, spinning at the wall and heading back. "Millions of people across our great land who want nothing more than to be left alone and pursue their own happiness of believing mean-spirited bullshit. Except society has evolved away from ignorance. And that's where we come in."

"How?"

"We make being shitty feel good again."

More glances and murmurs.

Another hand went up. "What are we supposed to do?"

Malcolm pounded the table again. "We lie."

A junior partner cleared his throat. "But in politics, everybody else lies. That's what has set us apart."

Malcolm smugly folded his arms. "Except they don't tell the Big Lie."

"What's that?"

Glide leaned forward and seized the edge of the end of the table. "We don't simply say something that's untrue. We make statements so insane that there's no possible intelligent response. Like arguing with some old fart in a rocking chair who claims we never landed on the moon. Any educated person can only laugh. Meanwhile, we've just won over all the non-moon-landing votes."

"Example?" asked the same partner.

"Most of our clients are against health-care reform, right?"

Nodding again around the table.

"Get those pens ready and take this down!" said Glide. "Tomorrow we send out this talking point to our top candidates: The government wants to create death panels to kill your grandmother."

The table laughed.

They weren't laughing long. Next meeting:

"*. . . I can't believe they bought it . . .*"

"*. . . Even Palin's quoting us . . .*"

"*. . . It's all over Fox News . . .*"

Glide swiveled side to side in his high-backed leather chair and puffed a fat cigar. "Remember you heard it here first."

"But how did you know?" asked their mass-mail manager.

"There's a new dawn in America! It isn't enough just to disagree with your opponent anymore. True patriots hate their fucking guts!" Glide got up and kicked the chair out from under a speechwriter. "Anger is sweeping the country! Tea bags from sea to shining sea! Voters everywhere exploding from frustration!"

"Why?"

"Because the facts don't support their beliefs. And we mean to fix that."

"But how?"

"Talk in code." Glide poured a glass of ice water from a sterling carafe. "From now on, the president is a socialist."

"He is?"

"No, but he's black."

"What's that got to do with anything?"

"Tons of people can't stand that the president is the wrong flavor."

"That's racism," said a pollster.

"And racism's not cool anymore," said Glide. "Even for racists. So we call him a socialist."

"That's nuts."

"The people we're trying to reach will get it," said Glide. "*Socialist* is the new 'N-word.' Have that imprinted on some stress balls."

## Chapter *TWO*

**TAMPA INTERNATIONAL AIRPORT**

A cab pulled into the departures lane outside Delta.

Two passengers got out with luggage, and the taxi sped off before Serge had a chance to pay.

Coleman jumped back to avoid getting a foot run over. "What the hell was that about?"

"Beats me." Serge clicked open the handle on his bag. "He was acting weird the whole way, ever since I hopped in the front seat with him."

"I think we're supposed to sit in back."

"And that's why I always sit up front." They walked through automatic doors. "It's about class struggle. You sit in back like King Tut, and you're saying, 'Dance, monkey.' But if you jump up front like equals, it's a bold statement that you'll tolerate B.O. to pull our country together."

Coleman got on an escalator under a sign: ALL GATES. "Then maybe it was when you handed him your gun."

"Could be a new driver," said Serge. "Anyone who works the airport knows you can't take guns on a plane. I could have just thrown it away, but I figured he's got a dangerous job and could use a piece. Even mentioned the serial number had already been filed off."

"You were being considerate."

"Plus I gave him an ammo box to get started and explained that those hollow-point bullets fragment and rattle around inside the body, so there's no way ballistic tests can connect him to anything I might have done."

"That's when he totally wigged," said Coleman. "Shaking real bad, nearly hitting that family unloading their car."

"Must have been carrying some emotional baggage from a domestic fight at home this morning over mysterious phone numbers on the bill that his wife called, and somebody named Loretta answered." Serge got off at the top of the escalator. "Hey, I'm not the one fucking Loretta, so he shouldn't be dumping his wife's shit on me."

"I heard you tell him that," said Coleman.

A bustle of people crisscrossed the hub of the main terminal. Others stared up at arrival and departure screens. Serge stopped for coffee. ". . . And a cup of ice on the side please."

"Iced coffee is more," said the young clerk.

"I didn't order that," said Serge. "Just regular coffee with ice on the side."

"That's still considered iced coffee."

"I don't want iced coffee. I want temperature control. I want a lot of other things, too, but I won't burden you with my agenda because there's a really long line behind me, except if you don't vote, please consider your grandchildren, who could end up in a bizarre futurescape with thought police zipping around ten feet off the ground on antigravity platforms, using pocket brain-erasers to curb individuality and coffee-clerk annoyance. Ice please."

She warily handed him a small cup. Serge walked to the preparation area, counted six cubes into his beverage, then drained the whole thing in one guzzle.

"I love airports!" Serge briskly rolled a suitcase toward the security checkpoint. "All the norms from the regular world are out the window."

"How so?"

"Like that tavern between those gates. People drinking in the morning." He looked at Coleman. "Okay, bad example. Let's go in this gift shop. To enhance the airport gift-shop experience, I pretend I'm a historical figure who's just been time-ported to the twenty-first century. I'm Leonardo da Vinci now. What would such a quotable Renaissance man say in a place like this? 'Five dollars for water from an atoll in the Pacific? Fuck me in the ass!'"

"Serge, people are staring."

The pair walked to the back of the security line. They produced authentic state driver's licenses with fake names acquired from a street broker who hooked them up with a contact in the motor vehicle office. Then they entered the queue leading to the X-ray machines.

"Coleman, here's another example of airport world. See that sign with pictures of prohibited items? Power tools, can of gasoline, a big ax, and my favorite: the Rocky and Bullwinkle bomb shaped like a bowling ball with the fuse actually lit."

"It's pretty funny."

"It's pretty freaky," said Serge. "They don't put up signs before there's a demonstrated need. Terrorists obviously ignore them, so they're meant to solve a problem from the law-abiding public. I mean, who were all these people bringing hatchets and chain saws to the X-ray machine?"

"Sir, excuse me."

Serge looked up at the next security guy checking boarding passes. "Yes?"

"Sir, did you mention hatchets and chain saws?"

"That's right."

"I didn't hear your full remarks," said the guard. "But I must warn you, there are serious penalties for making jokes about airline safety."

"Oh, I wasn't joking." Serge pointed back down the line. "We were just discussing your sign. That's the idea, right? You want people to pay attention to it. Most people walk right by, but not me. And I can't get my head around those illustrations. But then I've never been to Denver, so I don't know what's required to survive at that altitude. Maybe everyone drinking for breakfast in the airport bar has a snow ax and private supply of gasoline. And what's with that last item? Have you had to fire some X-ray people for letting cartoon bombs get through with lit fuses?"

"Please, just no more remarks."

Serge took off his shoes. "It's your sign."

Moments later, he stared up at a departure screen in Airside A. "Son of a bitch!"

"What is it?" asked Coleman.

"Our flight's delayed!"

"But only fifteen minutes," said Coleman.

"I've seen this movie before. 'Fifteen minutes' is code for 'at least three to five hours.' They know the plane's stuck in Pittsburgh, where they wrestled another drunk pilot to the runway, but they don't want an open passenger revolt, so they incrementally string us along fifteen minutes at a time, until you're across the international date line."

Serge paced in front of the departure screen.

Fifteen minutes later, Serge grabbed Coleman and pointed. "Sweet Jesus! They just added another fifteen minutes!"

"Serge, your face is that color again."

"Can't help it." More pacing. "If I'm told to be somewhere important at a specific time, I'm there with an extra wristwatch and breathing exercises to enhance my cooperation. But then they do it to you again! Every fucking airport and doctor's office teasing you along like strippers brushing your crotch with the back of their hand, because the *back* of the hand is the legal loophole. Probably learned that from airport security who pat you down that way so they can't be accused of groping. There are meetings going on somewhere."

"You might be getting worked up over nothing," said Coleman. "For all we know, that could be the last fifteen-minute delay."

"You're probably right," said Serge. "Let's find a seat and relax near screaming infants."

Two hours later. Serge sat near the gate with his head hanging back over the chair and his mouth open.

"Serge," said Coleman. "They just added another fifteen minutes."

"I have to kill myself."

"Maybe another flight attendant grabbed some beers and jumped down the emergency chute."

"Please strangle me."

"You need to get your mind off it."

"You're right." Serge jumped up and ran to the gate desk. "Excuse me? Could you tell me the true departure time for this flight?"

"It's what's on the screen."

"But it's changed eight times already."

"Those were unforeseen circumstances."

"Can you see if there are any other flights?"

"You'll forfeit your fare."

"Why?"

The gate attendant pointed at the departure board. "Your flight's going to be here any minute."

"You're absolutely right. *Any* minute," said Serge. "Like seven thirty-two tomorrow morning."

She glared.

Serge leaned over the desk and pointed down at her computer keyboard. "Could you please check for another flight? We have important business in Miami."

Another glare. She grudgingly addressed her computer.

Serge turned around. "Hey Coleman, come over here. You absolutely have to see this."

"What is it?"

"Something I can't get enough of." Serge pointed over the top of the desk. "An employee with four-inch-long chartreuse fingernails in a job that requires lots of typing." He looked up at the woman. "Better go for the five-inch nails, Lady Gaga. You're about to fry that keyboard."

Steam came out her ears. "I don't think I care for your attitude."

"Then my plan's working." Serge waved at the ceiling. "Fly me out of your life."

Gritted teeth. "All flights are full."

The departure board added fifteen minutes.

Serge stepped away from the desk and huddled with Coleman. "I'm going to get some entertainment value out of this."

"What kind?"

He approached the closed boarding door. "Not only are airlines cutting back on services and charging for bags, but they've begun treating their most valued customers like schmucks. The perks have become laughable."

"What kind of perks?"

"See that six-foot-long velvet cord separating two lines to get on the plane?"

"Yeah?"

"The one on the left is for their special first-class club. They're right next to each other, but there's no difference."

"Except the one on the left has a red carpet," said Coleman.

"It's *supposed* to be a red carpet," said Serge. "But it's just a red doormat. See? It's just a little rectangle with rubber weather stripping around the edge."

"You're right. It is a doormat."

"But not just any doormat." He gestured back at the desk. "In order to complete the charade, they guard that mat like the Shroud of Turin. I once saw this guy running late, and he rushed up with his boarding pass. But he unknowingly stepped on the Red Doormat of Total Ecstasy. There were no other people in line, but they still made him walk back around the cord to the other lane."

Serge took a step sideways.

"That's really weird," said Coleman.

"*A-hem!*" The woman with the fingernails.

"Yes?" said Serge. "How may I help you?"

She looked down. "Your left foot is on the Star-Elite Club carpet."

"Really? Thanks for letting me know . . . So anyway, Coleman—"

"Sir! You have to move your foot!"

Serge moved his foot. "This other time I saw airport maintenance guys fixing something in the ceiling, and they set up their ladder on the doormat, and the gate crew went completely ape-shit." Serge reached out with his leg and set a toe on the doormat, then quickly pulled it back.

"Sir!"

He looked over. "Yes?"

She flared her nostrils.

Serge faced Coleman again. "They started yelling at the maintenance workers: 'Move the ladder! Move the ladder!' 'What?' 'We're about to board a flight!' 'Can't they go around?' 'But it's the Elite carpet! . . .'" He set a toe on the doormat and withdrew it.

"Sir!"

"Is there a problem?"

Teeth gnashed.

"Serge," said Coleman. "She's getting really pissed."

"This is priceless." His toe touched the carpet again.

"Mister!"

Coleman looked out the window. "Our plane just pulled up. They're not adding another fifteen minutes."

"We rock now." Serge grabbed the handle of his suitcase and took a spot in the crowd.

Finally, their row was called. Serge walked around the correct side of the cord and handed his boarding pass to the woman with the nails. She tore off his stub with open hostility.

"Thanks." Serge reached back and stomped his right foot on the doormat, then took off down the gangway.

## MIAMI MORGUE

The lieutenant burst through the lab doors. "What's this nonsense you were babbling about on the phone?" He stopped to look around. "And what's that god-awful smell?"

"It's a morgue."

"I mean more than usual."

Forceps clanged into a pan. "Wanted to give you a heads-up because I know how sensitive you are to weird headlines."

A deep sigh. "What now?"

"Take a look at this." The medical examiner hunched over his work on the table. Dabs of menthol Vaseline under his nostrils.

The officer stepped closer. "The smell's even worse!"

A giggle. "Fish tend to do that."

The lieutenant studied the deceased on the steel table. "So what happened, pet detective? Someone murder a shark?"

"Remember the dead shark in the middle of Flagler Street from the TV news shows?"

"Which one? The guys keep throwing them around the city."

"Tuesday's shark." The examiner pointed toward a clear, sealed evidence bag. "That came from its stomach . . . Help yourself to some Vaseline."

The lieutenant dabbed his upper lip. "Looks like a mullet or something."

The M.E. used a pen to lift something from a metal tray. "Wearing a Timex?"

"That's an arm?"

"Most of one. I know it's hard to tell between the regular decomposition and digestion."

"Great. We got a shark attack." The officer added more dabs. "Chamber of commerce will love this."

"I don't think it was an attack."

"But you said it was in his stomach."

"Postmortem."

"The victim was already dead?"

"That's my bet."

"Okay, so he accidentally drowned somehow, and the shark came along later."

"Doubtful."

The lieutenant emitted a whine. "*Eeeeeeeee* . . . It's been a bad week. Can't you just call it a shark attack?"

The M.E. emptied the evidence bag into a tray and pointed with his pen. "This along the mid-forearm is the shark's bite line. I pulled these teeth out."

"Sure sounds like a shark attack to me."

The pen pointed farther up. "And here is where they used the hacksaw."

## Chapter *THREE*

**TAMPA INTERNATIONAL AIRPORT**

The flight was full.

Repeated intercom instructions about stowing luggage quickly and taking seats, but the aisle remained clogged by passengers struggling with overhead bins and non-bin-shaped bags.

Serge led Coleman to row 27. "Here are our seats."

A businessman was already sitting in the middle. "Would you like me to move so you two can be together?"

"No," said Serge. "We deliberately got the window and aisle seats. I'm big on looking outside at tiny buildings and stuff, and Coleman needs the aisle for emergencies. But coffee makes me pee like a Chihuahua, so we'll be switching seats a lot." He slid by the man's knees and plopped down. "Boy, there's really no legroom anymore. You don't mind if I stretch my leg out a little, or maybe a lot, to get around that partition and under the seat in front of you?"

Coleman tapped the man's right arm. "Do you know when they start serving alcohol?"

Serge tapped his left arm. "Coleman and I have a bunch to discuss, but don't feel like you're imposing. We'll just talk across the front of you, and you're welcome to eavesdrop and join in." He grinned and raised his eyebrows. "It can get pretty interesting! I was on a transcontinental flight with this one executive, having a great four-hour discussion on my favorite aviation disasters. Actually I was doing all the talking because I guess he was really interested in crashes, and then he couldn't wait to look it up on the Internet because he was trampling people after we landed. Like this one plane exploded off San Diego. But just the front part with the pilots blew off, and the rest of the plane kept flying perfectly straight for almost a minute . . ." Serge made a downward gesture with his right hand. ". . . before slowwwwwwwwwly nosing over into the sea. What would be going through your mind? 'Hey, I can see the new mall from here.' . . . We're going to Miami for the fabulous Summit of the Americas! Dignitaries and countless journalists from twenty Latin countries about to overwhelm the city, actually making Miami less diverse . . ."

Coleman tapped the businessman's right arm. "Going to be sick. My seat pocket doesn't have a barf bag."

The man dove for his own pocket and handed a bag to Coleman.

Serge tapped his left arm and stood up. "I have to pee. Excuse me." He slid by the man's knees.

Coleman held up a bag. "Serge, could you take this for me."

Two hours later.

Serge looked out the window.

At the Tampa Airport.

"Why the hell are we still on the runway?"

"They mentioned mechanical problems," said Coleman.

"Ten times."

*"This is your captain from the flight deck. The replacement part just arrived and we should be in the air in about an hour . . ."*

"Another hour!" said Serge.

"Serge," said Coleman. "You're grabbing his arm pretty tight. I don't think he likes it."

"Oops, sorry. I'll cope instead with a time-killing technique." He stood. "Excuse me, I have to get to the overhead bin."

Minutes later, Serge had an open laptop on his lap. He tapped the arm next to him. "Oh, Mr. Businessman, do you have any pen pals? Of course you do. But I just got my first one. He's from some wacky foreign country with exciting current events. And I think we're really hitting it off. I can be totally open and say the kind of things that make others hide from me, but he keeps writing no matter what. In fact, he contacted me first." Serge rotated the computer toward the middle seat. "I've scrolled back to the top of our message string. Check it out! . . . No, you're still staring at me. Look at the screen."

The businessman gave Serge a final glance, then turned toward the computer and began reading:

*Dear Sir or Madam,*

*It is with great trust and confidence that I contact you concerning a business transaction of large urgency. I am the nephew of Ishtwanu Gabonilar, who recently became deposed as finance minister of eastern Nabibiwabba province, prior to consummation of mineral lease with Swiss consortium that transferred funds of $100 million U.S. dollars prior to rebel offensive on the capital. With sad mourning, my entire family is disappear and believe executed. I require your assistance as such funds remain concealed in capital and must dispatch with trust to America before rebels discover. I cannot reveal source, but your name was recommended as person of extreme trust and dependency. For your services, you will received half ($50 million U.S. dollars). Awaiting your immediate speed response.*

*With much God bless,*
*Bobonofassi Gabonilar*

*Dear Bobonofassi,*

*Fifty million dollars! Holy fucking shit! My lucky day! How'd you get my name? Was it Coleman? Lenny? Who cares? The important thing is you got it. And perfect timing: I've been moping around lately over the oil spill while Coleman ran down my cell battery calling everyone for hashish, and we nearly got pinched when he shared a bottle of cheap rum outside a massage parlor with a drive-time radio personality who showed his wee-wee to an undercover cop, and we had to hide under some mattresses and walk home because they ran the plates on our stolen car after finding a teensy bit of blood in the trunk. Okay, a lot. Hey, some people bruise easily, others bleed. But it's always my fault, and then Coleman almost got busted again in the supermarket because he did 'shrooms and ten hits from a skull bong, and the grocery people grabbed him by the freezer with a gallon of triple-fudge ice cream, which we tried to say we were going to buy, but they found him on his hands and knees with his face right down in the pail like a beagle, and the shit was in his hair and other shoppers getting squirrelly, so they ordered me to give them all the money in my wallet and never come back, and that's why your timing is so great because even one million dollars right now would come in handy. Especially after the stock market whipped my ass like Sonny Corleone delivering a brother-in-law garbage-can beat-down (I love that scene). All my shares were in a friend's name, because I can't use mine right now, so I sit each morning watching CNN and the opening bell on Wall Street. And here's what pisses me off about the opening bell: "Special guests" ring it, all these rich, connected, oh-so-self-pleased, never-done-a-real-day's-work pussies grinning ear to ear up on that stand like Roman emperors while the whole country's on foreclosure-fire. And even worse, they have goofy guests: people in Star Wars costumes and the cast of Jersey Shore, like it's a big joke, this shit sandwich they're force-feeding Main Street. And then I hear that ting-a-ling again and see those smug motherfuckers, and this is what I finally figured out it means: It's a gleefully enthusiastic ringing of the funeral bell for the working class. And I begin calculating the trajectory of a perfectly tossed firebomb . . . Hold on, what am I saying? I'm here moaning about my insignificant problems, when you're the one whose entire family is rotting in a mass grave. And rebels never dig*

*good ones, so limbs are probably sticking out, flies buzzing around—*
*and the smell! Do I feel silly! Back to your problems: I'm on the case!*
*Please tell me at once what I have to do to help stop the rebels! (Don't*
*get me started on rebels—it's all: me, me, me, I need attention.)*

> *Your newest best friend in maximum trust,*
> *Serge A. Storms*

*Dear Serge,*

*It pleases me greatly for you kindness in my people's time of*
*necessity. The rebels are in much control and transactions limited.*
*For your assistance, I need you deposit $10,000. This is the*
*minimum to open numbered account among our trusted friends for*
*me to begin secure transfer of $100 million ($50 million to be your*
*gracious fee). Please advise when you have funds and I will forward*
*you account number and bank.*

> *Many Blessings,*
> *Bobonofassi Gabonilar*

*Dear Bobonofassi,*

*Ten thousand? Is that it? This just keeps getting better and*
*better! And to think I almost missed your e-mail between "Meet*
*hot singles in your area" and "Turn your trouser mouse into a one-*
*eyed python of love." I was distracted because of that new TV show*
Cougar Town, *which is actually Sarasota (there's a map of Florida's*
*Gulf Coast during the intro, if you need to check), and these smokin'-*
*hot menopause chicks are banging an entire city full of nothing*
*but young studs, except the average age of the guys in Sarasota is,*
*like, dead. Such inaccuracies make me crazy and my picture tube*
*now has a few extremely small bullet holes, but it still won't work*
*anymore. Was I overreacting? You can tell me, since we're going*
*to have a close cosmic connection for the rest of our lives, and even*
*longer (hope you're not in some religion where heaven is like a Jimi*
*Hendrix album cover with elephants wearing jewelry and a dancing*
*goddess flapping twenty arms). Can I call you Bobo? Speaking of*

dead, probably no word on your family. Better that way so you won't know about the torture. Rebels always start with the head. They use these face-spreaders. That's just mean. Of course I have a pair myself, but I always feel bad afterward. And maybe no TV isn't the worst thing. The other night I woke up and there was some old movie with a Cyclops. Remember when a bunch of films used to have Cyclops? And now nothing. What the fuck? Did you see Christopher Walken on Saturday Night Live? "More cowbell"? They should do something like that with Cyclops. Okay, enough yapping: Send me that account info ASAP! I'll be able to raise the ten Gs as soon as I reach Miami. And when this is all over, you should visit. Or maybe you should come right now, because I've become concerned about your safety. People say Miami's dangerous, but at least America doesn't have rebels. Actually we do, but they just wear funny hats and hold tea parties. No mass graves (yet). And if your family was tortured, the rebels are probably on the way to your house right now with the face-spreaders. You can always stay on our pull-out couch. Just think about it.

　　More Cyclops!
　　Serge


A businessman repeatedly tapped the flight-attendant call button over the middle seat of row 27.

A cheerful woman arrived. "How may I help you?"

"I have to sit somewhere else."

"I'm sorry, the flight is completely full—"

"*This is your captain again. We're still experiencing some very minor problems with the engines. The replacement part didn't fit right, so we're having another flown in from Atlanta . . . Meanwhile, please relax and I've instructed the crew to serve soft drinks and complimentary cocktails . . .*"

Two hours later.

Serge's hand continuously pressed the flight-attendant call button.

The woman returned. "How may I help you?"

"I have to get off the plane."

"Sir, nobody is allowed off the plane. We've already pulled away from the gate. Regulations."

"But you don't understand . . ."

A gentle smile. "It'll just be a little bit longer."

More tapping on the call button. A different arm.

The flight attendant looked at the businessman in the middle seat. "I want to sit somewhere else."

"As I informed you earlier, the flight is full."

Serge repeatedly tapped the button.

The attendant maintained poise. "Yes?"

"I can't go into all the details," said Serge. "But you really want me off this plane."

The businessman nodded hard in agreement.

"I'm sorry," said the attendant. "But they're just about—"

"*This is your captain again. The part from Atlanta fits, and we should be in the air in no time.*"

"See?" the attendant said cheerfully. "I told you it wouldn't be much longer."

"I still want to get off," said Serge. "Can't you just let *one* person go?"

"The rules are very strict," she said evenly. "After the doors are closed and cross-checked, absolutely nobody is permitted off the plane."

At the front of the jet, two men in uniforms stepped out of the cockpit. The main cabin door opened. Sunlight streamed in. The men left. The door closed.

Serge looked up at the attendant. "What the hell just happened?"

"The pilots got off the plane."

"Why?"

"They reached their FAA limits of how long they can work in a twenty-four-hour period. We're flying a new crew in from Cleveland."

"How long is that going to take?"

"Hard to tell because they're de-icing in a blizzard."

Serge rocked manically in his seat. "You don't understand. I really need to get off this plane."

The businessman leaned forward. "Please let him off the plane."

"I already told you that's forbidden. No exceptions whatsoever."

The attendant began walking away.

"Wait!" Serge called after her. "I'm not finished. I need to—"

"I'm sorry," said the attendant. "I can't talk to you anymore. I've also reached my twenty-four-hour limit."

She got off the plane.

# Chapter **FOUR**

## SOUTH OF MIAMI

Squawking green parrots in flight.

Other bright feathers.

Thousands. Macaws, cockatoos. Ninety-eight percent humidity. A higher number on the mercury.

The Metrozoo was known for its birds. Plus 1,200 other critters covering 740 acres on the distant underside of Miami, near the end of the turnpike. Hurricane Andrew was a jailbreak, tying up traffic with flamingos and zebras and the so-called AIDS monkeys. It was the oldest such attraction in Florida and the only subtropical zoo in the country.

Three animals started it in 1948.

Just past the zoo's entrance: an unassuming road with guard gates at intended intervals. The pavement leads through brush, past something called the University of Miami Institute for Human Genomics, before finally reaching what is now the Richmond Naval Air Station.

A smattering of widely separated buildings designate the secure area, some distinctly old by Florida standards. One of the earlier wooden structures was quite the scene from 1961 until it closed seven years later, although there was little fanfare.

Building 25.

Headquarters of Operation Mongoose, otherwise known as the CIA's campaign to overthrow Fidel Castro.

Sitting quiet for decades.

Until now.

"Let's take it round the horn," said field-station chief Gil Oxnart, striding hard into the room without waiting for the screen door behind him to bang shut. "Dazzle me."

The room used to have a conference table during the Johnson administration. Today, a square grid of penknife-scarred school desks.

A junior agent in the front row went first. Pages flipped in a single-spaced surveillance report. "Subjects departed primary location 0730, took Biscayne to Flagler, where said parties parked for secondary observation. Departed 0948, for safe house."

Oxnart flipped through a stack of telephoto eight-by-tens. "These aren't shit."

"Sorry, sir. Nothing happened," said the junior agent. "Except that last photo."

"What's this picture of a dead shark in the street?"

"Three guys threw it in front of the Costa Gordan consulate. I think someone was sending a message."

The chief tossed the photos back. "Ship them to Langley, computer section, but be discreet. Tell them it's personal business on company time . . . What else?"

"Departed safe house, 1820; Subject Alpha arrived home 1847. Subject Bravo, 1901."

"Keep up the good work, Huff."

"Sir?" asked the agent.

"What?"

"Why is our CIA station conducting surveillance on the other CIA station?"

"Because they're our biggest threat."

Call it the current climate. A long, depressing streak of revelations, press leaks, and congressional hearings. Waterboarding, rendition, black-box prisons, false-flag interrogations, Gitmo, naked human pyramids. The clandestine service had become a reality show. Rumors of war crimes trials, politicians outing agents. An already paranoid culture became even more compartmentalized and firewalled with career preservation. And since they now knew even less about what the rest of the Company was up to, the biggest worry wasn't overseas but the agent next door.

Station Chief Oxnart picked up an overlooked surveillance photo. "What's this?"

"Station Chief Lugar eating dinner," said a junior agent.

Oxnart handed him the picture. "Find out what this means." Then he clapped his hands sharply and addressed the rest of the room. "Look smart, everyone. We got the Summit of the Americas, and I want to be all over Lugar's men. Start with the airport. Make sure every inch is covered."

**MEANWHILE . . .**

*"This is Monica Saint James with Action News Eyewitness Eight, reporting live from Tampa International Airport, where, as you can see behind me, a Miami-bound flight has been stranded on the runway now for almost seven hours. Our station has received numerous cell-phone calls from passengers begging to be let off the plane . . ."*

The camera zoomed on the window of row 27, where someone was clawing at the glass.

*". . . Our own calls to the airline and transportation officials have all been met with 'no comment' . . ."*

Serge hyperventilated with his head between his knees in the crash position. He stood up and tapped the businessman, then slid into the aisle.

"What are you doing?"

"Getting everyone off this plane."

Serge walked to the back, went in the restroom, and closed the door.

A minute passed.

The restroom door opened. Serge peeked outside. Nobody looking. He quickly slipped back into his seat.

Soon a squat woman in polyester waddled to the back of the plane. She went inside the restroom. And came right back out, running up the aisle.

The woman grabbed the first flight attendant she could find and pointed frantically toward the rear of the plane. The attendant hurried toward the restroom.

Back inside the terminal, TV crews continued filming.

"... *Sources tell us there is a heated, backroom disagreement over the airline's handling ... Wait a minute. Something seems to be happening. It looks like the emergency doors have opened ...*"

The cameraman focused on yellow slides inflating. Passengers jumped from the doors and zipped down to the runway. Rescue vehicles raced across the tarmac.

"Thank God!" said Coleman, entering the terminal through their original departure gate and heading for the monorail to the parking lots and taxis.

"Hold up," said Serge. "There's one more thing I have to do ..."

The last passengers exited the aircraft, which was the signal for a standby tactical unit in body armor to rush aboard. They swept the plane and reached one of the restrooms. On the mirror, drawn in soap:

A bowling ball with a lit fuse.

Back in the airport, total chaos. News crews surrounded passengers getting off the monorail for firsthand accounts. "... *You wouldn't believe the smell! ...*"

And at the departure gate, calm was finally restored. A woman with four-inch nails headed back to her desk. She stopped and gasped. On the ground, a clean rectangle indicated the outline of a missing Elite Club doormat.

## Chapter FIVE

### MIAMI INTERNATIONAL AIRPORT

Blinking lights in the night sky toward the Everglades. A distant drone. Another Beechcraft full of weapons on its way to points south.

Limos continuously left the airport.

An orange-and-green Road Runner sat at the curb outside arrivals.

Coleman killed a Schlitz. "That really blew, driving all the way from Tampa."

"But it took less time than we sat on that runway yesterday. Planes are now dead to me. I hate airports."

"Me, too," said Coleman. "The magic toilets always flush before I can squat and get fully situated, and it sucks down the little paper covering I laid out, because the paper tongue in the middle hangs in the water, and then I have to get another, and it sucks that one down, too."

"Coleman, the whole key to airport life is tearing off the paper tongue first," said Serge. "It's against the rules, but you have to start fighting back somewhere."

"Serge?"

"What?"

"Then if we both hate it so bad, why are we at another airport?"

"My new job." Serge adjusted small opera binoculars.

"Job? Who hired you?"

"Those guys who threw me out in the street. Remember? Just after we got into town and I started taking photos of consulates."

"I thought you were kidding about getting hired. They told you to come to the airport?"

Serge shook his head. "When you're hired for such a sensitive intelligence position, they trust your judgment." He set the binoculars down and opened a laptop.

"What are you doing now?"

"Killing time until my mission starts." He began typing. "I'm writing to a pen pal."

Coleman cracked another beer. "You mean that guy whose family got abducted."

Serge shook his head. "Someone else."

"You're cheating on your pen pal?"

Serge continued typing. "I know it's not right, but the heart wants what it wants."

"Can I see?"

"Just let me finish this."

More typing. Serge finally hit the save button and passed the laptop across the front seat.

Coleman leaned closer and began reading . . .

Dear Sarah Palin, Almost President

Going Rogue . . . and making it look so hot!

First, I know others say it all the time, but I'm your number one fan. And I'll straight-talk like you always do: I'm writing you for a date. I've been following your career and there's no stopping the Palin juggernaut if you've got the right man behind you (which you don't). We both know the marriage is finished. You're so past that Alaskan Urban Cowboy phase. So here are my plans to manage *your life. Next phase: blockbuster movie star! It's a natural—all you need is the right vehicle. And I've got it! Are you ready? Are you sitting down?* All in the Family: *The Movie.* Can't believe *nobody's thought of it before. To update the show for our times, we gender-shift and make you Archie Bunker. They wouldn't even have to write your lines, just tape-record the speeches. Remember "Drill, baby, drill"? You pushed for offshore drilling, then after the spill you* opposed *offshore drilling, saying it was a dangerous idea that was forced by restrictions on arctic refuge exploration. No screenwriter in Hollywood has that kind of imagination. From there, everything falls into place. Instead of Edith, the guy you live with who drives the snowmobiles would be "Ed" the dingbat. And of course Levi is "Meathead." So let's start making some calls!*

*Meanwhile, I'll work on your PR. If we're going to be seeing each other, we have to be honest, so don't take this the wrong way: You tend to polarize people. There, I said it. But it's not your fault. The people polarize themselves. Everyone thinks baseball's the national pastime, but a big chunk of the constituency has always had a dick-hard need for second-class citizens, and the loss of white-only drinking fountains has finally caught up and made them lose their fucking minds. To watch the news (if you did), you'd think half the country was illegal Latin Muslims from Arizona holding gay marriages at the World Trade Center. But back to your polarity, which I'll boomerang to a super advantage. People think you're only about money. And just because you quit your old job. What's wrong with that? It's the all-American story. Hundreds of campaign volunteers working tirelessly on your campaign, residents counting on a diligent administration to steer the ship of state, but you saw Russia out your window and took a valiant stand against communism by selflessly bagging your responsibilities for millions in book deals and appearance fees. Now, that's character.*

*And if money's what it will take to get you to go out with me, so be it. I know this guy in Africa named Bobo, and I'm just about to come into $50 million, which I'll gladly split with you. In fact I might need your help on that because I think it's supposed to be* hush-hush. I'm sure you have contacts who can help me move the money, and we'll probably also need to get Bobo out before they use the face-spreaders. If I'm going too fast, you can just write all this on your hand.

Finally: the press. They're so unfair: "Which newspapers do you read?" "What parts of the Bush Doctrine do you support?" Those are disingenuous "gotcha!" questions. If they possessed any honesty or courage, they'd directly ask, "Do you read?" and "Do you know what the Bush Doctrine is?" So next time they give you some bullshit pop quiz, here's what you do, and trust me: America will be totally behind you on this. You kick 'em in the balls! (Or in Katie Couric's case, the twat. You know you want to. And then you can yell at her, "That's my Bush Doctrine, bitch.")

Can't wait for our first date! Please wear those jeans. Rrrrrrrow!

The Next Mr. Palin,
Serge

Coleman finished reading and looked up. "How are you going to get this to her?"

"I'll just send it through her website."

"So you really think you'll get a date? . . . Serge?"

Serge had become locked on the view through his binoculars. He tossed them in the backseat and threw the Road Runner in gear. "We're on!"

Fifteen minutes and ten miles later:

A limo sat on the side of a dark access road next to the Dolphin Expressway.

A carjacker with a shaved head threw the chauffeur over the trunk and stuck a gun in his ear. "Don't move!"

A second assailant in dreadlocks ran to the side of the stretch and aimed a TEC-9 in the back window. "Get the fuck out of the car or I'll blow your motherfucking heads off!"

The limo people watched the man outside with the submachine gun as if he were on TV.

"What are we going to do?" said the chief of staff.

"Is this glass bulletproof?" asked the president of Costa Gorda.

One of the bodyguards shook his head.

"Then I suggest we get out of the car."

A fist banged a window. "I said get the fuck out right now!"

A back door slowly opened. "We're coming out. Don't shoot."

The president emerged with raised hands. He was seized by his jacket and thrown face-first against the side of the vehicle.

Soon they were all lined up, hands against the roof. The shaved head grabbed two briefcases from the backseat, then went down the row taking wallets and watches.

In the commotion of the blitz attack, nobody had noticed an orange-and-green Plymouth roll up quietly without headlights and park on the shoulder under petticoat palms.

Serge reached in his backpack. "We'll have to move fast."

"What do we do?"

Serge pulled a pair of items from the glove compartment and slapped one in Coleman's hand. "Remember when we apprehended those thieves in Orlando? Just take this and do what I do."

Back at the limo, a bodyguard made a false move, and the dreadlocks gave him a skull crack with his gun butt.

Two dark forms staggered and swerved up the street toward the robbery.

The shaved head turned. "Yo! Reggie, check it out. It's our lucky night."

Serge and Coleman stumbled closer to the group.

A MAC-10 swung toward them. "Give it up!"

Serge staggered a few more steps, covered his mouth, and bulged his cheeks. "My tummy doesn't feel so good."

The dreadlocks kept his own gun aimed at the entourage and looked over his shoulder. "They're drunk."

"Stop right there!" ordered the shaved head.

But the pair continued weaving and stumbling, each headed toward one of the assailants.

When Serge was a few feet from the shaved head, he grabbed his stomach and bent forward.

"Don't you dare puke on me!" The robber jumped back a step, reflexively pulling up his arms, which meant the weapon was momentarily aimed at the sky.

"Coleman," Serge slurred. "Now."

"Now what?" said the robber.

"This!"

He got an eight-hundred-thousand-volt stun gun to the chest, dropping him to the street in a flopping seizure.

Midway up the side of the limo, someone else hit the ground with violent tremors.

Serge looked down at Coleman twitching on the pavement. "Shit." The battle would be decided in milliseconds. The dreadlocks realized the ruse and began swinging his TEC-9. Serge hit the ground and grabbed the other robber's gun.

*Pow-pow-pow-pow-pow* . . .

Before the carjacker had a chance to fire, the pavement around his feet was raked with Serge's salvo. He promptly dropped the machine gun and raised his hands.

Serge stood back up.

The Costa Gordan entourage went slack-jawed as Serge marched the attackers at gunpoint back to the Road Runner and forced them into the trunk. He slammed the hood and looked over at the group with a happy smile. "Show's over. You can relax now."

Heavy traffic whizzed by, out of sight, up on the expressway. An inbound 737 roared overhead as Serge strolled back to the limo past a row of shocked faces. He leaned down and helped a woozy Coleman to his feet: "You okay, buddy?"

Coleman nodded.

"What happened?" asked Serge. "Did he take it away from you?"

"No, I Tased myself." He rubbed the middle of his chest. "Forgot which way to point it."

"Don't embarrass me," whispered Serge. "These are important

people." Then he turned toward a tall man about sixty, balding on top with a thick gray mustache. "President Guzman?"

"Who are you?"

"Storms. Serge Storms." He extended a hand. "I'm attached to your consulate down here."

The president tentatively shook it. "In what capacity?"

"Security."

"I haven't heard of you."

"Just got assigned today." He bent down and picked up Coleman's dropped stun gun.

"So you work in our consulate?"

"No. In fact, it's best I not be seen near there."

"I don't understand."

"By *attached,* I mean unofficially. As far as you're concerned, I'm not attached at all." He winked. "And I was never here."

"So what *are* you doing here?" asked the president.

"Extra protection for the summit." Serge glanced back at his Plymouth's banging trunk. "Which you can never have too much of."

A block east, a black SUV rolled up and parked without headlights.

President Guzman rubbed his chin. "So you've been following us since the airport?"

"Just keeping a friendly eye."

The president joined Serge in looking back at the Plymouth. "That was close. I've heard of the crime around here."

"This might not have been a robbery," said Serge.

"Then what was it?"

"Who knows?" Serge made a lobbing motion with his arm like he was tossing a hand grenade. "Heard you've been having a little trouble with some rebels."

"My generals have all that under control now," said Guzman. "It's been blown way out of proportion by the press."

"Let it be blown," said Serge. "You'll get more foreign aid."

A block west, a second black SUV pulled up.

President Guzman squinted into Serge's eyes. "Foreign aid. Who are you really with? You're Latin, but the accent's American."

"Born and raised an hour north of here."

"So you're actually on loan from . . . the CIA?"

Serge just smiled again.

The president nodded solemnly. "I understand." He turned to his bodyguards in disapprobation. "You could learn something from this guy about real security. If it wasn't for him . . ."

Serge began walking back to his car with Coleman.

"Excuse me?"

Serge turned around. "Yes?"

"What are you going to do with the guys in your trunk?" asked Guzman.

"I need to find out who was behind this. We'll debrief them."

"But I mean after that?"

Another grin. "What guys in the trunk?" He resumed walking back to the car.

"One more thing," said the president. "Thank you."

"Just doing my job."

*Chapter* **SIX**

**MIAMI MORGUE**

The lieutenant stared in defeat at a shark and partially digested arm. "Is it too decomposed to get an ID?"

"Definitely."

The officer took a deep breath. "Then I guess it's the missing-persons files."

"Randy Swade."

"Who?"

"That's his name."

"But I thought you said—"

The M.E. stuck his pen into a tray and lifted a wristwatch. "Engraved."

"Why the hell didn't you tell me sooner? . . . Wait, where have I heard that name before?"

"Journalist for the *New Metro Loafing Times*."

"That weekly rag with ads for sex-chat lines and kits to clean urine samples?"

The M.E. dropped the wristwatch in the pan. "Went missing a

couple weeks ago in Costa Gorda. Found a passport and junk in his room."

"Now I remember," said the lieutenant. "They thought he got drunk at one of those spring-break bars that caters to underage American kids and then went swimming at night or some other misadventure."

"They got the misadventure part right." The M.E. snapped off his gloves and began washing up in the sink.

"You're saying the shark swam all the way back to the Miami River?"

"Of course not." The M.E. turned off the faucets. "I don't think Randy ever left Miami."

"But his passport and luggage . . ."

"Remember the investigative series he was working on for the paper?"

"I don't read that trash," said the lieutenant. "Nobody takes those conspiracy nuts seriously. All their articles about the CIA dealing crack."

"I know most of it's baloney, but still entertaining." He grabbed a hand towel. "Randy was writing about Miami being the arms-smuggling capital of the Caribbean basin. Fancied himself landing the next Iran-Contra scoop. He was naming some pretty big fish, excuse the pun."

"Luckily it's a matter for the Costa Gordan police."

The M.E. glanced toward the tray with the severed hand. "Looks like it just swam back into your jurisdiction."

"Great." A deep sigh. "Couldn't he have gotten robbed somewhere else?"

The examiner walked over and tossed the towel in a bin. "Lieutenant, if it really was his stuff in that Costa Gordan motel and he never left Miami, someone went through a lot of trouble."


## BISCAYNE BAY

Midnight.

All quiet on the water. The bay had been dark toward the east, but now a thin line of alabaster light appeared on the ocean's horizon, where a full moon prepared to rise over the Atlantic.

Toward the north, a magical white aura from the distant Miami skyline and, closer, the lights of Key Biscayne with the outline of the Cape Florida lighthouse anchoring its southern tip.

But the island remained a ways off, as did the mainland. Even farther to the south, the Ragged Keys and Boca Chita, the first dribbling specks of exposed coral that grew into the Florida Keys.

A luxury fishing boat drifted silently with the tide in one of the isolated spots of Biscayne National Park. Serge stood up on the bridge with a nautical map and a flashlight, waiting for the moon. Two would-be carjackers lay by the bilge, wiggling with hands tied behind their backs.

"We weren't going to hurt anyone!" "I swear we'll never do it again!"

"All my guests say that." Serge unloaded scuba equipment from one of the oversize duffels in the boat. "And they're always right."

The assailants stared at weight belts and mesh gear bags. "W-w-what are you going to do to us?"

"Thought we'd play a little game. You watch *David Letterman*? He leaves me in stitches!"

"Please let us go! We'll do anything! We'll pay you!"

"Shhhhh." Serge repacked the bag. "You won't be able to experience the peace out here."

A beer cracked. "Where'd you get this boat?" asked Coleman.

"Stan."

"Stan?"

"The High-End Repo Man. He owed me. You'll meet him later."

The moon finally rose, giving Serge needed illumination. He raised binoculars.

Coleman guzzled. "What are you looking for?"

Serge scanned the water. "A house."

"House?" Coleman crumpled the aluminum can. "But we're in the middle of the sea."

"It's one of our state's most fascinating and historic features." The binoculars stopped. "And there it is."

"What?"

"Stiltsville." Serge cranked the twin inboards and began motoring east just above idle speed. "A village of old wooden shacks on piers in the water."

"Way out here?" said Coleman.

"That's the coolest part." Serge pushed the throttle forward and brought the boat up on a plane. "Most pier houses simply extend from shore, or sit just a short distance from it. Not Stiltsville! In the 1930s, these crazy pioneers started building them far out in the bay on the edge of the open Atlantic, a harrowing distance from nearest land. At its peak there were dozens, but neglect and hurricanes thinned their numbers until now only seven are left standing. If it was daytime, you'd see a colorful collection of eclectic huts with wraparound decks perched in bright emerald-and-turquoise water."

The boat continued across the water without running lights except for the orange glow from Coleman's joint. "But why'd they build them so far from shore?"

"To party." Serge brought the boat around starboard.

"Hold it," said Coleman. "For a second I thought you said 'party.'"

"It was the first of many wild eras in Miami. The well heeled needed places to keep law enforcement at bay, and they held wild affairs at since-forgotten icons like Crawfish Eddie's, the Quarterdeck Club, the Bikini Club, and the Calvert. The area used to be called 'the Flats' and 'the Shacks,' until 'Stiltsville' stuck. Despite its remoteness, there still were frequent raids over alcohol and gambling. One outside porch got so crowded with partiers that it collapsed under the weight. They filmed episodes of *Miami Vice* there."

Coleman leaned eagerly and strained his eyes. "Do they still party?"

"No, most are now just private homes."

"Damn." A frown. "I wish I lived back then."

"You do in spirit." Serge looked back toward the bilge. "Guys, you might want to sit up or you'll kick yourselves for missing this. Actually you won't be able to miss it, thanks to my plan."

Coleman pointed with the joint. "Serge, I think I see one."

"Our destination." The boat came to port on dead reckoning. "Although most of the shacks are residences, I did a property-record search and this baby's only occupied a couple weekends a month. Some boating club owns it."

Coleman looked around. "Where are the others? You said seven."

"Spread out for privacy. Just like I'll need tonight. Plus it has the deepest channel."

The boat completed the rest of the journey without conversation, until Serge pulled off the throttle and threw a line around a pier. He lashed the vessel fast to the cleats.

"Everyone out!"

Serge hoisted his prisoners and rolled them onto the dock. Then unloaded gear. "Coleman, give me a hand with this cooler. It's super-heavy."

Soon, they were all snuggled inside the Stiltsville shack. Serge walked around the perimeter, propping open shutters, and soothing views of moonlit water poured in.

Silence. Only lapping waves against the piers.

Serge set a portable, battery-powered TV on the counter and raised the antenna.

Captives flopped around.

Serge rotated the antenna, trying to get snow off the tube. He looked back at the floor. "All that worrying isn't good for your blood pressure. We're in one of the most picturesque places on earth. You should look out the windows—very easy on the nerves. I've been waiting my whole life to get inside a Stiltsville shack."

A final twist of the antenna. Serge stepped back as the picture cleared. "There we go."

Coleman lit another joint. "It's *Letterman*."

"I saw previews this afternoon." Serge stood with hands on hips. "He's going to do one of my favorite bits."

On the tiny screen, Letterman tapped an index card: *"And now another edition of 'Will It Float?'..."*

Stage curtains parted to reveal a large, clear tank of water. Statuesque assistants stood on each side.

*"Tonight's item is an Ionic Breeze Air Purifier... Paul Shaffer, think it will float?"*

*"There's a lot of plastic. I think it'll float."*

Serge looked at the carjackers. "Well? Is it going to float? Come on—play along."

No response.

Coleman raised his hand. "I think it'll float."

"Me, too," said Serge. "Let's watch."

The models next to the tank threw the ionizer in the water. It immediately went to the bottom.

"Ooooo." Serge turned to the hostages. "Bad omen." He flicked off the set and unloaded the duffel bags. "But maybe you'll have better luck."

Their eyes only held questions.

"What?" said Serge. "You don't get it? We're going to play the home version of 'Will It Float?' Tonight's items? You!"

## MEANWHILE . . .

Spies never sleep.

Lights burned bright inside a converted 1960s safe house in Coral Gables. Cracked plaster, termite damage, boarded windows, new locks.

An emergency briefing.

The door flew open. Station Chief Duke "Nuke" Lugar. The nickname wasn't a compliment. His temper. "What the hell was this business near the airport tonight?" Fiery eyes swung toward a junior agent in the first row. "Belcher!"

The agent's hands shook as he opened his report. "Acquired subjects outside Miami International, 2108 . . ." He passed forward eight-by-tens.

"A black SUV?"

Belcher nodded. "That's Station Chief Oxnart's surveillance team. We took those from our own black SUV." He produced more photos.

"The president of Costa Gorda?" asked Lugar.

The agent nodded again. "We think they're working an arms deal with Oxnart. Probably using a front corporation."

"But I thought *we* were working the arms deal with them?"

The agent shrugged.

Lugar kicked over a chair. "That weasel's moving in on my turf—

and my promotion!" The station chief looked back at Belcher. "And what was this silliness you blathered on the phone about a carjacking?"

The agent fumbled more photos. "Here's Oxnart's black SUV on an access road near the Dolphin Expressway."

"What's he doing?"

"Looks like there was an attempt on Guzman's life, but it was foiled."

Lugar threw up his arms. "Great! Now he also gets commendations!"

Belcher timidly raised a hand.

Lugar clenched his teeth. "This better be good."

"Sir," said Belcher. "I don't think Oxnart foiled the attempt."

"Then who did?"

Trembling hands produced more photos. Night-vision close-ups of two faces.

"Who the hell are these guys?" asked Lugar.

"Nobody knows," said Belcher. "But we ran facial recognition and got a hit. The tall one was photographed taking photographs outside the Costa Gordan consulate yesterday."

"So Oxnart *is* working the arms deal! And he's now got his own man inside the consulate!"

"Doubt it," said Belcher. "These other photos show guards ejecting him from the building. They threw him to the ground really hard."

"You idiot! That means they hired him." The chief began pacing in thought. "This is a nightmare."

The door opened at the back of the room. A man in a hat took a seat.

"You're late," snapped Lugar.

"Sorry," said Mandrake. "Just got back from the bay. Picked up Oxnart's surveillance team near the waterfront and spotted two unknowns, but they had a boat and slipped our tail."

Lugar punched a wall. "Can't anyone do anything right?"

"I think this is important." Mandrake handed forward his own photographs.

"More mystery players?" said Lugar. "Dreadlocks and a shaved head?"

"The ones that attacked Guzman's limo. Here's another photo of them being marched onto the boat at gunpoint by our unknowns."

"Hey," said Belcher. "Those are the same guys from the consulate."

"You're a genius." Lugar resumed pacing. "Okay, we need to get out in front of this. What have we got so far? Oxnart's new agents are in bed with Costa Gorda, and they intercepted a hit team on Guzman. Then took them out on the bay at night. Standard procedure for interrogation and disposal . . ."

A new hand went up in the back of the room.

"Yes, Blankenship?"

"Sir, I think we may have this all wrong. Sometimes the simplest explanation is the correct one."

"What are you talking about?"

Another file opened. "After the facial recognition hit, I searched some databases and came up with a name. Serge A. Storms, wanted by state authorities for questioning in at least two dozen murders."

Lugar nodded. "Professional assassin."

"Don't think so." Blankenship flipped pages in a computer printout. "These look like garden-variety homicides. None of the victims appears to have any link to the intelligence community."

"That means he's good," said Lugar. "Maintained cover to protect the Company. If he ever goes down, it's just the work of one of this state's countless psychotic serial killers."

"I don't know . . ."

"You said two dozen murders?"

"Yes?"

"And he's never been caught? How's that possible unless he's sanctioned? With a sanitation team working behind him. I'm thinking Oxnart."

"So what do we do?"

"Cancel all vacations." Lugar uprighted the kicked-over chair. "Maybe we can turn this Serge character."

"Turn him?" asked Belcher. "But if you're right, he's already working on our side."

"Not turn him from the enemy. From Oxnart. Somebody with his talents needs to be working for *my* station."

# *Chapter* **SEVEN**

## BISCAYNE BAY

Serge walked across the Stiltsville shack and strapped something around the first captive's waist.

The man squirmed violently. "Dear God! Not in the water!"

"Relax." Serge snapped a latch. "Most people don't drown because they're bad swimmers. They drown because they panic. Humans are naturally buoyant. So as long as you keep your heads . . ."

"You just put a scuba weight belt around me!"

"That's right." Serge strapped a belt on the second hostage. "Now you're not naturally buoyant. Otherwise there'd be no point in the game."

Uncontrolled screaming and weeping.

"Jesus!" said Serge. "I'm never kidnapping you guys again. They're just five-pound belts, so you're only slightly non-buoyant . . . And that's what these are for . . ."

He smiled and held up mesh diving gear bags.

One of the captives stopped crying and sniffled. "What are those?"

"Your life preservers," said Serge. "Maybe." He opened the cooler. "All depends on what you put in them. Who wants to pick first?"

"What are our choices?" asked the second hostage.

"Tonight's 'Will It Float?' theme is Florida cuisine, starting with yummy tropical drinks like the mojita. And you can't have them without ice." Serge pointed down in the cooler. "There's a half-dozen ten-pound blocks in there. Who wants it?"

In rapid succession: "Me!" "Me!"

"I made that one too easy," said Serge. "Anyone who's had a tropical drink sees the cubes floating at the top of the glass, except weight belts aren't involved. So is their buoyancy enough? You make the call!"

"Can I change my answer?" asked the hostage.

"No," said Serge. "You buzzed in first. I don't make the rules." His head turned toward the remaining contestant. "That leaves you with this . . ." He opened another duffel and pulled out several shopping bags with loaves poking out the tops. "Miami is famous for her deeeeeee-licious Cuban sandwiches."

Coleman burped. "I had one of those once."

"I remember," said Serge. "You embarrassed the hell out of me."

"How'd I do that?"

Serge turned to his captives. "Dig this: We're on Calle Ocho in Little Havana, and Coleman points up at a menu board and says, 'What's a Cuban?' "

"I want to know what's going in me," said Coleman.

Serge rolled his eyes at the ceiling. "Anyway, there's twenty loaves of Cuban bread here. I let them get extra stale and hard to resist sogginess . . . Okay, everyone back out on the deck."

They had to be dragged.

Fifteen minutes later, Serge attached a final clamp and stood up. "Let the game begin!"

The captives sat with legs hanging over the side of the dock, hands still bound behind their backs. Each had a pair of mesh bags tied to their weight belts, respectively filled with ice blocks and loaves.

Serge knelt behind them. "One last thing. Regardless of the game's results, I built in a bonus round. I always like to give my students a way out. It's a pretty obvious and logical escape, just as long as you remember what I said before: Don't panic."

He slid sideways behind the one with ice, and looked up. "Coleman, your opinion? Will it float?"

"I think so."

"Me, too."

He gave a hard push, and one of the carjackers splashed into the water. And went under the surface.

Serge stood and scrunched his eyebrows. "Could have sworn he'd float."

"Look!" said Coleman. "He bobbed to the surface!"

"It floats!"

Serge moved to the remaining captive. "Coleman?"

"I don't think it'll float."

"Me neither."

Another shove and splash.

"Well, what do you know?" said Serge. "It floats. That's two for two."

The criminals stared up from the water, breathing heavy with relief. "Thank God! So you'll release us now?"

"Absolutely," said Serge. "You're free to go, anytime you want."

They looked around. "Uh, all right. Help us up."

"That's not the deal," said Serge. "Your freedom is built into the bonus round. Figure it out and it's joy time. Or come up with your own idea. Either way, I'll keep my word and not do anything to hinder your escape." He looked at Coleman and shook his head. "You give and give, but some people are never satisfied."

"Hey, I'm getting lower," said the one with the ice bags.

"I almost forgot," said Serge. "Ice floats. It also melts. Even faster in salt water."

"I'm begging you. Get me out of the water."

Serge took a seat on the edge of the dock. "Then come clean. Who are you working for?"

"What?"

"Who sent you to take out the president of Costa Gorda?"

"Nobody. We were just robbing them."

"Suit yourself," said Serge.

"Wait." The man had to tilt his head back to keep his mouth above water. "I swear I'm telling the truth."

"Bullshit. You're a spy!" said Serge. "For the last time, who put out the contract?"

"I don't know what you're talking about!" Coughing and spitting water. "You have to believe me!"

Coleman nudged Serge and whispered: "So he's really a spy?"

"Naw," said Serge. "Only another street-level stickup man. I'm just fucking with him." He faced the water again. "I'll make it simple for you. Was it the Marmoset or the Purple Gang?"

More coughing. "Okay, okay, it was the Purple Gang."

"See?" said Serge. "That wasn't so hard."

"Now get me out!"

"You have everything you need to get yourself out. Remember the bonus round: Don't panic."

*"Ahhhh!"* Glub, glub, glub. He went under.

Serge and Coleman stared over the side of the dock. One minute. Two. Three. Then a burst of bubbles hit the surface.

"Guess he didn't win the bonus round," said Serge.

"What was that business about the Purple Gang?" said Coleman.

"Just proving a point in support of prisoner rights," said Serge. "Torture doesn't produce reliable confessions." He swiveled his head left. "How are you doing with those loaves?"

*"Pleeeeeeeease!"*

"It's like the name of that movie," said Serge. *"Hope Floats.* Actually it dog paddles. Land's that way. Only a few miles."

"Little things are hitting me!"

"Those must be tropical fish. You should come out here in the daytime. Our coral reefs are magnificent!"

"More things hitting me! Are any of them dangerous?"

"Completely harmless. If I used meat, that would draw sharks. Bread only draws the little guys."

"Draws them?"

"Yeah," said Serge. "They like to eat it."

The captive looked around in the water at a growing swarm of tiny fish nibbling through holes in the mesh bag.

Serge and Coleman hopped back in the boat.

"Wait!" yelled the man in the water. "You can't leave me!"

Serge untied davit lines. "Remember the bonus round. Just stay calm."

Coleman leaned over the bow. "Wow! Look at those fish go at it. The loaves are almost gone."

Serge joined him up front. "They must love Cuban bread as much as I do."

Like the first captive, the man's head was tilted back, nose and mouth barely above the surface.

"Help—" *Glub, glub, glub.* Under he went.

The pair in the boat watched quietly. This time only two minutes until the bubbles came.

Serge started up the engine. "I would have bet anything at least one of them would win the bonus round."

"What was the bonus round?" asked Coleman.

Serge slowly pulled away from the dock. "What's the most logical thing to do in their predicament?"

"Hold your breath longer?"

"No, Coleman. Become buoyant again. Which means losing the weight belt."

"But their hands were tied behind their backs."

"And I put their belts on backward, so the release latch was right by those hands. If only they listened to me and remained calm." Serge gave the engines full throttle back toward shore. "Panic causes more drownings. That's what makes tonight's tragedy especially senseless."

# Chapter EIGHT

## THE NEXT MORNING

CNN.

*"With the second oil spill in the Gulf of Mexico entering its forty-third day, Congressman Bugler continues drawing flak for apologizing to the drilling company during this week's committee hearings, which political observers say could turn the balance in the upcoming elections . . . And now an odd news item from Tampa, where a dozen men are under arrest at a local hospital for illegally hunting coyotes within city limits."* The picture switched to a police spokesman. *"I've never seen anything like it in the middle of a highly populated area. We caught them red-handed with banned game bait available on the Internet. They claim some mystery men gave them free mosquito repellent, but we're not buying it. How do they explain the gun racks full of deer rifles in their pickups? And we're tacking on littering fines for all the empty beer cans. Luckily they were too drunk to hunt effectively and the coyotes got the upper hand. We'll be transporting them to jail as soon as their wounds heal."* The TV switched again to the anchor desk. *"We're going back again to Washington for continuing coverage of the political fallout from Congressman Bugler's comments of*

*sympathy for the oil companies . . . Wait a moment. We have breaking news. We're taking you live to the Office of Homeland Security . . ."*

Director "Rip" Tide walked briskly to the podium with a prepared statement. Behind him: twenty American flags and a large, vinyl thermometer.

*"I've called you all here today to announce we're raising the threat level. I can't reveal the nature of our intelligence or where an attack is most likely, so all citizens must be on increased vigilance wherever they work, play, or sleep. God bless the United States."*

A reporter held up a hand with a pen in it. *"But we're already at the highest threat level."*

*"That's why I'm announcing a new color."* The director reached in his pocket, pulled out a plastic square, and stuck it at the top of the thermometer.

Another reporter raised his hand. *"It's red, like the other one."*

*"It's a darker red."*

*"Not really."*

*"No, see, it's clearly darker."*

Reporters scribbled on pads. Another hand went up again. *"What's the name of the new threat level?"*

*"Red."*

*"Won't that be confusing?"*

*"No more questions . . ."*

Malcolm Glide turned the volume down on his office TV and picked up the phone.

"No, I will not be put on hold!" barked Glide. "I realize the congressman isn't in. I want you to deliver this message to him personally: Tell him to shut his goddamn mouth! . . . I know we're working behind the scenes to protect the oil company from its victims. That's exactly why he needs to go mute. Those were the strict ground rules from the beginning of his term: no press conferences, no interviews except Fox, and sit like a silent lump in the committee . . . Because he's fucking stupid! And I'm not going to let him throw this away! Do you have any idea how hard it was to get a moron like that elected?"

Harder than parting the Red Sea.

But if anyone could do it . . .

Two years earlier, in a large hotel ballroom somewhere south of the Mason-Dixon.

Election night.

Anticipation built all evening through the packed crowd. Finally it burst. A mighty, wall-shaking cheer went up. With 82 percent of precincts reporting, all three networks had just declared the winner in the Thirteenth District.

Max Bugler was now a U.S. congressman.

Balloons fell. School bands played. Champagne corks popped.

In the back of the room, Malcolm Glide received an unending series of backslaps as he puffed a fat cigar from Cuba, the embargo of which he staunchly supported.

It was an upset. A big one.

When the race had started, Max was the darkest of horses. His first bid for public office, no experience or idea what district he was in. But Max had a firm jaw and the last name of his father, a former governor.

If there's no hope of winning an election, a political party still needs to fill the ballot and turn out the faithful for other races. You use the strongest name recognition and hope for the least embarrassment. Max was a throwaway candidate.

They brought in Glide to minimize the embarrassment.

He burst through the doors at Bugler headquarters.

"Everybody stand up! Now!"

Chairs slid back. Staff glanced at each other.

"Thirty points behind! Have you all been circle-jerking in here? Where are we weakest?" He stretched out an arm. "You!"

"Me?" peeped a shaken staffer.

"You're fired!" yelled Malcolm. "Get out of my sight!" A finger aimed at the next person. "You! And you better not say, 'Me?'"

"War record?"

"Bingo! And don't say it like a question!" Malcolm clasped hands behind his back. "Continue."

"Well, our opponent, Hank Freeman, is a highly decorated Vietnam veteran. And our candidate's dad used his influence to help him, uh . . . not go to the war."

"Say it!" yelled Malcolm.

"Say what?" asked the shrinking staffer.

"We shoot straight in here!" shouted Malcolm. "Don't give some euphemistic 'not go to the war.' Say what everyone out on the street is saying!"

"He's a draft dodger?"

"I never want to hear that slanderous shit again! Get the fuck out!"

Running feet. A door slammed.

Glide plopped down in the chair at the head of a conference table. Other chairs began to fill.

"Did I say you could sit?"

They popped back up.

"Sit down!" Malcolm rubbed his cheeks hard with his palms. "So Freeman's a hero and our guy's a faggot. We got 'em now!"

Expressions around the table said they didn't understand.

"Who doesn't understand?" said Malcolm.

Nobody made a sound.

"Good. Because we don't need any amateurs who've never read Orwell." Malcolm pointed again. "You're fired!"

"What did I do?"

"You look weird to me. Out!"

The door slammed.

"We're going to flip this thing," said Malcolm. "Patriot is wimp. Wimp is patriot. Ideas?"

Silence around the table.

"Do I have to teach you everything?" He pointed again. "What's Freeman most known for?"

"Single-handedly stormed a machine-gun nest."

"He lied to get his medals," said Glide. "The nest was empty."

"But he won the Purple Heart."

"He shot himself in a cowardly attempt to be sent home."

"Both his legs were amputated."

"That means he was a *really* big coward," said Glide. "Made sure he'd go home. I want this viral on the Internet by Friday!"

A hand timidly rose. "How does that make our guy a patriot?"

"How'd he dodge the draft?" asked Malcolm.

"His dad got him in the National Guard."

"The same Guard that's now pulling five tours in Afghanistan?" said Glide. "Press release: Our candidate is proud of his war record performing highly dangerous service, and is deeply offended by anti-Americans who call our brave members of the Guard draft dodgers. If elected he'll courageously introduce legislation to extend their tours."

"But he served in Memphis."

"Memphis scares the shit out of me . . . Get to work!"

And now, two years later, the victory was political legend, forever cementing Glide's reputation. He dialed the phone.

"Rip? Malcolm here . . . Yeah, the thermometer looked great on TV . . . Listen, I need another favor . . ."


## SOMEWHERE IN CYBERSPACE

*Dear Serge,*

    *Most thanks again for your assistance. I just sent the banking account information. Did you receive? Please advise immediately when you have secured funds and make deposit.*

        *God's blessings upon you*

        *Bobonofassi Gabonilar*


*Dear Bobo,*

    *Great news, pen pal! I almost have the money. Even better: I've been in touch with Sarah Palin, and I think she can help us with the transfers and the rest of your problems. If you're watching TV and see her kick someone in the crotch, that's the signal she's on board . . . More good news! I didn't mention this before because of the stress you were under: I'm actually a spy! I've only been at it a couple days, but my first mission was a complete success except the hostages did some damage in my trunk. And Miami couldn't be a better place to launch my new career. City of international intrigue,* full of spooks since Castro. Did you know that at least three James Bond movies shot footage here? Do you get cable? But I know your next question: "How is being a spy good news for us?" Because I lied. I actually have the money, but a transfer is too risky right now. You'll be exposed. And here's where my excellent espionage training comes in: I tracked your IP address and found you're already in Miami. (Computer guy who works at the university owed me big.) Tell me where you are and I'll deliver the cash personally. Maybe we can meet downtown. Isn't downtown a trip? A skyline of gleaming bank towers and stylish office buildings that sprouted in the eighties building boom with laundered money from Noriega's Panama. And below on street level, sandwiched between skyscrapers, are all these funky little retail shops. There are only three kinds of stores: luggage, watches, and perfume. That's it. Just dozens of narrow joints selling American Tourister, Rolex, and Chanel. Someone told me the stores cater to people who fly up from the Caribbean for a ferocious amount of shopping. I've never visited where they live myself, but apparently the island life requires vast amounts of suitcases, being on time, and smelling better . . . Tell me where you want to meet, and I'll come armed to the teeth for your safety.

Waiting by the computer,
Serge

Dear Serge,

Much gratitude for your kind concern, but I am not in Miami. The bank transfer procedure is secure and utmost safe. Please use the account number I sent, and contact immediately upon deposit.

Blessings,
Bobonofassi Gabonilar

Dear Bobo,

Jesus, you're in more danger than I thought! I'm coming to your rescue! Sorry, but I also lied earlier when I said I only recently tracked you to Miami. I knew it from the beginning. It's just that a lot of these e-mails are scams from Nigeria. Obviously you made it out of East Bum-fuck and reached Florida, but had to conceal your location because of any relatives who might have escaped the rebels and are still in hiding back home. I'm guessing you're an exchange student because my computer friend narrowed the IP search to Coral Gables and the University of Miami. And the routing number on the account you gave me is also here—this big downtown bank just up the street. Change of plans: Too dangerous now to meet in public. E-mail me your location and I'll come there. Or maybe I'll just figure out your address first and surprise you. Meanwhile, stay put! (Maybe watch Burn Notice—seen it yet? Michael's mother is Sharon Gless from Cagney & Lacey. Who would have thought?)

> Your guardian angel,
> Serge

Dear Serge,

    I honestly am not in Miami. Please use the original money transfer plan.

> Bobonofassi

Dear Bobo,

    You're scaring me! I had no idea you were in such peril! I wasn't going to say anything, but Miami is also a huge rebels-in-exile city, so you're not even safe here. Clearly you're paranoid and don't know who to trust anymore. And since we've never met, a little lingering skittishness is more than reasonable. What if I'm with the cops? I might confiscate the money or worse. So to put your mind at ease, I'm attaching a bunch of newspaper articles about these unsolved cases where my name unfortunately came up (am I embarrassed!). Meanwhile, my IP guy is getting close to your exact location, but it might be too late. For the love of God, tell me where you're living! (Can't wait to see your house. Did you watch that thing on the local news where this guy in Florida furnished his place entirely with chairs and tables and beds made from FedEx boxes? The anchor people laughed about it, but the FedEx people were pissed. Then, at this other house, paramedics responded to a NASCAR fan who built *a roll cage around his toilet, with a steering wheel and a flat-screen TV on the wall so he could pretend racing, and he got too excited squeezing one off and had a stroke. Paramedic slang is a "commode code," but they left that out of the news. Anyway, the cage release got jammed and the ambulance guys had to use the jaws of life on his toilet. I'm starting to like NASCAR.)*

      *Ready to extract,*

      *Serge*


*Dear Serge,*

    *I truly appreciate all your efforts, but we have found someone else to assist us, and the money has already been transferred. We need no further contact.*

      *Bobonofassi*


*Bobo!*

    *Help is on the way! My computer friend just finished tracking. You're going under the name Rollo Tomagallu and using broadband connections at the school library and your off-campus house near LaJune Road. Since I now know your home address, it's too risky to continue this correspondence. Under no circumstances are you to e-mail me anymore. The next time we make contact, it'll be when I bring the money in person. Luckily I'm a professional (and now a spy!). The safest course of action, to avoid a counterstrike from rebel agents, is for me to sneak into your place under cover of darkness. So if some stranger wakes you in your bed at four A.M., don't freak out. It's just me. I'm guessing your room is the one on the southwest corner of the house. The light was still on last night when I was sitting outside in my car looking through the windows, and you were on the computer wearing a Nigerian soccer jersey. If I'm wrong, put some kind of school decal on the right window so I don't give one of your roommates a heart attack.*

      *Sleepless in Miami,*

      *Serge*

*Dear Serge,*

    *I am so sorry. This was all a scam. There are no rebels. I was just trying to make some money. Please leave me alone!*

*Dear Bobo (or Rollo),*

    *No can do. You're obviously cracking under the pressure and your judgment is shot—like telling me lies about this being a scam and violating my instructions not to e-mail anymore. So from now on, I'll be making the decisions for both of us. Have to move fast now. My advice to you: Just relax and go to sleep.*

      *It's almost over,*

      *Serge*

## DOWNTOWN MIAMI

"But, Serge," said Coleman. "I thought Sarah Palin was your new pen pal."

"She is." Serge led the way down the sidewalk along Biscayne Boulevard. "But she's also swamped with the rallies and hasn't been able to write back yet. In the meantime, I'm just a man. I have my corresponding needs."

"So writing to your other friend was like a pen-pal booty call?"

"Something like that." Serge opened his wallet and counted through cash.

"Holy cow!" said Coleman, peeking over his pal's shoulder. "Your pen pal just gave you a thousand dollars for nothing?"

"Not for nothing. To leave him alone." Serge finished thumbing through the fresh currency in his wallet. "Some people are too jumpy these days. That's why you have to cover their mouths after breaking into their bedrooms."

"So you knew it was a rip-off all along?"

Serge turned the corner onto Flagler Street. "Of course."

"Then why'd you answer his e-mail?"

"Needed start-up money for spying expenses," said Serge. "I'm not sure, but in all the spy movies, I've never seen them get a paycheck. It might take a while."

"Will a thousand be enough?"

"For openers," said Serge. "That's why I have a secondary plan. Miami is full of opportunities if you know where to look. That's why I need to come here every few months for a brain flush: all these different, layered worlds existing simultaneously, some off the grid, invisible to the average observer."

Coleman looked around. "Where?"

Serge pointed up at bank towers. "We're in the financial capital of Latin America." He lowered his arm and swept it across street level. "But down below are all these crazy shops."

"The ones with roll-down burglar shutters?"

"For when the yellow crime lights come at night and life clears off the streets like a nuclear winter," said Serge. "But during the day, a bustling economic furnace."

Coleman looked in windows as they walked. "But who needs this much luggage?"

"The island people." Serge pulled out a pamphlet for an art exhibit. "And they come in two styles: tourists and professional shoppers."

"Professional?"

"That's the hidden opportunity I mentioned. I had no idea until a few years ago, but there's a bunch of sub-budget hotels downtown, whose lobbies are completely full of giant cargo boxes. All these people with rope and packing tape. Barely room to walk."

"What are they doing?"

"The same thing *I'm* going to be doing soon to get more money." Serge pocketed the pamphlet. "Fill you in on the rest later. Right now the museum's coming up."

"Then why are you turning into this luggage store?"

"Shhhh! We're spies now."

A clerk smiled. "Can I help you find something?"

"Briefcases."

"Any kind in particular?"

"The kind that you have two of."

"We're well stocked in several brands."

"I'll take those two."

The pair headed west on Flagler Street.

"Why do we need briefcases?"

"For the museum." Serge trotted up steps toward the courtyard. "I love the art museum!"

They reached an expansive, elevated piazza with a mosaic of beige and Tuscan tiles. On the west end, the main Miami library; to the east, the Museum of Art.

"Stop here," said Serge. "We have to enter separately. I'll go first, and you come in ten minutes later."

"Why?"

"That's just the way it works. Then once inside, here's what you do . . ." Serge explained the plan. "Think you can handle that?"

"Piece of cake. So what kind of cool mission are we on?"

"No mission."

"Then what does your plan accomplish?"

"Nothing. Sometimes it's just about bursting with a zest for life and letting yourself become an unjaded kid again, playing fort in the woods, or spy in Miami. And sometimes your mission is just to act like a spy. Especially when there's no mission. Confuses the enemy into thinking there's a mission, which distracts them from your real mission. That's our mission."

"Does this have something to do with one of your Secret Master Plans?"

"Yes. I've got the tingles again." He showed Coleman goose bumps on his arm. "Something big is about to go down in Miami, probably during the summit, and only a spy can save the day."

Serge trotted toward the museum, and Coleman walked toward a wall on the far side of the courtyard that cut the wind so he could fire up a fattie.

"One, please," Serge told the ticket seller. He strolled through various galleries. Oils, acrylics, charcoals. The museum silent and empty. Only a handful of others: a family with two small children; a couple having an affair on lunch break; a man in a business suit staring at an abstract, then tilting his head to look at it sideways. Three guards in different doorways pretended not to look but seemed to be following Serge.

Serge reached the central gallery and took a seat on a large, continuous bench that formed a rectangle in the middle of the room. A Japanese garden sat inside it. Serge placed his briefcase on the floor.

Moments later, Coleman came in. He stood next to the businessman and stared at the abstract painting. "I am so stoned."

"Excuse me?" said the man.

"That painting." Coleman pointed. "Gremlins and flying snakes and naked chicks playing trombones while masturbating with wax fruit."

The man glanced at Coleman, then back at the painting. "I don't see anything."

"Because they hung it upside down." Coleman walked away as the man twisted his head.

Serge gazed up at a vibrant watercolor. Coleman clandestinely sat next to him. He placed his briefcase on the ground.

"Serge," said Coleman. "Why'd you pick a museum?"

"Shhhhh! We're not supposed to know each other."

"We could be strangers talking about art."

"Speaking of which, what's the deal with that guy you were talking to? His face is like an inch from that painting."

"I think he's a pervert."

"Museums naturally attract oddballs. The perfect place for spies to meet. They're always meeting in cultural attractions and other places where loitering is encouraged."

"Where'd you learn that?"

"*Get Smart.* People think it was a comedy but completely miss the Cold War subtext. I need a cone of silence."

"What about a shoe phone?"

"Got one," said Serge. "Made my own this morning with a cell phone." He took off his left sneaker, tapped a finger inside several times, then held it to his ear. He pulled it away from his head and peeked through the foot hole. "It's broken. What the fuck?"

"Maybe you can buy another."

Serge put his shoe back on. "That's already the third one I've gone through."

"Is it under warranty?"

"Yes, but the last time the phone people gave me some bullshit: 'You're not supposed to *walk* on it.'"

Serge grabbed the handle of his pal's briefcase. Coleman grabbed the other. They got up and left in opposite directions.

The businessman had moved on to the next painting. A hand in his right pocket. In the bottom of the pocket was a hole, where a wire led inside his shirt to his tie tack. The concealed hand pressed a button, taking photos with a pinhole camera.

When the room was empty, the man left the museum. He looked left: Coleman trotting down steps toward the Metro Mover. Stage right: Serge, fifty yards ahead, crossing the courtyard. The businessman picked up the pace.

Serge headed down Flagler Street. The man maintained a half-block separation.

Serge stopped to stare in the window of a luggage store. The businessman bent down to tie his shoe. Serge resumed walking. The man stood up.

At the corner of Miami Avenue, without breaking stride, Serge casually dropped the briefcase in a trash can and turned the corner.

The businessman began running. He reached the trash can and grabbed the briefcase. A black SUV screeched up to the curb, the man jumped in, and they sped off.

## Chapter *NINE*

### THE ROYAL POINCIANA HOTEL

Room 318.

Florida sunlight blazed through broken blinds.

The bed hadn't been turned down.

A fully clothed man lay on top of the covers with limbs twisted in various directions as if he'd fallen off a roof.

Eyelids fluttered in the harsh light.

The man pushed himself up with a groan. Blood on the front of his shirt. Where'd that come from? He went to get off the bed and fell to the terrazzo floor. He stood up and staggered toward the bathroom for a routine vomit to get a fresh start on the day. Then three aspirin and a chase of what was left at the bottom of the Jack Daniel's.

He coughed and felt a pain in his right side. The man raised his shirt and found a stack of bruised ribs. That's weird.

He walked to the window and shielded his eyes for a view of banks, a monorail, and the ocean.

"Where the hell am I?"

A look around the room. No remote control. His right hand turned the volume knob, clicking the TV on. A commercial for restructuring consumer debt. He went to the dresser for clues. A taxi receipt, gum, room key, airline boarding pass. A wallet with no ID, no credit cards, and fifty-six dollars. Three passports, all the same face. Chad Utley, Ireland; Roland Dance, Bahamas; and the real one issued by the United States.

The TV: "... *Dignitaries continue arriving as the Summit of the Americas returns to Miami...*"

A whapping sound from the unbalanced ceiling fan. It morphed into a louder whapping outside from a news helicopter on its way to a seven-car pileup on the Don Shula.

The man walked to the window and peeked out the blinds again.

"Miami... Shit... I'm still only in Miami."

He noticed a brown paper bag in a familiar shape, opened another bottle of Jack, and took it back to bed with him. Along with the authentic passport.

He took a slug, opened the passport, and examined the photo of a younger self:

Ted Savage, international persona non grata.

Ted had worked as a data analyst in the U.S. embassy in Costa Gorda. His CIA cover.

Costa Gorda was a success story of democracy.

Too much for some people.

The volcanic soil was rich down there, and the Caribbean nation exported impressive amounts of tropical fruit, coffee, and, of course, bananas. All of it shipped by American corporations with long-term land leases.

Fernando Guzman became president three years ago after a spotless election. Church bells rang. Firecrackers.

It was the kind of freedom certain people in Washington love to celebrate, except when it happens. Guzman had gotten the notion he was independent.

"As my first official act, I'm announcing wage reforms. Minimum two dollars a day."

Hit the export companies where it hurt. Phone calls. Campaign donations.

The companies needed to bend Guzman to their will. Which meant a CIA boot print in the country. And payments to the generals in case a coup was required. And in that case, the generals would need an enemy, real or imagined, against which to rally the populace.

Which meant rebels.

They actually existed. All fifteen of them. Camped in the mountains wearing Che Guevara T-shirts, smoking potent dope, and holding Marxist poetry slams.

The government knew where they were and left them alone because they were harmless and unworthy of the trouble, like Deadheads who remain in the field six months after the concert.

"Pepe, I'm hungry."

"So get some food."

"I think we're out."

"Did you check the ammo boxes?"

"Just crumbs . . . pass that spliff."

"Guess we have to go back down to the village"—where they posed for novelty photos with the tourists, in trade for chickens and vegetables.

"Viva la revolución! . . . *More beans please.*"

Meanwhile, President Guzman remained unyielding.

Time for hardball. And overnight, the ragtag mountain band of clowns became a full-fledged insurrection. At least on the local news.

Deep in the sanctum of CIA headquarters: "Are they really a threat?"

"No."

"Then do something."

They activated Savage. They picked him because he knew the terrain.

In the bars: "Señor Ted! What will you have?"

"Whiskey. *Dos.*"

In the brothels: "Señor Ted!"

"Is Conchita on tonight?"

In the alleys: "Special for Señor Ted. Forty dollars."

"Forty an ounce! When did prices go up?"

In the gutters: "Señor Ted. This is the *policía*. Time to wake up and let us take you back to the embassy."

"Wha—? Oh, thanks, Paco. Here's twenty for each of you."

They told Ted to write a report: Investigate the impending Communist takeover by a massive rebel force in the mountains.

So up the mountains Ted went, as he had done so many times.

A rustle in the brush.

Pepe jumped up, aiming an empty gun. "Who goes there?"

"Don't shoot. It's me." He stepped into the rebel camp.

"Señor Ted!"

Savage held up one hand. "I brought rum." Then the other. "And weed."

*"Arriba!"*

He came back and wrote the report. He fucked up. He told the truth: The country's soccer celebrations were a bigger threat.

Even worse, he leaked it to the press, just like he'd been told.

Disaster.

More phone calls. Discredit the messenger.

Two days later, all the networks went big with background dirt on the data analyst who had authored the "erroneous" report. Surveillance photos from the brothels and gutters. Almost as an afterthought, one cable commentator dropped what he pretended to be an idle comment. The report's author was CIA.

Outed.

They reeled him home.

No place to go, so he went places. Kentucky Derby, New Year's in Times Square, Mardi Gras. He didn't remember flying to Miami.

But now here he was. Savage lay back in his bed at the Royal Poinciana with a wet washcloth on his forehead and a bottle on the nightstand. "At least I won't get mixed up in any more trouble at this fleabag joint."

Two floors below, Serge led Coleman into the lobby. "Here's our hotel!"

Key Largo is commonly thought to be the beginning of the Florida Keys. But that's just the ones with the bridges.

Unconnected to land, stringing northward from Largo like little beads, are a scattering of small, mostly uninhabited islands that reach almost to Miami. Soldier Key, Sands Key, the Ragged Keys, Boca Chita, Elliott, Rubicon.

A forty-foot cigarette boat confiscated by the DEA departed Convoy Point and raced south across the bay. A giant rooster tail of salt water and foam sprayed behind the stern, its bow crashing over the swells.

Malcolm Glide held on to anything he could. "You've driven these things before?"

"Million times," said Station Chief Duke Lugar. "I just hope we don't have any leaks."

Malcolm looked around the deck.

"Not the boat," said Lugar. "Our operation. I've got my neck way out."

"Don't sweat it," said Malcolm. "We're airtight. How are the men coming?"

"Hungry for action."

A dotted line of mangroves came into view on the horizon. Lugar cut the wheel starboard, running parallel to the islands. "Fifteen minutes," said the agent. "I need to ask you something. Pretty sensitive."

"What is it?" asked Malcolm.

"We got a loose end in surveillance chatter that I can't seem to figure out," said Lugar. "Was hoping you could help."

The boat crashed down hard over a larger-than-usual wave rising from a shoal, knocking both men forward. Which meant shallower water, which meant they were getting close.

"So what's this loose end?"

"Could be a code name. Know anything about a Florida operative named Serge?"

"Serge?" said Glide. "Doesn't ring any bells. Why? What have you heard?"

"Picked him up on routine detail near the airport." Lugar pulled back on the throttle and threaded a coral channel. "At first we thought he was freelance, but it's beginning to look like he's working for Oxnart."

"Oxnart?" Glide knew all about the jealous rivalry between the station chiefs, because he'd personally nurtured it for leverage. He grabbed a railing as the boat took another jarring bounce. "In what capacity is this Serge?"

"Attached to the Costa Gordan consulate. Extra security for the summit," said Lugar. "But something's not right. I don't trust him."

Glide smiled to himself: *You mean you don't trust Oxnart.* "So what about him's not kosher?"

"Just this feeling I have. He suddenly shows up out of nowhere and foils an assassination against President Guzman." Lugar eased the throttle down to idle speed. He turned to Glide. "Did you have anything to do with hooking up Serge and Oxnart?"

"Me?" said Glide. He wished he did, the way it was under Lugar's skin. "Probably someone higher in the Company. You know Oxnart's talented and moving up fast."

Lugar clenched his teeth, edging the speedboat's bow into soft sand twenty yards from the shore of a small, unnamed island. He threw out the anchor. "This is as far as we go. It's not the kind of place that's got a pier."

"What kind of place is it?"

"A spot we use from time to time." The agent took off his shoes and hopped over the side in a foot of water. Malcolm followed as they splashed toward a break through the mangroves. In the distance, faint yelling and gunfire.

"You sure everything's airtight?" said Lugar. "Congress made these arms deals explicitly illegal. Not to mention if they found out what we're doing out here."

"I've taken care of everything," said Malcolm. "You just do your part."

Lugar splashed ahead in the shallowing water. "And it will really hit the fan if that geology report gets out—"

Glide grabbed him by the arm. "Where'd you hear about a geology report?"

"I just . . ." Lugar read the telegraph in Malcolm's eyes and caught himself. "What geology report?"

Malcolm released his arm. "That's better."

They reached the shore. A trail opened up, and the pair hiked through light brush until they found an open field.

All manner of menacing activity: guys with olive face-paint firing at silhouette targets, bayoneting straw bags hanging from trees, crawling through the live-fire obstacle course.

Malcolm looked around. "Did we bulldoze this land?"

"No," said Lugar. "About a century ago it used to be a pineapple farm. Most people don't know it, but back then America got almost all its pineapples from these islands."

A trainee in a foxhole lobbed something.

No sound.

"The grenade didn't go off," said Malcolm.

"About half don't because they're leftover army surplus from the Second World War," said Lugar. "We took what we could get."

"You mean the so-called pineapple grenades because of how the casings were scored?"

Lugar smiled. "Ironic."

"So when does the party begin?"

"They're flying out tonight," said Lugar.

Glide began walking toward the obstacle course. "Where'd you find these guys anyway?"

"Most worked out of front companies in warehouses around the airport. The rest were at the dog track."

# Chapter TEN

## DOWNTOWN MIAMI

A dingy 1930s hotel sat squashed between high-rise bank towers that lit up the night skyline. One of those old-style joints connected to the rest of the buildings on the block. Aqua with faded peach trim. Circular, nautical windows in a line under the edge of the roof. Its name displayed on a vertical neon sign sticking out from the corner of the third floor:

THE ROYAL POINCIANA

The sign was dark.

Inside the lobby: "I love these old hotels!"

"Serge, I think they're closed for repairs or something."

"Why do you say that?"

"All these huge boxes piled to the ceiling. They fill most of the lobby," said Coleman. "Broken plaster, rusty pipes, all those construction workers putting more stuff in boxes."

Serge looked toward an industrious squad of people wrapping the boxes with reinforced packing tape. "They're not renovating—they're shipping."

"Shipping?"

"Remember the professional shoppers I told you about?"

"Yeah," said Coleman. "You never finished explaining."

"Watch and learn."

Serge approached the front desk with bulletproof glass and a pass-through key slot. The man behind it looked twenty years older than his birth certificate. Stained Miami Heat T-shirt, stubble, and that hollow, gaunt type of face that reminded people of carnival booths. He watched a black-and-white TV with rabbit ears. A Spanish game show. Contestants wearing scuba suits in a vat of salsa.

"Excuse me?" said Serge.

Nothing.

"Hello? Can you hear me?"

The man laughed at the TV and choked briefly on his burrito.

Serge banged the glass. "Yo! Captain!"

The desk manager noticed Serge, stood, and wiped hands on his shirt. He leaned toward the round metal grate in the middle of the glass. "What?"

"I want in the pipeline."

"Pipeline?"

Serge pointed back at the people taping boxes.

"Oh, that," said the manager. He shook his head. "Don't think they're hiring. All of them work for stores in the islands, and most are family operations."

"Know all about it," said Serge. "They fly them up for sleepless, three-day shopping binges. But I'm already here. They'll save air fare. And when I put my mind to shopping, I can trample Joan Collins."

"Sorry," said the manager. "Can't help you."

Serge reached in his wallet and snapped a crisp hundred-dollar bill between his hands. He slid it through the key slot.

The manager held it to the light and stuck it in his pocket. "I'll make some calls."

"And I'll do advance recon so I'm totally prepared for my spree. What do they need?"

"Mostly luggage and electronics. But others take cabs to Walmart and Costco."

"What do they buy?"

"Everything. Paper plates, toothpaste, double-A batteries."

"That's actually profitable?"

"Like you wouldn't believe. They can't get normal distribution for American-brand goods, and a single can of Coke sells for five clams."

"Five dollars!" Serge whistled. "Even Starbucks doesn't have that kind of balls."

"There's this one guy who calls every month and pays me fifty to buy a laptop, but I'm not giving up that name."

"Understandable. We'll take a room. This is the perfect place to build up my immune system."

"Thirty dollars."

Serge fed currency through the slot, took a brass key, and got in an elevator. He slid the accordion metal cage closed.

Room 321.

A single queen bed with a six-inch depression in the mattress. The toilet seat lay on tiles under the dripping sink. The air conditioner was missing the front cover, displaying dust-caked condenser blades. Shouting and violent wall thumps from a fight in the next room involving five people and an ironing board.

"Serge, this is by far the dumpiest place we've ever stayed."

Serge slapped the bed, launching a small cloud. "I have just the fix." He reached in his suitcase and unrolled a Star-Elite Club red doormat inside the entrance.

Coleman reached in his own suitcase and removed a prosthetic leg with a Willie Nelson bumper sticker. He pointed at a splatter of spots on the ceiling. "Is that blood?"

"Yes." Serge unpacked the rest of his luggage.

"What kind of people stay here?"

"Two camps: the shoppers, and out-of-state tourists who book sight unseen, then huddle all night in mortal fear of crime and flesh-eating bacteria and flee at dawn."

The rotary phone rang.

Serge stared.

"Aren't you going to answer it?" asked Coleman.

"This could be the call I've been waiting for my entire life." Serge placed a hand gently on the receiver. "I hope it's the Wish Man. And I'm ready in case he only grants one wish. I'll say, 'More wishes.' Then I've got him. He'll have to answer to his people."

"You say that almost every time a motel phone rings, but usually it's just a complaint from another room. Or a hooker."

"Or both." He picked up the receiver on the ninth ring. "Serge here. Is this the Wish Man?"

"Sanchez from the front desk."

"Grant my wish."

"Got you plugged in for a shipment. Pick up the shopping list in the lobby."

"Be right down." He hung up. "We're on."


## COSTA GORDA

Midnight.

Moonless. The mountain highlands rose ruggedly in the center of the small Caribbean nation.

Silence under the stars except for croaking tree frogs and nocturnal, cawing birds.

Then: the distant drone of a C-130 Hercules air transport plane. No tail markings. Registered to a nonexistent consortium in El Salvador. The back-bay door wide open.

A crew member in a harness yelled over the engines and wind. "Thirty seconds!"

Next to him, a crouching row of camouflaged men with parachute static lines hooked overhead.

"Five seconds!" yelled the harness man. *"Go! Go! Go!..."*—slapping each man on the leg as they jumped out the back of the plane.

The aircraft quickly emptied, banked hard, and climbed steeply until it couldn't be heard.

Across the sky below, a sea of parachutes sprouted and drifted peacefully like airborne mushrooms. The drop zone was tricky in size and terrain, but the pilot was good. Only two guys had to be cut down from trees.

They gathered silk chutes and began a downhill trek behind their squad leader, who charted the way with a GPS. As they neared the coordinates of the reported rebel encampment, the leader called their translator to the front of the platoon.

He began shouting in Spanish: friendlies, allies, brothers, and most importantly, don't shoot.

Ahead, in an unseen configuration of pup tents, men stirred from sleep. "Everyone up! Someone's coming!"

When the paratroopers finally broke into the camp, they were met by a ragged, elements-beaten gang of insurgents pointing cocked Russian AK-47s.

The head of the paratrooper team whispered to the translator again. "Tell them we're on their side. We're here to help their struggle."

The translator translated.

The rebels looked confused.

"What's the matter?" whispered the squad leader.

"I'm not sure," said the translator.

"Tell them again."

He did.

More puzzled looks. The head rebel: "I'm sorry, we don't speak Spanish."

The squad leader took a step forward. "Ralph?"

"Henry?"

"What the hell are you doing here?"

"I was just about to ask you the same thing."

"We're on a secret mission to train the rebels." Henry glanced around. "Where are they?"

"You're looking at them."

"*You're* the rebels?"

"Station in Fort Myers sent us down last month."

"Where are the real rebels?"

"Got bored and left two weeks back."

"Where'd they go?"

"I heard them mention a bachelor party."

"This can't be the whole rebellion."

"Afraid so."

"What about the cocaine traffickers?"

"They also split."

"But intelligence says coke's still coming through."

Ralph grabbed a canteen off his belt. "We've had to start making their deliveries ourselves. I'm telling you, it's getting exhausting."

One of the other rebels raised a hand. "I want to go home."

Henry tossed his parachute aside in disgust. "Typical government operation."

A droning sound from above. They looked up.

Ralph raised night-vision goggles and peered through a break in the trees. "I don't see any tail markings."

"It's okay," said Henry. "That's our plane. It's circling around again for the supply-and-ammo drop."

"Covertly beefing up the revolution so the generals can seek military aid?"

Henry nodded.

Minutes later, large pallets of food and weapons floated down on giant parachutes and crashed through the trees.

"At least there's a silver lining," said Ralph. "We're sick of eating Spam."

He started toward the boxes. Henry grabbed him from behind.

"What's the matter?" asked Ralph.

Henry pointed skyward. Another drone from above. "Our plane again."

"Thanks," said Ralph. "Don't want me to get hit by more pallets."

"That's not it," said Henry.

"Why are you crouching down?" asked Ralph.

*Boom.*

A flaming explosion in the trees.

Everyone hit the ground.

*Boom. Boom. Boom.*

More trees ablaze.

Ralph turned his face sideways in the dirt toward Henry. "That's naplam!" He looked up at all the just-dropped pallets, engulfed in flames. "What the fuck's going on?"

"Blowing up the rebels' supplies," said Henry. "We have to disrupt their supply lines."

"They're hitting a little too close for comfort."

"Don't worry. They have our coordinates," said Henry. "Just a symbolic strike so the generals can show the people they're taking a strong hand to the revolution. They're supposed to miss the camp."

*Boom.*

A cluster of pup tents exploded in fire.

"They just hit the camp," said Ralph.

"They missed."

Ralph jumped up, yelling at his brigade. "Get that fire out before it reaches the ammunition."

The drone of airplane engines grew louder again.

"He's circling back!" yelled Ralph, hitting the ground again. "He's making another strike!"

Henry remained standing. Another wave of pallets floated down and crashed through the trees.

"More supplies?" said Ralph.

"For the rebel counter-offensive."

## *Chapter* **ELEVEN**

### DOWNTOWN MIAMI

Rusty trawlers and cargo boats sailed along the Miami River. Some going fishing, others destined for Hispaniola with crates of merchandise from Sam's Club to restock the bodegas.

On the southern shore of the river sat a mixed collection of warehouses, mechanics shops, and low-rent office buildings.

One of the buildings backed up to a marine repair yard surrounded by barbed wire. Stark concrete, tattered awnings, gravel parking lot, no outward hints of what might be happening inside. It had opened on Pearl Harbor Day. Occupancy hadn't topped 20 percent since 1967. It was about location.

Two stories, but the elevator was broken. A hallway ran down the middle of each floor, rows of offices on both sides. Windows facing the hall, shades drawn. In the middle of each door, another window with gold lettering. Most of the letters had chipped away, but some of the outlines remained. Bail bond, travel agency, title insurance, attorney-at-law.

The last door on the second story was the exception. Fresh gold letters:

### MAHONEY & ASSOCIATES, PRIVATE INVESTIGATIONS

Mahoney sat inside. The only associate was the fifth of rye residing in his bottom desk drawer.

The bottle currently rested atop the desk blotter, next to a rocks glass with two fingers of amber reinforcement. Next to a pair of crossed feet propped up by the black rotary phone. The sole of his right shoe was worn through. Adlai Stevenson.

The phone rang. Mahoney stared at it cynically. "Some boozy broad in a tight sweater with a weakness for the ponies?"

He answered on the sixth ring.

"Mahoney and Associates. Discreet investigations. Mumble to me . . . No, I don't need a free air-vent inspection for mold that could make me constantly tired." He slammed the phone down. "Shyster."

Since his fishing sabbatical in the Keys—and early retirement from Florida law enforcement—former agent Mahoney had returned to the mainland and set up shop with his dream job.

Unfortunately, it remained a dream. Two months, not a single case.

But if Mahoney wasn't making a living, at least he was living the life. An antique hat rack stood in the corner, topped with a lone, rumpled fedora. The desk chair creaked as he leaned back and propped his feet again, a wooden matchstick wiggling between his teeth. His necktie had a pattern of Route 66 signs. He opened a dime paperback to a dog-eared page.

Heavy footsteps approached from the stairwell at the end of the hall. Mahoney's eyes rose from the book. The toothpick stopped wiggling.

Footsteps grew louder. Mahoney's right hand silently slid open the top desk drawer, revealing a snub-nose .38 Police Special.

The brass doorknob jiggled.

The snub-nose cocked.

The door opened. Serge spread his arms. "Brother!"

A corner of Mahoney's mouth curled up in a rare smile. He slipped the gun back in the drawer and came out from behind the desk for a backslapping hug.

Coleman pointed at the bottle. "Can I have a drink?"

Mahoney produced another dirty glass. "Knock yourself out."

"He will," said Serge, grabbing a wooden chair from the wall and scooting it forward. "How's business?"

Mahoney went back and took his own seat. "Like selling turds to Roto-Rooter."

"Can't be that bad."

"Stinkaroo."

Serge looked back at the door and gold letters in reverse. "What about your associates?"

"That's show business."

"Then can I be an associate?"

"No cases." Mahoney shuffled a deck of playing cards. "And behind on rent. I can only pay you with the air in this office."

"You don't have to pay me. It'll be fun, get to hang out, reminisce old days." Serge picked up the hand Mahoney dealt. "Bet I bring you luck." He laid out a straight flush.

Mahoney threw down his own hand and dealt again.

Serge picked up the cards. "I know how you can score some money in the meantime to make the rent. And no work involved."

"Sounds shaky."

Serge pointed at the phone. "May I?" He picked up the receiver and dialed . . .

. . . South of Miami, a phone rang in an old building near the Metrozoo. "Allied Imports," said Station Chief Oxnart.

Serge hung up.

"No answer?" asked Mahoney.

"No, someone answered."

"Who was it?"

"I don't know," said Serge. "I just found a generic number for the CIA in the phone book."

"They're in the book?"

"Have to be in case someone wants to defect." Serge discarded the jack of spades. "They always answer like it's a wrong number in case it's a wrong number."

"Why'd you hang up."

"Now they'll trace your line." He pulled a folded sheet of paper from his pocket and picked up the phone again.

Mahoney watched as Serge made another dozen hang-up calls.

"Who are you phoning?"

"Consulates, for when they track your call logs." Serge pulled his digital camera from another pocket and set it on a ten-second, self-timed shot. *Beep-beep-beep* . . .

He dialed again . . .

"Allied Imports . . ."

Serge held the camera to the receiver. *Beep-beep-beep-beep*. And hung up. "Their sound technicians will be working on that for weeks."

"How's that score us moola?" asked Mahoney.

Serge waved around the inside of the office. "You've already hung a shingle with a physical business address. The CIA has front companies all over Miami doing clandestine work that they can't be connected to. But they can't stay open too long or they'll risk discovery, so they're always needing more. Eventually you'll be contacted."

"To be a front company?"

"Or a dummy front company."

"How's that different?" asked Mahoney.

"Dummy fronts *don't* do any clandestine work. They divert attention from the real fronts." Serge drew another card and laid out a full house. "So in a way, you're already a dummy front. Remember to mention that when you ask for money."

Another set of footsteps down the hall. Mahoney opened his drawer again.

The steps grew closer. Mahoney shut the drawer, recognizing the trademark sound of stiletto heels.

A knock on the door.

Serge opened it.

A boozy broad in a tight sweater with a weakness for the ponies.

Dark sunglasses. She plopped down in Serge's empty chair and began crying.

Mahoney pushed a glass of rye forward.

"Thanks." She drained it.

"See?" said Serge. "Told you I'd bring you luck. Your inaugural case."

"First things first," Mahoney told the woman. "Two hundred smackers a day plus expenses."

She nodded. "I'm good for it."

Mahoney flipped open a notepad. "Spill."

"It's my ex."

"What about the mug?"

She removed her sunglasses.

"Nice shiner," said Mahoney. "This a habit?"

"I keep changing apartments, but he always finds me." Sobs again.

"A man who manhandles women," said Serge. "That's my turf."

"But it's my first case," said Mahoney.

"Still is," said Serge. "I'll just do the preliminary legwork."

Mahoney turned to the woman. "You'll need to check into a hotel for a couple nights. We'll call."

Serge offered her his hand. "Let me walk you back to your car. I'll need to ask a few questions about this jerk."

"You're so kind."

They left.

Mahoney leaned back with his book. Coleman grabbed the bottle. A clock ticked.

Mahoney looked up. "What's taking him so long?"

They walked to the window. The detective parted blinds with his fingers. "Unbelievable."

Down in the gravel parking lot, in the backseat of a '57 convertible Ford Skyliner, two long legs in stilettos pointed skyward. Between, Serge's bare, bouncing derriere.

Mahoney drew back his hands, letting the blinds snap shut. Coleman opened them again.

Fifteen minutes later, Serge walked back in, whistling "Papa Was a Rolling Stone." He stopped at their stares. "What?"

"How'd you bang her?" asked Coleman.

"*Why'd* you bang her?" asked Mahoney. "Now she'll scram."

"No, she'll come back." Serge handed Mahoney a two-hundred-dollar retainer. "Besides, she asked me to. 'The customer is always right.' Right?"

"I'll give you a mulligan this time," said Mahoney. "But no more T-shots."

"Fair enough." Serge stood. "Guess I need to go have a friendly little chat with her ex."

Shouting from across the hall. One of the only other occupied offices.

"*Oh! Jesus! Why'd the hell you do that?*"

Serge turned around and looked out the window into a hall. A door slammed. A man ran by cupping hands to his nose. "*I'll sue you for every last penny.*"

Serge faced Mahoney again. "Whose office is that?"

"The Guy Who Punches People."

"You call him that because he has a temper?"

"No," said Mahoney. "It's what he does. Here's his business card."


**ONE MILE AWAY**

Seventh floor of a towering office building on Flagler Street.

The entire consulate staff sat anxiously around a massive oak conference table.

The protocol chief opened the door. "The president of Costa Gorda."

Everyone jumped sharply to their feet and stared straight ahead.

Fernando Guzman entered and grabbed the empty chair at the head of the table. "Please be seated."

They sat back down with synchronized precision. Before the meeting, rampant watercooler buzz about the foiled attack on Guzman near the airport. Heads sure to roll. They dreaded the moment the president would bring it up.

He didn't.

Instead, diplomatic minutiae and scheduling. Courtesy calls, cocktail parties, speech writing, an interview with the Spanish-language version of the *Miami Herald*.

A half hour later, it was over. The president closed a leather organizer and passed it back over his shoulder to his traveling secretary. Then he stood quickly—"Thank you for your attention"—and departed with the same abruptness.

The entire room exhaled with relief and began filing out with thoughts of liquid lunch.

President Guzman stood in the lobby with his mobile staff, running down afternoon appointments. He looked up. "Oh, Felipe? Could I have a word? In private."

Deer in headlights. "Me?"

Felipe Chávez. Consulate director and head attaché. Rumored to be heir apparent for the Washington ambassadorship. Or first in line for the chopping block over . . . well, anything that needed a scapegoat. Part of the job description.

Perspiration trickled into Felipe's starched collar as the pair arrived back in the conference room. Guzman closed the door. Then placed a hand on Felipe's shoulder.

Here it comes, thought the diplomat. Fired. Or worse, reassignment to Canada . . . The Canadians! Christ! The collar became soaked.

"You okay?" asked Guzman. "You're sweating like a pig."

"Just ate something hot."

"Good, because we've got a lot of work to do." Guzman's arm went all the way across Felipe's shoulders as he began walking the attaché in circles around the conference table. "I need someone like you close to me."

"You do?"

"Ever thought about a cabinet post? And not one of the little ones that runs the bus system."

Air sucked out of Felipe. The cabinet? That was bigger than an ambassadorship.

"Don't answer now," said Guzman. "Because that's in the future. I've got the rebels and traffickers to worry about, not to mention the generals. Right now I need someone I can trust who sees five moves ahead."

Chávez thinking: He can't possibly be talking about me.

"I'm talking about you." Guzman squeezed his shoulder. "You're why I'm standing here alive today. Razor-sharp instincts beefing up security."

"Security?"

"That crack field operative you sent as backup in case my idiot bodyguards weren't up to task, which they weren't. But you already knew that. You're going places." He pointed at the ceiling. "The top. But don't be looking at my office until I'm ready to retire."

"I wouldn't!"

"That was a joke," said Guzman. "So where'd you find this new agent."

Felipe blinked hard a couple times. "You mean Escobar?"

"Who's Escobar?"

Scooter Escobar, the young guy from the mail room, who was the spy in the consulate.

"I'm talking about Serge," said the president. "On loan to us from the CIA. Tell me—and this is very important—did they approach you first, or the other way around? Because if they came to us, especially in light of last night, it means they know more about my enemies than I do . . . So tell me, who approached you?"

"I . . ."

"Well?"

"I—I—I . . ."

"You can't answer a simple question like that?" He turned and pointed aggressively in Felipe's face. "This is exactly the sort of thing I'm talking about!"

Felipe lost color.

Guzman slapped him sharply on the back. "Always putting your president first. You know I can't be linked to the CIA or my opposition would rake me over the coals for being a Yankee stooge. You're willing to take the fall for me, and I'll never forget it. So before I forget, here's what I need concerning Serge . . ."

# Chapter **TWELVE**

## SCOOTER ESCOBAR

A sidewalk bistro in downtown Miami.

"You have to help me find out more about Serge."

"Why?"

"Because President Guzman asked the consulate director, and he asked me," said Scooter. "And because you're the only person I know who's actually met him. I think he's after my job."

"But your uncle's one of the generals. Your job's safer than anyone's."

"I don't know. He was pretty sore about the RPG explosion." Scooter tossed back another shot of tequila. "I think those arms deals he's running are pretty important."

"What arms deals?"

"Forget about it. I shouldn't have said anything."

"Then find out about Serge yourself," said the woman. "You're supposed to be the spy in the consulate."

That was the problem.

Always had been, even back in the old country . . .

. . . The top of the mountain sat in a cloud. A misty rain weighed down tree branches with dripping water. The jungle was thick, but the path clear.

An army detail hiked single file up the rocky trail in Costa Gorda. They weren't on guard. Didn't need to be.

Rustling in the brush off the sides of the trail. Twigs snapped. A louder sound. *"Ow! My ankle." "Shhh! They'll hear you. They're right there on the trail."*

The platoon commander at the front of the line smiled and kept marching. "Gee, I wonder where those dangerous rebels could possibly be hiding."

The soldier behind him tapped the commander on the shoulder. "Sir, they're right in those bushes. I can see their eyes."

"Pipe down," said the commander. "Just stay near me like we're joined at the hip. Anything happens to you and I'll lose this cushy job."

"But aren't we supposed to crush the rebels?"

"Shut up, Scooter."

Because if they did, they'd all lose their cushy jobs.

The rebels were down to a couple dozen. Low on food, out of ammo. They stopped reading poetry and had smoked so much dope that they'd forgotten where they put their guns.

It was the plum assignment. The entire platoon knew their rebel "search-and-destroy" missions were a joke and the lightest duty in their tiny army. Just stroll through the hills each day and head back to camp at night for steaks and beer. Nothing could mess it up as long as nothing happened to the rebels.

No rebels, no more missions. The platoon became the insurgents' fiercest protectors. Every last soldier was thrilled with the arrangement.

Except the one marching behind the commander.

"I hate all this hiking around."

"Quit complaining!" snapped the leader. "And don't do something stupid to hurt yourself."

It was the one burden the commander had to shoulder to keep his prized assignment.

The safekeeping of Scooter Escobar.

Escobar's father had been a territorial police chief until his untimely death involving a steep road, chickens, and Jeeps. Scooter was taken in as a youngster by his wealthy uncle, General Montoya Escobar, the most famous of all the generals, widely known for his vast landholdings, a consuming fascination with *Baywatch,* and herpes.

Scooter had always been the shame of the family, racking up school suspensions and hospital stays. The latter stemmed from his fondness for weapons. Any kind. He was obsessed and couldn't find his way around one if he had an extra set of hands.

They gave him a diploma for attendance, and Escobar began spending all his time partying in the beach nightclubs with knee-walking-drunk kids on spring break.

Then the scandal.

A gun went off in one of the clubs. Escobar's. He was the only person hit, left-hip cargo pocket, sending twenty packets of cocaine scattering across the dance floor and sparking a stampede, also involving chickens.

The general had seen enough. He decided Escobar needed some manning up.

"I'm cutting you off! You're going in the army first thing tomorrow!"

"But I don't want to go in the army."

"My decision's final! It's that or the street."

The youth pouted, then looked up. "Will I get a gun?"

Escobar was short, soft, and plump, but made up for it by being stupid and pushy about it. A light bronze complexion with black hair and silly bangs. He grew the first wisps of a mustache that looked like he needed a napkin. With family influence, he received extra attention at basic training. Three classes of recruits had passed through and Escobar was still there, dangling like a gourd from the chin-up bar. The training instructor went to his supervisor.

"I can't do anything with him. He's failed every physical."

"But he's the general's nephew."

"He's going to cripple himself on the obstacle course."

The supervisor sat back under a plantation fan. Then he waved his right arm in frustration. "Give him a pass and throw him in with a platoon. Who's got the lightest duty?"

"D Company."

And so Escobar marched through misty mountains, fiddling with his assault rifle and bitching nonstop.

"And stop bitching!" said the commander. "You're giving me a headache."

Escobar snarled and mouthed silent insults. He kept marching and watching the eyes in the jungle that nobody else wanted to see.

"Sir?"

"What!"

"Are you sure the rebels are harmless?"

"What rebels?"

"But they're so close. They could easily wipe out the whole platoon."

"Keep it in your pants."

Suddenly a deafening burst of automatic-weapon fire.

"Everyone down!" shouted the commander.

The platoon flattened on the dirt.

Except Escobar, who struggled to maintain a grip on his rifle, which was stuck on automatic and twirled him around in the middle of the trail.

The commander tackled him. "Gimme that thing!" He ejected the magazine and stuck it in his pocket, then shoved the rifle back in Escobar's stomach. "No more bullets for you."

From the back of the platoon: "Sir."

"What is it?"

A soldier pointed off the side of the trail. Muffled screams.

The commander made a quick hand gesture, and they charged the brush. Soldiers broke into a clearing, where rebels ran in circles of panic. The commander looked down, then up in astonishment at Escobar. "You killed a rebel. Do you have any idea how endangered they are?"

"I didn't mean to."

Back at base camp, the commander marched into a major's office, dragging Scooter by the scruff of his neck.

"I can't do anything with him."

"But he's the general's nephew."

"He killed a rebel."

"What!"

"The other rebels were so scared they ran off into the woods. My platoon had to hunt them down and force them back to their camp at gunpoint."

"We can't be having that." The major rubbed his whiskered cheeks in consternation. "But what about the general?"

"There's got to be some job that's idiot-proof."

"Wait." The major nodded and raised a finger. "I got it." He picked up the telephone. "Military intelligence."

The next day:

A plain, pastel-green government building in the capital of Costa Gorda.

"This is where you'll be working."

Escobar looked at an empty desk. "What do I do?"

"Sit."

The captain of intelligence left.

Escobar sat.

He looked out his door at a hum of diligent activity from some of the nation's top espionage minds.

He frowned.

A look around his office. Something in the corner. "What's that?"

Escobar walked over. He threw a switch on and off. He liked it. Next stop, a filing cabinet.

The captain of intelligence was deep in thought over reports of rebel desertion. Something had been gnawing at him for the last half hour. "What's that sound?"

The captain tracked it across the office until he arrived at the source. "What the hell is going on? I told you to sit!"

"Huh?" said Escobar, standing over a running document shredder.

The captain dragged him into the office of the director of Costa Gordan intelligence. "I can't do anything with him!"

"But he's the general's nephew."

"He shredded most of our files."

The director knew Escobar's entire history. He thought a moment. "I've got it." Quick scribbling on a memo pad. He tore off the top sheet and handed it to the captain. "Take care of this pronto."

"But I've wanted that job for years," said the captain.

"So have I," said the chief. "But none of us will have any job if we don't stop the bleeding."

They both looked at Escobar. He was bleeding. A stapler.

The captain nodded in resignation. "I'll handle it immediately." He stood at attention and snapped a salute. "First flight to Miami . . ."

## MIDNIGHT

"Put on your uniform," said Serge.

"Can't I just wear this?"

"First impressions are important," said Serge. "If I can wear the cape . . ."

An orange-and-green Road Runner drove west across Miami out to Sweetwater on the edge of the Everglades. A modest neighborhood of well-kept ranch houses and thriving palms that didn't need to be kept. Toys in yards. Above-ground pools.

Serge found a street running along the turnpike. He checked his notepad again and parked. "This is the place. We're on."

They strolled up the walkway. Serge knocked hard on a door that was rotten along the bottom from absent rain gutters.

A bowling-ball-gut resident answered with a Miller in his hand.

Serge elbowed Coleman. "He's even wearing a wife-beater."

"Wife-beater?"

"That stained tank-top T-shirt." Serge grinned big at the resident. "Are you Jethro Comstock?"

Jethro swayed on beer legs. "Whatever you're sellin', I ain't buyin'."

"Oh, we're not selling anything," said Serge. "Okay, we are. We're selling wishes. The first one's free. You wish we'll leave you alone."

Jethro drained his beer and stared at the cape. "Who the hell are you?"

Serge pointed at the *S* in the middle of his chest. "I'm Super-Serge and my sidekick is the Human Torch."

Coleman raised a Bic lighter and flicked it.

Jethro looked at the flames drawn in Magic Marker on Coleman's T-shirt, then back at Serge. "Get the fuck off my property!"

He started closing the door, but Serge threw out an arm and slammed it open against a wall.

"We're leaving," said Serge. "Right after you promise to leave Sally alone."

"Sally? The bitch!"

"Actually, that's a politically incorrect term," said Serge. "Chicks don't dig it."

"I'm going to seriously fuck you up if you don't get out of here right now."

"Sure thing." Serge flipped open his notepad. "Right after a few last details. Sorry, it's my job." He looked down at the pad and began reading. "You're not to go near your ex-wife ever again. Or call her on the phone. Or contact her in any way for the rest of your life. Or else." He smiled again. "Well, that about does it. We good?"

"Or else what?"

"Or else this!" Serge reached atop his head and flicked a switch, activating the revolving red beacon on his helmet.

"Blow me!"

The door slammed.

## Chapter THIRTEEN

**SOUTH AMERICA**

Surf crashed from the Pacific.

A beach house somewhere near the unmarked border of Chile and Peru.

Curtains flowed gently out a bedroom window.

Inside, a tall, wiry man with muscular shoulders from ocean swimming. He sat in boxer shorts at a computer. Fingers tapped. An Internet mail account opened.

Behind him, a local beauty slipped into a short, lavender sundress and counted out a thousand dollars on the dresser. "Same time next week?"

The man's head stayed toward the computer screen. He had a blond crew cut like the bass player in U2.

"You're definitely not the chatty type." The woman pocketed the cash. "I guess that's good."

More typing on the keyboard. The woman left. The computer

screen displayed a folder from the account. The man opened a draft e-mail. He hadn't written it. Only three trusted people had passwords to the account, and messages were delivered by saving them in draft form. So they wouldn't have to be sent by e-mail. So they couldn't be monitored.

He finished reading the message and hit delete. His expression never changed. He stood and began packing for Miami again.

Again.

And he was forced to discount his services this time. The last trip to Miami had been his first failure. Or half failure. The front end went seamless as usual, and the rest should have been even easier. That was the mistake. He underestimated. And he would never do it again. He folded socks into a suitcase and ran the details of the last job through his head . . .

. . . It all started with another typical Miami lunch crowd that filled an outdoor café and wrapped around the corner of the sidewalk. A valet hopped in a car. The maître d' carried leather-bound menus and led a party of four to a table with an umbrella.

A couple stopped talking as a waiter arrived with salads.

They watched him leave, then leaned forward and whispered.

Odd bookends. The kind where you look at the guy and wonder, How'd *he* get *her*? She downplayed the sex appeal with a white blouse, pink skirt, office shoes without heels, and black hair pulled back in a ponytail. But no disguising the exquisite Latin features. Across the table, none of the clothes fit right. Tie askew. His haircuts cost ten dollars, and he hadn't gone to his prom.

The woman slid a legal-size envelope across the table. "You sure they can't trace this to me?"

"Give you my word." The man stuffed the envelope in a canvas shoulder bag. "Is it all there?"

She nodded. "Balances, transfers, everything." She glanced around. "Now, what's this geology report you mentioned? I hadn't heard anything."

It was the man's turn to glance around. "Not here." He got up without touching his salad. "My contact's delivering it to me at the other place. Let's meet there at seven. I'll need your help finding out what it means."

He placed a pair of twenties on the table, climbed over the rope around the sidewalk tables, and headed up the street talking on his cell. "Carson? It's me, Randy. I'm just about finished with the story . . . Yeah, I'll be in tonight to file . . ."

Two hours later, the skyline glowed.

Restaurants filled.

A no-frills fish joint on the shore of the Miami River was busier than most. The wind carried a sizzling, fried aroma to the outdoor tables. Cajun spice. A man with a loosened tie and canvas shoulder bag sat in back with an open menu. He waved off the waiter for the fourth time and checked his watch again. He dialed his cell again. No answer.

The waiter returned. He looked at the customer's third glass of water. "Are you ready to order?"

"Give me another moment."

"Sir, we really appreciate you coming tonight, but we have a lot of people waiting for tables."

"My date's supposed to meet me. Must have been delayed."

"I'm sorry, sir, but I'm afraid I'm going to have to ask you to order or give up your table."

He looked at his watch. "Fine. Bring me something."

"What?"

Randy Swade handed the menu back. "I'll trust your judgment."

"Yes, sir."

The waiter left.

The reporter opened his phone again. Something caught his eye. "There you are. I thought you weren't going to make it." He closed his cell. "Did you bring . . ."

"This restaurant's too exposed," said the contact. "It's in the car."

"And I thought *I* was cautious." Randy slid out his chair and stood. "Lead on."

The guest did. He'd parked an extra block away under a drawbridge over the Miami River. Randy Swade got in the passenger side. And a man with a blond crew cut got in the other.

Fifteen minutes later, hands rubbed soap under the faucet of a restroom behind a fish restaurant. A man with a blond crew cut checked his face closely in the mirror. Only a slight fingernail scratch under his left eye. He turned off the faucet and returned to the dining room.

A woman with a black ponytail looked around like she was waiting for someone.

"Are you waiting for Randy?"

"Who are you?"

"His contact."

"Where's Randy?"

"Waiting in my car."

"But he told me to meet him here."

"I know, but he thinks he was followed. I told him he was imagining things."

The woman grabbed her purse and stood. "This is getting ridiculous."

He led her around the parking lot and up the empty street.

"Where the heck is your car?"

"Just a little farther."

The woman looked back, restaurant now out of sight around a bend, voices faint.

Her pace slowed. "I think I'm going back."

"My car's right there."

"Under the bridge? I don't see Randy."

"He's inside waiting for you."

She stopped and looked at drops on the ground under the car's trunk.

Red.

A man zipped a suitcase closed in a beach house on the Pacific coast of South America. What a screwup back under that bridge in Miami. His memory delivered a phantom pain to his healed left shoulder, where it had been dislocated. From now on, every woman, no matter how delicate in appearance, was to be considered a black belt.

He grabbed the phone and called a taxi for the airport.


## MIAMI RIVER DISTRICT

Serge sat across the desk from Mahoney. Feet propped up, hands interlaced behind his head.

From the other side of the hall: *"Ow! Shit, you broke my nose! Why'd you do that?"* A man cupped hands to his face. Footsteps trailed toward the stairs.

Serge jerked a thumb over his shoulder. "How does that work, anyway?"

Mahoney shuffled playing cards and pointed outside through the window at the office building's sign.

Serge stood and walked to the blinds. "Been meaning to ask about that. This building's almost empty, but the sign is full of company names. Pan-Global Enterprises, Consolidated Associates, Biscayne Trading Partners, the Dodd Group, and on and on. Did they forget to take them down?"

The king of hearts went on the desk. Mahoney shook his head. "That's our friend across the hall."

"The Guy Who Punches People? Which company?"

"All of them," said Mahoney.

"I don't understand."

Mahoney placed a queen on the king. "Real name's Steve Dodd."

"And he just punches people?"

Mahoney shuffled again. "Started as a hobby. Big attorney with the prosecutor's office, but the pressure of plea bargains and assholes got to be too much."

"I can relate," said Serge.

"Steve told me he quit his job, cashed in all his stocks for bail money, and whenever someone got on his nerves, he'd punch 'em. Said he used to take Prozac, but this is more effective. Blood pressure's down, never felt better."

"You mentioned hobby, but what about the business?"

The jack of clubs. "Word got around," said Mahoney. "If you want someone punched, you send them to Steve. Concoct some ruse about signing papers to get money or whatever."

"Sounds like a sporadic business," said Serge. "Constant interruptions for bail, court appearances, stays in county lockup."

"Used his criminal law experience and found a loophole. Now he's raking it in. Apparently there's a big market."

"What kind of loophole?"

"Why don't you ask him?"

The door opened. Steve stuck his head inside, rubbing knuckles. "Got any ice?"

Mahoney pointed toward the bucket next to the bottle of rye. "Have at it."

"Thanks."

"Excuse me," said Serge. "Mahoney was saying that you found some kind of loophole to punch people."

Steve wrapped cubes in a washcloth. "That's right. Supreme Court decision just a few years back declaring corporation same as people. So I created a bunch . . ."—pointing at the sign out the window—". . . firewalled assets and liability among them, and moved everything important offshore. Now the only people they can go after are the owners of the corporations."

"But you own the corporations," said Serge.

Steve shook his head and pressed the washcloth to his fist. "Another guy in Venezuela is doing the same thing. We own each other's companies. There's no extradition treaty."

Serge whistled. "Nice work if you can get it."

"Thanks again for the ice." He left.

Serge shrugged at his brother. "It's Miami."

"Speaking of which," said Mahoney. "How are you coming on my first case?"

"Definite progress," said Serge. "I don't think she'll be having any more trouble from him."

"How's that?"

"He thought he was dealing with amateurs until I turned on the red beacon—"

The phone rang.

"Mahoney here . . ." He listened, and listened. Mouth turning grim. ". . . Very sorry to hear that . . . Yes, we'll definitely do something."

Mahoney hung up and poured a stiff one.

"What's the matter?" asked Serge. "You don't look so good."

Mahoney stuck the bottle back in the desk drawer. "Just got off the phone with our first client."

"And?" Serge raised his eyebrows expectantly. "Bet she was thrilled."

"Not thrilled."

"Really?" Serge looked baffled. "What's she say?"

"Hard to make out because I think her mouth was swollen." Mahoney swirled the drink in his glass. "Sounded like her ex banged her up pretty bad."

"Motherfuck—" Serge dashed out the door, and Coleman followed.

"Serge!" Mahoney called after him. "Where are you going?"

A Plymouth screeched out of the parking lot.

Ten minutes later, Serge mashed the elevator button in a motel lobby. Over and over. "Screw it!" He ran for the stairwell and bounded up to the fourth floor three steps at a time.

Knocking on a door. Serge pressed his eye to the peephole. "Come on, Sally, open up. I can hear you in there." More knocks.

"Serge," said Coleman. "I hear footsteps."

They backed up. The sound of someone fumbling with the chain and locks. The door opened. She already had her back to them, walking across the room with arms folded tight. Stopped next to a broken lamp.

"Sally." Serge moved forward. "What's going on?"

She stared out the window with no reply.

"Sally, please look at me."

Then her head began shaking with sobs.

Serge lightly touched her from behind on the arm. A big flinch, pulling away.

"Sally . . ."

She finally turned around.

Serge stepped back with a gasp and bit his fist.

"Serge!" She stepped forward. Her tear-streaked face went into his chest with a desperate hug. But not before he saw the busted lip and the old, faded black eyes that had recently been replaced by new ones.

"Shhhh," said Serge. "Now just tell me what happened."

It took a long moment, but she regained her composure and slowly looked up at him.

Serge gasped again. "What are those red marks around your neck?"

"It's where he kept strangling me."

"Kept?"

"The first time I thought I was dead for sure. But he just wanted me to pass out, because I came to and he did it again, four or five more times. Said he wanted to show he had total control and could kill me anytime he wanted, which he definitely would do if I contacted you or anyone else again. And if I ran, he'd never stop looking for me no matter how far or long. And when he found me, he'd heat up a fire poker and . . . and . . ."

Serge's eyes clenched shut at what she told him next. His hands covered his ears. "No, I can't hear any more!" He pulled her arms away.

"Serge! I need you!"

But he was out the door.

Coleman caught up to him in the parking lot. He climbed in the passenger side of the Road Runner. Serge stared forward in the driver's seat. Rapid, shallow breaths.

"I've seen that face before," said Coleman. "What are you going to do?"

"We gave him a chance to listen to reason." He threw the car in gear. "But now it's Home Depot . . . and the toy store."

# PART II

*The* **PARALLAX
ENIGMA JACKAL
MANCHURIAN
SANCTION**

# Chapter FOURTEEN

## SOUTH OF MIAMI

Building 25.

Afternoon briefing.

Oxnart looked out across school desks. "Mandrake?"

An agent opened a file. "Maintained surveillance from Biscayne to the cultural center. Here are some pictures of him exchanging briefcases in the Museum of Art."

"Standard spycraft." Oxnart nodded.

Mandrake handed another photo.

"What's this?"

"He has a shoe phone."

"Old school." The chief handed the photo back. "Who'd he make the briefcase drop with?"

Another photo. "The chubby guy he was with at the carjacking."

"Then things are looking up," said Oxnart. "He might not be working for Lugar after all."

The agent stared down at his desktop.

"What is it?" asked Oxnart.

"There was a second briefcase transfer. A dead drop in a trash can at the corner of Miami Avenue." A hesitation before Mandrake produced more photos of a black SUV. "Lugar's boys picked it up. We saw the drop while taking surveillance photos."

"And you didn't try to intercept?"

"Of course we did, but their SUV was closer and got there first. We almost crashed into each other." Mandrake reached in his file. "Here's a photo of them giving us the finger as they sped away."

"Son of a bitch!"

The door opened. A breathless agent.

"Sinclair, you're late!"

"Sorry, Chief, but I just got the workups on those mystery phone calls to our station."

"And?"

Sinclair unfolded a printout. "Traced to this sketchy office building on the river. Then there's that beeping message—our sound guys are still working on it. And a bunch of other calls made to consulates. Bolivia, Costa Gorda, Colombia, Canada—"

"The Canadians! Christ!" said Oxnart. "Who's behind it?"

The agent glanced back at his notes. "Office rented to a private investigator, former state police agent named Mahoney."

"Who's that?"

Sinclair held up another photo. "Someone with an office that Serge was seen leaving."

"Of course!" Oxnart smacked a fist into his hand. "Now it all fits together. The airport, the phone calls, Serge. And an ex-law enforcement agent is the typical profile for someone behind a front corporation."

"Or a dummy front," said Sinclair.

"And Lugar's definitely running it! As if his horning in on my arms shipments wasn't enough!" He took a deep breath and made a sweeping wave in the air. "Fuck it. Go visit this Mahoney. Whatever they're paying him, we'll pay more."

"For what?" said Mandrake.

"Make it a front-dummy-front. That'll put a burr in Lugar's ass . . . And, Mandrake?"

"Yes, sir."

"Get a team together and work up intel on Serge."

"In case we need to take him out?"

"No, hire him. We can't let Lugar keep somebody like that . . . Everyone, get moving!"

Meanwhile . . .

In a converted safe house in Coral Gables.

An emergency meeting.

"Dunbar," said Station Chief Lugar. "What have you got on this briefcase?"

"Tailed Serge from the art gallery and intercepted it after he made a dead drop in a trash can, probably for Oxnart."

"Why do you say that?"

"Their SUV was already waiting, but we got the jump and cut 'em off at the intersection," said Agent Dunbar. "Almost crashed into us."

"Hope you flipped them off," said Lugar.

"Just like you ordered." Dunbar set the briefcase on his desk and flipped the latches. "Simple three-digit combination lock, so only a thousand permutations. I started with all zeroes and, well, it didn't take long. Double-O-Seven." He pawed through contents. "Souvenirs, postcards, and matchbooks and bar coasters—I'm guessing locations of more drops and meets—a tip sheet of places to eat like the twenty-four-hour Cuban sandwich shop at the corner of First and Third, probably a document exchange. And an invisible message. I was able to raise the ink with a thermal decrypter."

"Thermal?"

"A candle."

"Let me see that." Lugar stared at a smiley face and some words:

"We're still trying to decipher that last part."

"You can stop," said Lugar. "It confirms he's working for Oxnart."

"How's that?"

"Dunbar," said Lugar. "You actually have no knowledge of the history of the agency you work for?"

The agent shrugged.

"In 1961, JM/WAVE was the secret code name for the anti-Castro operation run out of Florida." Lugar handed back the message. "Headquartered south of Miami near the zoo in something called Building Twenty-five, where Oxnart's station is now located."

"So Serge really is working for him?"

"No," Lugar said sarcastically. "He's just some nut running around playing spy."

"What do we do about it?" asked another agent.

"It's gotten too risky now to hire Serge away from Oxnart," said Lugar. "That might be exactly what Oxnart wants, to get Serge inside with us as a double agent. Or worse, Serge has done something rogue to embarrass the agency. Then it's a game of hot potato: Whoever hires him last gets the blame. Either way, Oxnart's setting a trap."

"But what if it's not a trap?"

"Then we definitely need to hire Serge." Lugar picked up a lamp and threw it. Agents ducked; it smashed against a wall. "So we run a special ops to learn the angles and decide whether it's in our best interest to recruit Serge."

"What kind of special ops."

"Find out where he's staying. Which means we first need to find out where he is right now."

"Where do you think that is?"

Lugar stared into space. "Probably somewhere on a mission."

"We're on a mission!" said Serge. "Wake up!"

An orange-and-green Road Runner sat in the dark, just beyond the yellow lights of the turnpike's toll plaza.

"Coleman, *Coleman, Coleman* . . . Wake up, *up, up* . . . We're on a mission, *mission, mission* . . ."

Coleman remained motionless in the passenger seat, eyes frozen open.

"Coleman!" Serge violently shook his pal's shoulders. "Shit, he's dead! I knew he'd end up overdosing!"

Tears began rolling down Serge's cheeks. His head sagged until it rested on the steering wheel. "Why! . . ."

In the passenger seat, eyes blinked.

Coleman turned slowly in a deep fog, staring curiously at Serge shaking with sobs: "Why! Why! Why!"—pounding the driver's-side door with a fist—"My best friend's dead!"

"Serge," Coleman said with a slur. "I thought I was your best friend."

Serge's face snapped to the right. "Coleman! You're alive!"

"More than ever." Coleman came out of it much faster than usual. "That was freakin' radical, man."

"You gave me five heart attacks—I could have sworn you were dead!" said Serge. "Don't ever do that again! I'd almost blame myself."

"You mean just because you scored the drug, talked me into it, then injected my arm?"

"I'd still feel bad."

"So what was that stuff?"

"You know how normally I'm against drugs, but that was special medicine for a higher purpose."

Coleman grinned and raised his eyebrows. "Can I do it again?"

"No!" Serge declared. "This shit's very expensive and hard to come by. We only have enough left for the mission."

Coleman pouted.

"I only gave you some to gauge the correct dosage." Serge folded a map. "So what's the verdict?"

"Worked exactly like you told me, down to the last detail," said Coleman. "I was awake but couldn't move. Heard and saw everything."

"Perfect, because I wouldn't want my new star pupil to miss the show." Serge looked at his wristwatch. "It's time." He grabbed the gearshift.

The Plymouth wound through a familiar neighborhood on the edge of the Everglades. It stopped in front of a dingy ranch house with empty beer cans framing the front steps. Another pyramid of cans in the living room window.

"Be extra quiet," said Serge. "Grab those bags from the backseat. And don't slam the doors."

They lugged sacks up the front steps. "Serge, this is a whole lot more stuff that usual. What are you planning?"

"Child's play."

Serge set his bags on the ground and got out a lock-pick set. A few jiggles with the pair of steel tools. Then a few more. "It's not working. Too rusty."

Coleman reached and turned the knob. "It's unlocked."

They crept through the living room.

*Crash.*

"Coleman!" Serge whispered. "Quiet or you'll wake him."

"It's too dark," said Coleman. He stepped on something else, making a loud crunching noise. "There's stuff all over the floor. This guy lives like a pig."

Serge clicked on a flashlight. The beam swept an empty wall, then sports and swimsuit posters held up with tape. On the floor, more cans, pizza boxes. A coffee table made from produce crates supported a brimming ceramic novelty ashtray with a hardware ad and breasts.

"Leave the bags here. I'll only need my small one right now." He swung the flashlight. "There's the bedroom."

Serge turned the knob; hinges creaked. The beam hit a bearded face angled back over a pillow, mouth open, snoring like a car that wouldn't start.

"Excellent. Still asleep." Serge handed Coleman the flashlight. "Keep this on me. I need to see what I'm doing."

Serge reached in the small sack and arranged supplies out on the night stand. A small bottle with hospital markings and milky liquid. Diprivan. The tip of a syringe went through the port in the lid. Serge drew back the plunger, carefully monitoring calibration marks.

"Why are you taking so long?" asked Coleman.

"Because you're drifting with the flashlight."

"Sorry." Coleman re-aimed.

Serge was kneeling now, eyes close to the measuring stripes. "Have to make sure we get the same dosage I gave you. But he weighs more, so I'm recalculating in my head."

"Is that really the same stuff the doctor gave Michael Jackson?"

"One and only." Serge slowly extracted the needle from the bottle. "When I saw those news reports, I said to myself, 'I know what I can use that for' . . ." He stood next to the bed, clutched the syringe in both hands, and raised it high over his head. "I also just saw *Pulp Fiction* again. I love that scene where they inject Uma Thurman in the heart!"

"Jesus, Serge. You're going to stab him in the heart?"

"What? Not a good idea?"

"You're the doctor."

"Maybe you have a point. If I don't get it just right, he'll die immediately. And he's just the kind of jerk who would do something mean like that to us." Serge slid a half step toward the foot of the bed and raised the needle again. "One . . ."

"One," said Coleman.

"Two . . ." The needle went higher.

"Two," said Coleman.

"Three . . ."

"Three!"

Serge's fists came down fast and hard. He jumped back.

"Yowwwwwwwwwww!" A bearded face flew up from the pillow. "Motherfucker!"

Coleman crashed back into a wall.

Jethro Comstock stared down in bewilderment at a syringe buried to the hilt in the middle of his stomach. Then up at Coleman with the flashlight. "You're so fucking dead!" He flung the needle from his gut and reached under the pillow.

"Serge!" yelled Coleman. "He's got a big knife."

The man leaped from the bed. He pinned Coleman to the wall with a burly forearm across the chest, and put the blade to his throat, ready to slash.

Coleman closed his eyes.

He heard a knife bounce on the tile floor. The arm across his chest was gone.

Coleman slowly peeked out one eye, then the other.

Serge ran around the bed. "Right on time. Give me a hand."

They dragged Jethro into the living room and propped him up on a chair. Then began dumping out the contents of the Home Depot bags.

"What?" said Coleman. "No rope and duct tape?"

Serge held up the hospital bottle and syringe. "Because this is the rope and tape." Serge dipped the needle again, but only a fraction of the original dosage.

"So you're just going to keep him knocked out?"

"Not quite." Serge opened a box and removed a small electric fan. "It's a phenomenon well known in the medical community, but one which has only recently come to the attention of the ailing public."

Coleman repaired the joint he'd dropped in the bedroom fracas. "What's that?"

"What I replicated back in the car with my test run on you." Serge grabbed a second fan and a screwdriver. "Anesthesia Awareness."

"Thought it was just mellow trippin'."

Serge shook his head. "Some patients are put under for surgery. They appear to be totally out, but for unknown reasons, they're only paralyzed. They can still see, hear, and, most importantly, feel everything going on. But they're helpless to speak and communicate any discomfort."

"That would make getting your legs cut off really suck."

Serge snapped his fingers in front of Jethro's face. "Hello in there. I know you can hear, and you must have oodles of questions, but unfortunately you can't ask them, so I'll just go straight to Serge's FAQ . . .

First, we dropped in for another visit because I just spoke with Sally, and you apparently didn't respond to the courtesy of the red beacon." He leaned over and gave Jethro another injection in his left arm, then held the bottle to his eyes. "I usually tie up my contestants, but this stuff I'm pumping into you is—you guessed it!—the bonus round. It has a relatively quick half-life. Whenever I'm teaching a lesson, I always like to give my students a way out. After the lesson begins, there's a good chance you'll come out of the drug in time and be able to escape—if you're in decent physical condition, which doesn't apply to you. Sorry, the FAQ was written for the general population. Next question: When will the lesson begin? Believe me, you'll know. Now, if you'll excuse us . . ."

Serge went to work on the fans, four total. He left two intact, but unscrewed the heads off the others, so there was just the base and the bare rotating post that otherwise would swing fans in an oscillating rhythm back and forth across a room.

"Coleman, we need every chair we can find . . ."

A half hour later, everything in place. A configuration of furniture faced the captive at a range of twenty feet. The working fans sat atop the taller chairs. In front of those were the headless ones. They had been lashed sideways with duct tape to other chairs so that if they hadn't been decapitated, the fans would swing up and down. In front of those, a pair of stools held baking pans.

"There." Serge grabbed a gallon jug. "Just about ready . . ." He looked across the room. An empty chair. "Coleman! Where's our guest?"

"I think he went in the kitchen."

Serge raced around the corner and came back, gently guiding Jethro, who shuffled his feet and babbled blissfully like a toddler testing out new legs and sounds.

Serge eased him back down into the chair. "Here ya go, big fella. Now stay put this time." Another injection.

"Coleman, I need your help. And bring the lighter."

They pulled out another pair of chairs, setting one on each side of Jethro, and slid a coffee table up to his knees. Then Serge covered their surfaces with twenty large candles.

Coleman began lighting them. A warm, flickering glow filled the room. He held the lighter toward another candle with the Virgin Mary on its frosted glass holder, then crouched and stared eye level as he lit the rest. "Serge, there's all these saints and holy shit. What kind of candles are these?"

"Santería."

"I didn't know you were into that."

"I'm not." Serge grabbed the gallon jug and walked to the baking trays. "But if I turn up on spy radar, I'm covering my trail by letting them think we're connected to the Haitians."

"The Haitians are involved in this?"

"And now the moment I've been waiting for." Serge reached in the toy-store bag and removed a box from the Wham-O corporation.

"I remember those things," said Coleman.

"So do I." Serge ripped cardboard. "Wanted to use these when we were living that summer on Triggerfish Lane, but never got the chance."

"I didn't know they even made those anymore."

"Great ideas never die."

"But how's that going to kill him?"

"*Teach* him," corrected Serge. "And the perfect visual aid is the famous giant bubble wand . . ."

## Chapter FIFTEEN

### WASHINGTON, D.C.

The Capitol.

Two Marine guards stood rigid in the hall.

A marathon closed-door meeting of the intelligence subcommittee burned into the wee hours. Only those with the highest clearance.

Two people sat at the witness table.

Malcolm Glide leaned toward the microphone. "Unfortunately the Costa Gordan rebels have proven more resilient than we anticipated—"

"Excuse me," interrupted Senator Bancroft (D-Iowa). "I thought President Guzman assured us the rebel problem was under control."

"I'm afraid Guzman is believing what he wants to. Who can blame him? Guzman's an indispensable ally in a critical region of our hemisphere that could easily topple like dominoes if he tanks. We're receiving daily reports of assassination plots being hatched by the insurgents. If only the committee can approve additional funding so the generals can beat back the Communist tide before it reaches American shores."

The senator sat back. "I don't think we need to worry about Communists right now. Our apparatus is stretched thin as it is with the terrorists."

"Oh!" Glide nodded buoyantly. "We have terrorists, too." He turned toward the person next to him at the witness table. "Rip?"

Director Tide of Homeland Security stood and unfurled a large vinyl thermometer. He pointed at the top, where an extra length of vinyl had been taped on for another color square.

The senator took off the reading glasses sitting on the end of his nose. "What am I looking at?"

"The threat level has just been raised again," said Glide.

"It's just red," said Bancroft. "Like we used to have."

Glide shook his head. "It's a darker red."

"I thought we were already at darker red."

"That was last time," said Glide. "This is even darker. Boo!"

"This is ridiculous is what it is—a political ploy to exploit people's fears," said Bancroft. "I find it very interesting that the raising of the threat level conveniently coincides with your political interests, like distracting from oil spills or increased covert funding."

"Senator!" Glide said with feigned astonishment, placing a hand over his heart. "A little reverence, please. It's the national thermometer." Director Tide held it up again.

The committee broke out into partisan bickering.

A gavel banged. "Order! Order!" barked the chairman. "The gentleman from Iowa has one minute remaining."

"Thank you," said Bancroft, turning to the witness table. "I'm afraid I'll need more proof than you're offering..."

Malcolm pulled the microphone to his mouth. "Communists."

"... But I've seen the satellite photos," continued the senator. "And the foreign intelligence services—British, French, Brazilian—they all report the same thing. No rebel movement of any significance."

Malcolm slid the microphone closer. "The rebels are . . . in exile."

"Isn't that good?" asked the senator.

Malcolm shook his head. "Exile is scary. It has an *X*."

"I've heard enough," said the chairman. "Time to vote..."

The tally predictably fell along party lines. No more funding. The room stood. Politicians yawned and checked the time.

The director of homeland security covered his microphone and whispered sideways to Glide. "What about all those agents we have secretly in the mountains posing as rebels? The committee just cut off their money."

"I know."

"Then how are we going to get them home?"

"We can't."

"But that's a major scandal."

"That's why I need you to hold another press conference."


## THREE A.M.

A tiny, glistening bead of liquid appeared at the end of a hypodermic needle.

A finger flicked the syringe.

The front door opened.

"Found him flopping around in the bushes," said Coleman. He led the staggering, drooling hostage back to the chair and sat him down. "Serge, he broke two of the holy candles."

"I've got spares." Serge held up the syringe. "One more injection should do it."

He located a vein and hit the plunger.

"There." Serge tossed the needle at the wall like a dart and rubbed his palms together. "Time to play! And I've always wanted to play with those things since I was a kid!"

"The giant bubble wand?" said Coleman. "Those are a gas! The stoners and me would always buy one before we tripped." He moved his hands slowly through the air. "That huge blob pulsing and floating across the field, and one of the heads said it was his soul, and another dude said he was the devil and popped it, and we couldn't get the first guy to stop crying. Then we pulled out the other giant wand—the one with a hundred holes—and the field was covered with all these tiny bubbles, and the crying guy ran after them, biting the air. He's now a stockbroker. Serge, do you also have the other wand with the hundred tiny holes?"

"Right here," said Serge, pouring soap water into the baking pans. "That's why I got two sets of fans."

He turned them on.

Air currents. Curtains flowed. Candles flickered down inside their glass holders.

The fans' oscillating switches had been turned off, so they remained stationary, blowing straight ahead.

Then Serge activated the headless fans attached to the other chairs. Their oscillating switches stayed on. Duct-taped to the rotating necks were the Wham-O bubble wands. And since the bases of the latter fans had been secured perpendicular to the floor, their slowly rotating necks dipped the bubble wands down into the baking pans. Then lifted them up ninety degrees, where the regular fans blew out bubbles: a humongous, single blob on the left; hundreds of tiny ones on the right.

"Trippy," said Coleman. "Especially in the candlelight."

"Candles are the key," said Serge.

The wands dipped down again. More soap bubbles. They began popping on Jethro's chest and arms.

"So what's the deal?" asked Coleman. "We make him damp and sudsy?"

"No," said Serge. "This is just the trial round. And put that joint out!"

"But, Serge."

"No *buts*. You want to end up like him?"

"How can that happen?"

"Because the real lesson is about to begin." Serge clicked off the fans and dumped out the soap-water trays. Then he refilled them from a gallon jug. A familiar smell filled the air.

"I get it now," said Coleman. "When did you think it up?"

"You know how those big soap bubbles have a swirling, rainbow sheen on the surface?" asked Serge. "Got to thinking, where else have I seen that chromatic effect? Then it hit me. Time to go shopping!"

He approached Jethro. "I know you can hear me, but I need to make this quick because the summit's in town. You don't want to miss the summit! So here's the deal. Keep trying to move and maybe you can get away before my contraptions take effect. Or maybe not. Who knows? I just spitballed the calculations. But if you do get away, no more funny stuff with Sally or I'll come back and crunch the numbers with a computer. Any objections? Good . . . Oh, and one last kicker from the archives: Don't you love those great History Channel shows about B-17 Flying Fortresses making bombing runs over German ball-bearing factories? But you ask: How is that relevant? . . . Showtime!"

Serge walked back and switched on the fans.

The wands dipped into their pans.

They raised up. New, rainbow-hued bubbles floated toward Jethro.

The room grew slightly brighter in a series of tiny flashes. Then a big one.

"Cool," said Coleman. "Gasoline bubbles."

"Remember, the key is the candles," said Serge. "They don't have to actually touch the bubbles because the fumes are what ignite."

"Fumes?" said Coleman. "Are *we* in danger?"

"Of course not," said Serge. "Proper handling of flammable liquids requires plenty of ventilation. And I've got two fans. It's amazing how many people conduct unsafe lifestyles."

"The bubbles are exploding a foot or more away from him," said Coleman. "Isn't that too far?"

"Like when the Germans fired anti-aircraft guns, and the sky flashed nonstop with exploding flak during the B-17 raids," said Serge. "Throw up enough and some are bound to hit."

The living room: *flash, flash, flash* . . .

"Some hit," said Coleman. "But the bubbles are too small."

"I still wouldn't like it."

"Oooooo!" said Coleman. "A big one just singed him good."

"They're getting closer to the target."

"Some of the bubbles aren't going off. They're just hitting Jethro and making his shirt wet. Others are popping on the wall behind him."

"Not a good sign," said Serge. "They could be ignited by later bubbles."

"Cool! I gotta see that!"

"You won't."

"Why not?"

"Because we're leaving."

"Again? You never let me watch!"

"Coleman, this could get unpleasant. I'd rather watch bunnies and chickadees."

*Flash, flash, flash . . .*

"But, Serge!"

Too late. He was already out the door and running to the car.

Coleman lit a joint in the passenger seat and grumbled. Serge drove a short distance and parked at the end of the street before the turnpike entrance.

Coleman flicked an ash out the window. "Why are we stopping?"

"Plan our next spy moves." Serge opened a map. "The seasoned spy brings all of Miami into play . . ."

Behind them, the sky grew brighter.

"Why all of Miami?" asked Coleman.

"To provide the cover of confusion." Serge pointed at spots on the map. "This city's like Europe—all these utterly distinct cultural districts with severe borders."

Neighbors began walking out on lawns, pointing and dialing cell phones.

Coleman tapped another ash. A fire engine raced by. "But how do the different sections of Miami give us cover?"

"Throw off the enemy," said Serge. "The more places you conduct your ops, the more factions they think are involved."

Coleman leaned toward the map. "Like where? . . ."

The sky raged with light in the rearview. Sprays of high-pressure water. Another siren as an ambulance flew by. Onlookers yelling.

"Well," said Serge, counting on his fingers. "You got Little Havana, Little Haiti, Liberty City, South Beach . . ."

Three police cars zoomed past with all the lights going.

". . . Coconut Grove, downtown, Brickell, and the MiMo architecture district, to name but a few."

"What's that racket?" Coleman turned around and looked out the back window. "There's all kinds of cops and emergency vehicles. Everyone's standing on their lawns."

"This is kind of a rough neighborhood." Serge threw the car in gear. "We probably should get going before something bad happens."

# *Chapter* **SIXTEEN**

## COSTA GORDA

Another moonless night in the mountains.

"I'm hungry," said one of the rebels.

"I told you, we have to ration staples until they make another supply drop," said the squad leader. "Two spoons of Spam a day."

"Henry," whispered Ralph. "When *is* that next drop?"

"Don't know. Can't reach them on the high-band."

"We were only able to salvage two boxes from the last drop. The rest landed on the others still burning from the napalm."

"What do you want me to do about it?"

Ralph looked back at a waning campfire and audible groans. "The men are starving. Some are getting sick from eating the berries . . ."

On the other side of the encampment, more whispering among the lower ranks:

"I can't take this anymore."

"I'm so weak I can barely stand up."

"Guys!" Someone ran over with a small shortwave. "Just picked up the BBC. The intelligence subcommittee canceled our funding."

"But they wouldn't just leave us here . . . right?"

"What do you think? This is an illegal operation. We're expendable."

Eyes darted round the circle. Panic. "They've abandoned us!"

"What are we going to do?"

"I know this village at the edge of the next province. They must have food."

"How far?"

"About ten clicks past the river."

"What are we waiting for?"

Back on the command side: "Ralph, what are those guys doing?"

Ralph turned around. "Hey, where the hell do you think you're going?"

"We're hungry."

## DOWNTOWN MIAMI

This time, a shark was dropped in front of a Cuban deli with plastic Italian tablecloths. The chalk menu sat under a painting of a rooster.

A light afternoon crowd. In the back of the deli, at the very last red-and-white-checkered table, sat a young man from a mail room on the seventh floor of an office building across the street. His face was in his hands. Pork sandwich untouched.

"They're going to send me home!" said Scooter Escobar. "I just know it!"

"They're not sending you anywhere," said the woman seated across from him, picking through her avocado salad. "You've got the safest job in the whole consulate."

"But you've met this Serge character."

She sipped a glass of sangria. "Yes."

"Then you know what I mean."

"I know you're paranoid."

"But the president likes him." His head jerked back and forth looking for phantoms. "Why didn't they ask *me* to run backup security from the airport? I'm the spy in the office."

She set her fork down. "Listen, Scooter, your uncle's the general. You worry too much."

"That's easy for you to say." He leaned over the table and sniffed. "You have job security."

She did.

Felicia Carmen. All curves and hips and luscious red lips. A beauty mark. Long, curling jet-black hair, designed to make any man swallow his tongue and spit out deepest secrets, which was her job. The local honey trap in the Costa Gordan consulate.

The consulate was the ultimate brass ring.

Everyone wanted the Miami gig. It was a sexy city with easy lifting and all the perks. The rest of the local staff wrangled their assignments through politics. Felicia earned hers. Top performance reviews during stints in St. Kitts, St. Lucia, Montserrat, and Trinidad. On the short list for Miami.

Then Scooter jumped to the head of the line.

It wasn't fair.

Openings were few and far.

Then it accidentally became fair. Because . . .

Scooter arrived in Miami.

Word went back to the capital in Costa Gorda. "We've got a problem."

They added another opening.

Scooter required a full-time job, just to chaperone Scooter.

So Felicia arrived in town.

And for the first time, the tiny Costa Gordan consulate had a backup spy. And a spy's first priority is job security. She began spying on her consulate's head attaché.

"I'm telling you," said Felicia. "If they were sending anyone home, he would have mentioned something in bed."

Scooter sniffled back tears. "Did you use the vibrator?"

Felicia lit a thin cigar. "When that thing's in him, he tells me a bunch of secrets I don't even give a shit about."

"Was it on the high setting?"

"What's with always asking about the high setting?" She reached for an ashtray. "You're just trying to get a mental image of me."

Scooter grinned sheepishly. He glanced around again and dumped a tiny pile of white powder on the edge of the table.

"Wonderful," said Felicia. "That's going to help."

Scooter raised his face from the table and rubbed his nose. "I need it to calm down."

She shook her head and blew smoke rings toward a ceiling fan.

Escobar did another toot, then pulled an envelope from his pocket. He unfolded a single sheet of paper and handed it to Felicia.

"What's this?"

"The note Serge left for me at the consulate's reception desk." He tapped out more powder. "Remember? The first day he made contact, when our guys threw him out on the sidewalk. He said to give that note to the spy in the office." Scooter raised his head up and pinched nostrils. "But it's blank. I haven't been able to figure out what it means."

Felicia flicked her lighter and ran the flame back and forth under the paper. Tan lines slowly appeared on the page until they were solid brown.

"What are you doing?" asked Escobar.

"He wrote it in lemon juice. A child's trick."

"What's it say?"

She turned the page toward him. A smiley face over words:

HAVE A NICE DAY.

Escobar slid his chair back on saltillo tiles. "He's taunting me! He really is after my job!"

"That's the coke talking." Felicia crumpled the page and tossed it in her salad bowl. "You need to stop doing that shit."

Didn't listen. "I'm so screwed."

"Yes, you're a fuckup," said Felicia. "But your uncle always gets you out of everything."

"Not this time," said Scooter. "He's really pissed about those arm shipments."

"You started mentioning that before," said Felicia. "What shipments?"

"I did? I mean, I must have been thinking about the geology report."

"Geology report?"

"Did I say 'geology report'?"

"I'll let you see the vibrator."

Scooter brightened. "Really?"

"Sure." She passed him her purse. "And do some more coke . . ."

## MIAMI RIVER DISTRICT

A bottle of rye sat idle in a second-floor office.

Mahoney played solitaire.

The TV was on.

*"Stand by for a CNN special report."*

An anchorwoman appeared. *"Breaking news at this hour, which was captured in this exclusive footage from a cell phone by a local resident . . ."*

The picture switched to a shaky camera view of filthy, wild-eyed men in face paint and camouflaged military uniforms running through a peasant village, screaming and firing guns in the air.

*"Give us your food! We need food!"*

The anchorwoman provided voice-over: *"As you can see in these disturbing images, the rebel movement in Costa Gorda has launched a brazen offensive against the civilian population."*

Two of the men began chasing a goat.

*"Next, you will clearly hear the rebels shouting slogans in denunciation of the regime of President Fernando Guzman and promoting Marxist food redistribution."*

*". . . Our government betrayed us! . . ."*

*". . . We're rationing Spam! . . ."*

The anchorwoman filled the screen again. *"We'll bring you more as it becomes available . . . And to our independent i-Reporter in the village with the cell phone, a coffee mug is on the way . . ."*

The door opened.

Serge and Coleman came in and grabbed chairs. Mahoney looked up from the seven of hearts.

Serge pointed. "Nice bouquet."

A vase with a dozen roses sat on the corner of Mahoney's desk. Ribbons and a balloon: THANK YOU.

Serge read the gift card and slipped it back in the envelope. "Looks like your first client was a satisfied customer."

Mahoney stared.

"What?"

"They found her ex-husband's body." He turned off the TV. "Ruled arson. Some kind of elaborate contraption with fans, gasoline, and bubble wands."

"Not again."

Continued staring.

"What?" asked Serge.

"Something else," said Mahoney. "These two mugs came poking around this morning."

"Arson investigators?" asked Serge.

Mahoney shook his head.

Across the hall: *"I can't believe you punched me!"* A door slammed, running feet.

Serge glanced over his shoulder, then back at Mahoney. "So about these two guys?"

Mahoney reached in a drawer and tossed a thick brown envelope on the desk.

Serge peeked inside and whistled. "That's a lot of money. What's it for?"

"Said they wanted to hire me to be a dummy front company."

"What did you say?"

"That I already was one." Mahoney reached in the drawer and threw another fat envelope on the desk. "So they gave me that, too."

"Told you," said Serge. "What a city!"

A roar outside.

Serge glanced south. "That plane sounds awfully low."

They all ran to the window. "It *is* low," said Coleman. "It's going to crash!"

"Stan's got it," said Mahoney.

"You know Stan?" asked Serge.

"Who's Stan?" asked Coleman.

A twin-engine Grumman Mallard seaplane made an expert belly landing in the Miami River. Its amphibious wheels deployed, the aircraft rolled up a boat ramp, then taxied a short distance to the parking lot of Mahoney's building.

The pilot climbed down from the cockpit and trotted into the building. Soon, another set of footsteps down the hall. The door opened.

"Guys, could I get a hand with the tarps?"

Everyone went downstairs and surrounded the plane.

Stan threw a pair of thick lines over the cowling. Serge caught them and unrolled the tarp. He stuck a finger through a hole near the propeller. "Were they shooting at you?"

"They usually do." Stan threw more lines over the tail section. "Go-boat dropped me a thousand yards off a private island. Only took two rounds near the gas tank from private security while getting airborne. That's a piece of cake next to getting a twin-engine off a grass mountain runway by a cocoa-leaf farm. Or cracking the jewelry safe in a Coconut Grove master bedroom."

Coleman grabbed one of the lines. "So, Serge, what's this guy's deal?"

"He's the guy I mentioned before." Serge tugged hard on his own line. "Stan the High-End Repo Man."

"He repossesses airplanes?"

"And yachts and race cars."

"I didn't know repo men did that."

"Most don't." Serge tied a knot. "But it's this economy. Even the rich are missing payments."

"Former CIA," added Mahoney. "Now fronting 'Premier Acquisitions.' Got an office down the hall from me."

A commotion erupted at the corner intersection. Yelling.

Coleman lit a joint. "What's going on over there?"

Serge glanced. "Those are the Aggressive Beggars."

"Aggressive Beggars?" Coleman took a big hit and held the smoke.

"Miami phenomenon. Young, physically fit, capable of any work," said Serge. "But instead they wash people's windshields against their will."

*"Don't be a dick!"* yelled a man with a squeegee and cardboard sign. *"Give me some fucking money!"*

The light turned green. The beggar kicked a rear fender as the car took off.

"Serge?" Stan walked over with a set of keys attached to a small flotation device. "I'm slammed today. Going to pick up a Bentley, then two more planes. You game for freelance work?"

"I can't fly planes."

"Not a plane." Stan tossed him the keys. "Offshore racing boat, twin V-hulls, three Merc engines. Think you can handle it?"

"With my eyes closed."

"I'm guessing you'll be wanting to take her for a spin."

"But that would be unprofessional."

"It's okay." Stan secured the end of the tarp. "Just have her to Dinner Key by sundown."

*"Ow! Son of a bitch!"*

Everyone turned toward the intersection. A young man dropped a squeegee and grabbed his bleeding nose.

Steve Dodd walked back from the street, shaking his right hand to get out the sting.

Stan handed Serge a briefcase. "Know your way around a TEC-9?"

Serge flipped the latches and pulled out the compact machine gun. "I may have picked one of these up from time to time."

"Then I'll see you tonight. Now I've gotta make a delivery." Stan hopped in a Silver Cloud and sped away.

Coleman looked back and forth at the airplane, departing Rolls-Royce, windshield washers, Steve Dodd's fist, Serge's new machine gun. Three Nicaraguans came around the corner, tossed a shark in the intersection, and ran off. Coleman took another big hit. "Miami's far out."

"Mahoney," said Serge. "I may need a favor. But it will probably never come up."

"Oh, it'll come up," said Mahoney. "Mumble."

"It's my Secret Master Plan," said Serge. "And in my new line of work, the Master Plan needs a Backup Plan. That's where you come in . . ." And he laid it all out.

Mahoney tossed a toothpick. "That's the dizziest scheme I ever heard."

"But if I call you, you're in, right?"

"Aces." Mahoney began walking back to the building. "But I have one question. Those two jakes who paid for that dummy front business. Anything hinky involved?"

"Not yet."

"What's that mean?"

Serge just grinned.

# Chapter **SEVENTEEN**

## SOUTH OF MIAMI

Another TV was on.

"... *This is CNN reporting from Costa Gorda, where a crack American Delta Force has just been deployed to help President Guzman quash the rebel uprising...*"

The picture switched to a small band of rebels surrounded in the middle of the village. The Delta team's translator stepped forward.

*"Put down the goat and surrender."*

A tense pause.

*"We don't speak Spanish. Where are you from?"*

*"United States,"* said the Delta force commander. *"And you?"*

*"New Jersey. Do you have any food?"*

Back to the anchorman, holding a hand against the tiny speaker in his ear. *"Wait a minute. We have breaking news. We're going live to Washington, D.C...."*

The image switched to the press room at the Office of Homeland

Security. An empty podium flanked by flags and a vinyl thermometer.

Director Tide arrived from the wings and shuffled notes on the podium.

"Good afternoon. I've called you here to announce new airport security measures. In addition to shoes, all passengers must now take their socks off."

A hand went up. "What for?"

"I can't reveal that," said Tide. "But what I can disclose is that we're raising the threat level again. We're announcing a new color."

The journalists waited in silent anticipation as the director reached in his pocket and slapped a new plastic square at the top of the thermometer. He turned back around.

All hands went up in the audience.

Tide pointed at the front row. "Chuck?"

The reporter lowered his hand. "That's not a color. It's just a question mark."

"Correct," said the director. "It's the secret color."

The same hand went up again. "Why does it have to be secret?"

"Otherwise the terrorists win."


A hand went up. It reached a television knob and turned off the news.

Station Chief Oxnart faced the room.

"What have we got? Newcastle?"

"Couldn't find Serge. Lost him near Sweetwater."

"And you're still drawing a paycheck?" said Oxnart.

The agent nervously reviewed notes. "But we were able to outbid Lugar for the dummy front company on the river."

"At least that's something," said the chief. "Any day I can beat that asshole."

"Got something else," said Newcastle. "Might be Serge's handiwork. Arson murder in Sweetwater shortly after we lost the tail."

"Method?"

"From the police report, some kind of elaborate accelerant trigger."

Oxnart nodded to himself. "I'd expect nothing less."

"I don't know," said Newcastle. "It just doesn't fit."

"What doesn't fit?"

"The victim." He checked his notes again. "One Jethro Comstock, unemployed pipe fitter."

"Unemployed, my ass," said the chief. "He had to be connected. They don't send in an expert like Serge just for some lowlife." Oxnart narrowed his eyebrows. "Something's going down in Miami, and Serge is in the middle of it. I want to know what it is! . . . Can't anybody find out where he's staying?"

A phone rang. "Oxnart here."

It was the guard station.

"Send him through." Oxnart hung up. "Everyone look sharp."

A stretch limo parked in front of Building 25.

Station Chief Gil Oxnart was already waiting in the open front door. "Malcolm Glide, you crazy son of a gun! To what do I owe the pleasure?"

Glide bounded up the porch steps and shook hands, but his expression was dramatic.

"Something the matter?" asked Oxnart.

"Damn budget cuts."

Oxnart nodded solemnly. "Heard about that. Congress don't have a clue what's happening on the ground."

"I need your help."

"Name it," said the chief.

"Assassination plot. Big one."

Oxnart's head jerked back. He'd been waiting his whole life. "Who's the target?"

"President Guzman."

"Guzman? From Costa Gorda?" Oxnart snapped to attention. "You can count on me to stop it. Who's behind the plot?"

"We are," said Glide.

"What? But Guzman's our ally."

Glide shook his head. "Not a real assassination. Just a plot."

"I don't understand."

"Things are starting to move pretty fast with the summit. Something big is about to go down in Miami, and we haven't been able to put it together yet." Malcolm placed a hand on Oxnart's shoulder. "We need the assassination plot as a diversion. Disinformation to confuse the enemy until we can figure out what's going on."

"Any idea what it is?"

"Something to do with Costa Gorda." Malcolm squeezed Oxnart's shoulder. "Looks like the regime has become unstable. Between the rebels and the rumors of arms shipments."

"But we're helping ship the arms," said Oxnart.

"So the rumors are true."

"You're the one who told us to," said Oxnart.

"Then that's a double confirmation." Glide squeezed the shoulder harder. "You're a good man, Oxnart. I know everyone else is grooming Lugar, but you can go places."

"Thank you, sir."

"So I want to hear lots of chatter about this assassination."

"You got it."

"I knew I could count on you." Glide began walking toward the door. He stopped and turned. "Oh, and one more thing."

"What is it?"

"Have you picked up any intelligence about a new operative in town?" Glide played his cards close to his chest. "Probably a code name. Sounded like, um, Serge?"

Oxnart concealed a hard swallow. "Uh, no. Why? Should I?"

Glide shrugged. "Probably nothing." He continued out the door. "You know where to reach me, so don't call."

## DOWNTOWN MIAMI

Serge strolled confidently into the Royal Poinciana Hotel.

He leaned with an enthusiastic grin toward the desk manager behind bulletproof glass. "Hey, it's me. Remember? The guy you hooked up to do extreme shopping for those bodegas in the islands. Has my paycheck arrived yet? I'll bet they paid me a huge bonus for my exquisite taste."

The desk manager stared with an open mouth.

"What's the matter? You all right?"

"What did you do with the shopping list I gave you?"

"Threw it away, of course."

"You were supposed to use the list."

"That's what everyone thinks. So when they zig, I zag. Sometimes hop on one foot. Because you never know, right?"

"You sent them three hundred pounds of Florida souvenirs."

Serge smiled his widest. "Handpicked."

"They're not going to pay you."

"Come again?"

"I couldn't get him to stop screaming on the phone."

"Screaming?" Serge stepped back. "That must have been from joy. Probably sold the shit out of those palm-tree snow globes and seashell crucifixes."

"No, they didn't sell at all. Everything's being shipped back for a refund. And you pay the return freight."

"That can't be right," said Serge. "Maybe you had a bad connection. I'll make a few calls and straighten this out. Come on, Coleman . . ."

A half hour later.

Room 321.

Fierce sunlight streamed over the rattling air-conditioner.

A just-showered Serge came out of the bathroom squeaky-clean. Because he had showered twice "to get an edge on the others." He rubbed his hair with a towel. "Coleman?"

No reply.

He looked down at a pair of legs on the floor. One sock, one bare foot. He kicked the foot. "Wake up!"

Coleman startled. "Ow! Shit! My head!"

"Stop fooling around. We have a full schedule of spying."

"Serge, help me! I'm entombed!"

"You're under the bed."

Coleman wiggled his way out. "Beds often end up on top of me."

"Just hurry." Serge grabbed a stack of pages. "I've already had a busy morning waiting for you to come around."

Coleman fired up a joint and mixed vodka with tap water. "Doing what?"

"Kind of got carried away making more invisible messages. So I need to slip the extras under all the doors on this floor."

"What for?"

"The Miami experience! Some of the hotel guests are new in town. Why should we have all the fun?"

Coleman finished his drink and stuck a beer in each pocket of his shorts. "Ready."

"You're wearing what you slept in?"

"It's already on." He stubbed out his joint. "After you finish with the invisible notes, can we go to a bar?"

"Maybe later." Serge grabbed the door handle. "First we need to do some surveillance."

"On who?"

"Whoever we feel like." He stepped into the hall and locked up.

"What do you mean?"

"Once again, the majority of people lack imagination and miss out." Serge crouched down and slid a page under a door. "But at any time, you can simply decide to pick some stranger in a crowd and say, 'It would be a riot to follow that guy as long as I can and see what develops.'"

"You've done it before?"

"Many times. My record is four hours through several counties until the guy came unglued."

"Why'd he do that?"

"Near the end, I got sloppy and he spotted me." Serge crouched again and slid another page. "He sped up in his car, and I had to weave through lanes at high speed. Then I only *briefly* drove on the sidewalk, but I guess that made him uncomfortable. The surveillance turned into a chase."

"You chased him in traffic?"

"Not for long. He had no spy training and wrecked his car at the first light pole. So it was mainly a foot chase. And we're running through yards, jumping fences and ducking under clotheslines, and he keeps looking back and yelling, 'Who are you?' and I say, 'Just keep doing what you're doing. I'm going for a personal record.' But he ran in a police station instead."

Coleman crumpled a beer can. "Sounds like you could have gotten in a lot of trouble."

"There's no law against marathon following," said Serge. "Just as long as you respect others' privacy."

"Who do you want to follow today?"

"I like to pick the one person in public who's acting the most suspicious and paranoid." Serge bent down and slipped another page. "In any big city crowd, there's always someone like that. Then I help them."

"How?"

"By confirming their fears." Serge crouched and tucked a page under the door of room 318. "But who will that person be today? . . ."

On the other side of the door to room 318:

Agent-in-exile Ted Savage heard footsteps in the hall. He groaned and looked over the side of the bed. A sheet of white paper on the floor.

"What's this?"

He flipped it over. Blank on both sides. He knew the drill.

Ted ran a cigarette lighter under the page. Brown lines began to appear. He stared perplexed at a happy face as he continued with the lighter, revealing words at the bottom.

The lighter bounced on the floor. The page fluttered down as Savage stumbled backward onto the bed.

" 'JM/WAVE'! Jesus, they know I'm here! They're sending a message from Building Twenty-five!" He ran to the window, looking for parked vans concealing the capture unit.

Nothing in sight.

Ted ran for the dresser. Jack Daniel's empty. Back to the window. "Get a grip. You need to calm your nerves and focus. There has to be a bar down there." He scanned the street. "Remember your training! Think! What's the first move?" He looked back at the narrow slit under the door where the message had been delivered. "Abandon compromised location."

Ted snatched the note off the floor and dashed out of the room.

Two people stepped into the elevator. Serge grabbed the edge of the accordion metal cage and began closing it.

Pounding footsteps.

Serge reopened the cage and smiled. "Room for one more!"

Ted jumped inside, hyperventilating.

"Good afternoon!" Serge chugged from a thermos. "Don't you hate it when rude people won't hold an elevator when someone else is almost there, and instead slide to the corner so you can't see them and hit the 'Door Close' button? Steams me something terrible. Seen it a hundred times, but do I stand by idly during this cultural defilement? No! I'll already be in the elevator when it happens, the door closing on some family with kids. And the asshole who just hit the 'Door Close' button is heading for the fifteenth floor, and even if I'm going to the *sixteenth,* I'll hit the button to get off on two, but just before leaving, I'll mash all the other buttons, then jump out and yell: 'Have a nice tour of the hotel. Now get with the fucking team!'" Serge stared straight ahead and nodded. "Manners are important. That's how I roll."

Ted pointed at the unlit control panel. "We're not moving."

"Oh, right." Serge hit the button for the lobby.

Ted faced away, examining the secret note again.

Serge looked over his shoulder. "What have you got there?"

"Nothing!" Ted crammed it in his pocket.

"Sorry," said Serge. "My manners." A chuckle. "And I was just mentioning them. Life's funny that way, like you'll be using Reynolds Wrap on a sandwich, and suddenly a Burt Reynolds movie comes on TV. There are forces at work out in the universe that I don't understand. Do you drink coffee?"

Ted anxiously watched overhead numbers, awaiting escape into the lobby.

"Wait." Serge stared at Savage's profile. "I know you."

"Not me!"

"No, I'm positive," said Serge. "I never forget a face." The doors opened. "Have you ever done time?"

Savage sprinted out of the hotel.

Coleman popped some pills in his mouth. "That guy has serious problems."

"We could be in luck."

"How's that?"

Serge led the way onto the street. "The first person we met today might be the most suspicious. Let's follow him awhile and see if the pattern holds up."

Ted walked urgently down Flagler Street, checking each storefront for a bar. Only perfume and suitcases.

Serge trailed discreetly with hands in his pockets. "Where do I know him from? It's killing me."

Ahead, Savage nervously spun around on the sidewalk. Serge ducked behind a hotdog cart. "What really makes me curious is he knew how to raise the invisible ink on the message I saw when I peeked over his shoulder."

Coleman wrapped his fingers around an airline miniature of whiskey and sucked his fist. "Think he's a spy?"

"Not a chance, but it means he was an interesting kid like me doing all the science tricks with lemon juice and, later, gasoline." Serge stepped out from behind the cart. "He's on the move."

They shadowed Ted west.

A block behind, an SUV pulled away from the curb and drove well below the limit with a telephoto lens out the window.

A block ahead, Savage couldn't find a bar. But he had luck with a liquor store.

He came back out with four airline miniatures of whiskey in his pockets. Ted clutched one in his hand, glanced around the street, then sucked his fist.

"Now, *that's* suspicious," said Serge. "He's definitely our guy."

# *Chapter* **EIGHTEEN**

**MEANWHILE . . .**

Biscayne Boulevard.

Tourists strolled through Bayside Market with name-brand shopping bags. Some lined up for tours of the bay on large ferries, snapping photos of celebrity homes along Star Island. Stallone, Estefan, Shaq, Ricky Martin. Others ate lunch in Bubba Gump's and Hooters and carried takeout to the neighboring park.

Behind them, rows of colorful international flags flapped in the on-shore breeze. A loud din of construction. Workers putting final touches for the Summit of the Americas.

Near the sidewalk, a man in a hat sat on a park bench feeding pigeons.

Scooter Escobar ran across the boulevard. He took a spot on the bench and stared straight ahead. They exchanged newspapers. "You wanted to see me?"

"No," said the man, code name Raúl.

"Then why'd you set up the meet?"

"You're the one who called me. Are you still doing coke?"

"Yes."

Someone took a seat on the other side of Escobar. He smiled. "How are things at the consulate?"

"Who the hell are you?"

"Malcolm Glide, your newest best friend. I hear we're supposed to exchange newspapers." Glide set a folded *Herald* in Escobar's lap.

Scooter looked back and forth at the two men. "This was a mistake. I have to go."

He began to stand, but Glide pulled him back down. "Why the rush? It's a beautiful day. Old and new pals enjoying themselves. That's what life's all about."

Scooter wept in his hands. "I can't take it anymore."

Malcolm leaned forward for a view of Raúl. "Is he always like this?"

Raúl shrugged. A pigeon strutted for a piece of bread.

Malcolm put an arm around Escobar's twitching shoulders. "I've heard great things about you."

"You have?"

Malcolm nodded extra hard. "You're going to go far. Maybe work for us someday."

"Really?"

Another emphatic nod. "So when I hear someone as talented and dedicated as you might have a problem, I can't just stand by and not help."

"Problem?"

"Raúl filled me in. It's why you set up this meeting." Malcolm smiled warmly. "I mean, anyone can accidentally fire a grenade launcher."

"That's what I kept telling him," said Scooter.

"Telling who?"

"My uncle."

"That's right, the general. You let me have a little chat with him." Malcolm held two fingers together. "We're tight."

"It's too late." Weeping again. "I know they're going to send me home. They've already sent a replacement spy."

"You mean Serge?"

Scooter's head sprang up. "So it's true?"

Malcolm laughed. "Not remotely. Except I do need to talk to you about that. I'm scratching your back, but I have an itch, too. That's what friends are for. So I want you to go back to the consulate and act like everything's normal, and find out everything you can about Serge."

Scooter sniffled and wiped tears off his cheeks. "But I thought your government assigned him to us."

"Well," said Malcolm. "Things are a little confusing right now, especially with the assassination plot against Guzman."

"What!" said Scooter. "Someone's going to kill our president?"

"Oops, I shouldn't have mentioned that." Glide leaned closer and whispered, "Forget you heard anything."

"No problem."

Glide released his grip on Scooter's shoulders. "That's my boy! . . . Now let's all get back to work."

They exchanged three newspapers again and left in different directions.

## DOWNTOWN

Serge and Coleman continued west on Flagler.

It was slow going from perpetual stops; Ted Savage constantly twirled on the sidewalk and crisscrossed the street. Everywhere he looked, every face, every vehicle, every office window, suspicion lurked. That man at the cash machine? The woman selling roses on the corner? The mother with the baby stroller? Two teenage boys in white T-shirts running past him with a purse? The screaming restaurant owner chasing them? That plump guy a block back pointing at Ted . . .

"Put your arm down!" Serge snapped at Coleman. "He'll see you pointing."

"He started running."

"He saw you. Move!"

Coleman was soon a distant second to Serge. Two streets later, he caught up and fell back panting against a sandwich shop window. "Why are you stopping?"

Serge fed quarters in a slot. "To buy newspapers."

"But he's getting away."

"No, he's taking the stairs to the Metro Mover. The last one just left, so we have time."

"To read newspapers?"

"Not read." Serge let the spring door on the box slam shut. "We've been spotted, which means we need to take surveillance to the next level. We're going to employ one of the most sophisticated Cold War techniques . . ."

Serge explained the procedure as they climbed the public transit platform and reached the top just as another automated monorail car slid up on the tracks.

Ted was too focused on getting inside the sanctuary of the car to notice anyone else. He waited at the front of the platform, inches from the closed doors—*"Come onnnnnnn!"*—until they hissed open. Ted jumped into the futuristic pod, plopped down on a seat, and let his head fall back with a big exhale.

Others stepped in from the platform and filled the rest of the car. Business commuters, students, tourists, street urchins, fishermen. The car lurched, then quietly glided out of the station on twin elevated rails.

Multilingual conversations.

The tram swung south, sailing through an architecturally funky square cut in the middle of a condo tower.

"I took too many pills," said Coleman. "We just went through a building."

"That was real." Serge worked with his newspaper. "Just don't forget our stealth technique."

The route curved around Bayfront and north by Miami-Dade College. Stop after stop, people on and off. A black SUV following as best it could from streets below. Ted pulled another miniature from his pocket, waiting to use the distraction of the upcoming stop at Freedom Tower Station. He checked oncoming passengers and those already seated, then sucked the tiny bottle in his fist. Tension sheeted off Ted as his eyes wandered until they reached the bench seat at the opposite end of the car, where a couple of riders sat obscured by the newspapers they were holding up.

Ted suddenly choked on saliva and pounded his chest.

Staring back at him were two sets of eyes, each peering through a pair of circles cut in the newspapers. Ted jumped to his feet and ran to the front doors, trying to pry them open before the car had come to a stop at the next platform.

"He's on the move again," said Serge.

Newspapers flew. A race down the station stairs.

"Is this the chase part?" asked Coleman.

They ran diagonally through honking traffic on Biscayne. Under the overpass with I-395. Scrambling up the embankment, Serge closing in, Savage perpetually glancing over his shoulder. "Who are you guys?"

"Pay no attention to us," yelled Serge. "Just keep doing what you're doing."

"Get away from me!"

Serge reached the top of the overpass. "I remember now!" He stopped and cupped hands to his mouth.

A chain-link retaining fence ran along the highway. Savage leaped up onto it like a house cat hearing a garbage disposal.

From the rear. "Ted! . . . Ted Savage!"

# *Chapter* **NINETEEN**

## INTERSTATE 395

"Leave me alone!" yelled Savage, clinging to the highway fence.

"Ted!" shouted Serge. "I'm on your side!"

"Go away!" Ted yelled back. "You're . . . Wait, how do you know my name?"

"I'm a big fan."

"Bullshit! You're with the Company!" His fingertips went red to purple. "I know how this ends. You're walking along on a spring day, and a car pulls up. Maybe it's someone you know, someone you trust, and they ask if you want a ride . . ."

"This ain't that movie, Ted. Come on down." Serge took a step back to defuse the standoff. "You've been through a lot."

Coleman struggled up the rest of the embankment and lay down in the dirt. "I don't like the chase part."

Ted really wasn't looking forward to climbing the fence. He dropped and fell to his knees. Serge helped him up.

"Thanks," said Savage. "So if you're not in the trade, how do you know my name?"

"I didn't say I wasn't in the trade, just not with the Company."

"Then who *are* you?"

Serge clicked the heels of his sneakers together and gave a quick salute. "Serge A. Storms, patriot-in-waiting."

Coleman pushed himself up from the ground and walked toward Ted. "You need to mellow out. I have some coke."

"You do?"

Coleman poured a generous bump on the back of his hand and Savage vacuumed. He snorted deep with zooming eyes.

"Dammit." Serge steadied Ted. "He was spastic enough before."

"It's what he needed," said Coleman. "I know this territory."

Ted nodded. "Right, Miami. Should have known. World capital of ex-spook, paramilitary, soldier-of-fortune, dummy-front-corporation, back-channel, plausible-deniability, invisible-ink, yabba-dabba-doo . . ."

Serge smiled patiently. "Why don't I buy you a drink and bring you back down?"

"Now you're talking!"

"Me, too?" asked Coleman.

Serge seized his collar. "No more rocket dust for him."

"But he likes it."

"That's the problem." Serge straightened out his pal's shirt. "I've got a rare chance to pick the brain of a famous spy, and I can't have you turning it to hamburger."

Ted walked over. "So where are we going?"

"I know the perfect place." Serge led them back to Biscayne Boulevard and hailed a cab. "Just a mile or so down the road, but another world away."

"Where?" asked Ted.

"Churchill's," said Serge. "Heard of it?"

"Heard of it? I could have bought the place with my tabs."

A taxi pulled over.

"Churchill's?" said Coleman. "What's that?"

Serge and Ted looked at each other and laughed as they all got in.

The pastel Paradise taxi sped north. A small plastic palm tree stood on the roof. The driver jabbered nonstop on a cell phone in Swahili. A pine-tree air freshener on the rearview battled the jerk-chicken upholstery. The radio on "Classic Mo-Bastic Reggae! 107.5 FM, Miami!"

"So where do you know me from?" asked Ted.

"The news. I watch it all the time. Even when I don't watch it. I leave CNN on at night for white noise, but you know how you hear something in your sleep and it infiltrates your dream? And then Larry King is chasing me through a misty forest while Tori Spelling *reveals all*." Serge shook with the willies. "I can't leave it on anymore. Anyway, that's when I heard about your case. How you were 'outed.'"

"They betrayed me."

Coleman raised his hand. "I don't know what's going on again."

"You gave them your whole life," said Serge.

They turned left off Biscayne onto Fifty-fourth. Jimmy Cliff from the radio:

"*... The harder they come ...*"

"Then they got that TV prick to disclose my classified status."

"*... The harder they fall ...*"

Serge swayed to the music. "You're with friends now."

"*... One and all ...*"

"Serge." Coleman nervously tapped his shoulder. "Where are we?"

"Little Haiti. We're putting another distinct Miami district into play." Serge leaned over the front seat and handed the hack a twenty. "Let us out here."

"But we're still a few blocks from your stop," said the driver.

"I like to take in the neighborhood on approach. Here's another ten."

"It's your funeral." The cab screeched off.

Coleman looked around an arid landscape of sunken-eyed scavengers milling outside barricaded buildings. He clung to the nearest arm: "Serge, that guy coming toward us on the sidewalk is swinging a giant machete."

"Are other people around?"

"Yes, lots."

"Does it seem unusual to them?"

"No."

"Then it shouldn't to us."

Onward up Second Avenue.

Coleman pointed again. "There's one of those double-decker buses from that other country."

"England," said Serge. "See the building next to it? Churchill's, one of Florida's most venerable watering holes."

"Seems a little out of place in this neighborhood," said Coleman.

"Totally out of place," said Serge. "A British pub in Little Haiti catering to Goth kids. Non sequiturs rock my world."

They walked another block and went inside the pub's corner entrance beneath a large portrait of the former British prime minister and a sign: Under Old Management.

A block back, an SUV with tinted windows pulled up to the curb.

Coleman climbed a stool. "The bar's empty."

"An empty bar at midday is the perfect place for spies to meet. No eavesdroppers. And the arrival of any potential adversary can't go unnoticed."

They didn't notice two men in off-the-rack suits arrive at a table up front.

Ted looked around. "Where are the Goth kids you mentioned?"

"They only come out at night."

Bartender: "What can I get you fellas?"

"Bottled water," said Serge.

"Whiskey," said Ted.

"It's on me," said Serge.

"Make it a double."

The woman returned with drinks.

"Thanks." Serge twisted off the plastic cap. "Can I take pictures?"

"Knock yourself out." The woman returned to the end of the bar and took a seat in front of a TV: *"Our biggest-ever shoe and handbag intervention. Next on* Oprah.*"*

Serge clicked away with his digital camera, starting at the sailfish over the bar, hung against a faded Florida mural of egrets and gulls on a coastal marsh. It was a narrow joint, barely enough for the row of stools at the front, two end-to-end pool tables, and a small band stage for live weekend jams.

"So, Ted," asked Serge. "What brings you to Miami?"

"They dumped me."

"What do you mean?"

"I woke up and here I was."

Serge nodded. *"Burn Notice."*

"At least I think they dumped me," said Savage. "I was at the bar in New Orleans. Gets fuzzy after that."

Serge grabbed his water. "What's the last thing you remember?"

"Stumbling out of Cosimo's on Burgundy Street; next thing I knew I was waking up on top of the covers in a strange motel in another city and all my credit cards were gone. I had to turn on the TV to find out where I was."

Coleman tossed back his drink. "Been there, done that."

"Cosimo's," said Serge. "Another famous spy bar. Favorite of Lee Harvey Oswald while running his one-man Fair Play for Cuba Committee."

"You know your history," said Ted. "Anyway, looks like I'm stuck in Miami awhile."

"People should go to jail for what they did to you." Serge aimed his camera toward the back of the bar. *Click, click, click.*

One of the men in suits aimed his tie tack. *Click, click, click.*

"What's done is done," said Ted. "No use looking back."

Two more people came through the open door of bright sunlight. Local residents. The Haitians grabbed a pair of stools on the other side of Coleman.

Coleman turned and smiled. "So you guys live around here?"

The answer came in death stares. Coleman gulped. Murderous mouths, soulless eyes. The closest had a thick scar running from his forehead, over his eyelid, to his cheek.

Coleman managed a crooked grin. "I'll get back to you."

Ted reached in his pocket. "Serge, one thing you should know before we hang out anymore. You might be in danger." He unfolded the note with invisible ink. "JM/WAVE, the old anti-Castro operation. I think they're planning to set me up for some kind of fall."

"No, they're not," said Serge.

"Seriously, I understand these people. Now that they've neutralized me, I'm the perfect scapegoat for some rogue operation."

"That's my note," said Serge.

"Yours? What? Why?"

"Just gettin' my Serge on."

Ted felt someone poking his arm. He turned.

Coleman held out his hand. "Want to burn a joint?"

"Sure," said Ted. "But where? It's broad daylight. I saw some police cars on the way over."

"Got it covered." Coleman climbed off his stool. "I'm an expert at finding hidden places to blow numbers in public."

Ted hopped down. "What are we waiting for?"

Coleman felt someone poke his arm. He turned. The Haitians. A pair of giant, ivory smiles. "Can we come, too?"

"The more the merrier."

They went out the front door and circled behind the bar. Coleman found an alley with garbage cans and stacked beer cartons. They crouched.

A black SUV drove off.

## SOUTH MIAMI

Building 25. Nightfall.

Station Chief Gil Oxnart grabbed the podium.

"What have we got? Dresden?"

An agent opened a folder on his school desk. "Serge's previously unknown associate goes by the code name 'Coleman.' Picked up surveillance on Flagler Street, where subjects proceeded west on foot until boarding the Metro Mover."

"Classic move," said Oxnart. "Difficult to follow the monorail below on the streets."

"Had a heck of a time. Just about to lose him when they exited Freedom Tower Station, proceeding on foot to the 395 overpass." Agent Dresden passed a set of eight-by-tens. "Followed taxi to Second Avenue, where subjects exited north."

Oxnart turned to a city map on the wall, following the trail with his finger. "This route makes no sense, multiple modes of transportation, random pedestrian movement." He returned to the podium. "No healthy person has a lifestyle like that. We're obviously dealing with an experienced professional."

"Sir, we've picked up a third subject. Hold on to your hat." Another photo. "Ted Savage."

"The outed agent? That can't be a coincidence. They're planning something big."

Dresden reviewed his notes. "They held some kind of a meeting in Churchill's."

"Churchill's?"

"An old bar."

"Where?"

"Little Haiti."

"What on earth were they doing there?" asked Oxnart.

Dresden handed forward another stack of photos. "Took those with my tie tack."

The station chief studied them. "Who the heck are these two new local guys they're talking to?"

"Sir, we now have reason to believe the Haitians are involved."

"The Haitians! Christ!"

"We suspect those two new guys are ex-secret police under Baby Doc, the Tonton Macoutes."

"What kind of business does Serge have with the Macoutes?"

"Don't know," said the agent. "But it must be pretty important. They left the bar to secretly exchange something."

"Like what?"

"Don't know that either. Coleman's apparent specialty is conceal-ment. He made a flanking maneuver behind the bar, where we lost audio and visual contact."

"Jesus!" said Oxnart. "How far does this thing reach?"

"Pretty far," said another agent. "We've uncovered some kind of pipeline between Haiti and Costa Gorda."

"Why do you think that?"

"Because Serge has been making large, unknown shipments to both countries from the Royal Poinciana Hotel."

"The Royal Poinciana?"

"That's the return address on the manifests."

"You idiot," said Oxnart. "It's the hotel where Serge must be stay-ing!"

"Oh."

Oxnart began pacing. "We need to get our arms around this. Where were Lugar's boys during all that?"

Dresden handed over the last photos. "That's their black SUV." He smiled. "I don't think they got any pictures of us."

"Then we still have a shot," said Oxnart. "And I have a pretty good idea what Lugar's next move will be. The center of it all is the Royal Poinciana. Get a team together."

"How do you want us to approach it?"

Oxnart looked toward a pair of desks in the back of the room. "Shef-field, Winslow, this is your party. I don't want to know your plans."

"We're on."

"And realize you'll be flying solo. Absolutely no contact with the station until it's over. This mission doesn't exist, nor will it ever exist."

### ACROSS TOWN . . .

"The Haitians?" said Station Chief Lugar. "Christ!"

"That only scratches the surface," said Agent Bristol. "We've de-tected a secret network in the Caribbean, where Serge has been making clandestine shipments."

"How does Ted Savage fit into this?"

"Probably the scapegoat. Could have something to do with all the chatter we've picked up about an assassination plot."

"And we don't have anything on that either?"

Agent Bristol shook his head.

"Damn," said Lugar. "Something's in the air, and Oxnart's kicking our ass."

"Sir." Bristol raised his hand. "I think we can still salvage this, especially since we now know where they're all staying."

"You're right," said Lugar, snapping his fingers toward a pair of agents. "Manchester! Reed! Get over to the Royal Poinciana. Intercept protocol."

"Kidnap Serge?"

"Absolutely not. We don't know anything about his operation. If it comes from the top of our own agency, and we bollix it up, there go our careers."

"Then what do we do?"

"What I'm about to say, I never said." He stared down the agents. "Grab Savage, sweat him down."

"You're saying to abduct a private American citizen on American soil?"

"That's why you're on your own . . . This mission doesn't exist."

"Sir?" A younger agent raised his hand.

"What is it, son?"

"I don't know. I've been going over all these files, and I think we may have it all wrong." The agent unfurled a rap sheet. "I think Serge is just an eccentric criminal who somehow stumbled into things, and we've let our imaginations get away from us."

The room erupted in laughter.

"You still have a lot to learn," said Lugar. "That's the way it's *supposed* to look."

## *Chapter* TWENTY

**MIAMI INTERNATIONAL AIRPORT**

Rental-car counter.

The Littletons of Beaver Falls, Pennsylvania. Couldn't wait for vacation.

"We've never been to Florida before," said Nadine. "Always wanted. The children are at my parents'."

The rental clerk smiled. "You reserved a Taurus?"

"That's right," said Frank. "Here's my license and proof of insurance."

And so on through the rental procedure.

"Would you like to buy the tank at our special discount?"

"No, we'll fill it ourselves."

"Here are the keys," said the clerk. "Where are you staying?"

"Downtown," said Frank.

"The Royal Poinciana," Nadine added with excitement. "Sounds like a great place. The name alone—"

The clerk's expression changed.

"Something the matter?" asked Frank.

A smile returned. "No, everything's fine." The clerk placed a map on the counter and leaned over it with a red felt-tip. "Here's the best route to your hotel. I strongly suggest you don't get off the expressway until you reach your exit. Especially along here and here and here and definitely here."

"Why?" asked Frank. "Are those like bad neighborhoods with a lot of crime?"

"I'm not allowed to say that."

"We'd heard Miami has gotten better," said Nadine.

"It has," said the clerk. "You'll have a great time. Just stay on the expressway . . ."

A half hour later, a rented Taurus sat in a ten-dollar lot two blocks off Flagler. The Littletons' rolling luggage clacked through night streets.

"Look at Bayside. It's so beautiful." Nadine looked straight up. "And the skyline!"

Then they turned the corner. Luggage slowed. Eyes glanced around.

*"Hey man! Got a couple bucks?"*

"Don't look at him," said Frank.

Rolling sped up.

*"Yeah, ignore me, man!"*

They reached the address.

"This can't be it," said Nadine.

"There's the sign."

"Why isn't it lit?"

"Let's get off the street."

Luggage into the lobby.

"What are all those giant boxes?" asked Nadine.

"The website didn't mention they were renovating," said Frank.

The couple arrived at the reception desk.

"It has bulletproof glass," whispered Nadine.

"I know." Frank put his mouth to the metal grate. "Excuse me. We have a reservation. Under 'Littleton.'"

The night manager flipped through a box of cards and reached the

*L*s. There it was. Littleton. Three-night stay, but the manager pegged them as an early checkout at first light.

After a credit-card swipe, a key came through the slot.

They got on the elevator and stared at the empty bracket for the inspection certificate. "Is this thing safe?"

Frank closed the cage. "I'm sure we'll be fine."

They got off on three and stuck the key in a door. Frank felt for the light switch and flicked it. Roaches made a jailbreak.

They stood without speech. Then, Nadine: "My God!"

"So that's why the rates were so low."

"We can't stay here."

"Honey, I don't think we'll be able to find anything else at this hour." Frank looked at his watch. "It's almost eleven."

"I'm afraid to touch anything. Who knows what we'll catch."

Frank tried the air conditioner.

"Is it going to stay that loud?"

"At least it'll drown out the traffic." He grabbed his suitcase.

"You really expect me to sleep in that bed?"

"The covers are just old," said Frank.

"There's old, and then there's disease."

"Maybe we can spread all our clothes over it and lie on top."

Nadine went in the bathroom. A shriek.

Frank ran. "You okay?"

She shook with tears.

He looked in the doorway and placed a reassuring hand on her shoulder. "The last guest was just a little messy."

"And needed to be hospitalized."

"I'll go buy some cleaning supplies."

"Where?"

"Saw this drugstore a block over that was still open."

"Get bleach."

Frank grabbed the doorknob.

Thuds against the wall from the next room. Screaming. *Crash.*

Frank turned. "Make sure to keep the door locked. And don't unlock it until you're sure it's me."

"I'm just going to stand in the middle of the room and not move."

"Be right back."

The door closed.

Nadine stood perfectly still. Except for flinching at every new thud from the neighboring room. She decided to turn on the TV, using a sock to work the controls. Snowy picture, halfway into the local eleven o'clock report. "... *Police continue to dig under the house* ..." She changed channels. "... *A naked intruder armed with a sword* ..." Another channel. "... *Robbers wearing beauty-parlor hair dryers over their heads as disguises* ..." The sock clicked the set off.

She went back to the middle of the room to wait. And wait. Time slowed down.

But not that slow. She kept looking at her watch. Eleven-thirty. Midnight. Twelve-thirty. One. Tried Frank's cell phone twenty times. No answer.

Finally, a brave run down to the front desk.

"My husband's missing."

"What do you mean?"

"Gone. He went to the drugstore almost two hours ago."

"But the drugstore closes at midnight."

"That's what I mean."

The manager pointed at the wall behind him. "Sure he didn't go to Bayside? Hooters is still open."

"No! Do something!"

"Okay, okay. I'll call the police." He picked up the phone, then under his breath: "Probably find him at Hooters."

Lobby door opened. Three men strolled inside.

"What a great day we just had," said Savage. "Especially your underbelly tour."

"Glad you liked it."

"I'll never look at Miami the same."

*"Excuse me?"*

They turned. The night manager had his mouth to the metal grate in the diffracting glass. "Could you come over here?"

"Me?" said Savage. "What is it?"

"I need your key back. Unless you want to lose your deposit."

"But . . . my room."

The manager popped a pork rind in his mouth. "You didn't pay today."

"Got busy." Ted went for his wallet. "I'll pay now."

The manager chewed and shook his head. "Too late. Already rented it. Got your possessions in a bag back here."

"But it's my room."

"Not anymore. Some couple from Pennsylvania." He glanced toward a tearful woman standing off to the side.

"Why is she so upset?" asked Serge.

"Husband went to Hooters."

"Any more rooms?" asked Ted.

"Sold out. Big shopping group from Trinidad."

Ted turned to Serge. "What am I going to do?"

"Why don't you stay with us?"

"But the rooms are so small."

"Shoot," said Serge. "They got ten people stacked in most of them. And Coleman usually doesn't make it to the bed."


Two A.M.

Room 321 of the Royal Poinciana.

Serge jogged in place on the Star-Elite doormat.

Savage and Coleman sat cross-legged on the floor, taking turns sucking on an artificial leg with a Willie Nelson bumper sticker.

"Coleman? . . ."

Coleman looked up. "We made it a bong."

Downstairs in the lobby: A small crowd gathered around a commotion.

"Ma'am," said a police officer with an open notebook. "You'll have to calm down if I'm going to understand you."

Nadine Littleton took a deep breath. "I just know something terrible has happened to him."

"What about his personal habits?"

"What do you mean?"

"Has he ever done anything like this before? Strip clubs?"

"No!" More sobs.

"Ma'am, just routine. I need to cover all bases so we can find him faster . . . Does he have insomnia? Take any late-night walks?"

She blew her nose in a tissue and shook her head.

"What about enemies?"

"Oh, yeah. Lots."

"Really?" The officer got ready to write. "Who?"

"Everyone at the sales office since he got the new parking spot."

The officer clicked his pen shut. "We'll get a bulletin out. If you can think of anything else, please give us a call."

A second officer returned. "Nothing at Hooters." He looked at Nadine. "Mind if we keep this picture you gave us."

"Please just find him."

"We'll do everything we can."

"Thank you, officers." Nadine Littleton of Beaver Falls took the elevator back up to room 318.

## Chapter TWENTY-ONE

**THE NEXT MORNING**

A TV correspondent stood on the side of Biscayne Boulevard.

"... *And that's the latest from Bayfront Park, with the summit just two days away. Back to you, Jane.*"

"*Thanks, Gloria. And in other local news, police are seeking the public's help in locating a Pennsylvania tourist who disappeared after arriving at his downtown hotel last night...*"

A family photo of Frank Littleton filled the screen.

"... *Anyone with information is asked to call their anonymous hotline, five-five-five-TIPS. You may be eligible for a reward...*"

An abandoned corrugated-aluminum Quonset hut stood near one of the water-filled quarries on the edge of the Everglades. It had stored fertilizer at some point.

Property records listed the deed to Berkshire Holdings, Ltd., which was a front for an umbrella of contract operations financed with Cayman bank accounts replenished from untraceable cash deposited by CIA go-betweens with a paper trail that led to a table for six in the rear of Joe's Stone Crabs.

A man stripped to his undershorts sat tied to a chair in the middle of a back room. A naked lightbulb hung over his head. Blood from a forehead gash.

"You have to believe me," said the captive. "I don't know anyone named Ted Savage."

*Slap.*

"You were staying in his room!"

"Check my wallet. I'm from Beaver Falls."

*Slap.*

"How are the Haitians involved?"

"I just sell auto parts."

*Slap.*

"What do you know about the assassination plot?"

"The office will vouch for me."

*Slap.*

"How did you first meet Serge?"

"I don't know any Serge. You've got the wrong guy."

*Slap.*

Agent Manchester called Agent Reed aside. "You think maybe we *do* have the wrong guy?"

"Not a chance. That's Savage all right. You saw him come out of the room at the Royal Poinciana. And we doubled-checked the number, three-eighteen."

"But his driver's license says Frank Littleton."

"How many fake licenses do you have?"

"Five. But he doesn't look at all like Savage."

"So he had plastic surgery. The Company does it all the time."

"Okay, it's him," said Manchester. "But he's a lot tougher than they told us. I don't think he's going to crack."

"Any ideas?"

"Guess we'll just have to waterboard him."

"All right, we'll waterboard him."

They stood and stared at each other.

"Well?"

"Well, what?"

"I thought we were going to waterboard him."

"I don't know how to waterboard someone."

"Neither do I."

"We'll probably need a board."

"Okay, let's go look for a board."

They left the room and went outside. "I thought I saw a pile of lumber over there." Manchester walked toward the quarry.

A cell phone rang.

"Reed here . . . Oh, hi, chief. Everything's going great. We're just about to waterboard him—"

Screaming on the other end. Reed held the phone away from his ear.

Manchester leaned to listen. "Lugar sounds angry."

Reed brought the phone back to his head. "What do you mean we grabbed the wrong—? . . . No, I haven't seen any TV today . . . I can explain . . . Yes, sir . . . Yes, sir . . . No, sir . . . I understand, sir . . ." He hung up.

"What was that about?" asked Manchester.

"We got the wrong guy."

"That's impossible."

"It's all over TV. Missing tourist. And they spotted Savage on the street an hour ago."

"So what do we do with whoever's in there? We can't let him go and we can't kill him."

"That's what Lugar said. Told us to sit tight until he comes up with something."

"Do we still have to waterboard him?"

"I don't think so."

The agents went around the front of the warehouse. Reed slid open the squeaking freight doors and went inside. They headed toward the back room with the hostage.

"What will we say to him?" asked Reed.

"This is going to be awkward."

The room grew closer.

"Oh, Mr. Littleton," Reed called out. "There's been a teeny misunderstanding."

"We're very sorry," said Manchester. "I'm having lunch brought in. You like Chinese?"

Reed turned the knob and opened the door. "I hope you'll—"

An empty chair.

## THE ROYAL POINCIANA

Two police officers stood at bulletproof glass.

"Could you ring her room again?"

"If you insist." The desk manager dialed. And waited. "Still not answering."

"It's important."

"Something about her missing husband?" asked the manager. "Is he okay?"

"We think so."

"What happened to him?"

"It's better we spoke privately with his wife." Because they'd just received eyewitness reports of someone matching Frank's description running through the west part of town in his underwear, and the department was chalking it up to his having had a rough night. "Could you take us to her room?"

"Give me a sec." He hung a "Back-in-Five" sign on the glass and led the cops to the elevator. They got off on three. The manager knocked on the door of 318. "Mrs. Littleton? Are you in there?" Harder knocking. "Mrs. Littleton, the police are here. I think they have good news."

No answer.

"Open it," said one of the officers.

The manager sorted through a large metal ring of keys and stuck one in the knob. "Mrs. Littleton?" Opening the door . . .

"Sure this is the right room?" asked an officer.

"Positive. But it's empty, like nobody even stayed here."

"Did she check out?" asked the cop.

"No," said the manager, rubbing his nose. "That's odd."

They stepped back into the hall and headed for the elevator.

The door to 321 opened. A trio came out.

"Hold that lift!" said Serge.

They rode down with the cops.

"Where to today?" asked Savage.

"Thought we'd take a little drive," said Serge. "A most excellent Miami historic site. And a can't-miss for any true spy buff . . ."

## SOUTH OF MIAMI

Building 25.

Shades drawn. Ceiling fan whirled.

"Excellent infiltration," said Station Chief Oxnart. "Sorry you had to get slapped around."

"Thank you," said Agents Sheffield and Winslow, otherwise known as Frank and Nadine Littleton of Beaver Falls, Pennsylvania.

"Read your report." Oxnart fed it into a shredder attached to a burn bag. "Lugar's men must be in heavy shit to grab you off the street like that. They're protecting something important. What's your gut tell you?"

"They seemed awfully worried that we'd found out about Serge. Slapped me extra hard asking about him."

"So he is working for them after all?"

"Looks that way. The Haitians, too."

"Damn," said Oxnart. "The Lugar connection means Serge is on the level. Actually protecting Guzman. That must be what this fake assassination jazz was about." He smacked a desktop. "I never trusted that snake Malcolm Glide. He's been working with Lugar all along. And when Serge foils the so-called plot, they both get credit and we look like schmucks."

"I wouldn't be too sure," said Sheffield.

"Why do you say that?"

"Because they kept grilling me about the plot." The agent pointed to a bruised cheek. "I think they genuinely didn't know and were worried we'd found out about something they didn't."

"That makes no sense," said Oxnart. He suddenly raised a finger in the air. "Unless there's a second, real plot. And our fake plot is a diversion. That's it! Glide's setting me up to be the scapegoat!"

A hand raised in the back of the room. "I'm really confused now."

"So am I," said Oxnart. He turned around and grabbed a piece of chalk. "Let's diagram it out on the big blackboard . . ."

Meantime, a few miles away:

An orange-and-green Road Runner cruised south on the turnpike.

Serge took Exit 16 and sped west on 152nd Street, a checkered area below the city proper, where Miami bleeds into tomato farms, unpaved airstrips, gravel pits, and vast new subdivisions of shortcut construction methods and identical orange-tile roofs packed so close they seem continuous from a distance.

The eye of Hurricane Andrew came through here.

Serge pointed out the window. "There's the Metrozoo."

The Plymouth swung left. A road with a private entrance.

"This doesn't look like the way to the zoo." Coleman bent over to light a joint.

"Because it's not."

Coleman passed the joint to Savage. "Then where are we going?"

"I've always been fascinated by the Cuban Missile Crisis, partly because that's when I was born." Serge's hand was out the window, sailing up and down in the wind as he had done since childhood. "My granddad told me that while waiting in the maternity ward, they could hear the military trains rumbling south on tracks next to Old Dixie Highway. They carried all kinds of tanks and artillery and ran at night so it wouldn't freak out the neighbors, but everyone knew. Beaches down in the Keys covered with rows of mobile-missile batteries, all pointing at Fidel."

Coleman took a big hit and blew it out the window. "That would have been radical to lay out on the beach back then, get stoned, and look up at missiles."

"It was a special time," said Serge. "Remember that railroad crossing back there? Same tracks."

"Far out." Another joint-hit with a loud suction sound. "Shit. There's a dude up ahead with a gun."

"Get rid of the joint."

"That's a big fucking gun." The doobie flew out the window. "We better turn around."

"Negative. We're going straight."

"But that's a serious guard shack," said Savage. "And the guy's dressed like a soldier."

"Heightened checkpoint," said Serge, "because of this place's classified status."

"Let's get the hell out of here!"

"Shhhhh!" Serge applied the brakes and pulled up to the crossing-gate arm. "He's coming over."

The guard checked the windshield for a security-clearance sticker and didn't find one. He walked to the driver's side.

"Credentials?"

Serge grinned. "Don't have any except a universal respect for others."

The guard took an added step back, from training. "Why are you here?"

"History!" said Serge. "Always wanted to see Building Twenty-five. If those walls could talk! Operation Mongoose, CIA front Zenith Technical Enterprises . . ."

A hand went to the automatic rifle. "I must ask you to turn around."

"What? We can't see Building Twenty-five?"

"Sir, turn the vehicle around!" The rifle raised. "Immediately!"

"Look, we both know the drill. And in this line of work, sometimes it's best not to carry credentials, if you get my drift." Serge winked. "So if you wouldn't mind, could you go back in your little booth, pick up the phone, call the station chief, and say 'Serge is here!' I wouldn't want you to have to explain to him later why you turned me away."

The guard stared a second, then went in the booth.

"Serge," whispered Coleman. "Why on earth did you do that?"

"Because whenever they won't let me in someplace, I love to say,

'Call the person in charge and tell them Serge is here!' Done it a million times."

"Has it ever worked?" asked Savage.

"Never. But I get a big kick."

"So he isn't going to let us by?"

"Not a chance. Building Twenty-five's been mothballed for decades, and there hasn't been a station chief since 1968. That guard's probably just calling for backup. I knew it was a long shot seeing Building Twenty-five, but I'll happily settle for pulling up to the security gate at the former JM/WAVE installation and saying, 'Call the station chief!' The key to life is self-amusement."

"He's been on the phone a long time," said Coleman.

"Must be calling extra men in case they have to shoot out the tires."

"I want to turn around."

"Let me savor the moment a little longer . . ."

Inside Building 25, a phone rang.

"Station Chief Oxnart here . . . Front security? What can I do for you? . . . Could you repeat the last part? . . . He really said that? Those exact words? . . ."

Mandrake saw the chief's expression. "What's going on?"

Oxnart covered the phone. "Serge is here!"

"Where?"

He jerked a thumb toward the window. "Right at the front gate. As we speak."

"Jesus, what are you going to do?"

"What do you think I should do?"

Back at the guard shack:

"Serge," said Coleman. "I'm really scared. Let's get out of here."

"*Alllllllll* right. I guess that's long enough for the joy." He reached for the gearshift.

Ahead of them, the crossing-gate arm went up. The guard stepped out of the shack and saluted.

Coleman looked over at Serge. "What the fuck just happened?"

"There's obviously been some kind of mistake," said Serge. "A crack has opened in the cosmic star gate, and we're going for it!"

He hit the gas.

Inside Building 25:

"Hurry with the erasers! Get that shit off the blackboard!"

"What'll we say to him?"

"Play ignorant," said Oxnart. "Rule number one: Gather the most amount of information while giving up the least."

"I think that's his car now."

They ran to the window as a Plymouth Road Runner screamed up to the building and skidded into a parking slot.

"Back to the desks!"

Agents finished scrambling as three pairs of feet creaked up wooden steps outside.

A knock on the door.

Oxnart opened it. "How can I help you guys?"

"You must be the station chief," said Serge.

"Come again?"

Serge smiled and waved dismissively. "Just kidding. There hasn't been a station chief since '68." He walked inside. "So what's going on in here? Some kind of class?"

"Class?"

"History. This old building. Must have been turned into a museum when I wasn't looking—the perfect place to teach Latin American policy and espionage. University of Miami used to own it, so I'm guessing this is now an extension of their curriculum."

"That's right," said Oxnart. "It is."

"Makes perfect sense." Serge reverently ran a hand along a wall.

Oxnart followed him. "So tell me, Serge, what do you do for a living?"

"Uh, data collection. Zenith Technologies." He looked around at all the coats and ties. "They're not dressed like students." A chuckle. "You sure they didn't reactivate the station?"

A pause.

Oxnart laughed. "Ha ha ha ha ha."

Serge: "Ha ha ha ha . . . Too bad. I was hoping to get in on an operation where you slip diplomats LSD."

Coleman raised his hand. "I can get you some."

"Behave!" snapped Serge. He turned back around. "Sorry about that. Think we could sit in on your lecture . . ."

"I . . . don't think—"

"Ooooo!" said Serge. "I see a coffeepot. Stay right here."

Everyone murmured as Serge drained two Styrofoam cups and returned with a third in his hand. "Actually, I'd like to teach the class. What do you say?"

"Sir, we don't—" Oxnart stopped and thought: Gather information. "Sure, the podium's yours."

Serge ran to the front of the room. "Good morning, students! . . . I said, *'Good morning, students!'*"

They all looked toward the side of the room at Oxnart. He nodded. *"Good morning, Serge!"*

"Thanks! And I can't believe I'm finally here! Few know it, but this one building launched an economic boom that single-handedly transformed Miami from a sleepy frontier town to a major American city—the largest CIA field office in the world, with a yearly budget in today's dollars of almost four hundred million, employing thousands, buying up land, airplanes, creating a secret navy of fishing boats, and the laughs! Some teenagers threw firecrackers in a driveway, which was actually a commando safe house, and the kids fled in an explosion of automatic weapons. I've wanted to be a secret agent ever since I was a child and passed notes in class, but my teachers were nuns and experts in torture. I still toy with spycraft, like every Fourth of July, I make a copy of the Declaration of Independence, sign it, and mail it to the Queen of England in care of the British Secret Service. Next: evading capture. I need a volunteer to get me in a choke hold. You, in the second row, come up here. Now choke me . . . That's not choking. I can still breathe. That's . . . better . . ."

"Ahhhhh!" The agent jumped back, grabbing his hand.

"Forget all the fancy jujitsu stuff," said Serge. "Just remember the Rule of the Pinkie. Someone grabs you, don't fight the whole hand. Simply bend back the pinkie. Wherever the pinkie goes, the rest of the hand will follow. An exotic dancer taught me that. In fact, many ordinary citizens have used spy techniques for years and not known it. Hard to imagine now, but remember back when there was only one phone company, and long-distance minutes were droplets of gold? And you'd be traveling out of state and call home to let the folks know you made it okay, and say, 'I'd like to place a person-to-person call to *I. M. Safe*'? . . . Or when you keep a sex-addiction meeting under surveillance because they're the best places to pick up chicks." Serge looked around the room at suspicious eyes. "Okay, maybe that last one's just me. But you should try it. They keep the men's and women's meetings separate for obvious reasons. And there are so many more opportunities today because the whole country's wallowing in this whiny new sex-rehab craze after some golfer diddled every pancake waitress on the seaboard. That's not a disease; that's cheating. He should have been sent to confession or marriage counseling after his wife finished chasing him around Orlando with a pitching wedge. But today, the nation is into humiliation, tearing down a lifetime of achievement by labeling some guy a damaged little dick weasel. The upside is the meetings. So what you do is wait on the sidewalk for the women to get out, pretending like you're loitering. And because of the nature of the sessions they just left, there's no need for idle chatter or lame pickup lines. You get right to business: 'What's your hang-up?' And she answers, and you say, 'What a coincidence. Me, too.' Then, hang on to your hat! It's like Forrest Gump's box of chocolates. You never know what you're going to get. Most people are aware of the obvious, like foot fetish or leather. But there are more than five hundred lesser-known but clinically documented paraphilia that make no sexual sense. Those are my favorites . . ." Serge began counting off on his fingers. "This one woman had Ursusagalmatophilia, which meant she got off on teddy bears—that was easily my weirdest three-way. And nasophilia, which meant she was completely into my nose, and she phoned a friend with mucophilia, which is mucus. The details on that one are a little disgusting. And formicophilia, which is being crawled on by insects, so the babe bought an ant farm. And symphorophilia—that's staging car accidents, which means you have to time the air bags perfectly . . ." Serge chugged the cup of coffee he'd brought to the podium. "Did you know Gloria Estefan turned down a CIA gig while working customs at Miami International? Parts of *Casino Royale* were filmed here, *Thunderball*, too. *Goldfinger*. Please listen carefully as menu items have changed. Shark in the road, Queen of England, when nuns attack. The star gate's closing." He ran out the door with Coleman and Savage.

All agents dashed to the window and watched the Plymouth patch out.

"Is everyone just going to stand here?" asked Oxnart. "Or does somebody have an inclination to follow them?"

Four agents raced outside. The rest huddled around their chief. "What did you make of him?"

"Better than I thought," said Oxnart. "Took him no time to trace our infiltration at the Royal Poinciana. And the confidence coming right to our door—he was sending a message."

One agent pointed back at the podium. "But what was that bizarre presentation? Remember I said I thought he was just some crazy criminal?"

"A well-honed act," said Oxnart. "The most advanced method of holding back information is giving too much information."

"So you believe he knows this station's been reactivated?"

"Of course," said the chief. "You think he just drove up here on some silly history tour?"

"What do we do?" asked another agent.

"Can't go right at him now that he's onto us," said Oxnart. "But there is another lead we can follow up without detection—if Lugar hasn't already thought of it."

"What's that?"

"Pack some bags," said the chief. "We're going to the airport."

They headed out the door.

"At least now we know who's been sending all those messages to the British."

## Chapter TWENTY-TWO

**DOWNTOWN MIAMI**

A sheer, post-modern office building sat in the Brickell financial district.

Across the street:

Coleman repeatedly flicked a lighter for his joint.

"What's the problem?" asked Savage.

"I think it's dead." Coleman kept flicking. "Serge, what are we doing here?"

"Just keep your head down or they'll see us—before we *want* them to see us."

"Are we spying?"

"Yes."

"So this is part of your mission?"

"A different mission." Serge kept a keen eye on the building. "I have an itch I need to scratch."

"Itch?"

"I need sex," said Serge. "If I go too long, I become irritable."

"And this is why we're hiding in these bushes?" Coleman looked down at Serge's hands. "You're going to do it right here?"

"Not *that*," said Serge. "It would be creepy. Just keep crouching down and looking for women."

"But there are no women."

Serge pointed. "There."

The front doors of the building opened. A chatty group of attractive females spilled out, car keys in hand.

Coleman pocketed his empty lighter. "Who are they?"

"The meeting just finished."

Serge leaped from shrubbery and strolled across the street. "Excuse me?" he asked a redhead. "What turns you on?"

"Dendrophilia."

"What a coincidence," said Serge. "Me, too!"

They left arm-in-arm.

"Excuse me?" Coleman asked a brunette.

"Get lost."

"Will that turn you on?"

A half hour later, Coleman and Ted rummaged through a trash can, finding a book of matches with one left. Serge suddenly emerged from a landscaped park across the street. He ran back through traffic, pulling up his zipper.

Coleman struck a match that immediately went out. "Damn." He looked up. "So what was she into?"

"Trees," said Serge. "Luckily there was that park."

"Trees?" said Coleman. "How does that work?"

"I think I need an ointment."

Serge led them back to their hotel, scratching. "I remember a drugstore up the block."

They turned left on Flagler.

"There's a Walgreens," said Coleman.

They were in and out in a flash.

A tall woman with jet-black hair exited a luggage shop. Putting away her checkbook, not paying attention. And crashed into Serge.

He reached down and picked up his small drugstore bag.

"Oh! I'm so sorry!" said the woman. "That was all my fault. Hope I didn't break anything."

"Just rash cream," said Serge. "And it was definitely *my* fault. I always say that, even if it was your fault, because that's the kind of gentleman I am. Not like the other guys who bump into women and, regardless of liability, try to cop a feel."

"Serge." Coleman tugged his arm. "Harold, right?"

"Shhhh! Can't you see I'm talking to a beautiful woman who crashed into me and I'm turning it to my advantage with paralyzing charm, guilt manipulation, and previously applied deodorant?"

"Ask her what she's into," said Coleman.

"She's not from the meeting! And she can't know about that because most women consider waiting outside meetings a red flag, then go cold on you and spend the night at home with their cats eating ice cream and watching Meg Ryan movies."

"Gee, Serge, you sure know a lot about women."

"And they *especially* can't know that you know a lot about them." Serge turned back around with a nervous smile. "You didn't hear any of that, did you? If you did, I was talking about this great Meg Ryan movie where she bumps into a guy on the street who she mistakenly thinks waits outside the meetings, but in a heartwarming twist turns out to be the best thing that ever happened to her. So where were we?"

"You have to let me make it up to you." She adjusted a purse strap on her shoulder. "Can I at least buy you a drink?"

"No objection."

"Wait a minute . . ." She stepped slightly forward and looked him over. "Do I know you?"

"I'm not yet a household name—"

Her eyes widened. "You're Serge!"

"Or maybe I'm wrong."

"Serge, don't you remember me?" She tapped her chest. "Felicia, from the consulate. I'm the receptionist you asked to deliver that note. Sorry if I was aloof, but you wouldn't believe all the crazy people who walk in off the street. I had no idea you were working with us."

"I get it now." Serge nodded with a knowing grin. "The old pretend-accidental bump-and-greet in the street. You're the honey trap, sent to romance me and drop my guard. The next thing I know, we're in bed and you secretly inject my butt with a lethal isotope." He stopped and smiled again. "Okay, I'm game. Let's play spy."

She laughed and flirtatiously touched his arm. "I love a man with a sense of humor."

"Women always say that so they don't appear superficial," said Serge. "But it's only true if Brad Pitt is telling knock-knock jokes. Don Rickles eats alone."

"There's a place up the street I like," said Felicia.

They walked three blocks to a newly opened bistro. The maître d' appeared with hands folded in front of his stomach. "Will it be dinner or the bar?"

"The bar," said Serge. "We're playing spy."

The man gestured with an upturned palm. "That way. Enjoy."

They entered the lounge, and Felicia hopped on a stool like it was a horse she'd ridden her whole life. "Serge, what'll you have?"

"Water. Stirred, not shaken."

Felicia never had to wait for a bartender. He stood before her at the ready.

"Perrier for my friend," said Felicia. She ordered a fruity umbrella drink.

"What about me?" asked Coleman.

"And me?" said Ted.

"She didn't bump into you," said Serge.

"That's fine," said Felicia. "Whatever they want."

Two hours later:

*"Oh, Serge! . . ."*

*"Oh, Felicia! . . ."*

*"Faster! Harder! Faster! . . ."*

Serge thrust like a stallion in a ritzy hotel room across from Bay-front Park.

*"Oh, Serge! Whatever you do, don't stop!"*

*"I think I can handle that."*

*"Oh, yes! Faster! I'm almost there! . . ."*

Serge went even faster.

*"Oh God! Oh God! Say something horny! . . ."*

*"Knock-knock."*

*"Who's there?"*

*"Brad Pitt. I brought my cock."*

*"Oh God! . . ."*

Behind his back, a hand with ruby nail polish clawed his shoulder blades. A second hand rose in the air, gripping a syringe with a glistening needle.

## MIAMI INTERNATIONAL

An eight-seater prop jet took off from a short runway on a little-used corner of the airport. The all-white plane had no markings except a small tail number registered to a PO box in Key Biscayne. But it belonged to the U.S. government.

Binoculars followed the aircraft as it ascended into the clouds toward Florida Bay. The binoculars swung back to the foot of the runway as another pair of engines revved until the tower gave the go sign. The plane accelerated down the tarmac and lifted off in the same direction. Then another plane. And another, all banking south, with six more stacked up on the taxiway and others still arriving.

The binoculars lowered and hung by a cord around Oxnart's neck. He rubbed his head. "Are all these planes ours?"

"No," said Mandrake. "Maybe half, tops." The agent held an intercepted shipping manifest out of Miami. As each plane departed, he checked off another destination.

"The congestion's delaying our mission. I've never seen this part of the airport so busy." Oxnart raised the binoculars again and panned the distance across an open expanse of runway, heat lines wavering up from pavement. Mirage puddles. Weeds through concrete cracks. A lone, lost jackrabbit. Twin tanks of jet fuel anchored next to a small, rusty hangar. A departing plane filled his field of vision.

"Where can all these other flights be coming from?"

Another takeoff. Then a high-decibel shock wave. The jackrabbit stood on its hind legs in the middle of the runway and looked around, hundreds of yards from safety in every direction. In rabbit thought: Fuck me.

Oxnart's binoculars backed up.

"See something?" asked Mandrake.

He focused on the hangar at a thousand feet. "Uh-oh."

"What's the matter?"

Through high magnification, Oxnart watched another pair of binoculars staring back at him. "It's Lugar. That son of a bitch must have intercepted our intercepted manifest."

Across the runways, Lugar lowered his binoculars. "Oxnart. Shit. Must have gotten the manifest." He turned to a case agent: "Priority dispatch, all operatives. We have company. Code red . . ."

The agent took notes. "Which red? The darker one?"

"Shut up. Just tell 'em to be careful." Another jet roar. "Hit the ground fast and cover tracks."

From opposite sides of the runway, Oxnart and Lugar aimed binoculars skyward as the last of the planes flew off in a loose pelican-like formation toward the sunset.


## MEANWHILE . . .

A shout in a ritzy hotel room across from Bayfront Park.

Serge jumped out of bed and grabbed his ass with both hands.

"What the hell just bit me?"

Then he noticed the dripping syringe in Felicia's fist.

"I knew it!" Serge went for his pants bunched on a chair. And the gun in the pocket.

Felicia monitored her wristwatch.

Serge reached the chair. Then stumbled backward a couple steps. Stumbled forward. "Whoa, a little dizzy here . . ."

Felicia took him by the arm. "Why don't you lie down in bed before you hurt yourself."

"What did you stick in me?"

"That's not important. It's time to rest."

"But I'm not tired."

He fell facedown on the mattress.

Time passed.

Serge lay on his back. Eyelids finally cracked open a slit. Felicia dragged a chair to the bed: "That was just a little harmless truth serum. It'll wear off soon, and you'll be good as new. So let's start with the basics. What's your real name?"

He slowly licked dry lips. In dream-state slur: "Serge . . . Serge Storms."

"Who do you work for?"

"People in need, future generations, endangered species, lost tourists, the disenfranchised underclass, strippers with hearts of gold trying to support a child on a single income . . ."

"What is your mission?"

"To save the republic, cheer on the home team, stay ahead of the curve, read the warning signs, respect my elders, support the troops, spend more time thinking about landfills, harness the untapped power of avoiding all your relatives, try not to fart around women . . ."

Felicia looked toward the syringe on the dresser. "Maybe I gave him too much."

"Souvenirs, sunblock, sesquicentennial . . ."

Felicia sighed and looked at her watch again. Waiting for his gibberish to subside. ". . . Fancy fucking bathroom guest towels . . ." Finally the drug fell within parameters. She turned back to the bed: "What do you know about the plot?"

"Plot? Let's see, erratic time line, disjointed geography, arrive from Tampa, save Guzman, sink-or-float, blah blah blah, establish Scooter as the undependable wild card, introduce burned agent Savage as possible scapegoat, escalate CIA rivalry between Oxnart and Lugar as tension builds toward assassination at the Miami summit, some kinky stuff with a tree, bump into you, knock-knock . . ."

"Okay, that's enough . . ."

## Chapter *TWENTY*-THREE

### TWO HOURS LATER

Serge and Felicia strolled through chic South Beach. Beautiful people crowded sidewalk cafés along Ocean Drive. Every table a different language. German, French, Swedish, Portuguese from Brazil. Tiny portions of nuevo cuisine with sprigs of garnish arranged in tripods.

"Was that really necessary?" asked Serge.

"Sorry about sticking you," said Felicia. "Could have sworn you were a double agent sent to assassinate President Guzman. I had to make sure."

"But what would give you such a crazy idea?"

"Scooter Escobar." She lit a thin cigar.

"That idiot?"

"And he's getting stupider, arranging secret meetings with people he shouldn't."

"Exchanging newspapers on park benches?"

"It would be funny if it wasn't." She blew out a thin stream of smoke. "That's where he heard about the plot—from *your* people—and that you might be involved. He wasn't supposed to tell anyone, but he tells me everything."

"So you believe now that I'm on the level?"

Felicia smiled. "You were pretty funny when you were under. What's the whole anger issue with guest towels?"

"Used to be married. Long story," said Serge. "I don't approve of Tiger Woods, but I heard he had like eighteen bathrooms. How much can a man take?"

More gorgeous people in thongs and T-backs rollerbladed by. On the ocean side of the street, bodybuilders flexed at women in convertibles. Pink and lime lifeguard shacks shaped like time machines. A film crew from Japan shot a TV commercial for sake.

At one of the alfresco tables, a deal was being closed. A ruggedly handsome man with striking Latin features and long, sexy black hair dined with an equally attractive woman in a swimsuit. In two months, her *Sports Illustrated* photos would hit the stands, and she'd become a supermodel. But right now she was still an Above-Average Model.

The man reached across the table between their wineglasses and held her hand. She gazed dreamily into his eyes. Another typical Miami Beach afternoon tryst was about to spawn. In the Art Deco hotel rooms above the strip, 136 were already under way.

Men at other tables stewed with envy. The Latin hunk could have any woman in the place. What they didn't know—and the source of universal disbelief if they did—was that the oncoming liaison would be the playboy's first. Ever.

Oh, he could line them up in stunning volume and variety, but he'd just never been able to land them in the boat. Had nothing to do with his appeal or bedside manner. It was luck. The wrong kind. Always some crazy, blind-side against-the-odds interruption before consummation. And as with any statistical sample, somewhere in the world was the man who ranked absolute last on the standard-deviation coitus graph. That was this guy.

Johnny Vegas, the Accidental Virgin.

But hope springs eternal, and Johnny was at bat again with the bases loaded. As he held her hands and stared into those emerald-green eyes, it seemed nothing remotely could go wrong. The sun was high, and a balmy breeze ruffled the fringe of their table's umbrella. Sinful desserts arrived on a cart.

Three blocks south, Serge and Felicia strolled past the Colony Hotel.

Ahead, two men on the sidewalk, staring stupidly at the diners. A waiter asked them to move along.

"There you are," Serge called out. "We were supposed to meet at that corner."

"Serge!" Coleman came running over with Ted Savage. "I've never seen such great tits. There's been like forty-three so far."

"It's Ocean Drive," said Serge. "Nipple City."

"Serge!" scolded Felicia.

"Baby, don't crowd my facts."

Coleman stared at more breasts. "I never want to leave this place."

"Coleman, there's more to Miami than silicone."

"Like what?"

"Stay here long enough and anything can happen." Serge swept an arm over the beach mating frenzy. "Look at all these people. Their back-stories are arguably the most diverse and compelling in all the country, an international roll call of intrigue: TV producers, exotic-animal smugglers, money launderers, foreign agents, people on the run from Interpol, the ShamWow Guy. I'm getting pumped just thinking about all the secret life arcs surrounding us. Except in real life, it's impossible for me to know what's ticking behind all these five-hundred-dollar sunglasses. That's why I love to read novels about Miami."

Coleman's eyes seized on a passing bikini top. "Novels?"

"In novels, the omniscient narrator knows all secrets and reveals them." Serge watched a Lamborghini being valeted. "Sometimes I like to pretend that my own life has a narrator. I wish I could meet him someday."

"Why?"

"Because to me, narrators are the most impressive people on the planet. Every one of them outrageously intelligent and perceptive. They're like gods."

Serge was clearly a genius in all respects. They continued up the sidewalk. The group didn't know it, but they had, in succession, just passed the woman with the highest number of Botox injections, the largest wholesaler of human-growth hormone on the beach, the hotel with the top frequency of burglaries by maids, and the Most Laid Guy in Miami, which placed him thirty-fourth nationwide.

The Most Laid Guy was also the most unlikely. Just a regular Joe, maybe the corner barber or H&R Block man. Statistics again. Someone has to be the anomaly. Women didn't understand why, but they found themselves magnetically drawn to him in astounding numbers. A million males would have killed for what fell off his truck, but to him it had all become a burden. He sat alone with coffee and a copy of *Florida Architecture*.

"Pardon me," said a college cheerleader in town for a game. "Is this seat taken?"

"I'm trying to read."

And so on, until he'd eventually relent just to release the pressure.

The gang continued up the sidewalk, past a DEA agent on the take, an indicted boy-band manager, a paparazzo with inside information, a transgender with second thoughts, and a spy from Costa Gorda peeking over the top of a menu. He got up and began following.

Coleman bumped into Serge's back as they prepared to cross Thirteenth Street.

"Coleman, watch where you're going."

"I was looking up." He shielded his eyes. "These are some outrageous hotels."

"And every room holds a story." Serge gazed toward the top floor. "Things you could never imagine are going on right this second. Like that window there. I'd love to know what's happening inside."

Inside, someone had tied himself up with intricate knots and a gag ball in his mouth, where he'd remained alone and happily still for the last six hours.

Coleman looked around. "Who said that?"

"Said what?"

"Knots and gag balls."

"Maybe my narrator," said Serge. "Actually the proper term is *the* narrator. *My* implies a demeaning, possessive relationship, like he's an organ-grinder monkey. Narrators don't like that."

They don't. The spy from Costa Gorda grew closer. Felicia turned around. The agent ducked behind a potted tree at the News Café.

Coleman resumed walking. "Remember when they found the star of *Kung Fu* tied up and dead in that motel closet."

"David Carradine," said Serge. "Bangkok. The namesake of the *Kill Bill* movies."

"They said he accidentally got strangled during freaky sex with himself."

"Coleman, that's a private matter. He should be remembered for his impressive body of work."

"But it's so embarrassing." Coleman looked back up at the window. "If I ever thought I might die while playing with my dong, I'd make sure I could throw any devices across the room."

"That might just be the first time you've planned for the future."

"Planned? I've actually been practicing it. You were asleep."

"You *thought* I was asleep," said Serge. "I was wondering why I kept hearing bedsprings and then these little fur doughnuts began flying over my head and hitting the wall."

"I just don't want to be found in a motel room like Kung Fu," said Coleman. "How'd you like to be found in a motel room?"

"Let me take a wild stab at that," said Serge. "Alive?"

They started across the street. Three men approached from the opposite curb. White face makeup, black-and-white-striped shirts, and red berets. The trio tipped their caps in recognition as they passed Serge.

"You know those guys?" asked Coleman.

Serge nodded. "You heard of the Guardian Angels?"

"Yeah, vigilante group that protects people."

"Those three guys are from Tampa. They started their own group, the Guardian Mimes."

"You mean like the dudes from when you filmed those Clowns-versus-Mimes underground fight videos?"

"The same," said Serge. "I was worried they'd disband after we hit the road. Fortunately they've come back stronger than ever."

"Do you keep in touch?"

"Still got their numbers in my cell. I thought they tried calling a few times, but there didn't seem to be anyone on the other end."

Three more men in red berets came toward them on the sidewalk. Big, floppy shoes and rubber-ball noses. An exchange of knowing looks with Serge.

"The Guardian Clowns?" asked Coleman.

"I feel like a father." Serge unfolded his scavenger-hunt checklist and made an *X* next to "Wise Latina T-shirt," from the confirmation hearings of Supreme Court justice Sonia Sotomayor. He returned it to his pocket. "This is the end of Ocean Drive . . . Felicia, where to now?"

Felicia was facing the other way in frustration, hands on sensuous hips. "Scooter! Stop messing around! Get over here!"

The spy from Costa Gorda popped up from behind a Dumpster, glanced around, and ran across the street to them.

"What's with you?" asked Felicia. "When I said to meet us, I didn't mean follow us."

Escobar's eyes were still darting around. "They're everywhere. A spy can't be too careful."

"You're coked out of your skull."

"No, I'm not." Scooter gnashed his teeth. "Not a lot."

"Just don't do any more," said Felicia. "We've got important business."

Scooter took a step back. "That's Serge!"

"Everything's cool." Felicia set a brisk foot pace for the gang. "He's with us. Someone's been feeding you bad information, and I have a pretty good idea what's going on. I'll lay it all out when we get to our destination."

Serge walked up alongside. "What *is* our destination?"

"Spy."

"Not what we're doing. Where we're going."

"That is where we're going. But it doesn't open till late."

Back up the street, the Above-Average Model got an odd look on her face. She glanced around from their sidewalk café table.

"What's the matter?" asked Johnny Vegas.

"I don't know." She turned and looked the other way. "Just this strange paranormal feeling."

"What's it like?"

"An unusual pulling sensation," said the woman. "And I'm not one to believe in the supernatural, except I've never felt anything stronger . . ."

## LATER THAT EVENING

An eight-seater prop jet landed on a narrow dirt runway. Dense coconut palms. A small island with an inactive volcano.

Stairs flipped down from the side of the plane. A golf cart broke through palms on the edge of the clearing and gave the passengers a lift into town.

The driver smiled with a gold tooth. "Where to, señor?"

"Bodega," said one of Oxnart's men in a tropical shirt.

"Which one?"

The agent looked up. Blinking lights as another plane approached for landing. "Start with the closest . . . And step on it!"

The golf cart rolled back into the jungle.

The same scene repeated across the Caribbean Basin. Clandestine white Lears landing on dubious runways that rarely saw anything bigger than tourist puddle jumpers and smugglers' Cessnas. Then golf carts and antique jeeps appeared from the jungle, and more racing around the islands.

Two of Lugar's men entered a tiny sundries store on Costa Gorda. Cages of chickens, banana chips with Spanish labels. Guava paste. Santería candles. Cans of Coke for five dollars. The owner was a short, trim older gentleman in a lightweight yellow shirt and plaid shorts. Thin hair on top covering a port-wine birthmark shaped like a voting district. He parted rows of hanging beads from the back room and stepped up behind the counter. "Can I help you?"

The agents looked back and forth. Solemn mouths. "Souvenirs."

"Souvenirs?"

"Whatever you got."

Vague bewilderment from the owner. "We don't carry souvenirs."

One of the agents leaned over the counter and fiddled with a faded cardboard display that held two disposable lighters and twenty empty slots. In a low voice: "We understand you received a shipment from Miami." He pulled out a manifest and winked like they had a long-standing relationship.

"Oh, *that*." The owner chuckled. "Completely ridiculous. We're shipping it all back."

"Is it still here?"

"But it's taped up."

"We'll pay for the tape."

"Suit yourself." Back through bead strands.

He reappeared with a large, sturdy box and sliced open flaps. The agents dug through ashtrays, postcards, dashboard hula dancers, hourglass egg timers encased in Lucite, crucifixes made of seashells. The agents packed everything back up.

The owner laughed again. "Told you it was ridiculous."

"We'll take it all."

"You're kidding."

A pair of hundred-dollar bills said they weren't.

The owner folded the money and tucked it in his shirt pocket. "Nice doing business."

The first agent leaned forward again, holding another hundred out straight between his index and middle fingers. "If anyone asks, we were never here. And you never saw any souvenirs."

The owner pocketed the tip. "Who's going to ask?"

The men took their box and left without answering. The owner smiled to himself and shook his head, straightening the cardboard display on the counter.

Two more gringos came through the doorway and glanced around. "Have any souvenirs? . . ."

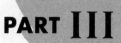

# PART III

# CLUB SPY

# *Chapter* **TWENTY-FOUR**

## MIAMI BEACH

Ocean Drive.

Changing of the guard. Nightlife. The sidewalk smelled like sex.

Lunch fare turned to fashionably late dinner. The jet set sniffed wine corks at outdoor tables facing the Atlantic. Haute cuisine. Micro-portions of pan-seared albacore, showcased with decorative, Spirograph swirls of lemon and raspberry sauce reaching the edge of the china, creating the illusion of a meal.

Someone had a more satisfying amount of eggs Benedict at the News Café. Cameras flashed. People still taking photos of the mansion steps where Gianni Versace was gunned down by Andrew Cunanan.

Johnny Vegas banged his forehead on a restaurant table as the Most Laid Guy in Miami left arm in arm with an Above-Average Model. They strolled one street over to Washington Avenue.

Club row.

The scene didn't start until midnight . . .

Every block, velvet ropes held back crowds pleading with bulky men in black shirts. Wires running from their collars to earplugs. Staring over the crowd's heads with stone expressions. From time to time, one of the security men pointed into the pulsing mob. The rope opened. A gleeful group ran inside. The rope closed. Ugly people stood for hours and went home.

Felicia and Serge strolled north on the sidewalk. She radiated the kind of visceral aura that meant never having to wait behind velvet cords. Serge was debonair, with enough poised carriage to ride her coattails. Not so with the trio trailing behind.

Coleman, Escobar, and Savage already contained a half-dozen drinks each, stumbling and weaving through waiting crowds.

*"Hey, watch it, asshole!"*

Serge turned to Felicia. "Sorry about that. They're a little rough on the edges but generally harmless."

"Forget it," she said. "I know men. Much worse. Those guys are lovable in their own way."

Serge looked back as the threesome divvied up pills. "They do seem to be hitting it off."

"Common interests."

The next club didn't have ropes to keep people out, so nobody wanted to get in.

Excitement built. Some kind of music video shoot in the street with ostriches, backup singers painted silver, and a giant, inflatable iPad.

Police cars with flashing lights penned in a crashed Porsche.

Another block, another film crew. A TV ad for rum that would only be seen in Uruguay.

Felicia and the gang skirted another hopping crowd behind a barrier. Limos pulled up. The under-nourished climbed out. Velvet rope unhooked. Air kisses. In they went.

"Who wants to exist like that?" said Serge. He turned around again. "Oh, no."

"What is it?"

"Where'd those idiots go?"

"I don't see them anywhere."

Serge sniffed the night air. "Follow the marijuana."

They arrived at a garbage-filled alley between buildings.

"What the hell are you guys doing in there?"

"Oh, hey Serge." Coleman took a big hit. "Just burning a quick one with my new friends. I didn't know spies did weed."

"Hurry up. You're keeping Felicia waiting."

"Almost done." Coleman rapidly toked a roach.

Then, yelling from deeper into the alley. A man in a ripped shirt ran past them onto the street.

"What's that about?" asked Coleman.

"Probably a mugging," said Serge.

Back up the alley, six people in red berets. Three clowns restrained the assailant, and three mimes silently pretended to punch him.

The guys rejoined Felicia. "Where is this place?" asked Serge.

"Next block." Felicia handed him a business card.

Serge stared at it, then flipped to the blank back side. "It just says, 'SPY.' No address or phone number."

"If you don't know, you're not supposed to come."

They crossed the street and stood in front of a boarded-up building.

"Looks closed," said Savage.

"Looks abandoned," said Serge.

"That's on purpose." Felicia walked around the corner. "Follow me."

They headed up a dark side street, then made a left down an even darker alley. Just past the third trash bin, Felicia approached an anonymous steel delivery door.

Four hard, evenly spaced knocks.

A metal slit opened. Two eyes.

"Hey Felicia." The slit closed. A voice inside. "It's okay. It's Felicia." The slit opened. "Long time . . . Who are those other guys?"

"They're with me."

"That's good enough."

The door opened.

"Wow," said Coleman. "What a cool club!"

Eyes adjusted in dim light that only came from the glowing bars and cocktail tables, fitted underneath with special diodes.

A waiter arrived.

Drinks.

"Serge," said Coleman, liberally splashing whiskey on his shirt like cologne. "Everyone who works in here is wearing an eye patch. Except that old bald guy sitting up in the DJ stand with a cat in his lap."

"It's SPY," said Felicia.

"It rocks," said Serge. "Like the lair of some larger-than-life Bond villain who holds the fate of the world for ransom. I always wonder how they can hollow out a volcano with nobody noticing, not to mention the four hundred lab workers in white smocks and clipboards, monitoring power levels on the giant laser used to shoot down satellites. How do they get hired? Where do they sleep and eat? I've never seen a cafeteria in the volcanoes. That would make it more realistic."

"Please," said Felicia. "We have important business."

"Right, business." He made a serious face. "You said you had an idea what's going down."

She leaned forward and motioned everyone else to join her. "About two weeks ago, I met with this reporter. He had a story about illegal arms shipments. But since his newspaper had a reputation for sensationalism, I thought it was just a wild tale."

"It wasn't?"

Felicia shook her head. "On a lark, I did some digging and found irregular bank records. So I met him again."

"What happened?" asked Serge.

"I gave him the records, and we were scheduled to meet a second time later that night when he would slip me some kind of geology report."

"Geology?" said Serge. "How does that figure?"

"I don't know."

"What did his report say?"

"Never got it."

"You were stood up?" said Serge.

"The permanent stand-up." Felicia knocked back a shot of tequila without making a face.

The guys were impressed.

She licked salt off the back of her hand. "I went down to the river, and this so-called contact of his was supposed to take me to him, but I saw blood dripping from the bumper first."

"That meant you were next."

"Those karate classes paid off." Felicia waved for the waiter.

Serge sipped his bottle of water. "So who was this guy?"

"Blond crew cut, never seen him before." Another shot of tequila arrived. "But I think I've heard of him. Freelancer who does contract work for the highest bidder. And not cheap."

"Whatever that reporter knew, someone wanted it to stay with him."

"And I think it leads back to the generals. They've never liked Guzman, and all they need is a push."

"Who's doing the pushing?" asked Serge.

"That's what I need to find out." She killed the second shot. "Only thing I know is it has something to do with the arms shipments. At first, all I had were the bank discrepancies and that reporter's suspicions, but a few days later Scooter told me about his uncle and actually seeing the crates in a Miami warehouse. You've heard of Victor Evangelista, the infamous weapons supplier?"

"Who hasn't?" said Serge.

"That's when I knew for sure. Then Scooter mentioned the plot against Guzman."

"I wasn't supposed to tell you that," said Escobar.

"Just keep your ears open and tell me everything."

"About what?"

"What we've been talking about!" said Felicia.

"Could you repeat it?" Scooter knocked over his kamikaze, flooding the small table.

Felicia grabbed his wrist. "Why don't you go sit with your friends at that table way in back while I finish talking with Serge?"

Scooter looked around. "Where?"

Serge pointed. "Behind the giant fake laser gun used to shoot down satellites."

The three amigos got up and Coleman winked at Serge. "I get it: you and Felicia." He made a circle with the thumb and index finger of his left hand, then pointed his other index finger and stuck it back and forth through the hole.

"Coleman!" snapped Serge.

"We're going . . ."

Serge covered his eyes. "I'm mortified."

"Don't be." Felicia edged her chair closer. "How long have you known him?"

"Since he was a pup." They both looked toward the back table, three arms waving drunkenly for a waiter. "I feel an obligation."

"I think it's sweet how you look out for him."

"So how'd you become a spy?"

"By accident. I was just this government secretary back home, but the bosses were always inviting me to these big parties. I was at a soiree in this compound on the side of a mountain, and some old jerk I'd never seen before is all over me, the kind that touches a lot." She shook her shoulders at the thought. "Just about to slap him when these other guys hustled me into the kitchen. Turns out the groper was running for vice president."

"And those others guys wanted you to get dirt on him."

"Wouldn't believe how much I got paid." She fiddled with her empty shot glass. "After that, I ruined five more candidates across the islands. Then Scooter needed a babysitter in Miami and here I am."

"I've always wanted to be a spy," said Serge.

"It's a joke," said Felicia. "Everyone imagines cloak-and-dagger, but ninety percent of the time you're spying on friends. Sometimes in your own office, everyone protecting their jobs. And not even good spying. Just a bunch of silly bumbling—"

A loud crash in the back of the room.

Serge turned. "What now?"

"Coleman crashed into the laser."

The other guys helped Coleman back into his chair. They guzzled drinks and slammed glasses down in unison. Then they all stood.

Felicia idly twisted a napkin. "I thought only women went to the restroom in groups."

Serge's expression sank. "I know where this is leading . . ."

## DOWNTOWN MIAMI

Dance music pounded from the clubs and Bayside Market. Streets jammed with honking taxis and limos. Summit traffic. One of the bridges across Biscayne glowed blue underneath from hidden neon lights.

Diplomatic staff and international trade lobbyists continued arriving at the most expensive hotels between the river and the causeway to the beach.

Registration desks stacked up at the luxury-suite high-rises on Biscayne. Except the line for platinum members. A man in an Italian shirt with a canvas shoulder bag opened his wallet on the counter. Fit, trim, dyed-blond crew cut like the bass player for U2.

The cheerful receptionist took his driver's license and credit card. "Welcome back, Mr. Peloquin!"—as if she personally remembered him, but the computer had prompted her greeting for a special repeat client. "How was your flight?"

He left his sunglasses on, exhaling hard through nostrils.

Her smile began to crack, and she rushed through the rest of the check-in. "Here are your room keys and drink coupons. Hope you enjoy Miami—"

The man snatched them before she was finished and headed for the elevators. Enjoy Miami indeed. He remembered his last visit. First the dislocated shoulder. And after all his trouble planting that reporter's belongings in a Costa Gordan motel—how was he supposed to know where sharks fed in Miami?

The elevator reached the fifteenth floor. A magnetic key card opened a door. The luggage he hadn't brought with him from the airport was already waiting in the room, courtesy of his employer.

The man slipped off loafers. Wallet and cell phone went on the nightstand. He reclined on the still-made bed, staring at a TV that he didn't turn on.

A vibrating sound from the nightstand.

He opened the cell phone. A text message.

"?"

He pressed a button.

" "

Arrival confirmation.

The cell phone closed. He picked up his wallet and took out the driver's license. The name said Dreyfus Peloquin. Nobody knew what it really was. Or what he looked like. A few grainy, ten-year-old photos had been floating around, but good luck. The closest thing to a name was an offshore answering machine periodically checked by another number in Argentina. Anything worth passing on got typed into a free Internet mail account and saved as a draft.

Conversely, Peloquin didn't know anything about who was texting him, just that the deposits in Switzerland had all cleared. It wasn't a first-name business.

Another driver's license came from a different part of the wallet. A different name, Winston Chabot. And a decidedly different look.

The man opened one of the suitcases on a table and unloaded packs of cash until he came to a metal box. He took it in the bathroom, squirted the contents of an unmarked bottle into his hands, and rubbed his face. Then he looked in the mirror and began tearing off his forehead and cheeks. He cranked sink faucets. Another nameless bottle and soon his hair was black. He held up the second driver's license.

Perfect match.

The new Mr. Chabot came back into the oversize bedroom. He was that peculiar blend of human who thrives on extreme adrenaline yet enjoys speechlessness. Good thing, because the suite was now his pampering prison cell until an undetermined time when the call came. If it ever came. He got paid either way, just to be on standby. Procedure called for him to stay in the room and not be seen. In Madrid, it had been over a month. And so began an arm's-length relationship with the room-service staff, which he quickly trained to knock, leave the trays outside, and wait for the fifty-dollar tip to slide under the door.

Chabot walked past the floor-to-ceiling windows. Most of the guests left the curtains wide open to enjoy the glittering nightscape of the Magic City, but these were pulled tight. In the distance, generators hummed. Floodlights. An around-the-clock crew continued final preparations on the main stage for the Summit of the Americas.

Another piece of luggage opened, this one with a custom-fitting foam liner.

With his left hand, Chabot removed the stock of an Israeli sniper rifle; with his right, he called room service.

# *Chapter* **TWENTY-FIVE**

## SPY

The DJ petted his cat.

A new song cranked. The *Mission: Impossible* theme. A giant laser lit up. Men in lab coats scurried around checking pressure gauges.

The men's room in the back of the nightclub was even busier.

Ted Savage, Coleman, and Escobar had made a beeline for the handicapped stall and barricaded themselves.

Escobar extended the Phillips-head on a utility knife and, moments later, Ted and Coleman pulled the mirror off the wall. It lay across the sink.

"Break that shit out!" said Savage.

Escobar dumped a baggie of white powder. "Hold on to your fuckin' heads, dudes. This is hundred-percent pure Peruvian flake. Couple lines of this primo blow and you won't be able to find your own nuts." He flicked open a giant barber's straight razor.

"Now, that's a freakin' blade!" said Coleman.

"Cut those cocksucking rails!" urged Savage.

Escobar sliced and diced. He pulled back the blade. "Who's first?"

Savage dove forward with a rolled-up twenty. A hard snort, then his head snapped back. Nose pinched between his fingers. "God*damn*. Where'd you get this shit?"

Escobar was already cutting Coleman's lines. "Had it flown up in the diplomatic pouch. Nobody checks. Nobody's allowed to . . . Your turn."

Coleman bent over . . .

Back in the lounge:

Serge drained a bottle of water. "So the consulate sent you to check up on me?"

"No, that was on my own," said Felicia. "With the generals and that dead reporter, I can't trust anyone. And Guzman's still a little naive. I'm doing this for my country."

"What makes you think you can trust me?"

"Because you're not in the spy business. You aren't connected to anybody, and I need independent help to see this through."

"But of course I'm a spy," Serge protested. "You injected me. That's like spy baptism."

"Come on." Felicia laughed. "That was when I *thought* you were hooked up. But you told me a lot when you were under the serum."

"Like what?"

"You're just a local guy who foiled a random carjacking. But everyone now thinks you're working for someone else, so you're playing along."

"What about me showing up earlier in your office?"

"Saw right through that."

"You did?"

"Of course. You noticed me on the street and wanted a date. Happens a dozen times a week. All kinds of stupid excuses to talk me up, like delivering a package to the wrong address . . . Except you were actually pretty funny—and cute—but I didn't want to let on."

"I can live with that account . . . So you know it was just a typical carjacking?"

"The simplest explanation is usually the right one. But in the diplomatic world, imaginations run wild."

"But you won't tell them, right? I'd kind of like them to go on thinking I'm Jason Bourne."

"I don't think I could convince them otherwise." Another laugh. "You've created quite a circular firing squad."

"How so?"

"Guzman likes you, because you saved his life from a so-called hit squad, and the head of my consulate likes you because Guzman likes you, but he hates you because he doesn't know your game and you might threaten his cushy gig in Miami, and Escobar thinks you're after his job—or used to—but he's more of a threat to himself and is now being courted by the CIA to find out more about you. And of course there's the local boob twins, Oxnart and Lugar. Then Victor Evangelista, who's dick-deep in gunrunning."

"Please keep talking to me like that."

"It's no joke. Vic's the key. We need to trace his shipments backward to the source and figure this whole thing out before another democracy's overthrown by multinationals." Felicia craned her neck around Serge, squinting toward the back of the club. "What's taking those guys so long?"

"Believe me, you don't want to know."

What she didn't want to know:

"Dear God, help me!" screamed Escobar.

"Holy crap!" yelled Savage. "Why the fuck did you do that?"

"Wasn't on purpose." Crying now.

"What do we do?" whimpered Coleman.

"Okay," said Savage. "Uh . . . Uh . . . First we have to remain calm."

"Then what?"

"I don't know."

Back in the lounge, Serge stretched and arched his back. "How do you get all your information?"

"Mostly from the head of our consulate. He's chatty in bed. Guy goes through Viagra like popcorn."

"Don't you love those TV ads for the stuff?" said Serge. "Especially the medical warnings: 'Discontinue use if experiencing diminished eyesight.' I mean, who's schlong out there is so limp it requires blood to be diverted in such quantities that the room starts to go dark?"

"Serge, come back to me," said Felicia.

"What?"

She gently placed a hand on his. "I know who you are."

"Right, I'm not a spy."

"No, I'm talking about everything." She lit a dark brown cigarette. "Police records, psychiatric diagnosis, the *bodies*."

"How's you learn all that—allegedly?"

"I'm a spy."

"But if you know my whole history, you're . . . not afraid to be sitting here?"

She formed her mouth into a circle and blew smoke rings toward the ceiling. "Natural attraction has no master. You can't diagram it logically."

"You're attracted to me?"

"Jesus, Serge. You're otherwise so intelligent." She rolled her eyes. "Do I have to spell it out for you?"

"I don't . . . I mean, you . . . me?"

She stubbed the cigarette. Her hands disappeared.

"What are you doing?"

A huskier voice. "What do you think I'm doing?"

Serge seized the sides of the table with his hands. "Whoa!" He glanced around to see if anyone was watching.

The voice became even throatier. "You enjoy that?"

"But we're in the middle of a club full of people."

"I like it that way. Public places."

"Paraphilia?" said Serge.

"And dangerous situations, particularly espionage. That's why I was so good wrecking political careers." Felicia's mouth neared the side of Serge's head. "Are you getting in the mood? I'm in the mood. In fact . . ." She whispered the rest, then plunged her tongue in his ear.

Serge watched her other hand move to her own lap. He gulped with diminishing eyesight.

"Serge, let's do it right now, right here! I've never been so ready! Nothing could turn off my—"

A restroom door crashed open. Three men ran screaming back into the lounge.

*"Serge! . . ."*

*"Help us! . . ."*

*"We're in trouble! . . ."*

Serge's head slumped to his chest. Eyesight returned.

"Serge!" yelled Coleman. "You have to do something!"

Serge closed his eyes. "Go away."

Felicia grabbed Serge by the arm. "Look at all the fucking blood!"

"What?" His head perked up. "Holy shit, all three of you are covered in it! Where's it all coming from?"

"Mainly Escobar," said Savage.

"Where's he hurt?"

Savage and Coleman pointed at Escobar's left hand, wrapped in a giant toilet-paper ball like a red boxing glove.

"What the heck happened to his hand?" said Serge.

"He cut his finger off," said Coleman.

"Call 911!" Felicia shouted to the bartender.

Houselights came on.

"How'd he cut his finger off?" said Serge.

All three went back to crying and stomping their feet.

Felicia jumped up and applied pressure to Escobar's hand. She looked back at Serge. "They're ripped on blow."

"For openers," said Serge. He grabbed Escobar by the shoulders. "The doctor is on the case. This can be fixed with microsurgery. Where's your finger?"

"Got flushed down the toilet," said Escobar. "You really believe they can fix it?"

Serge closed his eyes tight again. "Why did you flush your finger down the toilet?"

"Wasn't on purpose," said Escobar.

"Yeah," said Coleman. "We were dumping all the coke to get rid of the evidence because of the problem with his finger, and it just fell in."

"But Coleman really tried to save it," said Savage. "His arm even got stuck."

"That's why there's so much blood," said Escobar. "We had to stop and get Coleman's arm out of the toilet first, and couldn't attend to the other wounds."

"Other wounds?" said Serge.

Savage displayed his left hand. "Me and Coleman cut ourselves on the broken mirror. That's why Scooter lost his concentration and cut his finger off."

"Back up," said Serge. "How did the mirror break?"

"I leaned against the sink," said Coleman.

"How did you break the mirror leaning on the sink?"

"The mirror was lying across it," said Escobar.

"Why was the mirror on the sink?"

"There was no other place to put it," said Coleman.

Ambulance sirens. A burst through the club's secret door with a stretcher. "Who's hurt?"

Serge pointed in different directions. "Those two are just scraped. The short one lost a finger."

"Where is it?" asked an EMT.

"On the way to Biscayne Bay."

They hoisted him onto the gurney. The lounge's door flew open again.

Ambulance sirens faded into the breezy night.

Felicia looked at Serge with regret. "Rain check?"

Serge managed his best smile under the circumstances. "I'll look forward to it."

She headed toward the door. "I need to check a few things out. Let's meet again tomorrow and put my plan in motion."

## Chapter *TWENTY-SIX*

**THE NEXT DAY**

Edge of the Everglades.

Isolated. Buzzing insects. Melting heat.

A cloud of chalky dust kicked up in the distance and drifted west behind an orange-and-green Plymouth.

The gravel road swung south. A lone metal building appeared.

"That's the warehouse," said Scooter.

Felicia gestured toward a smaller dirt road. "Go around back."

Serge pulled up tight along the rear of the structure and parked beneath a ventilation fan frozen with rust. "You sure this is the place?"

Felicia grabbed a crowbar and opened her door. "We'll soon find out."

They walked around the front to a gravel lot. Coleman took a slug of Southern Comfort and passed it to his new buddies. Serge picked up a charred hubcap. "This used to be a nice car . . ."

". . . And here's one of the bumpers," said Coleman.

"And a blast crater," said Savage.

"Scooter," said Felicia.

"What about him?" said Serge.

Felicia approached the warehouse entrance. "He blew it up."

"Scooter blew up a Ferrari?"

"It was an accident," said Scooter. "The thing just fired."

Felicia jammed the iron bar in a latch and popped off the padlock.

"Coleman," said Serge. "Stand lookout by the car. Just knock on the metal wall three times if you see anyone."

They slid open a door on screeching tracks. Shafts of sunlight hit the floor.

Serge stopped in the middle of the empty building and looked around. "You probably didn't know this about me, but I have a thing for women with crowbars. Actually not a thing. Crowbars just seem to come into play."

Felicia wasn't listening. She squatted down near the back.

"What is it?" asked Serge.

She stood and rubbed something between her fingers. Tiny pieces fluttered to the floor. "Sawdust."

"I'm guessing they weren't making cabinets."

"That's the spot," said Scooter. "Where they were checking the crates. I told you."

Felicia reached down again and picked up a scrap of plastic. "Packing shims from an RPG."

"The one that malfunctioned," said Scooter.

Felicia turned slowly and nodded. "Evangelista's place."

"Victor Evangelista?" said Serge.

"Ostensibly a respected businessman, highly connected politically. Rumors have been rampant for years, but nothing proven. And a lot of people who were doing the talking aren't able to anymore."

"I know his backstory," said Serge.

"Then you know he's arguably one of the biggest gunrunners in the hemisphere," said Felicia. "According to the rumors, Victor's been playing all sides for years. The generals, CIA, even the rebels."

"That's a short life expectancy."

"Normally," said Felicia. "Except everyone *wants* him to play all sides."

"I don't understand."

"CIA fronts pay him to secretly arm the generals, because Congress won't let 'em do it themselves. And both the generals and the CIA want him to arm the rebels."

"That doesn't make sense."

"Welcome to spy town." Felicia lit a thin cigar. "The rebels are a joke. Unless our governments arm them, they're worse than harmless, except when they come out of the mountains to beg for food or wash people's windshields."

Serge whistled. "If we armed all the windshield guys in Miami, you got an apocalyptic wasteland. Or more so."

"They have no choice but to arm the rebels."

"Why?"

"Because any regime bankrupt of even the slightest intelligent ideology needs to see enemies where there aren't any."

Serge nodded. "Glenn Beck."

"These are volatile times for my country," said Felicia. "It's no secret that for decades, our government—make that the generals—has been on the take. First it was letting drug smugglers pass through. And now guns. Except the volume of the traffic is far more than the junta and rebels could use in ten lifetimes. It's obvious that Costa Gorda has become a weapons pipeline and money-laundering haven for every tinhorn south of Mexico—and brings great shame to me and my homeland."

"Shades of Noriega." Serge placed a consoling hand on her shoulder. "But isn't it good that at least the guns are moving on and not staying in your country."

"No. It means more millions to skim for the generals, which means more power, which means they're able to override any legitimate democratic vote of the people. That's why the election of President Guzman worries so many."

"He's a good man," said Serge.

"Incorruptible," replied Felicia. "But he didn't get elected without also being an expert politician. Everyone's holding their breath over just how long his finesse can juggle the generals. Especially the generals."

"And I thought our politics was rough."

"I'm betting the military will eventually get too nervous and do something stupid, like a coup. Or a bullet." Felicia dropped the cigar and crushed it out with her foot. "My country's biggest hope is to expose the generals' financial network to the world. Except that seemed impossible until now. We've got to follow this trail wherever it leads."

"So you're a patriot," said Serge. "Even shorter life expectancy."

"I can take care of myself."

"You're the one who mentioned a bullet."

"But we're way up here in Miami. What can happen?"

Suddenly a crash through a side window of the warehouse. Serge knocked Felicia to the ground and shielded her with his body. "Stay down!"

He pulled a .45 pistol from behind his back and twisted toward the window.

Someone was crawling through the small opening.

"Coleman!" yelled Serge. "What the hell are you doing in the window?"

"I think I'm stuck." A grunt.

"You were supposed to stand lookout by the car."

"I got lonely."

Serge pointed the gun toward sunlight. "But the door's wide open."

A pause. "Serge?"

"Yes?"

"What am I doing in the window?"

"Talking to me."

"Does Felicia have any weed?"

"I don't think so."

"I'm going to wiggle back out now," said Coleman.

"Hope it works out for you."

A grunting sound. Then Coleman thudded to the ground outside. *"Ow."*

Felicia got up and brushed off. "We probably need to get moving."

"What was that?" asked Scooter.

"What was what?" said Serge.

"Thought I heard voices."

"I hear them, too," said Savage. "Does Coleman talk to himself?"

"Yes," said Serge. "But it's the language of children raised in the forest by animals."

From the rear of the warehouse: three knocks on a metal wall.

From the front: *"Who left the door open?"*

"Shit." Felicia spun. "The back door! Hurry!"

They raced outside. Serge quietly eased the exit shut, just as the first backlit silhouettes slid the front doors the rest of the way open for a motorcade of white vans.

Felicia crouched behind the Plymouth. She looked up at the ventilation fan. Voices again: *"We don't have all day. Get busy with those crates."*

*"The planes are waiting. It's a tight window."*

Serge whispered sideways. "Recognize them?"

"The first sounds like Victor," said Felicia. "The second's familiar, but I can't place it . . . Where are you going?"

"Follow me." Serge crawled on hands and knees to the corner of the building. He flattened himself and peeked around the side.

"See anything?" Felicia slithered forward in the dirt for her own look.

"No, just the back end of a white van . . . Get down!"

"What is it?"

A trail of dust coming up the gravel road. Five black SUVs. Serge aimed a small digital camera. *Click, click, click.* The dark vehicles pulled around the front of the warehouse and disappeared. From the ventilation fan: the sound of car doors slamming.

*"You're late! . . ."*

"I know the second voice now," said Felicia. "It's that Lugar character. His Miami station must be the one supplying Evangelista."

"I'm new to this business, but I think this is a good time to split."

"Unless we want to follow them . . ."

## BUILDING 25

A dozen tables pushed together. Agents breaking stuff open with pliers and hammers and razor blades.

"Where's Bamberg?" asked Oxnart.

The sound of a car outside. "There he is now," said an agent twisting the head off a dashboard hula girl.

Bamberg came through the door and dumped a box on an empty table.

"That the last of it?" said Oxnart.

"Except for what Lugar got to first."

Another agent cracked open a snow globe with a leaping dolphin. "What are we looking for anyway?"

"Maps, account numbers, microfilm. Who knows?" said the station chief. "Just keep looking."

An ashtray shattered. "But we're running out of time."

Oxnart checked his watch. "Damn. We're just going to have to pack it up and take it with us in the vehicles . . ."

Meanwhile:

"Step on it!" said Felicia. "You're going to lose them!"

"I'm doing my best," said Serge.

"How hard can it be to follow five black SUVs?"

Serge leaned over the steering wheel. "Except we're in Miami."

"So?"

"Miami drivers are a breed unto their own. Always distracted." He uncapped a coffee thermos and chugged. "Quick on the gas and the horn. No separation between vehicles, every lane change a new adventure. The worst of both worlds: They race around as if they are really good, but they're really bad, like if you taught a driver's-ed class with NASCAR films." He watched the first few droplets hit the windshield. "Oh, and worst of all, most of them have never seen snow."

"But it's not snow," said Felicia. "It's rain. And just a tiny shower."

"That's right." Serge hit the wipers and took another slug from the thermos. "Rain is the last thing you want when you're chasing someone in Miami. They drive shitty enough as it is, but on top of that, snow is a foreign concept, which means they never got the crash course in traction judgment for when pavement slickness turns less than ideal. And because of the land-sea temperature differential, Florida has regular afternoon rain showers. Nothing big, over in a jiff. But minutes later, all major intersections in Miami-Dade are clogged with debris from spectacular smash-ups. In Northern states, snow teaches drivers real fast about the Newtonian physics of large moving objects. I haven't seen snow either, but I drink coffee, so the calculus of tire-grip ratio is intuitive to my body. It feels like mild electricity. Sometimes it's pleasant, but mostly I'm ambivalent. Then you're chasing someone in the rain through Miami, and your pursuit becomes this harrowing slalom through wrecked traffic like a disaster movie where everyone's fleeing the city from an alien invasion, or a ridiculous change in weather that the scientist played by Dennis Quaid warned about but nobody paid attention." Serge held the mouth of the thermos to his mouth. "Empty. Fuck it—"

Felicia grabbed the dashboard. "Serge!"

He slammed the brakes with both feet. Then deftly tapped the gas, steering into the skid and narrowly threading the intersection.

The centrifugal force threw Felicia against the passenger door. "Did you see that moron slide into the bus stop? He almost got us killed!"

Serge floored it and stuck his head out the window. "See some snow, motherfucker!"

They continued south as the sun began baking rain off the streets with a familiar smell. Serge skidded through another accident-littered intersection, head out the window again. "Traction, pussy!"

"Serge, pay attention."

"To what?"

*Bam.*

Slightly crumpled hood. Radiator steam. Felicia glared at Serge.

"Hey, he stopped short. This is what I'm talking about."

"Thanks." She stared out the window. "You lost them."

"Not yet," said Serge. "Back at the warehouse they mentioned airplanes, and from where we are, that narrows it considerably."

Felicia pointed at increased steam blowing over the windshield. "But our car."

"Just a paint scratch." Serge threw it in reverse and looked over his shoulder. "Miami residents don't know how to drive after accidents . . ."

A rotund man in a custom Tommy Bahama shirt gazed skyward from the runway. A Coast Guard rescue helicopter took off for a rescue. Another idiot trying to cross the sixty miles to Bimini in a single-engine fishing boat.

A damaged Plymouth sat outside a fence with the hood up. Serge refilled the radiator with a gallon jug. Coleman, Scooter, and Ted lay on their backs in the weeds, passing a joint and staring at clouds.

"Far out."

Felicia stood next to Serge with binoculars, panning the Opa-locka Airport. "There's Evangelista and the white vans. But I don't see Lugar's guys or their vehicles."

"Don't look now," said Serge. He grabbed her for a deep, hard kiss as five black SUVs raced by and sped across the tarmac.

She pushed him away and raised the binoculars again. "A plane's landing."

"Lugar's crew must have gotten tied up in traffic, too," said Serge. "Told you we'd make it in time to see the shipment depart."

Felicia watched the Beechcraft taxi to a stop and the stairs flip down. Men from the vans went to the plane. Doors opened on the SUVs.

"That's weird," said Felicia.

"What's going on?"

She handed him the binoculars. "Take a look."

"That is weird," said Serge. "They're *un*loading the plane. And they're putting the crates back in the same SUVs."

Felicia grabbed the binocular's back. "Those aren't the same SUVs."

"Of course they are."

She shook her head. "The others didn't have the same window tinting. And I don't see Lugar anywhere."

"Tinting?" Serge clicked away with his digital camera. "Nobody's eyesight is that good from this range."

"Mine is and . . . wait, someone's got a briefcase. He's handing it to Evangelista." She adjusted the focus. "I know that guy. It's Oxnart, from the other CIA station."

"I remember him from Building Twenty-five," said Serge. "Lugar's rival."

"What the hell's going on?"

## Chapter TWENTY-SEVEN

**THREE A.M.**

Washington Avenue. South Beach scene in full swing.

Crowds hopped behind velvet ropes. Limos arrived.

Felicia and Serge strolled up the sidewalk, trailed by the bumbling trio. Scooter wore a hospital bandage on his left paw.

"I'm having trouble getting my head around this," said Felicia. "Arms coming and going."

"What's the plan?"

"I'll tell you when we get inside . . ."

The gang reached a corner and zigzagged into a dark alley. Four hard knocks on a steel door. A metal slit opened.

SPY.

Scooter Escobar raced for the back of the club and ordered drinks. Ted and Coleman joined him behind the laser gun. Felicia and Serge grabbed their regular table. The DJ waved down at her from his Blofeld perch and cued up a techo-dance version of the Johnny Rivers espionage classic.

Serge glanced at the Three Musketeers in the rear. "Let's hope it goes better this time."

"I think it will," said Felicia. "They had that fear-of-God look."

"Never stopped Coleman. He once broke arms on consecutive nights."

"At least Escobar doesn't think you're a foe anymore," said Felicia. "And they gave him a meaningless promotion for summit security to keep his uncle happy."

"Is Scooter really necessary?" Serge uncapped a bottle of water. "He's bad chemistry. Coleman and Ted don't need any more encouragement."

In the back of the club: "Check it out!" Scooter revealed an eight ball of cocaine under the table.

"Scooter's part of the plan," Felicia told Serge. "He's our entrée with some of the people on the other side that I need in order to fill in the missing pieces. They've started meeting him on park benches trying to get intel on us."

"And they trust him because he's untrustworthy?" said Serge.

"That's the picture."

"*. . . Secret agent man! Secret agent man! . . .*"

Serge leaned forward on elbows. "So what's next?"

Felicia unfolded a summit schedule on the table. "First order is protect Guzman. He's heavily guarded and impossible to reach except for two openings. The grand summit ball, and the final big speech onstage at Bayfront Park. We cover those two events, and otherwise we're free to continue tracking the arms."

Serge sat back in his chair. "Uh-oh."

"What is it?" Felicia looked around. "What's wrong?"

He pointed toward the laser. "They going in the restroom together again. Let the show begin."

"Serge." She reached and held his wrist. "There's something else important I have to tell you."

"You can't quit me, baby?"

"This part is really serious." She squeezed his wrist tighter. "You might be in grave danger. I want you to think hard before continuing on with me."

*". . . Odds are he won't live to see tomorrow . . ."*

"What's to think about?"

"Some stuff Escobar forgot to mention after the last time they mined him for information. They were asking about you in the same breath as the Guzman plot. I've seen the pattern before. Honduras, Bolivia. Here's how it happens: If a plot succeeds, the shooter will be dead within the hour. That might be you."

"Except I'm not going to shoot anyone," said Serge. "So I'm safe."

She shook her head. "Doesn't have to be the real shooter. Just a scapegoat. The proverbial lone gunman they've set up. With your criminal record and out-of-the-blue coziness with Guzman after the carjacking, you came to them on a platter."

"That's sounds too random."

"Because it is," said Felicia. "At first I thought the scapegoat was Savage—and probably he was. But you became a much better fit."

"You knew Savage was in town?"

"The entire intelligence community knew. The guy's a total screwup. That's his specialty: the all-purpose patsy, taking the fall for shit across the hemisphere for so long we can't remember. He thinks they burned him, but they're just keeping him on ice until the next blame-trip." Felicia signaled for another drink. "When he hit town last week, everyone was like, 'Okay here it comes. Something big's going down and the windshield's hitting Ted again.' Except it's never been anything so big that he'd be eliminated. You may have just picked the worst possible time to fill his shoes."

"But I'm all about timing."

Meantime:

In the restroom, a rolled-up twenty vacuumed a mondo line of Colombian Idiot Dust. Ted Savage snapped upright and grabbed his nose. "Fuck me!"

"My turn!" said Coleman. His face went down.

Escobar tugged Savage's arm. "Check this mother out."

"Holy cow! That's a freaking cannon!"

"You like it?" Escobar turned the black, nine-millimeter pistol over in his hand. "New military model only issued to special forces. Even fires in mud and shit." He ejected the clip and popped the top cartridge. "See the star formation on the tip of the bullet? Got an explosive charge, illegal everywhere. The bullet fragments like a tiny grenade, and what would normally be a tiny flesh wound to the shoulder will take an arm clean off."

"How'd you get it?"

"Received a huge promotion." Escobar held the gun to his face and stared down the barrel with his right eye. "Security for the summit. Guess they wanted the best."

Back in the lounge, the DJ cranked Paul McCartney.

Felicia knocked back another shot. "... And you'll need to be fitted for a tux."

"What for?"

"The big Diplomats' Ball at the summit tomorrow night."

"You're asking me out on a date?"

"... *Live and let die!* ..."

"This part's business," said Felicia. "For Guzman's safety."

"But I don't have any credentials. How will you get me in?"

"I can put us on the list. We'll make a great couple."

Serge pumped his eyebrows. "Then after that a real date?"

"If nothing goes wrong between now and the end of the ball."

"What could possibly go wrong?"

"... *Said live and let die!* ..."

*Bang.*

The restroom door crashed open. Two men came screaming through the lounge. Savage and Coleman ran up to the couple, crying and flapping their arms.

"Calm down," said Serge. "What did you go and do now?" He looked around. "Where's Escobar?"

Louder crying, pointing back at the restroom with shaking arms.

Serge noticed their shirts. "Blood again? How'd you cut yourselves now?"

Felicia jumped up. "They didn't cut themselves. That's spatter."

Savage wiped tears. "It was an accident." He lifted his shirt to show them the giant pistol he'd spirited out of the restroom.

"Are you crazy!" Serge glanced around fast and snatched the gun. "The bartender's already calling the cops."

Felicia took off running with Serge close behind.

They pushed open the men's room door and froze.

"Dear God!" said Felicia.

"What a mess!" said Serge.

"Where's his head?" said Felicia.

Distant sirens.

She grabbed Serge's arm. "We need to get the hell out of here."

## COSTA GORDA

Clouds drifted below.

Poking from their wispy curls was a steep mountain rising high into the jungle rain forest. Lush, humid, loud with colors and birds.

Jutting off the side of the mountain, just above the cloud line, sat a mansion. Red barrel-tile roof. Walls of coquina, hewn and helicoptered up. A courtyard with twin rows of palms down the sides of an elongated pool. At one end stood a towering bronze statue of General Montoya Escobar, which appeared handsome, august, and nothing like the general. At the opposite end of the water, just inside a granite balustrade that prevented a sheer drop into the tree canopy, stood the general himself.

A lone bird of prey circled above.

On the far side of the compound, a series of hollow booms.

"Pull!"

A clay disk sailed over the trees. A general in a jacket with leather elbow pads raised a vintage double-barrel.

Boom.

Soldiers with machine guns patrolled atop walls and down in the jungle paths around the base of the compound.

General Escobar lifted his arm above the balustrade. A peregrine falcon circled a final time over the mountain and came in for a talon landing on Montoya's glove.

The same scene every weekend, a collision of class and crass. Dom

Pérignon, skeet shooting, falconry, and art masterpieces throughout the residence, where all the TVs were on *Baywatch,* and the pool full of naked women and drunk old generals peeing in the shallow end.

Or at least the TVs were usually on Pamela Anderson. Today they carried dubbed-in satellite reception from Miami.

"... *This is Eyewitness News Action Seven Noon Report. We take you to South Beach and the site of an unfortunate fatal accident* ..."

Another channel.

"... *Action Eyewitness Nine, from just off Washington Avenue, where police are releasing few details outside a club ironically called SPY* ..."

Another channel.

"... *Unnamed sources identify the victim as Scooter Escobar, an intelligence agent attached to the Costa Gordan consulate, who is also the nephew of a five-star general—*"

A hand turned off the set. A trusted colonel walked across the patio to Escobar. "They're ready."

Escobar released his falcon for more airtime.

His inner circle left the skeet-shooting platform and sat solemnly around an outdoor table at the base of a fountain featuring swans and Greeks. Other lesser generals staggered from the pool in Speedos and picked up the idle shotguns.

"*Pull!*"

*Boom.*

They went round the circle at the table, expressing deep condolences, which Escobar accepted with solemn nods. Then he angled forward with folded hands. "Gentlemen, this was no accident."

One of them looked toward the house. "But they said on television—"

Montoya held up a hand. "Forget what they say. It was a message."

"From who?"

"No confirmations yet, but I have a pretty good idea. There's a new player in Miami. Close to Guzman. Word of our plot has obviously leaked out."

A travel attaché held up a photo from consulate surveillance. Someone being thrown out the door and to the ground.

"What do we do?" asked the general on his left.

"Move up the schedule. The summit ball is tonight."

"What about this new player?"

"If we're lucky, one stone, two birds."

*"Pull!"*

*Boom.*

Escobar looked over his shoulder and snapped his fingers. An aide promptly appeared and placed a solid-gold telephone on the table.

A general raised his hand. "But the summit ball . . . I mean, won't that attract a lot of attention?"

"That's why we create a diversion." Escobar finished dialing and raised the receiver. "This is Escobar, give me the head of internal security . . . Carlos, I need a favor. Yes, television . . . five minutes will work . . ."

From the other end of the table: "General, who would you like us to use?"

Escobar hung up the phone. "Who's available?"

"We already have our top asset in place."

"Hate to burn that one in case we have to abort," said Escobar.

"There's the backup we always keep in Miami."

"Let me see the files . . ."

*"Pull!"*

*Boom.*

Soon the table was covered with classified reports on rice paper. Discussion, advice, debate . . . then a voice from the house: "Sir, it's coming on TV."

They left the scattered documents and went inside. On the largest flat-screen plasma, a Costa Gordan broadcast from the capital: *"Breaking news at this hour as a surprise rebel offensive has raised the national threat level . . ."* The camera swung to a large vinyl banner of a chili pepper with a fresh, dark red square at the top.

*"Pull!"*

*Boom.*

An explosion of falcon feathers.

# Chapter **TWENTY-EIGHT**

## DOWNTOWN MIAMI

The Performing Arts Center.

Stretch limos stretched around the block.

Back doors opened. Couples emerged in tuxedos and evening gowns. Heavy on diamonds and elective surgery. The limos pulled away and more rolled up.

VIPs entered the historic Olympia Theater and passed through the metal detectors cloaked in decorative cloth. Guards at three security checkpoints examined credentials and matched invitations against the guest list. Police snipers perched on adjoining rooftops.

The Diplomats' Ball.

A man in a white tux approached the first checkpoint. Nobody looking at him. Because of the Latin bombshell on his arm.

"These credentials . . ." said the first guard, glancing back and forth at his lists. "I'm sorry, but I'm afraid I'll have to ask you to step aside." He got on the radio.

A limo longer than the others pulled up. Camera flashes. Passengers emerged and arrived at the checkpoint. Security men snapped to attention. "Good evening, President Guzman." No need for his papers.

Guzman looked to the side. "Is there a problem?"

"Sir," said a security agent with a clipboard. "They're on the list, but he doesn't have the correct color badge."

"It's okay." Guzman threw a smile off to the side. "I'll vouch. They're with me."

"Yes, sir, Mr. President."

Guzman put an arm around Serge's shoulders and looked over the gleaming tux. "You clean up pretty well."

White-gloved waiters circulated with sterling trays of hors d'oeuvres, caviar, and crystal champagne flutes. Someone tinkled a grand piano. A hundred overlapping conversations under eighteenth-century oil paintings in gold frames.

"Glad you could come," Guzman told Serge.

"You kidding? I'd have made it if I had to crash this thing."

Guzman laughed. "Not much chance of that with all this security."

"That's what they said about Obama's state dinner when that hot blond chick and Dom DeLuise slipped through to meet the president, knocking Balloon Boy clear off the front pages. Did you hear about Balloon Boy down where you live? I want to be Balloon Boy. I've made some rough sketches."

Guzman laughed heartily again. "That's why I'm glad you came. You're a real person I can have a normal conversation with. I'm required to attend these parties, but I hate them. The more wealthy and powerful the guests, the more vapid the chitchat. Plus, everyone's so guarded, worried about slipping and saying the wrong thing because everyone else in the room is a potential enemy for career and social standing."

"Except if the party goes late and everyone gets plowed," said Serge. "Then it's completely surreal. When the working class gets hammered, they throw beer bottles at the banjo player and break their necks on mechanical bulls. But if the A-list goes in the bag, you see things you can't make up, like walking in an unlocked bathroom, and someone on the museum board is jerking off in a cummerbund."

"Might want to keep your voice down," said Guzman. "But go on. I'm enjoying this."

"I made this one shindig in Ocala. That's Florida's horse country. Limos arriving at a giant mansion on a hill surrounded by pastures and stables, and in the beginning it's all very sophisticated bullshit with everyone in formal wear. Except the woman of the house greeting her guests at the door in riding boots. And the riding helmet. And holding the riding crop. And I'm like, we get it. You want attention. Isn't it enough that everyone knows you're ridiculously rich with stables full of racehorses? No. She has to dress like she'd just finished a fucking steeplechase. And she's one of these types with a fake Martha's Vineyard accent who has to introduce herself to everyone with *three* names. 'I'm Meredith Astor Farthington, of the Providence Farthingtons.' And I roll my eyes, and go, 'I'm Serge Alexander-the-Great Storms, by way of Hobbit-Town.' Then I look over her equestrian outfit and say, 'I guess nobody else got the memo that this was a costume party. What were you last time, a pirate?'"

Guzman covered his mouth to suppress mirth.

"And here's something I learned about the rich: They're so touchy," Serge continued. "After my little joke at the door, the woman's face turns all red, and that riding hat was about to start spinning on her head like a teacup. I decide to disappear in the crowd. Fast-forward three hours: blue-blood, wall-hugging drunk time. Remember me saying these people get surreal? Most people don't realize how tall a horse actually is. I'm a little over six feet myself, and I'm looking eye level across a sea of bald and gray skulls packed like sardines in a humongous living room. And suddenly this big horse neck and head sticks out of the mob! That Missy dame I met at the door must have been worried we'd forget she had horses, so she brought in Mr. Ed and just let him roam, all these aristocrats slidin' in horseshit. I'm hanging back and digging it with the bartenders. This can't possibly get any better! Guess what? It got better! The woman still doesn't have enough attention. She has to *ride* the horse. Indoors. Through a crowd. Now, it's her house. You think she'd know where all the chandeliers are. *Bam!* Right in the nose! She flips off the back of the thing into the fireplace. So they're throwing drinks trying to put her out, and the horse rears up and busts the bathroom door clean off the hinges, and it gallops over a table of food before diving through the bay windows into the swimming pool, and these other people run over and lift the bathroom door off this unconscious guy with no pants and a cummerbund. Man, that dude had it right when he said, 'The rich are different from you and me, and in more ways than having more money.'"

Guzman caught his breath from laughing. "Who said that?"

"The guy at the interstate ramp who washed my windshield."

"Let's go to the bar. I'm thirsty."

Working through the crowd, snatches of dialogue: *"Can't say enough about that dress . . . Oh, he's more than just our gardener . . . spending the summer in Aspen . . . Here's the number of my stylist . . . Remington's been accepted at Andover . . . More than a gardener? I'll say: banging her rear door in the greenhouse . . ."*

They reached the bar. "God," said Guzman. "Did you hear all that drivel on the way over?"

"I can see why you dread these gigs." Serge requested ice water in a martini glass. "Not a single interesting conversation in the house."

In the back of the room: "They really are going to assassinate him?"

"Shut up!" said Malcolm Glide. "Jesus, people are around!"

"But the generals have lost their minds. I just got word Montoya went on the warpath after his idiot nephew shot himself, and they held a secret meeting at his house in the mountains."

Glide grabbed a glass of champagne off a passing tray. "It's their internal business."

"Not if it happens here. That could ruin everything."

"And it could ruin everything if you don't stop yapping and someone overhears."

"I also heard they moved up the schedule," said Victor Evangelista. "Which means it could be here. Tonight. At *this* ball. And our people lost track of Serge. That's no coincidence, going off the radar just before a sanction."

"Serge?"

"Our intel thinks he's who they're going to use. They placed him close to Guzman with the foiled carjacking that they no doubt used as a setup."

"You worry too much."

"You should, too," said Evangelista. "If the generals pull something stupid, it could expose the shipments, everything, even the you-know-what—"

"Shut up! Fuck!"

"But we'll go to prison for life."

"Look, if it makes you feel better, I'll place some calls tomorrow and smooth this out," said Glide. "Meanwhile, relax and enjoy the party. There's no way Serge could get in here with all this security."

"You really think so?"

"Definitely," said Glide. "Now calm down before you give yourself a heart attack."

"You're probably right." Evangelista took a deep breath and removed his hand from his beating chest. "Serge is probably a million miles away."

A spoon began hitting a glass.

*"Excuse me! Excuse me, everyone! May I have your attention? I'd like to propose a toast . . ."*

Glide mumbled to his left. "Who is that? I don't recognize the voice. And I know everybody here."

"I can't see him. Too many people in the way."

"I'm going to stand on this stool."

At the opposite end of the room, a man in a white tux stood on another stool in front of a baby grand piano.

Glide grabbed his head. "It's Serge!"

"He's doing a toast? Holy God, we're going to jail . . ."

Serge raised a cup of coffee and looked down at hundreds of people. "When I said 'toast,' I meant plural. I've got a few. Okay a ton. There's so much to say that I typed it up on shelf paper, like Kerouac writing *On the Road*." He set the cup down, then grabbed the edge of a paper spool and let it unroll to the floor. "First, a big toast to all you fine people for putting the *Latin* in Latin America. To be completely honest, Americans are terrible with geography. You're just a vague group of interchangeable countries on the map where all the men are required to grow mustaches. But we're neighbors and have to start mending fences somewhere." Serge craned his neck. "Is Guatemala here?"

A hand in the middle went up.

"Sorry about the CIA coup in '54," said Serge. "Ouch! And it was launched right out of here in Florida, instigated by the United Fruit Company. And over bananas, literally. It would be funny, except it really happened. Okay, it's still funny. Condolences . . . Chile?"

Another hand went up."

"Sorry about Allende and '73," said Serge. "It was the government, not us. We weren't paying attention. You're just too far away and half the people think you're Argentina . . . Panama?"

Another hand.

Serge smiled. "You look like that guy in the Dos Equis ads, the Most Interesting Man in the World. I was pining for that title, but hey, how's the Canal Zone coming? Colonial ways die hard, but we did eventually get that one right. And the invasion was just a phase . . . Venezuela?"

A hand. "Over here."

Serge shook his head and wagged a finger. "Venezuela . . . Venezuela . . . You've been a bad boy, like at the United Nations, saying you could smell sulfur at the podium where George Bush stood the day before, like he was Satan. Personally it cracked me up, but wrong room, okay? Remember Khrushchev banging a shoe in '61? " He looked out across the rest of the guests. "The point is, we all have our differences, and the United States isn't the only one with dirty hands. Human rights, death squads, street kids in Rio, the 'disappeared,' Madonna playing Eva Perón. Hey, we all make mistakes. That's how nature made us: fight, eat, and diddle. But when it comes to fighting, real enemies aren't always nearby, so instead we quarrel with our neighbors, the people most like us who should be our best buddies. It's happening all over the world. Some Arabs hate the Jews. Not most, but I'm sure you've heard the stories. Except a Jew isn't always handy, so they split into Sunni and Shiite and attack each other. And over what? I guess who hates Jews more. Christianity? One word: Ireland. And all across the U.S., red and blue states. Even Florida, at a church up in Gainesville: 'What would

Jesus do? Burn the Quran!' It's in our blood—evolution tells us we have to hate somebody. Most scientists agree on this except creationists, who hate evolutionists. But I've got the answer: We just shift our primal directives to eating and diddling, because a well-laid dude with a stomach full of lobster Newburg ain't strapping on any suicide vests, if you know what I mean, and I think a few of you out there do . . . All right, I see I'm losing some of the wives out there tonight, so on with the big toast, which I hope will soon become the unofficial slogan of the summit." Serge raised his coffee cup and voice. "Let's give each other slack!"

The audience stared.

"Come on," said Serge. "Get those glasses up!"

Guzman raised his. "Everyone! Glasses up!"

They complied.

"That's more like it," said Serge, raising his own goblet higher. "To slack!"

*"To slack."*

"Louder!"

*"To slack!"*

In the back of the room, Malcolm Glide slapped himself in the forehead. "This is a disaster."

Victor Evangelista collapsed against a wall. "I feel faint."

# Chapter **TWENTY-NINE**

**MEANWHILE . . .**

Four blocks from the Diplomats' Ball, a high-rise hotel overlooked Bayfront Park.

On the fifteenth floor, a man who had dyed his blond crew cut lay on the bed, watching a blank picture tube. The bed was made and the man was clothed. An empty room-service tray by a lamp.

A cell phone sat on the nightstand. It remained still.

One floor below, another man lay on his bed. Another TV remained off.

The cell phone on his nightstand began to vibrate.

The man flipped it open and read a text message.

"!"

He closed the phone and walked to the dresser. A black leather bag rested open.

The man checked the contents, zipped it shut, and headed out the door.

Victor Evangelista grabbed Malcolm by the lapels. "We have to do something! Serge is making a scene!"

"Let go of me!" Glide shoved him. "We need to keep our heads until we can get an undercover detail in here."

"For what?"

"To capture Serge," said Malcolm.

"And then?"

"Get him to one of our black-box locations and find out what he knows."

"What if he doesn't talk?"

"Either way, he won't see the sunrise." Malcolm dialed a cell phone for reinforcement.

"But look at all the attention he's getting," said Evangelista. "It's too high profile to make a move."

Malcolm closed his phone. "Chill out! Serge finished his toast. Now he'll just fade back into the obscurity of the crowd."

"That makes sense. We'll hang tight. Time is on our side . . ." Victor stopped and glanced around. "Is someone playing the piano?"

At the front of the room, Serge's fingers tickled the ivories as he scooted the stool up to the baby grand. ". . . And now, to celebrate our new era of slack, I'd like you all to gather round while I play an inspirational song for global understanding."

"But, Serge," whispered Coleman. "You don't know how to play the piano."

"They don't know that." Serge finished warming up and cracked his knuckles. "This song has just a few simple notes at the beginning that I taught myself, and when they start singing along, no one will notice the rest . . ." He looked up. "Everybody ready? . . ." A few slow, repetitive notes on the keys. Serge cleared his throat:

*"Hey . . . Jude! . . ."*

"Jesus!" said Evangelista. "He's playing 'Hey Jude.'"

"We have to hurry," said Glide. The pair began working their way along the walls past steam trays.

"I can barely move in this mob," said Evangelista. "Look how far the entrance is."

"We'll get there," said Malcolm. "Just stick behind me . . ."

They continued pushing forward, brushing past a man with a black leather bag going the other way.

". . . *Naw . . . naw . . . naw . . . naw-naw-naw-naw . . . naw-naw-naw-naw . . . Heeeeeey Jude . . . .*"

Glide and Evangelista finally broke through the crowd. They reached the sidewalk in front of the Olympia Theater and waited for a black van.

Back inside, everyone crowded round the piano, getting sloshed, joining in. The song reached its climax.

Serge jumped up and kicked out the stool, banging the keys like Jerry Lee Lewis. ". . . *Jude-ay! Jude-ay! Jude-ay! Jude-ay! . . . Yowwwww-www! Owwwwwwww! . . .*"

More drinks grabbed off trays and downed. Everyone singing along at the top of their lungs.

Serge hit the keys a final time, stood, and bowed to wild applause.

Guzman slapped him on the back. "I didn't know you could play the piano."

"Neither did I."

The president laughed again. "You're quite the people person. I could use someone like you."

"I have to take a squirt."

"And you always get to the point."

A line of people shook Serge's hand as he headed for the restroom. Felicia trailed behind.

"Just be a minute," said Serge. He ducked in the door. Seconds later, he stood whistling at a urinal. He stared at the ceiling. Then the floor. "What the hell—"

His urinal was next to the handicapped stall. On the floor, barely visible below the partition, the edge of a dress shoe. Turned sideways.

"That's pointed the wrong direction for anything good." Serge finished his business and tried the stall door.

Latched.

He got down on hands and knees. Inside, a man slumped on the floor. And a black leather bag.

Serge wiggled underneath and felt veins on the man's left wrist. Then checked the bag.

The bathroom door burst open.

"What's up with you?" Felicia looked him over. "And your tux is filthy—"

"It's the doctor!"

"Who is?"

"How they're going to take out Guzman!"

"Slow down," said Felicia. "What's going on?"

"Does Guzman have a regular personal physician?"

"He always travels with one, but we use several different ones."

"The real one's dead in there. Handicapped stall," said Serge. "The bodyguards won't be alert to the doctor. We have to find Guzman—and a guy with a black leather bag."

They rushed back into the ball.

"What about the dead guy?" asked Felicia.

"I left the stall locked and pulled his leg inside so nobody would find him," said Serge. "If panic breaks out, it'll make the killer's job that much easier."

Felicia reached in her clutch purse. "Take this." She slipped a small .25-caliber automatic in his hand.

"There's Guzman!" Serge waved urgently.

Guzman cheerfully waved back.

"He doesn't understand," said Felicia.

"We have to get to him!"

They began pushing their way through the crowd. "Sorry . . . Apologies . . . Sorry . . ."

Felicia grabbed Serge's arm and pointed another direction. "There's a guy with a black bag. He's heading toward Guzman."

"And he's closer." Serge dispensed with apologies. Shoving people, spilling drinks.

"He's almost there," said Felicia.

"So are we."

"We're not going to make it."

"Failure isn't an option," said Serge. "Guzman!"

"He still can't hear," said Felicia. "The music's too loud."

More drinks spilled.

"The guy's reaching in his bag," said Felicia.

"What the fuck is that thing?"

"Pneumatic hypodermic gun."

"Shit, Guzman's back is to him." Serge elbowed past a waiter. "He can't see it coming."

President Guzman shook hands with an attaché from Ecuador. "Haven't seen you in a while."

"Congratulations on your election."

"Thanks." A smile. "But now the hard part . . ."

The man with the black bag inched closer. The last person between him and the president stepped out of the way. Clear shot. Nothing but the back of Guzman's tux.

The Ecuadoran attaché took a sip of champagne. "So how are the generals treating you these days?"

"We've resolved some differences," said Guzman. "But there's always going to be that with the military."

The glinting tip of a hypodermic gun neared his back. Two feet. One. Six inches. Finger on the trigger.

The fake doctor felt a small barrel in the middle of his back. And a voice over his shoulder. "I wouldn't do that. Put it back in the bag."

He did.

"Now start walking," said Serge.

The man remained still.

Felicia poked his ribs lightly with the tip of a stiletto blade extending from a lipstick. "I'd listen to him."

This time he began moving.

All three ended up back in the restroom. Serge gave Felicia the gun and crawled under the stall again. He unlatched the door. Felicia pushed the man inside.

"Interesting," said Serge. "There's a dead guy on the floor and no reaction from you. Most innocent people would comment."

"You're pointing a gun."

Serge glanced casually at his hand. "Just a formality."

Felicia shoved the man into a wall. "Who sent you to kill Guzman?"

"What are you talking about?" The man rubbed the back of his head. "I'm his physician."

"Sure you are," said Serge. "Then what's the deal with the hypodermic gun?"

"Oh, *that*," he said, nodding. "The president was complaining of fatigue. Lack of sleep from all his appointments here. I was going to give him a vitamin-B injection."

"Serge," said Felicia. "What are you doing?"

"Going through his bag."

"I see that. What for?"

"We're going to have fun," said Serge. "What have we got here? Maybe I can use this. And I can definitely use this . . ."

"Serge!" Felicia looked around quickly. "We don't have time. Someone could walk in here any minute!"

"This will be express fun." He reached in his pocket and tossed something to her. "Bind his hands behind his back."

"Plastic wrist restraints?"

"Always carry some to parties," said Serge. "You never know what the theme's going to be."

Felicia pulled the strap tight as Serge laid out medical supplies atop the toilet tank. "So you're really a doctor?"

"Absolutely."

"But maybe your certification has lapsed in this country." Serge picked up a blood-pressure tester. "So I'm going to give you a field exam to see if you're still up to snuff."

Serge wrapped the tester around the man's neck and fastened the Velcro. "They always put these on people's arms. But the neck is much more accurate." Serge began squeezing the black rubber bulb. "Wow! You're off the charts!"

". . . I . . . can't . . . breathe . . ."

Serge eased off the pressure until the slightly deflated ring hung loose around the man's neck.

The man trembled uncontrollably. "Dear God! Please don't strangle me!"

"Strangle you?" said Serge. "Never. What gave you that idea?"

"So you're going to take this thing off me?"

"Didn't say that." Serge grabbed an empty syringe and a small surgical vial. He slipped them under the blood-pressure wrap, one on each side of the man's trachea. Then he squeezed the bulb a couple times to hold them in place.

Felicia stared in confusion. "What are you doing?"

"Placing braces beside his windpipe because we wouldn't want him to stop breathing." Serge smiled big in the man's eyes. "How's your breathing?"

"Okay."

"Felicia, your purse."

She tossed it. "What are you looking for."

"Here's a lipstick. And a nice fat pen." He held them up to the man's face. "This is your medical recertification test. If you really are a doctor and not an assassin, this should be a breeze and I'll let you go. I always like to give my students an escape clause." He stopped to grin again. "Don't you just love the suspense?"

Felicia nervously peeked over the top of the stall at the restroom's outer door. "Will you hurry?"

"Don't sweat. It's just a one-question test." Serge turned to the captive. "And here's the question. Answer right, and I'll take that thing off your neck and you're free to leave. Now, I'm going to reinflate that tester to the max. But first I'm going to place these two items next to a blood vessel to relieve the pressure. And that's the name of my new game show: *You Pick the Blood Vessel!*"

"So if I pick right, nothing will happen to me?"

"No, you'll pass out. That's definite." Serge began squeezing the bulb again. "But I'm a trained professional. I'll catch it in time and cut you loose. You'll come back around pretty quick."

"And if I guess wrong?"

"You won't pass out."

"That doesn't make sense."

"It does if you're a doctor." Serge squinted at him. "You wouldn't be lying to me about that, would you?"

"Serge!" said Felicia.

"Almost done." He turned to the captive. "What? No idea?" A frustrated sign. "Okay, I shouldn't be doing this because it's against contest regulations, but here's a hint." Serge tapped two different spots on the man's neck. "Jugular vein or carotid artery."

Silence.

Serge squeezed the bulb. "If you don't pick, I'll do it for you."

"Okay, carotid."

"Interesting choice." He slipped the lipstick and pen under the inflation ring. *Squeeze, squeeze, squeeze, squeeze . . .*

"He's not passing out," said Felicia.

*Squeeze, squeeze, squeeze.* "No, we're well past that point."

"Look at his face! It's completely red."

"Purple's up next," said Serge. *Squeeze, squeeze . . .*

Eyes bulged. Then his whole head began vibrating like a paint-can shaker in a hardware store. Spastic tremors through all limbs, feet slapping the tiles.

The outer restroom door opened.

"Serge," Felicia whispered. "Someone's here."

An undersecretary from Montevideo stepped up to the urinal. The thrashing in the adjoining stall couldn't go unnoticed. "Is everything okay in there?"

Felicia intentionally fell back against the stall's wall with a loud moan. *"Mmmmm, yes, oh yes, baby . . ."*

The undersecretary chuckled to himself. He'd been to a lot of these balls. He zipped up and left.

Felicia stared down at a foot still twitching from residual death rattles. She seized Serge's hand. "We're out of here! Now!"

They sprinted back to the ballroom, then composed themselves in the doorway and resumed walking at a casual pace.

"What on earth did you do to that guy back there?"

"Long explanation," said Serge. "But a great dinner story. Involves the history of Florida Championship Wrestling and the infamous sleeper hold. We'll grab a bite later."

On the other side of the room near the main entrance, Victor Evangelista hung on to a brass railing. "If this goes sideways . . ."

"Shut up," said Malcolm. "These guys know their job." He turned and gave a nod.

Five new men slowly fanned out across the ballroom around the central axis of President Guzman.

Guzman smiled. "Serge, where have you been?"

"I'm like a cat. Whenever I'm in a new building, I have to explore."

Guzman smiled. "Then you haven't seen the *whole* building."

"Why do you say that?"

"Because if you had, I'd be able to tell." Guzman looked toward Felicia. "Why don't you take her and check out the other big room through that ornate door. It's the mini-expo where countries tout local goods and attractions."

Serge glanced through the door. "Burlap sacks of coffee beans must be Colombia. The colorful, twirling carnival dancers, Brazil."

"Machu Piccu diorama, Peru, obviously," said Guzman.

"Wait . . ." Serge took a couple steps left to see farther into the room. "I don't believe it. A horse! A real horse!"

"Argentina," Guzman said with a grin. "Was waiting for you to notice."

"What a coincidence! Come on, Felicia, this is a gas."

Guzman watched with amusement as the couple departed. The president's mouth slowly turned down as Serge approached the archway. A certain simultaneous confluence of movement had begun. Funneling behind Serge. A guy here, another there and over there, deliberately scattered in the vast crowd so nobody would give a second thought unless they were Secret Service. Or a politician who gave a lot of speeches in public. Guzman continued observing the men, whose converging vectors defied random cocktail-party mingling. "This is not good."

Guzman quickly gathered his own security detail from the loose pocket surrounding him. He pointed through the arch and snapped orders.

"But, Mr. President, you'll be unguarded."

"Rodriguez and Acevedo, stay with me," said Guzman. "The rest of you, move!"

On the far side of the expo room, next to the Juan Valdez impersonator, Serge stroked a horse's mane. "Hey there, fella. You like canapés? Try these . . ."

The horse lapped Serge's hand.

Glances shot back and forth across the room, slight nods exchanged in a five-point spread formation. The tallest agent in the capture unit uncapped a tranquilizer needle concealed in a fountain pen.

The pattern tightened toward Serge.

Behind them, a second pattern flowed in the same direction at a faster pace. It filtered between the men in the first formation like a basketball team getting back in transition for defense. It was man-to-man coverage. The one with the needle was first to hit the ground from a stun gun in his ribs.

And so went the element of surprise. Malcolm Glide's intercept team knew they had company, and they weren't hard to identify. Guzman's security chief hit the floor from a wicked right cross. A wholesale brawl broke out; the startled crowd began shrieking and running. Another of Guzman's agents took a hard blow to the temple. Just before going down: "Serge! Catch!"

Serge looked over from the horse. A small stun gun flew through the air. Serge snatched it, about to make a break.

But two of Glide's boys had gotten through. Serge dropped the first with a loud *zap*. Then he made his move. He grabbed Felicia's hand. "Up we go." The second capture agent raced forward with his own stun gun. He lunged and zapped, but Serge saw it and dodged.

The sizzling electrical arc missed him. And hit something else . . .

Back in the main room, President Guzman watched a screaming, panicked crowd stampede through the doorway. Followed by Serge, atop a wildly galloping horse with a fresh stun-gun burn on its hind quarter.

Felicia held on tight from behind. "Chandelier!"

"Got it," yelled Serge. They ducked.

The trusty steed took the corner, continued galloping down the lobby carpet and out the front doors of the Olympia Theater.

Two tourists stood on a street corner.

"There's a guy in a white tuxedo racing up Flagler on horseback."

"It's Miami."

# *Chapter* THIRTY

**THE NEXT DAY**

South of Miami.

Felicia checked her watch.

Serge checked his camera. "This is going to be so cool! I haven't taken pictures here since they filmed the TV show."

"We're not doing this for your entertainment." Felicia watched traffic signs. "Take a left."

"I know the way." Serge slipped the camera in his pocket. "You sure have a hard-on for this Evangelista character."

"He's the biggest arms dealer in Miami, and he's threatening to destabilize my country!"

"Maybe that's a tad dramatic," said Serge. "Ow, you popped me in the ribs."

"Your own government is in bed with him!"

"Now wait a minute. That would be illegal."

"The Iran-Contra Affair was illegal and look where that led."

"Ollie North got a cable-TV show. Haunting."

"I'm not amused." Felicia pulled out a scrap of paper with coded times and locations. "We need to finish tracking these shipments before the big summit finale."

The Road Runner turned into a wooded entrance and pulled up to a booth. "Four tickets, please."

Felicia looked up the road. "There's another black SUV. Give me your camera."

"Now you're talking."

Felicia snapped photos as they drove by.

Serge parked with the rest of the tourists. Actually only two others because it was an educational Florida attraction with no water slides or tiki bars.

Coleman hopped from the backseat. "I've seen this place before."

"Television." Serge began walking. "It's the historically designated Charles Deering Estate, over four hundred majestic acres on the shore of Biscayne Bay. Now a museum. The ceiling of the south porch is inlaid with seashells."

"Check the size of that freakin' lawn!" said Savage.

"And to the left are the landmark rows of palm trees made famous every Friday night in the opening credits of *Miami Vice*." Serge stroked one of the trunks. "It's like I'm at the Vatican."

"Stop screwing around!" yelled Felicia. "Let's go!"

Serge caught up with her at the front door. "Where are we heading?"

She marched inside. "The wine cellar."

The quartet trotted down stairs.

A Latin man in a guayabera came the other way up the steps. He glanced suspiciously at Felicia, then looked back down at a tourist pamphlet.

Serge turned and watched the man depart. "You know him?"

"In passing."

Serge winked at Coleman. "Told you spies meet in museums."

"Wine cellar?" asked Coleman.

"Deering liked his grapes, but it was Prohibition." Serge grabbed a wooden support and swung it back and forth. "So he built this bookcase that secretly rolls out to reveal that giant safe door."

"The wine is in the safe?"

"The safe is a subterranean party room."

They slipped inside the half-foot-thick metal door with ancient tumblers and entered the clandestine space. Curved, concrete bunker roof supported by brick arches. Walls covered with custom woodwork creating a thousand individual slots.

"Whoa!" said Coleman. "Look at all the wine bottles!"

"And recessed tables that conveniently fold down for festivities."

"What's Felicia doing?"

She was at the back of the room, reaching in a cubbyhole. Four rows down, sixth wine bottle from the left. A tiny square of paper unfolded in her hands.

Serge went over. "Fan mail from some flounder?"

"My friend in the stairwell." She mentally decoded the symbols, then handed the paper to Serge. "Destroy that."

He tore it in pieces and handed them to Coleman. "Eat these." Then back to Felicia: "What did it say?"

"It's happening sooner than I thought."

"Where?"

"Right here, right now." She looked around. "But why this place?"

"Maybe because it's got spy history. At least in fiction." Serge looked up at the ceiling. "The estate is all coming back to me now. In Season Two of *Miami Vice*—eighth episode titled 'Bushido'—Lieutenant Castillo used the estate as a safe house before retreating to the grove of palms for his climactic confrontation with a Russian secret agent named Surf . . . Where'd Felicia go?"

Coleman dropped an antique wine bottle, but Savage made a nice save with his foot. It bounced harmlessly. "She ran up the stairs."

"You two stay here." Serge took off. He reached the front steps and made a sharp right for the logical location. Sprinting across the expansive open lawn that stretched down to Biscayne Bay.

"There you are." Serge ran up to where Felicia was hiding behind one of the palm trees in the landmark grid. "This is exactly where Castillo hid from Surf."

She grabbed a fistful of his tropical shirt and yanked him behind her. "Get out of sight."

"What's going on?"

"Hear that?"

"Yeah, sounds like an aircraft . . . And there it is. A seaplane."

Another sound.

The pair scooted farther around the tree. Two heads peaked out from behind the trunk, stacked on top of each other, as five black SUVs raced past them toward the waterfront.

"This is my favorite feature of the estate," said Serge. "On the outcropping at the very back of the lawn, Deering built a seawall inlet from the bay in the shape of a giant keyhole."

"Quiet!"

"The airplane's too loud."

It was. The plane did a belly flop in the boat channel and motored through old coral heads into the keyhole. The SUVs were already backed up with open doors. Crates came out.

So did members of the museum staff, who trotted down to the shore wanting answers.

Badges flashed. Federal.

Good enough answers. They left.

"Did you see who that was?" said Felicia.

"Agent Lugar again," said Serge. "What the hell is going on?"

The plane finished loading and began taxiing away for takeoff. It lifted from a froth of waves, banking serenely over Key Biscayne before catching a flash of sunlight and disappearing into the clouds.

"Get back," said Felicia.

The pair ducked behind the palm as five departing SUVs sped away.

## MIAMI MORGUE

Two bodies on metal slabs.

A homicide detective burst through the doors.

The medical examiner put down a sandwich and grinned. "Good news. No sharks today."

"I'm not laughing. What the hell happened at the summit ball?"

"Two dead guys."

"Already know that," said the detective. "I was there when they wheeled them out of the restroom."

The examiner gestured at one table. "That guy was a doctor from Costa Gorda. Identification in his medical bag. He took a large injection of tranquilizers and potassium. Knocked him out and stopped his heart like that." A snap of his fingers. "We found a hypodermic gun half full of the stuff"—he pointed at the other body—"in that guy's medical bag. Been used in assassinations."

"So dead guy number one killed dead guy number two?"

"Looks that way."

"Then who killed the first guy?"

"Don't know, but I'd love to meet him," said the examiner. "Haven't seen this technique before. Heard about it from TV as a kid, but thought it was just make-believe theatrics."

"TV?"

"Florida Wrestling. Practically the granddaddy of the sport in America. Broadcast in the sixties from the Fort Hesterly Armory and the Sportatorium in Tampa. Gordon Solie, Jack and Jerry Briscoe, the Army of Darkness—"

"Okay, okay, I get it. I grew up here, too. What's that got to do with the stiff?"

"One of the most feared maneuvers was the dreaded sleeper hold. Someone like Dusty Rhodes would apply it with forearms on the top and bottom of the head. Then the nemesis passed out, and an antidote maneuver had to be applied to wake him up. Except that last part really was showbiz. The 'sleeper' is a choke hold, but it doesn't cut off air like the others; it cuts off blood. If the hold actually was applied, the victim would wake up on his own when blood returned to the brain."

"Then why didn't our pal here wake up?"

The examiner giggled. "This is where it gets cool." He held up an evidence bag containing random everyday items. "These were used as braces and placed under this blood-pressure tester that was wrapped around his neck. Next to the windpipe."

"What the hell for?"

"Why else? So he could apply a sleeper hold, of course. Once I saw the Great Malenko—"

"You're driving me insane! What killed him?"

The examiner raised another bag.

The detective scrunched his eyebrows. "Lipstick and a pen?"

"That's why I want to meet this guy. We've got a new, more exciting version of the 'sleeper' on our hands." He tossed the evidence bag aside. "The whole contraption was designed not to cut off blood to the brain, but *from* the brain."

"You lost me."

The coroner stuffed the rest of the sandwich in his mouth and talked as he chewed. "Compress everything, and you got a classic 'sleeper' pass-out. But compress only the jugular, and leave the carotid open . . . Blood keeps flowing upstairs with no place to go."

"That's a murder?"

"Ever had your car radiator boil over?" The examiner wiped mayo off his mouth with surgical gauze. "In his case, ultramassive intracranial hemorrhage."

"I don't know what that means."

"His head exploded from the inside, like a stroke, except times a hundred."

"And that makes you smile?"

"Must have been interesting to watch."

## Chapter THIRTY-ONE

**THAT NIGHT**

A camera flashed, illuminating blue-and-gold bas-relief friezes along the top of a vintage Art Deco landmark.

Another flash. This time from a Bic lighter. Coleman fired up a toke from a prosthetic leg with a Willie Nelson bumper sticker. "What is this place?"

"Historic Dinner Key." Serge raised his camera again. "Just south of downtown on the shore of Biscayne Bay. Used to be an island, but they filled the gap to Coconut Grove."

"What's that building you keep taking photos of?"

"Miami city hall." Another camera flash. Serge uncapped a thermos of coffee. "Wasn't always city hall. That just started in the fifties, but—and this staggers the trivia-hungry mind—it used to be one of the largest airports in the world!"

Smoke drifted across the parking lot. "That little building?"

"The old Pan Am terminal was the main connection between

North and South America." Another camera flash, swig of coffee. "And the other structure over there used to be an airplane hangar that became the public arena where Jim Morrison of the Doors was arrested for exposing himself in 1969, and later the Floridians of the ill-fated American Basketball Association played home games. Can you freakin' dig it?"

"Yeah, buildings." Coleman exhaled. "But where are the runways?"

"Weren't any." Serge drained the rest of the thermos and raised arms. "It was the golden age of seaplanes, like the Sikorsky F-40s and of course the Brazilian Clipper. Passengers boarded from floating barges. Charles Lindbergh landed his Lockheed here in '33 after a transatlantic flight."

Felicia came running around the corner of the building. "What's with all the camera flashes? We're supposed to be on surveillance. And I could smell the dope all the way down to the dock!"

Coleman and Savage waved and smiled. Serge ran in a circle.

"Serge!" she snapped. "What are you doing?"

"Dribbling an invisible basketball and grabbing my crotch. It's a history mash-up."

Coleman took another hit. "The Doors."

"Knock it off!" said Felicia. "Just got a tip from the Canadian consulate. Might be our big break."

"The antique, winged Pan Am clock still hangs in the city council chambers." Serge pointed. "Let's take a look through the windows, shall we?"

"No!"

Serge pointed another direction. "Then can we fuck behind the hangar?"

"No! . . . How can you be aroused at a time like this?"

Serge looked down at his sneakers. "I drank coffee and there's a bunch of old stuff around. That usually does it."

"Hurry! They should be here any minute." She looked back up the road. "And we already have company. Don't turn around."

Coleman turned around. A black SUV sat in the darkness on the shoulder.

"Are they the people we're waiting for?" asked Serge.

"No, another interested party taking surveillance photos. If my hunch is right, that's part of their plan." Felicia ran around the side of city hall and led them down to the waterfront. Binoculars went to her eyes. "Coleman, what the hell are you doing?"

Coleman was down at the edge of the bay, floating something out into the water. "Catch and release. I'm setting the fake-leg bong free so it can drift to distant places where someone else can enjoy it. That would be far out."

"Just stay alert." A propeller sound in the distant sky. Felicia raised her binoculars again. "There it is now, on schedule . . . Oh, Serge, take me!"

"I thought you said this was an inappropriate time to be aroused."

She caressed her left breast. "Espionage, danger, remember?"

"Right." He pointed. "Behind the Jim Morrison hangar."

The pair took off in a sprint. Serge stopped and turned around. "Coleman, what the hell do you think you're doing?"

"Coming with you."

"Coleman!"

"I won't watch. Much."

"Go back to the parking lot with the walkie-talkie and do what I said."

"Poo."

Moments later:

*"Oh God! Oh yes!"* shrieked Felicia. *"Faster! Faster! . . ."*

Serge was on top, thrusting at maximum speed and looking out over her head with binoculars. A Grumman Mallard made a splash landing in the unseen waters, one of the few seaplanes in recent years to visit Dinner Key.

*"Don't stop!"* Felicia dug her fingernails into Serge's neck. *"I'm coming! I'm coming! Oh my God! I'm coming! . . ."*

A walkie-talkie squawked next to her head.

He grabbed it. "Serge here. Come in, Coleman."

"Are you still fucking?"

"Yes, what's up?"

"Nothing. I was just trying to picture it."

"... *I'm coming!* ..."

"Was that Felicia?" asked Coleman.

"She's busy."

"Can I listen?"

"No. Call back when you have something."

Serge set the walkie-talkie down and grabbed the binoculars again. The Grumman eased up to the dock ...

Over in the parking lot, Coleman kicked a pebble.

Three white vans pulled up the circular drive and took a side road that led around behind city hall.

Coleman keyed his walkie-talkie. "Serge?"

"What?"

"I'm hungry."

"So am I, but you don't see me stopping what I'm doing."

"Hold on," said Coleman. "I couldn't hear you. Three white vans just drove by."

"Did you say three white vans?"

"Yeah, like we saw at that other place. Can we order a pizza?"

"Coleman, you were supposed to be on the lookout for three white vans."

"I thought it was six polka-dot cement mixers."

"Coleman ..."

"The vans are heading your way. Now they *are* becoming polka-dot cement mixers, melting together in a big, glowing blob that's yodeling through a 'crazy' straw to my soul."

"You dropped acid, didn't you?"

"No, I would never ... Is it obvious?"

"Dammit, Coleman!" Serge jumped to his feet.

Felicia sat up with a wild mane of sex-hair. "What's the matter?"

"Here come the vans." They watched from the shadows until the vehicles passed. "And Coleman's tripping. Hope you enjoy surprise parties."

"Tripping?"

"It's like herding infants in traffic. Last time he filled his underwear with lightbulbs and played a solitaire version of 'duck-duck-goose' for two hours."

"Why?"

"I don't even ask anymore. There's Victor Evangelista."

They looked down toward the dock and couldn't miss Vic's billboard of a Tommy Bahama shirt. Van doors opened.

"Look," said Serge. "It's Agent Oxnart again."

"They've started unloading the plane," said Felicia. ". . . Six, seven, eight . . ."

"What are you doing?" asked Serge.

"Counting . . . eleven, twelve, thirteen . . ."

"Why are you counting?"

"Shhhhh, you'll mess me up . . . seventeen, eighteen . . ." She zoomed in with the binoculars. "And the branded codes in the wood. I just figured it out. I can't believe it."

"Figure out what?"

"Those are the same crates."

"What do you mean?" said Serge. "They're refilling similar boxes?"

"No, they're the exact same ones. See for yourself." She handed him the binoculars. "From the warehouse to Opa-locka to the Deering Estate to here. Lugar, Oxnart, Lugar, Oxnart." She shook her head. "None of the arms ever left the city. They're just running laps around Miami. And every time Evangelista gets paid on both ends . . . That's the real reason we were detecting so many more guns than my country would ever need."

"Told you it was a typical CIA operation."

Felicia took a hard breath. "This is worse than I thought."

"What?" said Serge. "I thought you'd be happy the weapons aren't reaching Costa Gorda."

"That's when I thought the arms were the goal. But they're just a means to an end, and I don't know what the end is."

"Why do you say that?"

"Because Evangelista would be dead for sure if he was pulling this double rip-off on his own. Our generals and your agents would be tripping over each other to put a bullet in him." She stared at the stars. "Someone much bigger is behind this, with a bigger agenda."

"And you don't think it's the generals?"

Felicia bit her lip. "Just this feeling I have. Something the dead newspaper reporter mentioned that I can't get out of my head."

Serge covered his eyes with both hands. "Please, God. This isn't happening."

"I didn't know you cared so much about my people."

"Not that." Serge nodded toward the dock. "Infants in traffic."

"Coleman's going down there and talking to them? What the fuck!"

"Surprise."

"Do something!"

Serge raised his walkie-talkie. "Coleman, you need to get out of there!"

Felicia tugged Serge's sleeve. "Why isn't he answering his walkie-talkie?"

"It's in his underwear."

Coleman looked down at his talking crotch. "Trippy."

Felicia jumped up. "I've got to stop him!"

Serge grabbed her arm. "Beyond the point of no return. Best to let it play out."

"But he could wreck everything."

"Usually it gets so weird, people just dismiss him as a street loon."

"He's patting them on their heads."

"Duck-duck-goose."

"They're aiming guns at him!" said Felicia.

"The game is more competitive than I remember."

The hatch closed on the plane. Mooring lines uncast for emergency takeoff.

"See?" said Serge. "Evangelista's intervening and trying to cool them out. Maybe he's done LSD and knows the score." Serge keyed the walkie-talkie again. "Excuse me, Mr. Evangelista. Please don't harm my docile friend. He's just on acid."

Felicia and Serge watched in the distance as Victor stared down at Coleman's pants. *"Who the hell was that?"*

"Uh-oh," said Serge. "More guns."

Shouting in the distance again. Evangelista firmly extended his arms to regain command of the troops. "No! No shooting! It's a critical time for our operation back in Washington. Put the safeties back on—now!"

A goon in a jumpsuit pointed an Uzi at Coleman. "But he saw everything. First Scooter and now this."

"He's just a drug addict!" yelled Vic.

"What about the voice in his pants? . . ."

The arguing between Evangelista and his men escalated. The plane began taxiing off in Biscayne Bay. A heated shouting match.

Felicia squinted from behind the hangar. "What on earth is he doing now at the back of that van?"

"Oh, Coleman," said Serge. "Not even you . . ."

One of the jumpsuits pointed. "Look!"

Everyone turned to see Coleman with an RPG on his shoulder.

Victor held out a calming hand. "Easy with that. Try not to make any sudden moves. You don't want to touch anything."

The Grumman lifted off from the water.

Coleman touched something.

*Wooooooooshhhhhhh.*

Everyone ducked.

The rocket-propelled grenade streaked across the night sky, exploding through the seaplane's left wing and fuel tank. The fireball lit up everything for miles, and debris plunked down into the water like flaming rain.

The launcher hung loose by Coleman's side. "Far out."

The Road Runner screeched up. Felicia jerked him into the car. Tires squealed.

Evangelista: "They're getting away!"

Everyone ran to the vans and patched out, but the Plymouth was already gone.

## Chapter THIRTY-TWO

### THE ROYAL POINCIANA

The elevator reached the bottom floor, and Serge opened the accordion cage.

He led Coleman and Ted through the lobby. They suddenly froze.

"Felicia," said Serge. "What are you doing here? We weren't supposed to meet for another two hours."

"You've picked up a tail. The guys we ditched last night at Dinner Key must have traced your hotel." Her eyes shifted. "And one of them is already in here. Tan windbreaker. Don't look."

Coleman looked.

"Dammit," said Serge. "He always does that."

"It's moot anyway." Felicia felt inside a shoulder bag for her purse gun. "They know you're staying here. You were made before you got off the elevator."

"Suggestion?"

"The only option is a shake. And since they've already acquired us

284

visually, it'll be a hot pursuit." Felicia made sure her shoulder bag was zipped tight and clutched fast to her side. "From your police record and knowledge of Miami, I'm guessing you've been here before."

"My specialty." Serge bent down to double-tie his sneakers. "Everyone ready?"

Felicia looked toward the lobby door and took a deep breath. "Lead the way."

From the rear: *"Excuse me?"*

They turned. The hotel manager waved a stack of note cards behind the bulletproof glass. "Mr. Storms, you have a message. Actually several." He slid them through the metal slot. "From the owners of those bodegas you shipped all that stuff to."

Serge sighed. "I told you I'd get all their money back. I just need a little more time."

"It's not that," said the manager. "They canceled the refund requests. And want to double their next orders."

"What happened?"

"Completely sold out," said the manager.

"Which ones?"

"Every island. Said they've never seen merchandise move so fast."

"Serge!" said Felicia. "We have to get going!"

They did, hitting the sidewalk in a sprint and making a sharp right behind Serge's lead.

Seconds later, a man in a tan windbreaker ran out to the curb. He waved hard for a black SUV parked across the street. The vehicle screeched up.

One block west, Felicia hit her aerobic jogging pace, one of the few ever to keep up with Serge. "Where are we headed?"

"Foolproof way to lose a tail in Miami." He dashed through an empty intersection without breaking stride. "We're bringing another of the city's cultural districts into play."

"How far away is it."

"Pretty far."

"I don't think Ted and Coleman will make it." She looked back. "And here comes the SUV."

"No problemo," said Serge. "The final destination is miles off, but the star gate's coming up quick. Fifty feet."

"Star gate?"

"The free People Mover."

Serge and Felicia ran up the stairs to the monorail platform. She looked down over the railing. "The SUV's parked right below the station."

Serge hopped on the balls of his feet. "This is going to be so much fun!"

Ted and Coleman finally staggered up the steps. "We can't go on." "We're gonna die!"

A monorail pod pulled up. Doors opened. Serge gave them a shove. "In you go."

The tram pulled out. An SUV began rolling on the street below.

"We're moving too slow," said Felicia. "And there are so many stops. We'll never lose them."

"Yes, we will," said Serge. "That's the job of our escape guide. He'll be our control agent. I just need to make contact."

"Who's that?"

"I don't know yet."

"Then how will you recognize him?" asked Felicia.

"Random street person. Preferably homeless."

"You're looking for someone in disguise?"

"No, the real thing," said Serge.

"I don't understand," said Felicia. "Is he expecting you?"

"No," said Serge. "We've never met. And probably never will again."

"Now I'm totally confused."

Serge surveyed fellow commuters in the pod. "Street people are the best to help you navigate a city's underbelly and lose tails. Plus they don't cost much, but you have to break the payment up in small pieces or they'll simply run away. Just as long as you keep feeding them ones and fives like bread crumbs, they'll remain loyal protectors like the family dog with bacon treats."

Felicia stood up. "This is ridiculous. We're getting off, and I'm taking charge."

"Trust me," said Serge. "It's one of Miami's untapped resources, convenient and ubiquitously located all over the city like newspaper boxes or trash cans. And especially in the People Mover because it's free and air-conditioned, like a mobile public library."

Felicia stepped to the doors as they approached the next station. "Coming with me or not?"

Serge's eyes locked on the rear of the pod. "Here's our guide now." He walked to the rear of the car and took a seat next to a lean, forty-year-old black man with bloodshot eyes and laceless sneakers. His tattered Miami Hurricanes jersey had been selected from the bottom of a storm-water culvert. Clutching a brown paper bag.

Serge smiled and extended a hand.

The man stared at it with disdain. "Who the fuck are you?"

"Serge Storms. You must be my contact agent."

"Agent?" The man's eyes widened as he shrank back into the corner of the molded bench. "Don't hurt me! Don't take away my thoughts!"

"Why would I do that?" asked Serge.

"Because you're with the CIA. I told them at the shelter, but nobody would believe me."

"I believe you," said Serge. "I'm not with the CIA, but I am *running* from them."

"You, too?"

Serge spread his arms. "It's exhausting."

The man tapped his left temple. "They have implants."

Serge rubbed the side of his own head. "Mine still hurts."

"It'll go away." The man removed a grungy Marlins baseball cap. "I lined the inside with tinfoil. You should get one."

Serge held out his hand again. This time they shook.

"Name's Jimmy," said the man.

"Jimmy . . ." Serge pointed at the brown paper bag. "Can I buy you another?"

"Sure."

"Okay, we'll need to find a liquor store."

"What are you talking about?"

"Your bag."

"I don't have booze in here."

He handed the sack to Serge, who glanced oddly at Jimmy before reaching inside and pulling out five paperbacks. "Kurt Vonnegut?"

"I read all the time." Jimmy nodded at the books in Serge's hands. "And that guy knows the real shit, man! The whole fuckin' lay-down: time travel, other planets, alternate planes of existence. You need those if you're going to survive in Miami."

"Couldn't agree more."

Jimmy took the books back. "So when was the last time you saw the agents?"

Serge pointed down out the window at a side street running parallel to the monorail. "There they are now."

Jimmy leaned toward the safety glass, then covered his mouth in horror. "One of the black SUVs! We have to get out of here. Follow me!"

The next platform approached. Serge waited with Jimmy just inside the pod doors and grinned at Felicia.

She exhaled with dwindling patience.

The doors opened . . .

Five minutes later, Coleman looked out the back window of the city bus. "Still following us."

The bus slowed at the next stop. Jimmy stood up. "Time to switch transpo."

One block behind. A passenger in a black SUV with binoculars: "They're switching again. First the People Mover, then a public bus, and now a jitney. How much training does Serge's new contact have?"

"I don't know, but do you see where we're heading?"

The passenger lowered his binoculars. "Liberty City? At night?"

"The home of the Miami riots," said the driver. "One of the highest crime rates in America, and birthplace of some of the biggest rappers ever to grab a mike. The contact agent is probably their go-between with that faction. They've diversified into all kinds of other underworld endeavors."

"The rappers are involved? Christ!"

"Just keep watching."

He raised them to his eyes again. "You sure you want to go into Liberty City? We can always say we lost them."

The driver's knuckles turned white. "Just don't think about it."

The passenger adjusted his binoculars. "They're getting off the jitney. And running across a vacant lot to where another bus is just pulling up at that stop."

"Standard evasion. Hang on!"

The driver raced to the next intersection and made a skidding turn, then another, putting them at the bus stop on the other side of the lot.

"Where's the bus?" asked the driver.

"Up there two blocks. Stay with 'em."

"I'm trying to, but there are a lot of cars."

"Where could they be heading?"

The bus took a left on Seventy-ninth Street and drove beneath the interstate.

"We're getting deeper into Liberty City."

"And they're getting off the bus. They're starting to run again."

The SUV blew a red light but got jammed up in traffic. Cars filled both lanes. The driver of the SUV leaned on the horn. Occupants of the vehicles in front of them got out . . .

Serge and the gang ran up a dark sidewalk. Shadows in alleys, vacant people milling outside a fortified convenience store. Youths in white T-shirts rode bicycles in circles. The bicycles were too small for them.

Three blocks back, traffic cleared. The SUV began moving again. It passed I-95 pawn and the Tropicana Club. "Where'd they disappear?" said the passenger. "We need to go faster."

"You try driving with busted headlights and a cracked windshield."

They stopped again behind other cars, but no horn this time. Some of the alley people approached the van.

"Screw this," said the driver, making a screeching U-turn and racing back toward Biscayne. "I mean, we really did lose them, right?"

The passenger stowed his binoculars. "That's what my report will say."

Serge smiled. "Told you we'd lose them."

Coleman looked around the inside of a dark room and clutched his buddy's arm. "But where are we?"

"Hot Nitez." Serge grinned again at the three unamused bouncers blocking their path. Thick, folded arms, neck tats, detachable brass-knuckle belt buckles.

"Serge," whispered Ted. "We're the only white people."

"I'm not prejudiced."

"I'm scared."

The largest bouncer took a step forward. "What are you guys doing in here?"

"Just boys 'n the hood," said Serge.

A stiletto snapped open. "And you just walked into the wrong club."

"Oh, it's the right club," said Serge. "Bet Luther Campbell got his start here. Big Supreme Court case. I'm down with 2 Live Crew."

"You're 2 Dead Crew." A lascivious grin with diamond teeth. "But the lady can stay for my personal tour."

"Get your fucking hands off me," said Felicia.

"A tiger. I like it."

From behind: *"Man, they're cool! They're cool!"*

"Shut up, Jimmy!" said the bouncer. "You crazy bringing these crackers around?"

The new arrivals at the door had everyone's attention. Conversation at all tables ceased. Even the rapper onstage stopped and strained for a view around his microphone.

Big hands began seizing them.

"Hold it a minute!" said Serge. "There's no need for that. We heard it's open mike night."

The bouncers laughed. "Did you hear that shit? Our boy here thinks he can flow."

"Oh, I can rap all right," said Serge.

"And I'm George Wallace."

"Make you a deal," said Serge. "Give me the mike, and if I roast this joint, you let us go home."

"Shit, you get over and we'll *give* you a ride home," said the first bouncer.

The second bouncer smiled with diamond teeth. "Even let you pick the cuts on the car system."

Coleman tugged his shirt. "Serge, you know what you're going to sing?"

"No idea."

"Serge!"

"Relax. Rap is all about improvising, and I do my best work under pressure . . . I just need your help."

"Me?"

"After each couple verses, we'll do a short, two-part chorus. I'll elbow you when it's your part."

"What do I say?"

"Whatever pops in your head." He looked at the bouncers: "And I'll need coffee . . ."

A minute later, Serge was at the mike. If the place was quiet before, it was now a tomb. A clubful of people stared with latent violence.

"Wow," said Serge. "Tough room." He killed his coffee and turned to a DJ at the turntable. "Give me something upbeat . . ."

Synthesized music throbbed from a dozen industrial speakers.

Serge shuffled quickly in place, shooting gang signs. Then a hyper set of jumping jacks and push-ups.

The audience exchanged odd looks.

Serge finished warming up with a series of somersaults toward the center of the stage, jumped to his feet, and grabbed the mike:

> *Serge is back, Jack, with all new facts*
> *The South Beach Diet and bikini wax*
> *Burmese pythons, the pit bull attacks*
> *Cunanan, Shaq, German tourists in T-backs*

*I roll like Ricky Martin in "La Vida Loco"*
*Caught the Mariel down to Calle Ocho*
*Dissed the TEC-9s, and the dealers with the blow*
*And the motherfuckin' drivers who have never seen*
*snow.*

*Serge:* Miami's trivia pimp is just the way that I rap.
*Coleman:* Look at all the black people. I think I'll crap.

*Brazilians, the Euros, and all the Latin foxes*
*Winning their hearts with all my souvenir boxes*
*The beautiful ladies are what propel my rants*
*From* The Golden Girls *to the chicks with implants.*

*Survived the hurricanes and the oil spills*
*Syringes on the beach and OxyContin pills*
*The hookers, crackheads, meth freaks with bad gums*
*Saw the Orange Bowl come down with the Sterno bums.*

*Serge:* I'm stormin' ashore with all the rhymes you'll ever need.
*Coleman:* Is anybody out there holdin' any weed?

*Smacking down the predators with just one hand*
*While rockin' out to KC and the Sunshine Band*
*The Dolphins, the Marlins, the Panthers, the Heat*
*Geriatric brawls at the shuffleboard meets.*

*Janet Reno, Don Johnson, cigarette boats*
*City-hall bribes, stolen election votes*
*Anglo flight,* dos cervezas, por favor
*Got my OCD buzz on like an epileptic whore.*

*Serge:* Packin' cameras, my pistols, Florida DVDs.
*Coleman:* The other night I spit up in my BVDs.

*You're welcome for a visit, but you better not laugh*
*Carjackings, race riots, drug informants sawed in half*
*Cavity searches and the AWACs aircrafts*
*Bales in the surf and the refugee rafts.*

*The Gables, the Grove, cruisin' Biscayne Bay*
*I float like a flamingo, and sting like a ray*
*Givin' preservationists all of my hugs*
*And only anal love for the litterbugs...*

Serge and Coleman bowed. The crowd came to its feet in wild, unending applause.

Ten minutes later. A low-riding Cadillac DeVille cruised out of Liberty City with the top down. Serge, Felicia, Coleman, and Ted all crammed in the backseat of the whip. Giant chrome hubs. Amped stereo system with magnum subwoofer in the trunk, pumping out the tunes:

*"Sweet home Alabama..."*

*Chapter* **THIRTY-THREE**

**NEXT MORNING**

Felicia had the wheel.

Ten more blocks, then a red light at Eighth Street, more commonly known as "Calle Ocho," the main drag and social artery through Little Havana.

"Where'd you get this tip?" asked Serge.

Felicia sped up to make a yellow light. "Someone deep in our military."

"That you slept with?"

"Don't be disgusting. It was a hand job."

Coleman tapped Serge's shoulder. "I miss Ted. Why'd we leave him at the motel?"

"Because you gave him all those pills. He'll regain consciousness." Serge turned back to Felicia. "So where's this fool's errand taking us?"

"Fifteenth Avenue."

"Fifteenth?" said Serge. "You don't mean Máximo Gómez?"

The next thing Serge knew, Felicia was pumping quarters into a parking meter. "We need to keep an ultralow profile. I can't stress that enough. There are way too many people around. Absolutely no unnecessary attention."

Serge stood on a street corner, staring at a gold bust on a marble pedestal. A man in a military jacket with a wildly bushy mustache. A brass plaque: GENERALISSIMO MÁXIMO GÓMEZ, 1836–1905, *LIBERTADOR DE CUBA*.

His trance shifted to the public park behind the statue and a living tradition of the old days. Under the shade of awnings, dozens of old, espresso-fueled Cuban men in straw hats sitting around special tables, playing furious games of dominoes.

"Serge!" said Felicia. "Were you listening?"

"Right, no extra attention."

Minutes later: Everyone's attention on one particular table. An excited crowd clustered tight behind the chair of the man holding court.

"Now, this is how you play dominoes!" said Serge, lining up the little white rectangles. A chorus of urgent Spanish whispers.

In the background, a wall with a mural of Latin leaders from some past hemispheric summit. In front of the wall, a bench. Felicia sitting, shaking her head.

Serge extended an arm without looking. "I need more!"

Someone slapped a leather case in his hand.

"Espresso me!"

Someone else held a tiny thimble of jet-fuel coffee to Serge's mouth. Felicia sagged.

It took another ten minutes, but Serge finally reached the last domino, gingerly setting it on end. "Now observe and regale."

His index finger dramatically reached for the last rectangle, slowly tipping it over. And they were off! The initial row of dominoes fell like, well, dominoes, then forked and broke into multiple lines, snaking, curving, making jumps, reaching another table that had been pushed over, until they were all down, and the underlying pattern took shape: the island nation of Cuba in red, white, and blue, below a motto. CASTRO SUCKS COMMIE COCK.

A mighty cheer went up.

Everyone pressed forward to shake Serge's hand and slap him on the back.

"I'm his best friend!" said Coleman, who immediately had a giant cigar stuck in his mouth while another person lit it.

Felicia remained alert. The crowd began to disperse, revealing someone she hadn't detected before. A bulbous man in a Tommy Bahama shirt wiped his brow, departing toward Calle. She stood up on her bench, drawing on years of surveillance training, taking in the audience as a whole and filtering its movement for the one who stood out.

She found him.

Another bench near the gold statue. A man rose with a folded newspaper, pulled the brim of a Panama hat down low over his eyes, and headed in the same direction as Evangelista. Carrying a briefcase.

Then she saw Coleman weaving erratically across the patio. "Uh-oh."

He crashed into Serge, knocking him against the table and scattering the dominoes that spelled *cock*. Cuban expatriates scrambled to realign them.

"Coleman!" said Serge. "Watch it, man."

Coleman wavered on his heels, pupils like pinholes. He held out the cigar. "What's in these things?"

"Where'd you get that?"

Felicia ran over. "We gotta split. They're on the move."

"Who is?"

"Evangelista and his contact."

"You saw the contact?"

"Not his face. They're heading west on Ocho."

Serge jumped up. "Coleman, we have to—" He looked around. "Coleman?"

Coleman stared upward with a smile of total peace. "My nuts like this." His eyes rolled back in his head and he toppled over.

"Coleman!"

Felicia dashed for the street. "I'm going ahead. Call you on your cell..."

## CALLE OCHO

Coleman grabbed a lamppost and panted. "Why did Felicia have to take the car?"

"Coleman, you never smoke a cigar in Little Havana. They're stronger than the coffee." Serge shielded his eyes against the sun and looked up the street. "Enough rest. We need to shake a leg!"

Coleman pushed off from the pole and began staggering again. "How much further?"

"Farther. Three blocks."

"I don't think I can make it."

"You're acting like vultures are circling."

Coleman pointed at the sky. "What are those?"

"Vultures. Don't look up anymore."

"I think I'm going to faint."

"See the restaurant sign up there?" Serge dragged him toward it. "Cuban cuisine."

*"Versailles?"* asked Coleman. "Is that Spanish?"

"No, ironic," said Serge. "Like back at the Official Little Havana gift shop—in arguably the most virulent anti-Communist enclave in the world—selling souvenir domino sets 'Made in China.' My own people no less...Just keep walking."

"Serge?..."

"Whoa!" Serge dashed over and yanked him back onto the sidewalk. "Try to stay out of traffic."

Coleman tripped over the curb. "How come you always know where you are in Florida?"

"Lots of hours with maps, photos, and an aggressively encouraged obsessive-compulsive order."

Coleman stumbled forward. "Don't you mean *dis*order?"

"Only when it's a bad thing," said Serge. "But those people have problems. Like the ones who hoard newspapers and magazines until their homes are stacked to the ceiling with little place to walk until the piles eventually collapse, and the bulldozers find them crushed to death by their own shit. That's why I only collect small souvenirs like pins and matchbooks."

"Has it ever collapsed on you?"

"Yes, but I only twisted an ankle," said Serge. "Speaking of geography awareness, did you notice all the double street signs around here?"

"Double?"

"Saturating idiosyncrasy throughout Little Havana." Serge steadied Coleman by the arm and continued west. "There are the regular designations on the signs like Fifth Avenue and Tenth Street, and then second memorial names, mainly Cuban patriots, prominent politicians, a Brothers to the Rescue pilot shot down by a MiG, and José Canseco. The sign for Miami Sound Machine Boulevard kept getting stolen until Gloria Estefan's solo career took off. Her father actually participated in the Bay of Pigs." Serge pointed various directions. "They've used up so many signs that they're running out of space and starting to triple up, like Southwest Seventh Street/Claude Pepper Way/Calle Simón Bolívar . . . Don't think too hard about it and just let the magic wash over you . . ."

Coleman stopped at another lamppost. "How come Little Havana looks so different from all the other places we go in Florida?"

"All the signs are in Spanish?"

"No, I get that," said Coleman. "Just something . . . *off*."

"I know what it is," said Serge. "Look around and it'll hit you."

Coleman slowly rotated in place on the sidewalk. Transmission shop, pawnshop, bakery, nail salon, *farmacia,* meat market. He stopped turning when he was facing Serge again. "Still can't place it."

"No chain stores!" said Serge. "All independent mom-and-pop's. Not a single Rooms-to-Fucking-Go in sight. Isn't it heaven?"

"I think I'm dying."

Coleman didn't die. But he wasn't attractive when they finally reached air-conditioning and the maître d's stand inside Versailles.

A spiffy-dressed man cradled menus. A professional smile. "Two for lunch?"

"Three." Serge angled his head toward a table. "The rest of our party's already here."

"Right this way . . ."

The maître d' led them on a winding course through the dining room, toward a seated woman staring daggers at them.

"Great," Serge said sideways to Coleman. "Another chick pissed at me. The pattern of my life."

"Maybe she has gas," said Coleman.

"No, it's chicks. I'm always in trouble without a clue. Married men are geniuses."

"Could be her time of the month."

"You might have something there." Serge nodded to himself. "That would explain it. When it's the wrong day—grab a helmet! I just give 'em all my money, point at the door, and say, 'Call me when *The Exorcist* is over.' Now I feel guilty for misjudging her . . . On the other hand, if she isn't on the rag, I'm unfairly being taken advantage of for my sensitivity."

"Why don't you just come right out and ask her?"

"Used to do that, but funny thing: Even if the answer's no, it only seems to make things worse. You and I freely exchange information without getting huffy."

"I always warn you not to come in the bathroom when I'm spanking my monkey."

"Exactly," said Serge. "But women clearly don't want that kind of data. And then they barge in without knocking and have a problem with *that*."

"They don't understand because they use appliances."

"Better pipe down now—we're almost there."

They arrived at the table.

Serge manufactured his most engaging smile and pulled out his chair. "Sorry, we're late."

Coleman pulled out his own chair. "Are you on your period?"

"What!"

Serge chuckled awkwardly and punched Coleman in the shoulder. "Ow."

Serge scooted his chair in and opened a menu. "What looks good?"

Felicia stared down at her own menu. "Notice the corner booth by the front window?"

"Yeah," said Serge. "Evangelista, eating alone."

"The contact went to the restroom before you arrived."

Coleman nudged Serge and giggled. "Spanking it."

"Serge!" said Felicia. "What's wrong with your friend?"

He shrugged. "I keep trying to explain the off-limit topics around women, like how a lot of guys walking down the street are mentally undressing you gals and fantasizing tittie-fucks."

"Serge!"

"Just giving an example of an off-limit. How else will you know what a gentleman I am?"

"This is serious." She glanced again at Evangelista's table. "That's the contact's briefcase next to his chair."

"Recognize this contact?"

"Yes, but I don't remember where." Felicia turned a page in her menu. "American. I think he's famous or something. Was hoping you could peg him when he comes back."

"Do my best." Serge squeezed lemon into his water. "Whoever it was did me a favor by picking this place as the meet point. I could eat anything in here, especially the palomilla steaks."

Coleman knocked over a glass. "Didn't break. No foul . . . What's so special about the joint?"

"Versailles is the cultural dining epicenter of Little Havana. It's an off hour right now, but at peak times, this place is a humming hive of exile political debate."

"Looks like a regular restaurant."

"You know how CNN sends reporters to barbershops in Iowa and interviews customers for the common man's opinion of current events?"

"You mean the customers who wear fishing hats that say 'Kiss my bass'?"

"Those are the ones," said Serge. "And whenever something happens in Cuba, they send the camera crews here."

"Don't look," said Felicia. "But his contact just came back."

Serge intentionally knocked his fork on the floor, copping a glimpse as he bent down.

Felicia pretended to read her menu. "Know him?"

"Uh, yeah." He looked down at his own menu. "I think you might want to consider dropping this business."

"What business?"

"The whole thing. Your arms pipeline and whatever mystery's behind it." Serge reached across the table and placed a hand on hers. "Might be a good time to walk away. Make that run."

She pulled her hand back. "This isn't like you. What's the problem?"

"Evangelista's contact. I know him." Serge shifted his eyes toward the other table. "And you don't want to."

"I'm not backing off. It's my country."

"And this is my country," said Serge. "I know how the game is played. And the players."

"So bail out if you're scared. I'll go it on my own."

"I'm not scared. But I wish you'd be just a little bit."

Felicia dismissed him with an offhand wave. "The generals disappear people all the time in Latin America."

"Trust me on this. The guy has so much money and influence, he could make an entire city block in Miami disappear, no questions asked."

Felicia picked up her menu again. "So who is this prince of darkness?"

Serge picked up his own. "Good way to put it . . ."

While they were talking, Evangelista picked up the briefcase and left. He strolled west up the sidewalk past the restaurant's windows. A few minutes later, the contact finished a glass of water and departed eastbound.

Felicia threw a twenty on the table and got up. "We need to get moving."

They reached the front door. A call from behind.

"Excuse me," said the maître d'. "You have a message."

"I do?" said Serge.

He handed him an envelope.

Serge tore open the flap. "Who's it from?"

"The gentleman at that table." He tilted his head toward the empty one that had yet to be bussed.

"Which gentleman?" asked Serge. "The big one in the tropical shirt?"

"No, the other."

Serge unfolded the note and read. He didn't speak.

"What is it?" asked Felicia.

Serge looked up. "You're not going to believe this . . ."

## Chapter *THIRTY-FOUR*

**ONE HOUR LATER**

A '68 Plymouth rolled through a quiet neighborhood in Little Havana. Modest ranch houses and haciendas. A dog barked, trash cans at the curb for pickup, chain-link, Mexican tiles. The Road Runner continued, only one occupant in the car.

Serge slowly turned onto Southwest Ninth Street (also Brigade 2506 Way) and pulled to a stop in front of a quiet stucco home with the address 1821. He unlatched a gate, walked up the steps, and opened the front door without knocking.

Inside: long rows of bookcases, tables with maps, walls covered in photos and flags. At the rear of the room, a solitary man in a business suit stood with hands clasped behind his back. Reading a plaque.

Serge stepped beside him and stared at the next plaque. "Nice day."

The man laughed. "Kind of weird meeting in the Bay of Pigs Museum. But from everything I've heard about you, actually not. How'd you find this place?"

"It's on my rounds. And I could count on it to be empty. No respect for history." He pointed through double glass doors. "See all the color pictures of older men on the side walls in that meeting room? They're the patriots. The black-and-white photos of younger men behind the podium are the martyrs."

"Whatever. The whole reason I wanted to meet—"

Serge interrupted by holding up a hand. He looked down at his own tropical shirt and the invasion brigade souvenir pin affixed over the pocket. Then at his contact's empty lapels. "Where's your pin?"

The man laughed again. "I know you must recognize me. Let's get down to brass tacks."

Serge cleared his throat and tapped the top of a small glass souvenir case. "The pin. It's our signal."

"You're joking."

"I never joke about national security." Serge turned around. "I'll go back outside, and we'll start again."

The man sighed as Serge left the building.

Moments later, the door opened again. Serge crossed the room.

The man tapped his lapel pin. "Happy?"

"Yes." Serge fiddled with the area over his own pocket. "Now take off your pin before our code signal is detected by enemy agents."

"We're in an empty freakin' house."

"Ahem . . ."

"For the love of . . . Fine, whatever you say."

The pin came off and went in a pocket.

Serge smiled. "So imagine my surprise when I got your message at Versailles. What on earth could the one and only Malcolm Glide want with me?"

"We've been watching you."

"I've seen the black SUVs."

"You're good," said Glide. "And President Guzman trusts you. That's important."

"Don't bullshit me. You may scare other people." Serge formed a steely glare. "I know you'd like nothing better than for his administration to topple so you and the generals can have the whole sandbox to yourselves again."

Glide nodded with pursed lips. "I know why you think that. Because that's exactly how I want it to look."

Serge's eyebrows knotted. "What?"

Malcolm gestured at the map table. "Have a seat. What I'm about to tell you has the highest security classification. Not even the FBI. And only the very top of the CIA."

"Right, and you're just going to spill it to me."

"Guzman's in extreme danger."

"From you."

"Like I said, I know how it looks."

"It looks like you're a disgrace to our political system. All those smear campaigns, preying on voters' worst fears."

"What can I say? I'm the best." Malcolm sat back with a coy grin. "I know we're on opposite sides of the philosophical aisle. But I was hoping that would make my proposition seem all the more credible."

"You mean work with you? Now *you're* joking."

"That right-wing political stuff is just business. It's also the reason why they came to me."

"Who did?"

Malcolm shook his head. "Can't reveal that. But they said it was the perfect cover. You know about the arms shipments?"

"Yeah, you're ripping off the American people and destabilizing the legitimate democracy of one of our neighbors. You should go to jail for life."

Malcolm leaned forward and folded his hands. "Have you ever asked yourself why none of the weapons ever leave Miami?"

"You're in cahoots with Evangelista ripping off your partners in crime?"

"Serge, the arms can't leave Miami. *That* would be destabilizing. Meanwhile, I've gained the trust of the generals and Evangelista in a way no covert agent ever could."

Serge formed a sarcastic mouth. "They came to you because you're a prick?"

"Precisely. We're building an airtight case. Bank transfers, taped conversations, everything."

Now Serge leaned forward. "Okay, purely for sporting value, what's this proposition? But realize that if I get half the chance, I'll use it against you and nail your ass."

"Fair enough." Malcolm nodded again. "The case is coming together like planned. Except things have started moving too fast in Costa Gorda. Guzman's pushing through all these reforms. I told him it was crazy. Just wait and be patient, and he'll get everything he wants. Right after our case . . ."

Serge's eyebrows went up. "You talked to Guzman?"

Malcolm nodded harder. "He knows everything I'm doing. And he's got the generals shitting themselves."

"So where do I come in?"

"The summit. The best time for a coup is when the president is out of the country. And after that idiot Scooter killed himself, the generals moved up the schedule. They already tried to hit him at the Diplomats' Ball."

"I know."

"I know you know. I sent in a capture team for you," said Glide. "But lucky for us—and Guzman—we didn't succeed. That was some nice work of yours taking out the asset."

"I have no idea what you're talking about."

"In any case, what you did at the ball changed my mind about you," said Malcolm. "And I need your help."

"What for?"

"They're going to make another attempt at the big summit finale at Bayfront."

"Know who they're using?"

"Evangelista."

"That's the smart move," said Serge. "He must have contacts with all the top freelancers."

"We think the hitter he hired is already in town, but his whereabouts . . ."

"So why don't you pull Guzman out of the summit?"

"Won't budge. Says his nation's enemies will win."

"I like him more and more."

"Then help your country," said Glide. "Make sure they don't succeed."

"But if you and everyone else can't find the shooter, how can I?"

"It may come to more drastic measures," said Glide. "These things go down to the last hour, even minute."

"Cut the head off?" said Serge.

"And the mission collapses." Malcolm sat back and folded his arms.

"You're actually serious," said Serge. "You want me to do Evangelista?"

"Only as a last resort. Right now he's too valuable. We've never gotten so deep inside the Latin American arms network. All his houses and mobile phones are tapped, even his yacht and the car that got blown up. Can't tell you how hard it was to wire the second Ferrari."

"One question: Why me?"

"Because of your particular skill set. I've gone over your police record." He pulled a packet of folded paper from his jacket. "Did you really kill all these people?"

Serge grinned like a schoolboy. "We may have had words."

Malcolm flicked his wrist. "I don't want to know. They all look like regular crimes, and the odds are astronomical that you've never been caught. So the only answer is you had clearance—and protection. Plus the trail is so insane and random. Only a completely organized mind with ten million dollars of government training could have meticulously planned every last detail of a madman's profile . . ."

"But I really am insane."

"And that's exactly what you'd be ordered to say. You have discipline, deny everything." Malcolm returned the document to his jacket. "But we went over your record ten times. Never seen an operative so thorough. No trail to the government whatsoever."

"And? . . ."

Malcolm paused and stared earnestly into Serge's eyes. "If things go south, you're expendable. The perfect patsy."

Serge smiled for the first time. "I knew that was the answer before I asked the question. And you were honest about it, so we're halfway to trust."

Malcolm stood abruptly. "Great. Glad to have you on board."

"I said *half*way."

"Realize that," said Glide. "We wouldn't want you if you just went by what I've said here today. When we meet again, I'll provide solid proof."

"Where do you want to meet?"

"You pick again. I'm sure I'll get a laugh."

Serge picked.

Malcolm laughed. "I was right. Tomorrow at one?"

"Thirteen hundred." Serge pressed a sequence of buttons on his wrist. "I'm resetting my watch to military time. You should, too."

"Why?"

"Because we're within a day of the strike. I learned it from the TV show *24*." He clicked a last button. "We're now on Serge time."

## Chapter *THIRTY-FIVE*

### THE BIG DAY

One P.M.

"Can I help you find anything?"

A man in a tailored suit set down a five-hundred-dollar purse. "No, just looking. Wife's birthday."

"Please let me know if you need any assistance."

A curt nod.

The saleswoman left.

Another man picked up a purse.

Malcolm Glide turned and checked his watch. "Serge, right on time." He smiled and tapped his lapel: Miami Seaquarium pin.

Serge nodded his approval, then opened his mouth.

Malcolm stopped him: "I know . . ." He removed the souvenir and stuck it in his pocket.

"What have you got?"

Glide reached in another pocket and looked around the department store to make sure no one was in earshot. "First time I ever met in a Saks Fifth Avenue."

"The Dadeland Mall. History motivates me."

Glide glanced around again. "But it looks brand new."

"Not the store." Serge held palms out in midair. "The space. It speaks to me."

"What's it saying to you now?"

"Nothing. That would be crazy." Serge chugged a 7-Eleven to-go cup. "Before Saks, this was the location of Crown Liquors, where, at two twenty-eight P.M. on July eleventh, 1979, two customers pulled machine guns from paper bags, spraying the store with eighty-six rounds and cutting down a pair of rivals in a scene no less brazen than the Wild West or Prohibition-era Chicago. It has since been dubbed the first shots fired in Miami's so-called Cocaine Cowboys War."

"That's all very interesting," said Glide. "But—"

Serge suddenly dropped the empty Styrofoam cup and staggered backward like he was being riddled by bullets.

Salesclerks ran over, helping him up from where he'd fallen and taken down a rack of blouses.

"Sir, are you okay?"

"I got it from here," said Malcolm. "My friend's prone to seizures." Then he turned to Serge and helped straighten out the front of his tropical shirt. "Man, you are *good*."

"Thanks."

"No, really." Malcolm bent down and picked up what he'd dropped from his pocket. "A few seconds ago, when you were lying there under women's clothes, I initially thought, 'Maybe I've been wrong about this guy. He actually is off his rocker.' Then it hit me. I've never seen such exquisite technique before."

Serge made a sweeping motion with an invisible machine gun. "Don't be fooled by cheap imitations."

"What brilliant spycraft! Most people check for surveillance tails by secretly peeking around. But you go the opposite direction, way over-the-top."

"That's where I live."

Malcolm turned his neck. "See how absolutely everyone in the store is staring over here like there's something deeply wrong with you?"

"I've gotten used to the popularity."

"It's perfect! Surveillance teams are trained to avert their gaze. But when you create this kind of public spectacle that's so weird and embarrassing, it would be abnormal *not* to look. Then anyone who isn't paying attention stands out like a sore thumb, and you've nailed your tail." He turned again. "As you can see by the crowd's universal disgust, we haven't been followed."

"You mentioned solid proof."

"Obviously I can't let you keep this." Glide handed him a large brown envelope with a bulge in the side, then turned toward a row of white doors. "You can check it out in there. And these are your credentials."

Serge grabbed a shirt off a table and went inside the nearest dressing room.


## TWO P.M.

Biscayne Boulevard. North of the Herald Building. Beemers, Saabs, city bus with a vodka ad. A crew in safety vests worked jackhammers. Salsa music echoed from alleys.

An attractive woman in a pantsuit sat on a bench along the 2100 block. Pedestrians walked by. Another rude suggestion. She checked her watch, just like the minute before.

2:02.

A screech of tires.

Serge hopped out and took a seat on the bench like he didn't know her.

"You're late," said Felicia.

"Got caught in traffic . . . taking pictures."

"At least nobody's following us—" Felicia cut herself off. "Check that. We have company."

"Where?"

"High noon across the street. That guy with the telephoto camera taking pictures this way."

"He's not following us," said Serge. "He's following the building."

"Building?"

Serge arched his neck back over the bench and aimed a small digital camera straight up. "*That* building." *Click, click, click . . .*

Towering behind them stood a vertical glass rectangle perched on a pedestal. Running up the side, blue-and-white patterns of leaves like a giant ceramic kitchen tile. One of those buildings that looks old and new at the same time: designed to be futuristic when it was christened in a bygone era.

"What so special about that?" asked Felicia.

"The Bacardi Building, crown jewel of the recently embraced MiMo architecture movement during the fifties and sixties."

"MiMo?"

"Contraction of *Miami Modernism.* Buffs are constantly coming out to take photos. And spies always meet in culture."

"To hell with the building. What did you find out at Dadeland?"

"Shit's on. It's going down this afternoon during the big outdoor summit gathering at Bayfront Park."

"So Glide's really on the level?"

"As level as they come. He showed me the files. All the bank records, photos of Evangelista meeting the generals and an assassin called the Viper. Plus taped phone conversations with same. Most of the stuff exactly matched what you've developed—and more."

Felicia jumped up. "We better get moving."

"I'm ahead of you."

They dove in the Road Runner and raced south. "Have a plan?" asked Felicia.

"I scouted the area around the summit. Too many high-rises within eight hundred yards of the amphitheater. Even an average shooter . . ."

"Then what are we going to do?"

"People picture snipers' nests like Oswald resting a rifle on a window ledge of the School Book Depository. That was amateur hour. True pros set up way back in the room for concealment, with highly calibrated rifles on stands in steady vise grips. Then they fire the kill-shot through an open office or hotel window ten feet in front of them."

"So we just look for an open window," said Felicia. "In this heat, there shouldn't be a lot."

"Except the window only has to be open a few inches for the shot. And like I said, there are a lot of buildings." Serge reached into his pocket. "Here are the credentials Glide gave us."

"What are you doing now?"

Serge had a cell phone to his head and waved for her to be quiet. "Mahoney? Serge here. Remember the backup plan? . . . Time to back it up. Bring all you got . . . Yeah, and call the Volkswagen Boys."

Serge hung up and hit the gas. "Things are going to start happening fast from here on out."

Things did.

Other phones rang in Miami.

Building 25. "Agent Oxnart . . . What? . . . When? . . . Right." He hung up. "Everyone, code black. Bayfront. Move!"

A former safe house in Coral Gables. "This is Lugar. . . . Where? . . . We're on it." He hung up. "Bayfront. Directive Omega . . ."

A cell phone buried deep in a pants pocket: "Evangelista here . . . Change in plans? . . . Who? . . ."

*Chapter* **THIRTY-SIX**

## DOWNTOWN

Mass confusion.

Ten times worse than when the arena lets out after a Heat play-off game.

Flashing lights, police cars everywhere in the middle of streets, sealing the entire grid. Motorcycle cops zipped down the middle of the evacuated roads ahead of limos with bulletproof glass and flapping flags on fenders.

The Road Runner got stacked up twenty deep under the I-95 interchange. Police with batons waved drivers back in the direction they'd come.

"We won't be able to get anywhere near the place," said Serge.

Felicia stuck her head out the window. "We're not even moving."

"You look like the running type," said Serge.

"But we still have to park."

"I hate to do this." Serge cut the wheel. "Hold on to something."

The Road Runner broke out of traffic, jumped the curb, and crashed through a chain-link fence. Serge downshifted and drove sideways along a forty-five-degree embankment beneath the overpass.

The police saw him, but with the traffic chaos, only the motorcycle unit could get to him, and they were tied up on escort duty. Bums and bottles scattered ahead of Serge's front grille. He cascaded down a grass berm and skidded to a stop in the mushy edge of a retention pond. Driver's door against a tree. Tires spun, spraying mud.

Serge removed the keys. "That's as far as this train goes."

1433 military time.

Bayfront Park.

Amphitheater.

Festive. Standing room only. A crushing sea of people in light clothing filled every inch and spilled down the esplanade. Disposable cameras raised in the air above heads. TV trucks. Balloons. Schoolchildren in native costumes, waving flags on little sticks.

On the opposite side of the street, in small, constitutionally roped-off squares, tiny groups of protesters quarreled with one another and thrust homemade signs at passersby: "IMMIGRATION NOW! " "STOP IMMIGRATION! " "FREE CUBA!" "NEED CONCERT TICKETS!"

A band played a national anthem that included flamenco guitars and bongos. A president approached the podium. He led a vibrant little country with no armed forces that Americans couldn't find on a map. The president raised his hands to acknowledge the applause, then introduced the national soccer team that had just defeated Zimbabwe. Louder cheers . . .

Two people urgently pushed their way through the crowd without great success.

"How are we going to find the shooter with this mob?" Felicia checked the official schedule. "Guzman's the sixth speaker."

"I need to get someplace high and scope angles." Serge looked around. "Over there. The roof at Bayside Market."

"Hooters?"

"See that rifle barrel?"

"A sniper!"

"Yes, but one of ours," said Serge. "Stay close and grab the back of my shirt. This'll be rough going."

The pair began plowing ahead. "Excuse me, excuse me . . ."

*"Hey, watch it, fella!"*

*"What's your deal?"*

"Coming through. Excuse me . . ."


1438.

On the fifteenth floor of a downtown high-rise hotel, a room-service tray sat in the hall.

The guest hadn't left the room since Tuesday. Lying on the bed, staring with patience at a textured pattern on the ceiling, and wondering about the tool that had been used to create it.

No complaints from his neighbors. No TV or sound of any kind. One of the few people who could go a week without speaking a word—not on the phone, not to the hotel guy delivering his food, not even to himself. He liked it.

The room remained dim with curtains pulled.

A cell phone vibrated on the nightstand.

He checked the text message.

"#."

Thin leather gloves slipped over hands. The hands checked the tightness of the mounting bolts on a five-leg titanium stand that held a Galil 7.62mm Israeli sniper rifle. The cap came off the scope.


1441.

Serge and Felicia finally broke free from the suffocating mob and ran up an escalator.

A woman in tight orange shorts smiled. "Table for two?"

Serge flashed the credentials Glide had given him. "Which way to the roof?"

"That employee door to the kitchen and up the stairs."

They took off again, jumping two and three steps at a time, reaching the roof with clothes that smelled like buffalo wings.

A two-man tactical team heard the access door crash open. The one not manning the rifle swung and aimed a pistol. "Freeze! Both of you!"

Serge held his badge high and ran toward them. "Government agent."

"Stop right there. Let me see that."

The one with the rifle glanced over. "Who are they with?"

The spotter studied the laminated photo ID with a bar code. "OCI."

"OCI?" said the marksman. "I've never met one of them before. What the hell are they doing here?"

The other handed back the badge. "What *are* you doing here?"

"Got an intel intercept. Thirteen hundred hours. Assassination plot on President Guzman."

"We haven't heard anything."

"Just came in," said Serge. "Looks like freelance flew into town. I'm guessing one of those windows across Biscayne."

"You mean one of those *thousand*?"

"Got an extra pair of binoculars?" asked Serge.

They began scanning facades of bright, reflecting glass.

The spotter finished one bank tower and went to another. "When's Guzman speak?"

Serge worked his way down an office building. "Sixth."

"I think it's too early to find him," said the spotter. "If this guy's any good, he's not going to open the window until Guzman's at the podium."

"What can it hurt?"

Down on the street, motorcycles revved, lights flashed. Police on foot opened the gates for more limos, including one with the national seal of Costa Gorda.

The dignitaries were met backstage at the amphitheater in a large, open-air tent. Handshakes, champagne, caterers circulating with shiny trays. Stereo speakers piped in the live program from the stage, a joke about sugarcane export policy.

Across the street, in a fifteenth-floor hotel room, a cell phone vibrated.

A hand in a leather glove flipped it open to a text message: "!"

The cell flipped closed. The room's guest walked over to the window.

# *Chapter* **THIRTY-SEVEN**

**1503**

Binoculars made another sweep from the roof of a building full of chicken, beer, and breasts.

"This isn't good," said Serge.

"We still have at least an hour," said the spotter. "Three more speakers before Guzman."

Serge took a full breath and lowered his binoculars. Thinking. Eyes wandered the teeming summit grounds. Families, faces, food carts. The stage and the next marching band assembling below the side steps.

Serge's eyes stopped. "Uh, what's that tent?"

"Where?" asked the spotter.

"Down behind the stage."

"Oh, that's the secure greeting area."

"Shit!"

"What's the matter?"

Serge quickly raised the binoculars and shortened focus. "It's open-air. I can see everybody. Including Guzman. And if I can see him . . ." His binoculars swung back across the street.

The spotter followed suit. "The shooter's not going to wait for the speech?"

"The podium shot is Hollywood stuff," said Serge. "Would you wait?"

They started again with the nearest line of buildings, entire hotel windows filled their fields of vision. A curtain opened.

"Think I got something," said the spotter

"What is it?"

"That one, fifteenth floor, third from the south."

Serge locked in with his own binoculars and watched a couple rip off each other's clothes and put on costumes from the Napoleonic Wars.

"Sorry," said the spotter.

More panning. More open curtains. More personal choices. Binoculars reached the end of the floor and paused again. In a circular, high-magnification view, another pair of curtains, but these were barely parted. The window behind them opened six inches.

"This looks interesting," said the spotter.

"Where?" asked Serge.

"Third room from the end."

"That's him," said Serge. "Looks like an Israeli Galil seven-point-six-two. When did the window open?"

"Just a few seconds ago."

"He's going for the shot now! Take him out!"

Serge kept his binoculars trained on the window. "What are you waiting for? Take him out!"

The spotter and Serge simultaneously looked over at their own sniper, slumped with an entry wound between the eyes.

"What the—!"

A tiny explosion with a fine mist of blood. Then the spotter toppled over from a bullet through his forehead.

Serge glanced quickly at the hotel, then grabbed Felicia by the arm and pulled her down flat below the lip of the roof. Another tactical round flew through the space where they had just been and pierced the coils of a rooftop air-conditioning unit.

"Downstairs!" Serge led her scrambling on hands and knees across roof pebbles to the access door. He reached up for the knob just as another slug punctured the metal a few inches from his hand. They tumbled into the stairwell and ran down to the street.

"What now?" said Felicia.

"To the hotel!"

"That'll take too long."

"Anything else will take longer. And Guzman's still exposed in the tent."

They sprinted through the marketplace, hurdling police barricades and darting between limos on Biscayne Boulevard. Into the hotel lobby and onto the elevator.

Serge's hands shook impatiently as he stared up at slowly ascending numbers. Ten, eleven, twelve. "Come on!" . . . finally . . . fifteen. They jumped out and dashed down the hall.

A maid stuffed soiled towels in her cart.

"Federal agent!" Serge flashed his badge. "Open this room! Now!" *"No inglés."*

Serge saw her universal magnetic door key hanging from a string on the side of the cart. He snatched it and pulled his pistol.

The maid screamed and ran off in a manic duck waddle.

Serge held the card over the slot. His other hand gripped the gun. Hearts pounding. He turned to Felicia, already poised with her own weapon. "Ready?"

She nodded fast, eyes boring through the door.

Serge slipped the card down. Green light. They burst in.

"Don't move!" yelled Serge.

Silence.

Empty, like it had never been slept in.

Felicia swung her gun in the bathroom. Nothing. "Sure we got the right room?"

"Positive. Window and curtains open a half foot." Serge knelt on the carpet. "And look: rug indentations from the feet of the rifle stand. He was here all right."

"Now he's gone." She ran to the window. "And Guzman's still out there."

She bolted from the room, and Serge chased her onto the elevator.

Doors opened in the lobby. She started running for the entrance, but Serge grabbed her from behind. "He would have gone out the back."

They ran around the pool and through a gate to the parking lot.

"What are you stopping for?" asked Felicia.

"Look."

A stream of thick red blood dripped from the corner of a Dumpster. Serge pushed the lid open. "This shortens our search considerably."

"You sure that's him?"

"Recognize his face from the binoculars across the street. And those are shooting gloves."

Felicia looked inside. "Hey, that's the same guy who killed the reporter by the river—and tried to kill me. What the hell's going on? Why's he dead?"

"The penalty for failure. He followed standard procedure by clearing out once the sniper nest was compromised. And his bosses followed procedure by cutting ties."

"But what about Guzman?"

"Safe," said Serge. "Standard procedure also calls for canceling the mission after the first miss. Until next time, when they try again somewhere else."

"We better get over there anyway," said Felicia. "Still haven't reported the two men we lost on the roof. Since we still don't know the full picture, it's probably best I pass it through my own country's security detail."

"Hold up," said Serge. "I haven't had a chance to ask. Since there's a break in the action."

"What?"

Serge dropped to a knee. "Will you marry me?"

"Serge! This is a crazy time!"

"Doesn't that mean no?"

"No, it means it's a crazy time." She pointed. "There's blood streaming from a Dumpster behind you. Whatever happened to a quiet dinner?"

Serge stood and shrugged at the growing red puddle. "It's our culture. This whole go-go lifestyle."

## 1517

A SWAT team swarmed a rooftop at Bayside Market. A walkie-talkie: "Team three is down! Repeat, team three is down!"

The bulletin came over the radio in a black SUV as it screeched up to a barricade on Flagler. "We've already lost men," said Agent Lugar. "He could be anywhere, so fan out. And don't trust Oxnart. We don't know what side of the play he's on."

Four doors opened. Agents took off running in six directions.

Three blocks the other way, another black SUV. Doors opened. "Move out!" yelled Oxnart. "And keep an eye for Lugar's team . . ."

A Volkswagen Beetle pulled up behind the SUV. Twelve men got out wearing red berets.

## 1522

Serge and Felicia walked back across Biscayne Boulevard at a more leisurely pace, waving credentials at checkpoints. This time they avoided the impassable crowd by walking up the VIP drive next to slow-rolling limos and entering the rear of the tent.

A smiling caterer. "Champagne?"

Felicia shook her head and looked around. "I don't see the president."

"Relax." Serge aimed an index finger. "He's up there. Back of the stage. Must be on next."

The current speaker gave a commendation medal to his minister of coffee.

"I see our head of security," said Felicia. "Wait here . . ."

Another caterer with a bow tie. "Hors d'oeuvre?"

"Oooooo!" said Serge. "Do I see water chestnuts in there? That's always a fearless statement!"

The caterer glanced back dubiously and walked away empty-handed.

Serge munched snacks from a full silver tray resting on his left arm.

He strained for a peek at some kind of loud commotion back at the security checkpoint.

*"Whoops. Losing a little balance again . . ."* Someone fell over, taking down one of the potted palms flanking the entrance. Then a tent pole. The corner of the vinyl roof collapsed on minor cabinet members from Paraguay.

Serge finished chewing. "Coleman?"

Someone else at the checkpoint. "It's okay, fellas. He's with me."

"He's stinking drunk," said one of the guards, replanting the tent pole. He sniffed the air. "And your breath doesn't smell so good either."

Ted Savage flashed a smile and his freshly laminated badge.

A second guard checked it. "Go on in."

"Ted!"

"Serge!" He ran over. "What are you doing here?"

"Was about to ask you the same question."

Ted held up the badge again. "Just got reinstated. Someone canceled my burn notice."

Coleman grabbed two glasses of champagne from a passing tray.

Another water-chestnut delight went in Serge's mouth. "But why are you at the summit?" *Munch, munch, munch.*

Ted leaned to whisper. "My first comeback mission." *Wink.* "It's a secret. I'm on backup security."

"It's safe with me . . . I need to find Felicia. Will she be surprised to see you."

He walked off.

"Don't be long," Ted called after him. "Coleman's about to become a two-man job."

"I usually just roll him under a table," said Serge. "These have the long tablecloths that reach the ground, so he won't be bothered."

A tap on Ted's shoulder. He turned. "Can I help you?"

One of the guards from the checkpoint. "Did your badge say 'OCI'?"

Ted smiled again and held it up.

The guard handed him a half-dozen pages. "These just printed out in the mobile command post. Flash bulletin. Color cartridge was low, but I think the threat level's a new red."

Two blocks away, a powder-blue '54 Skylark pulled up in the alley. Mahoney looked over his shoulder at his office mates. "Do your thing."

**1538**

Serge returned with Felicia. He looked at Ted's hands. "What's that?"

A rare sober expression from Savage. "You need to see these."

Serge gave him a look, then grabbed the pages and began reading.

17 DEC—1518—MIAMI SECTOR
URGENT
Echo: Team Bravo neutralized
Assets: Two, location Zulu
Echo: Unknown Mark. Unknown Flag. Delivery: Israeli Galil
      7.62. Neutralized.
Assets: Same
Protocol: Whiskey Tango
Germination: Immediate

ALL SECTIONS: TOP PRIORITY

Serge rapidly flipped through the rest of the bulletin. He raised his head with a blank stare. "This is the two-man team we lost on the roof of Hooters."

"Yeah," said Felicia, pointing behind her. "I reported it in."

"Look at the time stamp on the bulletin," said Serge. "It's before we even got back across the street."

"So someone else found them before I could report. So what?"

Serge turned to the third page. "Here's a suspect photo-grab from the surveillance cameras in the restaurant. My head's turned, but it's a pretty good likeness of you."

"It would make sense that they got that out," said Felicia. "Of course we'd be suspects before they knew who we really were. But I'm sure it'll all get cleared now that I filled in my people."

"How do we clear *this* up?" Serge turned to another page. Details on the body of a would-be assassin found in a fifteenth-floor hotel room with his rifle still in its stand.

"That must be a mistake." Felicia looked at Serge in confusion. "His body was in the Dumpster. And the rifle was gone. You were there. Am I losing my mind?"

Serge didn't answer—simply turned to the final page and another photo.

"Hey, it's me. And you're in the background," said Felicia. "Remember? When I was standing in the assassin's hotel room window and looked down to see if Guzman was still safe in the tent? But that's a really long-range shot. Who could have taken it? . . ." She took a step back. "What the fuck's happening?"

"Someone has gone to a lot of trouble."

"We're being set up?" said Felicia.

"And not by amateurs."

"Son of a bitch! I knew you should never have trusted that Malcolm Glide!"

"It's not him."

"Of course it's him!"

Serge shook his head. "Look at the back of the stage. Guzman's still breathing. It would only be a double cross from Glide if your president had already been hit and they needed patsies."

"So who then?"

Serge looked out the tent at the hotel across Biscayne Boulevard. "Whoever booked that room on the fifteenth floor."

"Why would they come after us?"

"Maybe your arms investigation . . . Maybe anything . . . But whoever it is knows we're protecting Guzman. That's why they had to scapegoat us ahead of time. We were spotted at Dinner Key and tailed to Liberty City—"

"Back up. You said 'ahead of time'?"

"Before the hit on Guzman. It's still on."

"I thought you said they cancel after a miss."

"I've been wrong before."

"I have to warn them!"

From the other side of the tent, security officers with suspect photos from the flash report. *"I think I just saw them over there."*

"Uh-oh," said Serge.

"What do we do?" said Felicia.

"Quick." Serge raised a skirt of white linen. "Under the table!"

They both dove beneath.

"Serge," said Coleman. "What are you doing down here?"

"Shhhhhhh!" Serge pointed underneath the tablecloth at shiny cop shoes.

"Excuse me?" said a police officer.

"Yes?" said Savage.

The bulletin photos again. "Have you seen these people? A witness thought they saw you talking to them."

Ted gave the pics a closer look. "Seem familiar, but I'm not sure."

The officer looked around. "Are they still here?"

"No." Ted gestured out a tent flap. "Left a while ago. Said something about a flight to South America."

"Thanks." The officer walked away, talking in a radio mike.

The linen table skirt lifted. Ted's face upside down: "Coast is clear."

Felicia crawled out and dusted herself off. "We have to stop the speech."

"We have to get him out of here," said Serge. "I doubt they'll use a sniper twice. The backup plan will probably be up close and personal."

"Someone near the stage?" said Felicia.

"Or on it."

They turned to move quickly toward the rear of the tent.

Nope. Cops gathered with printouts and arm motions.

They turned left.

Other officers huddling with pages.

To the right.

Someone else handing out more pages. In fact, in every direction, everyone seemed to be studying photos of Serge and Felicia.

Serge reached down for a hem of linen. "Everyone, back under the table!"

Coleman turned his face in the dirt. "Weren't you just here?"

"Shhhhh!" said Serge. "I have to think."

"So what's the plan?" asked Ted Savage.

"Now pinch-hitting in the bottom of the ninth." Serge placed a hand on his shoulder. "We need your help."

"Me?"

"Bases are loaded and Casey's at bat."

## 1521

Serge adjusted a bow tie. "How do I look?"

"Perfect," said Ted.

Felicia balanced a silver tray. "They just gave you these uniforms?"

"Said I needed them for undercover agents." Ted grabbed a flute of champagne off the tray. "I love my new badge!"

The pair worked the tent in a sinuous route, circulating with trays that allowed them to make abrupt detours without suspicion when officers approached . . . gradually working toward the back of the stage.

More agents appeared; the couple made about-faces on opposite sides of the tent, crisscrossing again in the middle.

"This is like Pac-Man," said Serge.

"Shut up," said Felicia.

Finally, the goal line. They stood halfway up the side steps, where it wasn't unusual for the help to stop and listen to a few words, maybe snap a picture.

"I don't see how anyone can get through the net," said Felicia. "The place is crawling with security."

"But looking for us."

"True."

The crowd burst into applause. The bald president of a former French colony smiled and raised his arms in appreciation. The left side of his military jacket was weighed down by countless, impressive medals representing the accomplishment of buying a lot of medals.

Felicia watched the president being spirited off to waiting blondes. "That means Guzman's next."

The president of Costa Gorda walked toward the podium to a stout ovation.

Serge took a heavy breath. "Why the hell does he have to give this stupid speech with all that's happened?"

"Because he's a real leader." Felicia began clapping. "This is why the people love him."

The crowd became one massive, undulating organism. Tiny flags waved. Cell phones held up to capture the moment. A giant beach ball bounced in back. After repeated acknowledgments from the president, they finally settled down.

"Look at that mob," said Serge. "It's like a rock concert without the mosh pit . . . Wait, I was wrong. Those kids flying around over there."

"The Young Independents," said Felicia. "They *really* love Guzman."

The president addressed the microphone. *"Good afternoon . . ."*

A louder roar went up.

Serge examined faces onstage, back and forth. Relatives, traveling assistants, cops, paramedics. Felicia checked the front rows of the crowd, cheering citizens, children on parents' shoulders, news photographers.

"Nothing out of place," said Serge.

Felicia's eyes swept back the other way. "We need to stay alert. Anything could happen."

And things happened, as they are known to do, in fast order.

Clouds rolled in across what had just been a clear sky. Wind began to whip. The park dimmed.

*"I think they're wearing caterers' uniforms. We saw them heading toward the stage."*

Felicia watched security closing in. "What do we do now?"

"Pray for pandemonium."

"What's that noise?" asked Felicia.

Ripples of thunder from across the bay.

The crowd held programs and anything else over their heads.

"Starting to rain," said Felicia.

"Regular afternoon shower," said Serge. "Never seen snow."

Outside the perimeter on Biscayne Boulevard, drivers lost traction and slammed through police barricades, scattering screaming pedestrians.

More yelling from the street as protesters used the opportunity to break free from their cordoned-off squares, attack one another, and hurdle the smashed barriers toward the amphitheater.

The security net that had been tightening on Serge and Felicia turned and ran from the stage.

Other agents rushed back to the main entrance of the VIP tent, where Guardian Mimes clogged the checkpoint, frowning and pulling their pants pockets inside out to show no credentials.

The aggressive windshield washers arrived, squeegeeing limo glass. *"Give us money!"*

Another fracas. Young women chased someone running south on the sidewalk.

"Leave me alone!" yelled the Most Laid Guy in Miami.

Johnny Vegas sat on the curb and tossed a bouquet in the gutter.

A platoon of Guardian Clowns pushed through the crowd and squirted people with plastic lapel flowers. "Out of the way! This is serious!"

The High-End Repo Man jumped in a driver's seat, speeding off in a stretch and running over a shark. A prime minister in back held on to the door. "Hey, you're not my driver."

Clouds continued gathering. Sky almost black. Wind howled.

Another set of screams from a large circle that quickly opened in the audience for the Guy Who Punches People.

More security responded from the stage.

A wild brawl broke out at the VIP tent, where police arrested the Guardian Mimes and charged them with nonviolent assault because they had pulled their punches.

"This isn't good," said Felicia.

"It's perfect," said Serge.

Remnants of the dispersed security force finally spotted Serge and Felicia and drew guns. *"There they are!"*

Lugar's men spotted the security and drew guns. *"Freeze! Drop the weapons!"*

Oxnart's team arrived and pointed guns at everyone else. *"Nobody move! Who's who?"*

Guzman became distracted from the various commotions and lost his place, then refreshed himself with notes and continued about climate change.

Something caught Felicia's eye. The curtains on the far edge of the stage slowly parted. "Serge! To your left! What's *he* doing here?"

"Evangelista?" said Serge. "Shit, he must be the backup plan, coming to finish the job himself."

"He's advancing from the other side of the podium!"

"He's reaching in his pocket!"

Ted Savage and Coleman came up the stairs, both a little unsteady. "Anything good going on?"

"Not now, Ted!" Serge reached under his shirt.

So did Felicia.

So did Evangelista.

They saw a glint of metal against the fat man's stomach.

"He's got a gun!" yelled Felicia.

She was right. A .380 Ruger. Evangelista's hand curled around the grip.

Serge and Felicia pulled their own pieces.

From the back of the stage and down in the audience, dozens pointing: *"They've got guns!"*

Instant panic.

Stampede. Screams.

Guzman stood frozen at the podium, bewildered by unseen events. Evangelista approaching from the right side of the stage; Serge and Felicia from the left. The president's bodyguards tried to get to him, flailing through the crazed mob running helter-skelter across the stage.

"Evangelista's still advancing!" said Felicia.

"He's got the gun out! He's aiming!" Serge swung his own pistol left and right. "Guzman's in the way."

Felicia braced her shooting arm, repeatedly shifting stance as innocent heads bobbed into her line of fire. "I can't get a shot off."

Serge's free hand shoved someone aside. "Neither can I."

Someone could.

*Bang, bang, bang . . .*

Hysteria became bedlam, then a circus, and finally a madhouse.

Half the people hit the ground shrieking; the rest ran blindly into things and dove off the front of the stage.

Serge stood on tiptoes for a better view.

An empty podium.

"Guzman!"

Serge and Felicia rammed through the mob like blitzing linebackers. They reached the pile of bodyguards behind the podium.

"Is he hit?" asked Felicia.

"No."

"Felicia," said Serge. "Look!"

Evangelista lay splayed out on his back. Silent eyes wide. Spreading pool of blood. Bullet through the heart. Gun still in hand.

"You shoot him?" asked Serge.

"No," said Felicia. "Never fired."

"Neither did I," said Serge.

"Then who did?"

Somewhere below in the trampling of feet, a meek voice: "Serge?"

"Ted? Is that you?"

"Down here."

Serge pushed through more people, then looked back. "Felicia! It's Ted! He's been hit!"

"Serge?" said Ted.

He bent down and cradled Savage in his arms. "How bad is it?"

Ted shook his head. "Did I get him? Is Guzman safe?"

Serge glanced back at Evangelista's body, then the bodyguards whisking Guzman down the stairs to a waiting limo.

"Yes, Ted. You saved him."

Ted smiled weakly. "Good. I think Evangelista got me back, but at least I nailed him first. I succeeded in my last mission."

"Hey buddy." Serge stroked his arm. "You got a million more jobs ahead. Just stay with me."

Ted just smiled again. "Thanks, Serge."

And he was gone.

# EPILOGUE

## CNN

*"Good evening. Officials are reviewing security procedures tonight after a failed assassination attempt on the life of Costa Gordan president Fernando Guzman at the prestigious Summit of the Americas in Miami. The plot was foiled this afternoon by a quick-thinking federal agent who was tragically killed in an exchange of gunfire with the assailant . . ."*

Serge looked up from his portable TV. Someone approaching on the sidewalk.

He hopped to his feet, ran around the table, and pulled out a chair.

"Serge . . ." said Felicia.

"Have you thought any more about my question?"

"Serge . . ."

"You said dinner, so here we are!" Serge swept an arm from the street to the sea. "Sidewalk café on Ocean Drive in beautiful South Beach. Coconut Palms. Sand. Male models rollerblading in scrotum-huggers."

"Serge . . ."

"You already know Coleman, and this is Mahoney. They're going to be my best men. I know you haven't answered yet, but I'm an eternal optimist at love. What do you think about a night beach wedding with tiki torches and Creedence Clearwater music? I already ordered coffee—"

"Serge!"

"What's the matter, baby?"

"Everything's gone south. I just found out—"

"Hold that thought," said Serge, turning up the TV.

". . . *Meanwhile, congressional leaders are calling for increased national security spending in light of today's developments, and the threat level has been raised to an unprecedented pixelated red, which can only be seen in high-def . . . Joining us tonight is conservative campaign strategist Malcolm Glide.*"

"*Thanks for having me, Jane. As the unfortunate events in Miami clearly demonstrate, the nation is far from safe, even in our own hemisphere. That's why my elected colleagues are introducing an emergency bill for immediate and massive arms shipments to our staunch military allies in Costa Gorda.*"

"*Excuse me, Mr. Glide. But weren't you the lobbyist for the scandal-ridden contractor in Iraq that misappropriated over a billion dollars and whose missile guidance systems chronically malfunctioned, directing rockets back to our own troops?*"

"*Jane, when the nation is at war, it's no time to undermine the morale of our corporate officers.*"

Serge smiled at the set. "Have to admit he's good."

"Serge!" Felicia grabbed his wrists. "Glide *did* set you up."

"No, he didn't. I saw the files."

"And I saw ours . . ."

TV: "*. . . Meanwhile, funeral arrangements are being finalized for prominent Latin businessman Victor Evangelista, an innocent bystander who was accidentally killed by stray fire during the assassination attempt . . .*"

"Huh?" said Serge. "Didn't they find his gun? . . . Oh well, first casualty is the truth. Guess someone high up decided it would be too embarrassing if his ties to Washington came out."

"Evangelista was on our side," said Felicia.

"What are you talking about?"

"Federal agent," said Felicia. "He was the one working undercover for our governments, not Glide. *He* was amassing evidence against Malcolm and his companies. And he was just days away from taking down everyone, including half our generals. They couldn't let that happen."

"But . . . that . . . what? . . ."

"Serge. There was an assassination plot all right, but not against Guzman. The real target all along was Evangelista. Everything Glide did was designed to take Victor out of the picture. He played all of us: you, me, Ted, a whole daisy chain of dupes."

"But then why did Evangelista have that gun?"

"Like I said, federal agent. He was there protecting against the plot. My guess is that Glide fed him your name and photo, and when he saw you on the other side of the stage, his gun came out."

"And then ours came out," said Serge. "Beautiful."

"They must have figured that even if he fired first, one of us would be left to get him."

"Except poor Ted was the one who got the shot off," said Serge. "And took a bullet from Victor in return."

"That's where it gets worse."

"How can it possibly get any worse?"

"Where did the bullet come from that hit Savage?"

"Evangelista, of course."

Felicia shook her head. "Our security got Evangelista's gun. Never fired. And no GSR on his hands."

"Then who shot Ted?"

"My money is on an undercover plant in our own bodyguard detail."

Serge shook his head fast to clear the fog. "I'm getting dizzy."

"Serge," said Felicia. "During a plot, there's always a backup gunman."

"Why?"

"To kill the first shooter and cut ties for deniability," said Felicia. "You're big on history. Ruby shoots Oswald. And back when Aquino landed in the Philippines and that soldier shot him on the runway, and then that other soldier shot *him*."

"So Glide set me up as the scapegoat, except Ted took my place?"

Coleman raised his hand. "Can I get a drink?"

Serge and Felicia in unison: "Shut up!"

TV: *". . . Meanwhile a massive manhunt continues tonight in South Florida for the would-be assassin who remains at large this hour and is believed to be in the Miami Beach area."*

Serge grabbed his head. "I can't believe this was all about stupid gun shipments."

"It wasn't," said Felicia. "Remember when I thought the guns were just a means to something bigger? They were. The business with the dead reporter that kept nagging me. The geology report he was supposed to slip me before they killed him."

"That's right," said Serge. "You mentioned it."

"I finally got a copy from one of my sources in our interior ministry."

"So spill."

"Oil," said Felicia. "They discovered a new field off our coast. I guess the petroleum companies are getting too much grief from your country over what's happened in the Gulf. So they went looking for an easier government to ply."

"And Glide?"

"All his candidates are backed by huge oil lobbyists. He simply expanded his dealings offshore to Costa Gorda. The guns never had to leave Miami. That was just designed to raise money and pay off the generals, because no matter how big that oil field is, Guzman wasn't about to let those drilling rigs anywhere near our coral reefs."

Serge looked oddly at the tiny TV screen. "But . . . if Glide actually was trying to set me up . . ."

Then a flash of recognition. His eyelashes fluttered as recent images strobed through his brain: the security film at Hooters, the photo of Felicia in the hotel room window, more probable images yet to come from stage cameras.

His eyes shot toward Felicia. "Oh my God, you're right! Evangelista really was the target!"

"So you finally believe me?"

"Except you're wrong. They weren't setting me up. They were setting you up. *You're* the patsy."

"Me?"

"Works better. You're a foreign national. Probably dummy bogus evidence linking you to the rebels. Think: Who sent you to Miami in the first place?"

"Scooter's uncle, the general, to watch out for him . . . Oh my God."

TV: *". . . Authorities are looking for this woman caught on various security cameras . . ."*

"That's me!"

Serge stood. "We have to get you out of here."

"This can't be happening." She rested her forehead on the table.

"It'll be okay. We'll talk to Guzman." He stroked her hair. "Felicia?"

Blood ran between his fingers. A man ran across the street.

"Felicia!" He shook her hard. Down to the ground she went.

A curdling yell echoed off the Art Deco hotels and sidewalk restaurants.

*"Noooooooooooo!"*

## BISCAYNE BAY

Midnight. A million stars.

Several serious yachts anchored in one of the few deep channels.

Lights on. Music carrying across the water. People in evening wear filled the back deck of the largest vessel. Slow dancing. A radar dish rotated above the cabin.

One of the couples climbed off the stern and onto the swim platform, then into a smaller boat that ferried them back to their own yacht. Other couples followed. Vague voices calling back to their host as lines cast off.

A party winding down.

*"Thanks for having us, Mr. Glide . . ."*

*"Congratulations on the funding bill . . ."*

*"Here's a check for the best candidates money can buy . . ."*

Laughter at the last remark.

A magnum of Dom Pérignon hung by Malcolm's side as he waved toward the last guests motoring off into the dark bay. He went back inside and plopped onto a spacious leather couch. A radar screen showed tiny blips where his visitors made their way back to their respective boats. A sixty-two-inch plasma TV was on CNN.

"... *In other news, fifty thousand barrels of oil a day continue to spew into the Gulf of Mexico, while cleanup crews prepare for a spectacular nighttime burn of a corralled section of the petroleum, which should be visible from Pensacola to Fort Myers ...*"

Another laugh from Malcolm. He emptied the rest of the magnum. Three people appeared in front of him. The live-aboard captain, mechanic, and cook.

"Will there be anything else, Mr. Glide?"

"No, that's it. Good night." He tilted his head, indicating that they were blocking his TV view.

They disappeared to their berths below.

"... *Breaking news at this hour: Authorities are reporting the discovery of a body believed to be that of the foiled assassin from the Summit of the Americas in Miami. Speaking off the record, officials have identified the deceased as Felicia Carmen, a member of Costa Gordan intelligence who is suspected of being a double agent with recently uncovered ties to the country's Marxist rebels. With shades of the Versace slaying, Ms. Carmen herself was gunned down in a brazen daylight attack on Ocean Drive. Police are seeking this man ...*"

Serge's face filled the screen.

A sedate smile from Glide as he drained the last of the champagne—"never saw it coming"—then rested his head back over the couch and closed his eyes.

A new green dot blipped on the edge of the radar screen.

Another yacht.

No running lights. Drifting in blackness fifty miles off the coast of Tampa Bay.

"How long you going to need it?" asked Stan the High-End Repo Man.

"We'll be heading back before you know it." Serge glanced at a seaplane moored to the bow. "Thanks for flying us over. We never could have made it in time from Biscayne to the Gulf in that speedboat."

"Don't mention it," said Stan. "But next time give me a little advance warning when we're transporting some guy who's tied up."

"I didn't think it was unusual."

"In your case, you're right."

Serge looked over the rear of the vessel at a small, shore-excursion boat lashed to the stern. "How much does one of these dinghies cost?"

"Why?"

"It won't be coming back."

"Don't you ever change?" The repo man wiped his hands on a rag. "Forget about it. I'll just file insurance, lost at sea."

"I owe you."

"Yes."

"You might want to get back to the plane," said Serge. "Some people don't want to see—"

"Already on my way." The repo man climbed down onto a pontoon, then into the cockpit.

Lines cast off. A propeller began to whirl, and the plane scooted across the water until it lifted off into the unseen night over the Everglades.

Serge turned the other way. "Now, as you were saying?"

"I swear I didn't betray you!" pleaded Malcolm Glide. "I thought we discussed the risks—that you might be the fall guy if things turned sour."

Serge had been disappointed. It was almost too easy kidnapping

Glide off his boat near Stiltsville in Biscayne Bay. But irony always brought his spirits back. He grabbed the handle of a large crank, making one slow clockwise turn.

Iron gears clicked. The dinghy lowered a foot.

Serge leaned toward Malcolm. "Except you planned for everything to go sour all along."

"Stop cranking!" yelled Glide. "On my mother's grave! Espionage has many layers, very complex. It's not what it seems!"

"It seems Felicia's dead. She was my almost-fiancée." Another crank.

The small boat lowered another foot and stopped with a shudder.

"That wasn't supposed to happen!" said Glide. "I told them to leave her out of it, but those generals are crazy. You try dealing with Latins."

"What am I? An Eskimo?" *Crank.*

"I didn't mean it that way!" Malcolm looked down at his trussed-up body, fastened securely in the dinghy's middle seat with boat straps and chains, no hope of movement. "I'll give you money!"

Serge looked behind him. "Coleman, you want money?"

"Sure!"

Serge turned back and grinned at Glide. "Too bad you didn't double-cross Coleman." *Crank, crank, crank . . .*

"Please stop cranking! . . ."

Serge stopped cranking and placed a hand on his heart. "Okay, you've touched me." He grabbed something from the bilge and vaulted over the stern into the dinghy. "I'm going to show you mercy."

"You are?"

"I know, I should have my head examined."

"Thank God!" said Malcolm. "You won't regret this!"

"Lift your feet."

"What?"

"Just lift them."

He did, and Serge unrolled something. "You can put 'em down now."

Malcolm rested his feet on a new surface. "What's that?"

"The red Star-Elite Club carpet." Serge climbed up from the dinghy and back over the stern. "Now you're traveling in style."

Glide began blubbering again.

"Jesus, be a man!" Serge resumed cranking. "It's not that bad."

"It isn't?"

"Not for me. You're pretty fucked." *Crank, crank, crank* . . .

Tears flowed with abandon. "What are you going to do?"

"Teach you about nature. Like this holy body of water and all the majestic shorelines surrounding her . . . Isn't it peaceful?"

"I had nothing to do with the oil spill! I just lobbied candidates with scientific facts!" Glide wriggled in vain against his bindings. "It's never happened before! It was the scientists!"

"Scientists told you that all the other countries were wrong when they demanded PB install a remote-controlled shutoff valve?" *Crank, crank, crank.* "And your candidates voted to let them go without valves to increase profits? And cap liabilities in case of a spill?"

"I'm begging you. Don't kill me!"

"Oh, I won't kill you . . . I'm not *that* upset about the Gulf."

"You aren't?"

Serge set the lock on the winch and leaned against the lever, staring up at constellations. "That would be egotistical. Humans tend to view everything in terms of their own insignificant life spans. But in the long run, Mother Earth takes care of herself. The big wheel keeps on turning."

Malcolm sniffed back sobs. "That's what I always say."

"Right-o. Nature spawned you to pee in the pool. And nature created me to cross your path. See? Mother's always right . . . Or at least: When she's not happy, nobody's happy." Cranking resumed without stopping. So did the crying.

The hull hit the water. Serge hopped down into the dinghy again and pull-started the engine. "I know what you're thinking? How in heaven's name can I steer?" He stepped back onto the yacht. "Fret not. Serge is your pilot. I drilled bolts, freezing the rudder, so you'll sail straight as an arrow."

Malcolm choked back emotion. "To where?"

"Your crowning achievement!"

Coleman stood in the yacht and shielded his eyes. "It's started. I need to smoke some dope to dig this." He rolled a number.

Serge looked up and squinted. "You can almost feel the heat from here." He reached into the small boat and slammed the throttle forward. "I love an oil burn just before dawn."

The dinghy sped away as screams trailed off into the distant waters.

"Look at him go!" Coleman took a deep hit. "But he's heading right for the flames."

"Imagine the view."

"Didn't think we'd be able to still hear him yelling from this far . . . Oooo, he just caught on fire."

"That's rarely positive," said Serge.

"Still screaming," said Coleman. "How long will he be alive?"

"Longer than you'd actually think."

A ring of fire engulfed the western horizon. In the middle, a spike in the flames, and a screaming voice heading toward the center of the burning oil.

"How'd you think of doing this to him."

"Actually he's doing it to himself. If it wasn't for his political shenanigans, he'd just be on a long, windy ride until the gas tank ran out and someone found him drifting in the morning."

"But the gas tank won't run out?"

"No, it will," said Serge. "But all at once. You get such bad gas mileage in a burning spill."

Coleman exhaled a toke. "Still screaming."

*"Ahhhhhhh! . . ."*

"Coleman, what are you doing?"

Coleman was hanging over the side of the boat. "I see something floating." He retrieved a prosthetic leg with a Willie Nelson bumper sticker and packed it with pot.

*"Ahhhhhhh! . . ."*

*Boom.*

Serge smiled at the rising fireball. "Energy for a brighter tomorrow."